MW01232024

DAY OF
WRATH

DAY OF WRATH

William J. Coughlin

DELACORTE PRESS/NEW YORK

Published by
Delacorte Press
1 Dag Hammarskjold Plaza
New York, N.Y. 10017

Manufactured in the United States of America

First printing

Designed by Terry Antonicelli

Library of Congress Cataloging in Publication Data

Coughlin, William Jeremiah, 1929–
    Day of wrath.

    I.   Title.
PZ4.C858Day   [PS3553.O78]   813'.54   80-11328
ISBN 0-440-02152-9

1

beginning

chapter one

farrell savings bank

THE Mack Avenue Branch of Farrell Savings Bank was small compared with the bank's other offices. It shared a decaying stretch of Mack Avenue with its neighbors: bars, secondhand stores, and dingy wholesale outlets. However, the branch did business, at least just enough to justify its existence. It was a convenient bank for the workers of the three large manufacturing plants that, like squat gray cathedrals, dominated the area.

Like the street, the bank building, built in 1928, was old and worn. Inside, they had retained the old-fashioned polished-wood tellers' windows, although bulletproof glass had been installed in place of the old decorative iron grills. The glass was merely psychological, just to help dispel the anxiety of the staff working behind it. A robber could easily hop up onto the wide counter running the length of the tellers' cages and merely step over the glass partition. There were other protections, such as an armed uniformed guard, a retired policeman, who stood in the customer area keeping an eye on anything suspicious occurring around the high marble writing tables. The bank had installed silent alarms at each teller's cage, and television cameras set near the ceiling recorded the scene below.

The Mack Avenue Branch had been robbed twice. The bank employees had followed the procedure taught them by management: They offered no resistance, giving the robbers whatever they wanted. Even the guard, as per instructions, had raised his hands. Lives, said the bank manual, were more important than money, although this was more of a public relations position than the bank's basic attitude. During both robberies the silent alarm had been set off, and the small television cameras caught the action each time. But police had been busy on each occasion, and officers responded only after the robbers had departed.

However, one robber had been caught that same day while trying to hold up a gas station. The other bandit had escaped and was still officially wanted.

All the bank employees had been present at each of the robberies. The guard, the three women working as tellers, and the branch manager, who doubled as a loan officer, all considered themselves veterans—but they were nervous veterans. Since the robberies the silent alarm had been set off at least a dozen times due to nerves or unfounded suspicions. Still, the bank staff felt it was better to be safe than sorry.

Friday was their big day. The Mack Avenue Branch provided check cashing service on Fridays, payday for the men and women at the plants. Every Thursday night an armored car delivered $150,000 to the branch. Another delivery was made early Friday afternoon. The two deliveries were for safety, because it didn't pay to tempt fate by keeping too much cash in one place at one time.

Friday, then, was the very best day to rob the Mack Avenue Branch of Farrell Savings Bank.

The three men in the Volkswagen had studied the bank branch and they knew about Friday. Friday mornings were slow, the main rush didn't begin until eleven o'clock or later. After that the place was crowded.

They had parked the Volkswagen a block down from the branch. From that vantage point they could see the handful of people waiting for the bank to open at ten o'clock.

"I still think we'd do better if this was a group effort. Everybody should have a hand in this." The man behind the steering wheel was a tall, slim blond. He was handsome and at a distance might be taken for a bright and eager college student. However, closer up the blue eyes betrayed a steellike hardness, and the "college boy" was really a man of about thirty years of age.

"Shit, if we brought everybody, it would look like some goddamned Chinese fire drill. This is a quick job, Larry. Just need a few people. Get in quick, get out quick, that's the best way. Too many people would fuck it up." The black man was as tall as the blond driver but with a thicker, more powerful build. He was dressed in work clothes, a black knit cap perched on top of his close-clipped skull.

"Johnson is right. We've done this before. If you keep it simple, it works." The third man, seated in the back of the automobile, was also white and blond, but his hair was the color of dirty straw. He was shorter than his companions but very muscular. His square face was placid, as if his facial muscles had forgotten how to register emotion. He too was dressed in work clothes. He had a sawed-off shotgun, part of its barrel and stock having been shortened, concealed under a loose-fitting jacket. His name was George Hagen.

"Me and Hagen did all right the last time, you got to admit that," the black man said to the driver.

"Yes, but you didn't get much money. We need operational money."

The black man shifted his weight but kept his eyes on the line of people at the bank. "We'll do better today. I figure that place must have a quarter million dollars at least."

The driver shook his head. "Less. I've been watching for the last two Fridays; just counted the people going in and estimated what they might be cashing. I'd guess they probably have maybe a hundred or a hundred fifty thousand delivered Thursday night. The Friday afternoon delivery is the big one."

"Too many people to hit the place in the afternoon," Hagen said. "Somebody's liable to panic. Crowds are hard to handle." His voice was flat, carrying no hint of any emotion.

Jesse Johnson, the black man, seemed tense. He lit a cigarette and puffed nervously. "There they go," he said.

The small collection of people were admitted to the bank. It was ten o'clock.

"Shall we go now?" the driver asked.

"Don't be in such a hurry, Gormley," Johnson said to the driver. "Let some of those people do their business and clear out. The fewer in there, the better. We'll go in a few minutes." Johnson checked his revolver again, twirling the cylinder to make sure that it was loaded. He did it without thinking, a repetitive gesture that betrayed his growing excitement.

"Let's go over everything one more time," Gormley said.

"Oh, shit," Hagen protested from the rear seat. "Look, these things sort of just happen, Gormley. Everything will work out just fine. We'll be quick and smooth."

"One more time," Gormley said quietly. "Just in case things don't go so smoothly."

Johnson snorted. "Okay. We got us a stolen little Volkswagen, right? You let us off in front of the bank and make a U-turn. Wait across the street. We hit the bank and get our bags filled." Both men had cotton bags tucked inside their shirts. "We get the money, go across the street, and take off. We change cars. You and Hagen take the Plymouth, and I drive the old Cadillac."

"Okay."

Johnson snubbed out his cigarette in the car's ashtray. "If things blow up, we'll shag-ass out of there, and you pick us up." He paused, staring at the bank down the street. "If things should really blow up, you get the fuck out of there. The others will need you more than we will, right?"

"Right," Gormley replied.

"What do you think, Hagen?" the black man asked.

"It's time, Johnson. It is time."

"Then let's go get them mothers." Johnson forced a grin. "The World Liberation Army needs some of their capitalistic money."

Gormley started the Volkswagen, carefully pulling out into the street. He stopped in front of the small bank. Several people were coming out. It was a quiet day, and not many people were out on Mack Avenue.

Johnson got out of the car, the revolver concealed in his waistband. He held the seat forward, and Hagen crawled out, twisting to keep the shotgun out of sight in the folds of his jacket. Johnson slammed the door, and they started toward the bank.

Larry Gormley was surprised at his own sense of calm.

He let a large truck go by, then drove a half block, turned around, and returned, parking in a loading zone diagonally across from the bank, from where he could see the entrance. He kept the motor running.

When Johnson and Hagen entered the bank, seven customers were inside. Four were middle-aged women, looking as worn and bleak as their surroundings. One old man was arguing with a teller about a utility bill. The bank guard was watching the quarrelsome old man. In line behind one of the women was Gino Marchetti, the owner of Marchetti's Bar and Grill. He was there to deposit the previous day's profits. Like most bar owners, he had a restricted license to carry a pistol, which allowed him to take the weapon with him to and from the bank. He had a heavy .357 Magnum revolver stuck inside his trousers in a waist holster.

Patrolman Roy Sonaberg, assigned to the Accident Prevention Bureau and therefore in plain clothes, was making out a check. He needed some money for the evening. He was taking his wife and her parents out to dinner.

Patrolman Sonaberg saw the two men come in. His practiced eye noted that one was a black man, a touch over six feet, two hundred pounds, wearing work clothes and a black knit cap. The other, a white man, was shorter, had dirty blond hair, a thick neck, a muscular build, work clothes, a worn jacket much too big for him. Both men were in their late twenties or early thirties.

Hagen walked up to the guard. The shotgun came out in an easy, almost graceful motion. He jammed the barrel into the man's fleshy side. "Freeze," he said.

"Okay," Johnson called from the front of the bank as he drew his pistol, "this is a holdup. Just do what you're told and no one will get hurt."

Marcella Weaver, a teller, slipped the safety cover off the silent alarm bell with her toe, then applied full pressure on the chrome floor button.

"Don't raise your hands, just keep them where I can see them," Johnson commanded.

Hagen reached around the bank guard and took away the man's pistol. Hagen stuck the pistol into his own waistband. The guard was red-faced and wheezing, beads of perspiration began to pop out on his forehead.

"My friend has a shotgun," Johnson said. "If you try anything, he'll blow you into little pieces, got that?"

One of the women customers answered yes in a loud, almost hysterical voice.

The old man at the teller's window glared at Johnson and Hagen, transferring his anger from the utility company to the robbers.

Patrolman Sonaberg stood perfectly still, his hands stretched out on the marble table. He could feel his palms becoming wet.

Johnson grabbed the top of the cashier cage and swung himself up onto the counter. He looked down over the glass at the three women tellers and the manager. They stood still looking straight ahead.

"All right, ladies," he said as he swung himself over the partition into the tellers' area, "I want you to fill up these bags with money." He landed lightly on the floor, displaying a surprising agility for a man his size. "And I want you to do it very fast."

"Do what he says." The white-faced manager's voice was flat with fear.

The silent alarm had been transmitted to the police dispatcher, who had put it on the air.

The precinct patrol car assigned to that sector was only a few blocks away when the radio announced a possible holdup in progress. The East Side cruiser, a special car that answered all dangerous runs, was also only minutes away. Both cars responded.

The scout car officers were unconcerned, supposing that there was just another drunk at the bank. It was becoming

routine. The people at the bank were jumpy, robbery conscious, overreacting to the slightest problem. The driver
of the scout car made a slow, careful turn and headed for
the bank. They could see the bank's entrance as they
approached.

Inside the bank Gino Marchetti was sweating. He had a
reputation as a tough man. He ran his bar with an iron
hand in a neighborhood where only an iron hand could
survive. It would be embarrassing to be caught in a holdup,
to be armed and yet do nothing. The people would think
him a coward, and that would be bad for business.

Marchetti decided he would shoot the bandit holding
the shotgun first. He pretended to scratch his neck with his
left hand as his right slowly moved for the butt of the
heavy pistol. The man with the shotgun was behind him
and to his left. He would have to draw, turn, and fire.

His heart was beating wildly as his hand closed around
the grip of the revolver. He had never fired the weapon
before but felt confident of his abilities. He was good with
weapons. In the army he had earned a marksman's badge.

Gino Marchetti pulled the large revolver. It seemed
twice as heavy now. He brought the barrel across his body
as he turned. The shot sounded like a cannon. The noise
of his own gun frightened him, numbing his mind. He saw
the bank guard slam back against the wall. He knew he
had hit the wrong man. The shotgun pointed at him as he
spoke. "Oh, Christ, I'm sorry . . ." The blast hit him in the
face. He fell against the woman next to him. Covered with
his blood and brains, she began a low mournful moan as
she regarded herself in horror.

Hagen racked the shotgun quickly, loading it again. He
glanced down at the guard. The man's dead eyes stared at
the wall. The front of his uniform shirt was marred by a
small bloody stain in the center of the chest.

The acrid smell from the gunfire began to fill the small bank.

The scout car had just pulled to the curb several doors from the bank when the officers heard the shots. One policeman excitedly reported their position and that they had heard "shots fired." He requested backup units. Guns drawn, the officers got out of the car, moving quickly to a neighboring store's doorway, from which they could cover the front of the bank.

Across the street Larry Gormley watched the policemen. It was going wrong, very wrong.

The cruiser heard the "shots fired" call. The senior officer, a tall, thin policeman with a skull face, known as Merry-Go-Round Wexler, took command. "Pull into that alley behind the bank," he told the driver. "We'll cover the back."

The other officers in the cruiser racked their shotguns and made ready as their car slid into the alleyway.

Inside the bank Patrolman Sonaberg felt sweat running down his back. Two citizens had been killed in his presence. He was an armed police officer. He didn't want to do anything, but that would be hard to explain later. He was a sworn officer, not a civilian; it was a matter of duty. He wondered who the dead man was who had tried to shoot the robber. He didn't look like a cop.

Sonaberg watched the man with the shotgun. He was the key. The other man was behind the bulletproof tellers' area and wouldn't be able to get a shot at him. The policeman decided he could worry about him later.

Behind the tellers' cage the women were frantically filling the sacks the robbers had brought with them.

The blood-covered moaning woman irritated the man with the shotgun. "Shut up," he snarled, showing emotion for the first time. "Shut up, you old bitch!"

Sonaberg drew the pistol quickly, cocking back the hammer as he leveled the barrel at the robber's chest.

"Don't move, I'm a police officer!"

Hagen's eyes met his, but the shotgun did not swing in his direction.

"Put that gun on the floor," Sonaberg commanded.

Hagen looked over at Johnson, who was moving quickly toward the door leading to the customers' area.

Sonaberg's voice was strained. "Move!" He knew the man with the tellers would react quickly. It would all be a matter of timing. First one, then the other.

Hagen shrugged. He slowly began to squat, holding the shotgun in front of him. He placed it gently on the worn tile floor.

"Get up and kick it away," Sonaberg said.

Hagen flipped the weapon with his toe; it skidded a few feet away.

Sonaberg turned as he heard the door open. Johnson had thrown open the door between the customers' and staff areas but had not stepped through. "Throw out your gun," Sonaberg snapped.

Hagen shot him, the bullet catching Sonaberg in the shoulder and spinning him before he fell. The policeman's pistol looped into the air and clattered to the tile floor. Sonaberg was fully conscious. He realized he had forgotten about the guard's pistol. It was a stupid mistake, just stupid, but at least he had taken some action, had carried out his duty.

Sonaberg lay still, feeling the pain begin to burn through his arm and shoulder.

Outside on Mack Avenue the policemen, crouched against the storefront, heard the shot and then acted more on instinct than on thought. Larry Gormley watched as one officer moved to the front of the bank. He smashed the glass with his pistol, taking care to keep back from the edge of the window. "Police," the officer shouted through the broken glass. "Come out with your hands up!"

"That tears it," Johnson said as they heard the policeman's call. "Let's get the fuck out of here." He grabbed several of the full bags.

"Hey," Hagen said, "let's keep these people as hostages. We can work something out."

Johnson shook his head as he came through the partition door. "No way, baby. They probably only got a couple of guys out front. We'll get out the back and shag-ass out of here."

"But hostages—"

"Come on," Johnson insisted, cutting Hagen off. "We still got a chance." He hurried toward the barred door at the rear.

Hagen hesitated. He looked down at the wounded man on the floor. Blood welled from the man's shoulder wound. "You really a cop?" Hagen asked.

Sonaberg was in pain, his eyes slits, his teeth clenched. "Yes," he said.

"Cops are pricks," Hagen said in a conversational tone. He pointed the revolver at the man's head and calmly pulled the trigger. The shot echoed loudly through the small bank.

"Come on, Hagen!" Johnson had the rear door unbolted. "Let's go!"

Hagen turned and ran, following Johnson out into the alley.

They faced shotguns. The cruiser men were waiting, their hard eyes challenging.

Johnson looked around, shrugged, and then dropped his pistol. Hagen hesitated, but all the barrels swung toward him. He too dropped his gun.

"Hey, we surrender," Johnson said. "We consider ourselves prisoners of war and demand that we be treated accordingly."

"You what?" Merry-Go-Round Wexler asked as he advanced.

"We are officers of the World Liberation Army," Johnson's voice took on the tone of a proclamation, "and this has been a revolutionary act to assist the people—"

Merry-Go-Round Wexler expertly snapped a blow at Johnson's jaw. The big Negro spun around like a top. Wexler nailed him again as he turned. Wexler's ability to do this had earned him the name Merry-Go-Round.

Hagen just watched, registering no emotion.

"Hey, knock it off," one of the policemen hissed, "here comes the lieutenant." Another police car came bumping into the alley. Wexler stepped back.

On Mack Avenue Larry Gormley watched the policemen enter the bank. It was all over. He turned off the motor, climbed out of the Volkswagen, and casually walked away.

He walked toward Warren Street to catch the bus. It meant they would have to move their headquarters again. Somehow they would have to get money and more guns. And if Johnson and Hagen were alive, they would have to do something to help them.

It was just a setback, Gormley thought to himself as he stepped aboard the bus. Revolution was never easy, and there were always setbacks, but he had complete confidence in their ultimate victory.

the information desk

THE information desk for the Criminal Court Building was situated in the middle of the large stone and tile lobby, the first thing you saw as you entered through the revolving doors. The information desk was a round, four-foot barricade of polished dark wood. Inside it a police officer sat on a revolving chair. It was his duty to direct people to the proper courtrooms and to answer any questions.

The job belonged to only one man. Most of the questions were already answered by a large building directory against the west wall, but they needed a job for Big Red Mehan. Big Red had been a good cop, but arthritis had begun to melt his ankle joints, and he could handle nothing more than a sit-down job. He was well liked and well connected within the police department, so special care had been given to Big Red's problem. The information desk had been the answer. Mehan was fat, florid-faced, and most of his red hair had departed from his shiny pink skull. He liked the job. Talking to people had always been a big thing with him, and now he could work a full eight-hour shift at full pay doing what he liked the best.

With his red, round face protruding over his wooden fortress, he presided over the comings and goings of the criminal court like a life-size puppet, his raspy voice squeaking out obscene observations on the parade that passed before him.

He talked to a young attorney who lounged against the wooden rail of the information desk, drinking coffee from a cardboard cup.

"Ya know why they call this place 'the Zoo'? I'll tell ya why, it's because all we ever get here is the goddamned animals. We got everything but the fuckin' peanuts here. Look at that broad over there, the big black one with her fanny against the wall. Ya see her? Jesus, big as a fuckin' elephant, but not as smart probably. Livin' on welfare, bunch of kids dumb as her. An animal. I dunno what the fuck she's here for. Might be welfare fraud, maybe a witness against the dude she's living with. With animals like that, it could be anything.

"And look over there, comin' through the door. That's attorney-at-law Archie Cominsky. Look at the way he rolls when he walks. Stretch those long arms of his a few inches more and slip that potlicker a banana and you'd have a dressed-up monkey.

"Didja see that crowd going up for that sentencing in Judge Abrams's courtroom? Man, I been here almost five years and I think they compose a cross section of everything that ever walked in here. Fruitcakes, the whole fuckin' bunch of them.

"Ya know, maybe I could start selling peanuts here. Give that mean blind son of a bitch who runs the concession stand some competition. Shit, I'd probably make a million dollars.

"The judges ain't much better than the rest, what a crop of loonies we got running this outfit. Every year it seems to get a little worse. When old Judge Harper or Judge Sullivan was alive, things were better. Now we got mostly a collection of nuts. Whole joint is screwy, ya know, but it's fun. Everyday I get to see new animals. It's like working in a zoo, but without having to shovel shit, ya know? It's a good job."

"What's that, lady?" Mehan inquired of the thin black woman whose eyes looked anxious and lost.

"Where is Judge Perry's courtroom at?" she repeated softly.

"You a defendant?"

She shook her head. "No, my son."

"Oh, too bad. Well, take those elevators over there. The courtroom is number ten, and it's on the fifth floor. Just turn right when you get off the elevators."

She nodded her thanks and shuffled off.

"Nice old woman. Polite. Her kid is probably a prick."

a matter of sentence

THE clerk smirked as the judge peeked out of his chambers into the crowded courtroom. Just like an actor counting the house, the clerk thought to himself.

It was almost time to start. The clerk stood up, stretched his short stout frame, and wished he could be in any one of a dozen other places rather than have his morning spoiled by listening to flatulent oratory. But a job was a job. He struggled into his suit coat and, with short, rapid steps, strode out of the office into the courtroom, taking his place at the long desk below the judge's bench.

It was an explosive situation, so almost half the crowd was composed of assigned uniformed police officers. Some looked bored, some looked nervous, the mood depending on each man's anticipation of what was to come. The newspaper people were out in force, jammed around the press table like piglets to a mother sow. They looked relaxed, happy with the expectation that they had a soft assignment, a predictable story, easy to write. A buzz of soft laughter and low conversation rose from the mass at the press table.

The clerk unlocked the desk drawer and extracted the case file. It was ready; he had carefully checked to make sure that all entries were up to date. He knew that lawyers complained about his abrupt manners but never about the way he kept track of the court's business.

The civilian part of the crowd, jammed into the wooden rows of seats at the back of the courtroom, had already been carefully searched in the hallway. Despite all the precautions, they still looked dangerous, a motley collection of costumed, strutting humanity representing almost every screwball "cause" in the city. This was to be their arena, the theater they had selected to prance out their carefully chosen roles.

John Patrick Rooney had been a court clerk for almost thirty years. He had buried four judges and hoped to bury the one he worked for at the moment. He had never liked judges.

Rooney knew all the players in the groups milling around in the rear of the courtroom. They always turned out for the big cases, the ones with publicity. Max Schmidt, the resident Nazi nut, was there; a flabby middle-aged man surrounded by his following of flawed young men, their pimply faces grimly set, trying to mimic the maniacal fierceness of the German SS men they aped. Flowing long white hair encasing a narrow, buck-toothed face marked attorney Melvin Markowitz. Markowitz described himself as a civil libertarian, the press described him as a left-wing radical, and the police described him as a loud-mouthed nut. He fitted all those descriptions. Markowitz's crowd was made up of pale, short-haired young women wearing horned-rimmed glasses—almost a uniform—and pimply-faced youths who sneered at the Nazis.

A pimple contest, Rooney thought to himself. All the rest of them were there too: the black radicals, the black conservatives, and the white court watchers. Just as moths arc attracted to a flame, the screwballs came flocking when they knew television would be present. Rooney had seen it all before. Each leader hoped only for a few well-chosen shouts to be recorded for the six-o'clock news. The prospect of an actual interview was considered heaven on earth.

Rooney squirmed on the rubber ring. The thing helped his hemorrhoids, but he could never get used to it. He sighed to himself. It was show time.

"Might as well bring them in, Charley," he said to the gray-haired court officer.

He had said it in a low voice, but the whole crowded courtroom seemed to quiet down in anticipation. Charley gathered a few bulky policemen, and they returned to the courtroom with the two defendants.

They were escorted to chairs behind their lawyers, where the officers ceremoniously removed the handcuffs that bound each of them. However, they were immediately surrounded by a sea of blue police shirts.

George Hagen and Jesse Johnson—locally their names, Hagen and Johnson, had become household words—awaited their sentencing.

Their efforts to rob the Farrell Savings Bank had resulted in the death of a bank guard and the murder of a policeman and a customer. They claimed to be soldiers in the World Liberation Army—not enlisted men, either—one was a colonel and the other a field marshal. Because the murders had been committed while in the perpetration of a felony—robbery armed—they had been charged with first-degree murder, and the death penalty had been requested by the prosecution.

S. Harry Flynt, the Chicago-based radical lawyer, had descended from the heights of his national reputation to defend them. It was the beginning of summer, news was slow, so the trial and the antics of S. Harry Flynt had provided some spark of interest and color during the news lull. He made fiery speeches and was even thrown into jail briefly for contempt of court. But the end result had been the same as most cases the great man defended, the jury had found them guilty as charged.

The new Death Penalty Act just passed by the state legislature called for a second jury to determine whether the ultimate penalty was to be exacted. That jury, hearing of the heartless murder of Patrolman Sonaberg, quickly recommended death. Under the law the trial judge had no discretion, he had to send the doomed men to the gas chamber. Sentencing was just a formality. However, the news was still slow, and although everyone knew what was going to happen, the media was giving the event full coverage.

Rooney kept a weather eye on the office door. He was good at it after all his years. He popped up just as the judge came into view, his black robe flowing about him.

"All rise," Rooney called in a tone of voice that implied instant doom to anyone who let his or her seat stay in contact with the wooden benches. "The criminal court is now in session, the Honorable Herbert Abrams presiding." He sang out the phrase in a sort of nasal song.

Rooney didn't have to turn around, he just listened as the judge eased himself into the great, squeaky leather chair behind him. "Be seated!" Rooney snapped out the words quickly, punctuating them with a rap of his gavel on the wooden block. It sounded like a pistol shot, and he was amused to note that several of the more nervous police officers jumped at the sound.

"*People* versus *Hagen and Johnson*," Rooney intoned through his nose, giving the words a disinterested sound, like a railroad conductor calling the next stop.

John Patrick Rooney parked himself back on top of the rubber ring. He had completed his part in this theater of the people; now he was content to sit back and let someone else star for a while.

Judge Abrams waited dramatically before speaking. Then, good showman that he was, he kept his voice low, forcing those assembled before him to strain to hear his words.

"Let me say at the outset that this is a court of law and not a circus. I will tolerate no demonstrations or outbursts of any kind from anyone. Is that clear?"

"Oh, go fuck yourself," Defendant Hagen called out in a bored voice. The crowd laughed, and there was a ripple of applause.

Judge Abrams never changed expression. He looked as cool as ice. He had expected just such behavior and was prepared to handle it. "Can't you control your clients?" he growled at S. Harry Flynt.

"Control them?" Flynt cried as he popped from his chair. He too had his act ready. "Control them? You are about to send these two boys to their death, and you ask me to control them? They have a right to scream at the injustice that is on display today. They have a right to cry out—"

"Fuck you too, commie," one of the neo-Nazis called from the rear. He was grabbed by a burly officer and shoved out of the courtroom.

"There can be no due process, no fair hearing, not when counsel for the defense is subjected to vile and insipid cries of hate. It is the basis—"

Judge Abrams held up his hand to stop Flynt. "Better wait," he said, his tone almost friendly. "I see one of the newsmen can't get his tape recorder working."

Flynt's head spun around, and he looked over at the press table. He studied the group for a moment before he realized that no one had a tape recorder. His face grew red, and he exploded in a torrent of words.

Judge Abrams leaned back, his face dignified, his attitude interested yet impartial. It was his mask. It would be a long, tedious day, for Flynt was incapable of saying anything briefly. Although he appeared attentive, Judge Abrams allowed his mind to wander to more interesting things. He contemplated the cool beauty and promise of the lovely Mrs. Sam Cohen, who, with luck, would be his before the tennis season ended. It would all depend upon his practiced skill and the continuing neglect by Dr. Cohen of his deliciously beautiful wife.

It took Flynt three hours to finally finish his remarks. Defendant Johnson, his black face continually angry, had kept pace with his lawyer's talk, crying out "right on" and "amen" at appropriate times. Defendant Hagen had given in to boredom: His blond head rested on his chest, his eyes closed and his breathing even. He was asleep.

"Bring the prisoners forward," Judge Abrams commanded, acutely aware that lunchtime had passed. The officers woke Hagen up and brought both men before the bench.

"You heard the remarks of your counsel, Mr. Flynt. Is there anything you wish to say before this court passes sentence?"

"You fish-peddling Jew bastard," Defendant Johnson shouted, "I'll pass sentence on you! I hereby sentence you to be shot in the nuts until you are dead!" It was a scream of hate.

Nervous laughter rippled through the back of the courtroom. Johnson turned angrily. "You think it's funny, you motherfuckers? You think it's funny! You won't think so when the World Liberation Army executes this little Jew prick!"

Another "fuck you" brought instant ejection of yet another of the crew-cut crowd.

Judge Abrams turned to Hagen as if he hadn't heard Johnson's remarks. "How about you?" he asked Hagen, his voice almost kindly.

Hagen yawned. "He's not kidding, you know." Hagen's

voice was still sleep-filled. "They will get your ass." The words were spoken in almost the same kindly tone as the judge had used. The lack of emotion in the words made the threat strangely chilling.

Judge Abrams glanced over at the press crew. They were all writing furiously. It would make good copy, this death-threat business, and you couldn't buy that kind of publicity. He had a moment's concern but quickly put it out of his mind.

The judge coughed gently to clear his throat. "Each of you has been convicted of first-degree murder. The jury selected for that purpose saw fit to recommend the death penalty. Your actions can only be described as cold-blooded and—"

"Oh, fuck off," Johnson growled.

Judge Abrams felt his temper rise and he fought an impulse to reply in kind. He controlled himself. After all, he really held the ultimate trump card. "It is the sentence of this court that you both be taken to the state prison located at Tecumseh and there, at six o'clock in the morning of September fifteenth next, you shall be executed in the manner provided by statute."

"You going to be dead long before that, you honkie bastard!" Johnson screamed.

Even before they got the prisoners out the door, John P. Rooney jumped up and, in a voice that defied any protest, he called, "This honorable court stands recessed," cracking his gavel against the wooden block.

Some of the reporters clustered about S. Harry Flynt, who loudly proclaimed a national drive to free the "political" prisoners and to stop the death penalty. He was just warming up for the television cameras that waited outside in the hallway. Some of the reporters trotted after the doomed prisoners, hoping to get a few extra angles for their stories. The rest of the newspapermen chatted with the affable Judge Abrams, who, although threatened by a terrorist army, remained cool and detached and displayed a ready wit.

All of which disgusted John P. Rooney and caused his hemorrhoids to throb even worse.

the world liberation army

THE headquarters of the World Liberation Army had been moved to a cheap furnished apartment above a porno bookstore. The landlord, the operator of the bookstore, thought the group were probably using the place for some kind of offbeat sex. Had he known it was political, he would have been appalled—that sort of thing could bring trouble.

The windows were closed so that no one could hear what was said within the apartment. The day was warm, and the quarters were ovenlike. The atmosphere inside had been tinted blue with the curling, pungent smoke of marijuana cigarettes.

"I still say we have to do something." Alice Mary Brennan spoke, her words slightly slurred. The oldest of the group, nearing forty, she had started out in a convent looking for a way to serve mankind. Then came a stint in the Peace Corps, and following that service she was slowly converted to becoming a more radical activist. She had been jailed in Canada for protesting the seal hunts, and from the contacts in jail and other underground connections she had eventually ended up as a leader in the World

Liberation Army, pledged to bloody revolution. She had the title of secretary of defense, cabinet rank. Alice Mary Brennan was thick and heavy-limbed, physical gifts from ancient Irish ancestors, who had had to work with their bodies. "We must do something," she repeated, looking at the dull faces staring at her with vacant eyes.

"Can't do nothin' cause we ain't got no money and no guns," Flash Johnson said. His first name was Coleman but everyone called him Flash. He was Jesse Johnson's younger brother. He lacked the revolutionary zeal of his brother, coming into the "movement" primarily because it was a good vehicle to get white women.

"We'll get money, goddamn it," Albert Martin snarled. He had been appointed secretary of the treasury and was touchy about the fact that they were broke. "But hitting a lousy bank is all wrong. There's just too much protection, too much heat." His thin chest, bare and hairless, heaved with the effort of talking. "We'll have to look for smaller targets, an all-night drugstore or a supermarket. They're always good for a couple of thousand."

"Whatcha goin' to hold 'em up with? Your dick?" Flash Johnson laughed so hard at his own wit that he fell over sideways, his head coming to rest on the bare thigh of Thelma Sturdevant, who had pulled her skirt up to cool her long legs.

"Be quiet, General," Alice Mary snapped. "You know I don't like that kind of language."

"Don't care much for dick neither," Flash Johnson replied petulantly. She was the only female member with whom he had not scored. He would have been more resentful if she had neglected to call him by his proper title. He liked being a general.

"When Larry gets back from L.A., then we'll get moving," Al Martin said.

"How you know that dude's ever comin' back, man? I

mean, he's been gone one hell of a long time. The cops might have offed him, ya know?"

"He'll be back," Thelma Sturdevant said dreamily. She shifted a bit to compensate for the weight of Flash Johnson's head on her leg. "Larry will be back. He'll read about the sentencing and he'll come right back. He knows we need leadership."

"Leadership?" Flash Johnson sat up. "Where the hell was our leader when they was trying my brother and Hagen? Shit, he took out of here like a striped-ass ape. He's probably out there on the coast laying half the women in southern California. Ain't much of a leader, no way."

"He went out there to get money and guns," Alice Mary said. She inhaled deeply on the joint passed to her by Al Martin. "If he's successful, we'll be ready to hit the court and take care of that judge who sentenced your brother and Hagen."

"That won't do my brother no good." Flash Johnson's eyes were red from the smoke. "Shit, won't do any of us any good, even if we were able to pull it off."

"But your brother ordered it," Alice Mary protested.

"Woman, he just wasn't thinking, that's all. Damn, even if we did manage to knock off that asshole judge, we would get so many bullets through us we'd look like cheese." Flash shook his head. "And if we did it, man, then they would really give it to my brother and Hagen. I mean even the fuckin' Supreme Court would be so pissed off that they'd come down to the prison just to watch them die."

"Well, do you have a plan?" Thelma asked, her voice sleepy.

"Look, you girls can hustle your ass a little, you know, just turn a few tricks, that's all. Then, as soon as we got enough money for a gun—and that don't take much—Al and me will hit Miller's Cut-Rate Drugs. On a Saturday night that place is good for a nice two-thousand-dollar score, easy."

"And then what?" Alice Mary's voice was filled with anger by his suggestion.

"Oh, I don't know, maybe live off the money for a while, hustle a little more ass, hit another store. Something like that."

The heat was oppressive. Alice Mary struggled to her feet. She was overweight and had an awkward time rising from the hard wood floor. She looked at the bearded Martin; the thin black; and the sweaty, half-dressed blonde. "I came here to help lead a world revolution," she began. "When I first met you people, you were pledged to revolution and social justice and you were ready to die for your beliefs. Now you are just disgusting!"

"It's just this fucking heat," Al Martin said, getting up. "I'm going to get out of here for a while, just to cool off." He paused. "We'll wait for Larry before we do anything on our own."

"How long we going to wait?" Flash Johnson asked, his arm now around the shoulders of Thelma Sturdevant.

Alice Mary's voice was hard and icy when she spoke. "A week, no more." Her eyes challenged the others.

Flash shrugged. "Suits me."

Al Martin looked as if he wanted to protest, then he nodded slowly. "Okay, one week, no more." He looked down at the blond girl being fondled by Flash Johnson. "That okay with you, Thelma?"

She looked up at him with vacant eyes; her facial muscles sagged from the relaxing effect of the marijuana. "Huh?"

"We wait one more week for Larry before we do anything else, okay?"

She didn't fully understand but nodded her assent.

Alice Mary walked out of the apartment with Al Martin after he had put on a wrinkled shirt. They hardly noticed that Flash was undressing the lethargic Thelma as they left. They had seen it all before anyway.

"Are all terrorist gangs this well organized?" Alice Mary asked sourly as she followed Al Martin down the dark, narrow staircase to the street.

"Don't let Flash bother you," Martin said softly. "We have a job to do, and we'll do it. That judge is as good as dead."

His quiet dedication reassured her, and she felt much better.

the supreme court

LIKE many other large industrial cities, the manufacturing center of the state had a separate criminal court with jurisdiction over all crimes committed within the city limits. Other courts served the civil needs of the millions who lived in the area, but criminal justice depended entirely upon the activities conducted within the walls of the Criminal Court Building. The criminal court, despite the fact that it provided its judges with full rank and high judicial salaries, was regarded by most as no more than a glorified police court, and lately it had come to be called "the Zoo" by all who were closely acquainted with that institution.

Its halls were filled with the scum of the city's underside. Junkies, winos, pimps, prostitutes, holdup men, and killers thronged through its corridors. The veteran defense lawyers, although their garb ranged from seedy to gaudily expensive silk suits, shared a mutual trait: They were smart, aggressive, and loud. The prosecutors, on the other hand, were usually young, inexperienced, and easy marks for their more skilled opponents. The policemen and detectives who moved through this human river were universally grim and irritable. The court's hallways at the end of the day were empty tunnels littered with squashed cigarettes, crushed potato chips, and debris of every kind imaginable.

Monied lawyers wrinkled their noses in distaste at the mere mention of the criminal court. It was no place for a gentleman. If they needed criminal work done, they hired one of the loud silk-suit types to do it, feeling distaste at even this isolated contact.

So "the Zoo" was the last thing Justice James Tingle expected to discuss in the quiet, posh surroundings of the state's supreme court, its highest tribunal.

He was called James "The King" Tingle, and he had become accustomed to posh surroundings. It hadn't always been so. A poor black, he had worked his way through college and law school following World War II with the help of the GI Bill. He had landed a job as a law clerk with a black firm and then had passed the bar just in time to fill the need that suddenly developed for black candidates in political parties hungry for the growing black vote.

First had come his election to the state senate. It was a job he hated, but it did add to his power and prestige in the black community. As populations shifted, he campaigned and won a term in Congress. He liked Washington but was dismayed at the length of time required to achieve power and rank. He ran for the state supreme court and was elected, the first black lawyer to achieve that honor. He had served as justice of the supreme court for almost five years.

He was big, both in height and width. Tingle stood a full six and one-half feet tall in his stockinged feet. His weight had become enormous, but he carried it well on his large frame. He enjoyed life and lived it in high style, a style that had earned him the title "King." He tried to be worthy of that name, living expensively and well. A big, boisterous man, loud and outgoing, he either charmed people or overwhelmed them with his noisy manner and earthy humor. Publicly, however, he presented an entirely different front. He made it a point never to smile in a photograph, and he was careful not to display his rough humor whenever he was in front of television's unforgiving eye. In his campaign pictures he looked like an oversized black angel, serious, just, and fair. It was a good image for the voters, and he tried to protect it despite his natural tendencies the other way.

The outer office of the chief justice was manned by an elderly, birdlike woman who had served the court longer than any of the justices. She was absolutely terrified of Justice Tingle and dreaded having to call him. When he came stalking through the office door in response to her summons, she felt a chill of fear as he walked by, winking an eye at her. Somehow the gesture seemed more threatening than friendly. The big man passed into the private chambers of H. Raymond Buckington, the state's chief justice.

"Hey, Buck, what's up, man?" Tingle knew that the wealthy, blue-blooded Buckington liked to imagine himself as "hip" and felt especially favored if Tingle talked to him in what he considered to be "street language."

His friends called him Buck to his face, but when he wasn't around, and especially among lawyers, he was dubbed Beaver Buckington because of his protruding upper teeth—his mother thought it made him look British and never had the flaw corrected. Buckington was an official "liberal," despite his inherited millions, and his legal opinions were universally on the side of the workingman.

Sometimes he had to call a labor leader late at night to find just what side the workingman was on, but as soon as that was established, they could count on Buck Buckington to rally to the cause.

He loved the minorities as classes. He favored all black causes and had been honored many times for his stand on civil rights. Privately he avoided most of the blacks he knew, since he did not understand their speech half the time.

Buckington's life had been isolated, and he really had no idea of what went on in the great outside world. Buckington believed that he knew all about men and women, their hopes and problems. He sincerely believed it. But James Tingle knew the man's limits. Buckington, not knowing any better, would accept the world of blacks as explained and interpreted to him by James Tingle. Tingle was as close to Buckington as the chief justice ever allowed any minority person to get. This had proved very useful to King Tingle.

A small man, trim, white-haired, and sixty, Buckington looked the picture of a chief justice. The other members of the court had voted him into the job because he looked like a chief justice and because he made nice, harmless speeches.

Buckington smiled up at the huge black man and nodded at a large leather chair. As soon as Tingle was seated, Buckington got up and dramatically closed the chamber door.

"What's happening, baby?" Tingle laughed. "You got a bottle hidden away, or what?"

Buckington smiled warmly. His protruding teeth caught the overhead lights and gleamed his pleasure at what he thought Tingle might have considered a fine joke. "James," he began in his high-pitched voice, "I'm afraid we have quite a problem on our hands."

Tingle's protective instincts came alive like revolving radar antennae. He had three quarreling girl friends, a mountain of gambling debts, and his liver was, according to his doctor, beginning to die from all the alcohol he consumed. He wondered which "problem" had gotten to the ear of the chief justice.

"It is that criminal court in the city, James," Buckington said, much to the relief of the large black man. "They have a clogged docket down there. It takes almost a full year for a defendant to be brought to trial, and the jails are full with people who can't make bail and who may be innocent. The newspapers are beginning to take notice. And, as you know, the supreme court has responsibility for the proper administration of all the courts in the state, and that includes the criminal court. Oh, I know that most of that duty is only on paper, but nevertheless the papers will come after us. So, James, we must do something about the criminal court, and we must do it quickly."

"Shit," Tingle said. "All that court needs is more judges. Say, Buck, we have superintending control over all the judges in the state, why not send a flock of those jackasses up north down there? That should do it."

The chief justice shook his head. "Ever since Judge Yimburg got mugged down there, I just can't get as many volunteers as I used to."

"Order the bastards to go!"

"I can, of course, but the outstate judges complain that the criminal court judges don't do enough work. Those who have been down there say there isn't a judge around in the afternoon. They say they will pitch in if the regulars do their part. They do have a point, James."

"Whole bunch is just a shiftless mob of no-goods. None of them remember how to do a day's work. That's what the trouble is." He knew Buckington considered every judge but himself to be lazy, so the statement would be quickly accepted as just another bit of authentic street wisdom.

"You have put your finger right on the sore spot, James. Yes sir, you and I have always thought alike. If we can get those criminal people to work, it could solve the whole situation."

"Mule won't work less somebody whacks it with a stick." Tingle hoped that offering sounded folksy enough.

The chief justice chuckled. "Wisdom, James, the true wisdom of the people. James, I am going to give you that stick, and I want you to go down there and whip that mule!" The beaver teeth gleamed once more.

"Hey, man!" Tingle started to protest. He wanted no part of "the Zoo."

"Please, James, it's the only answer. You are the only man who can do it. The job requires the forceful presence of a supreme court justice, and I know you have the respect of many of those people." Buckington meant the black judges, and they both knew it. "Think about it, James."

Tingle shifted his bulk, causing the expensive chair to shriek in protest. His mind worked like a computer. If he were successful, it could be a political gold mine for him. He could establish a reputation as a take-charge administrator. If unsuccessful, it would go down as a good try. He couldn't really lose. And he could control the docket. Suddenly he realized he was being handed an honest-to-God, real gold mine by Buckington. The man who had complete control of the criminal docket could "take care of" cases, and that would mean money, big money, enough money to settle his debts, perhaps more. He could end up rich!

Tingle nodded thoughtfully. "If you feel it's the only way, Buck," he said at last.

Buckington was delighted. "Oh, I do, James, I do. And

you will have the full power of the supreme court behind
you. You will be the czar down there. We'll have a slow
summer here anyway, so we can get along without you for
a while, and you'll be doing a real service for justice."
Buck Buckington would also feel more comfortable if
James Tingle was out of town during the annual supreme
court golf outing at the Kingsbrook Country Club. They
would admit him, black or not, of course, but it had always been a bit of a strain before. Now everyone could
relax and have a good time.

The large black man stood and extended his huge hand
to the chief justice. "I'll do a good job for you down there,
boss," he said, grinning.

Buckington's teeth gleamed again. "I know you will,
James. I know you will."

Both men, for entirely different reasons, were genuinely
pleased.

chapter two

the world liberation army

JUST like Santa Claus, he arrived in the middle of the night, his bag packed to capacity. He had made it two days before the deadline ran out, although he had no way of knowing that a deadline for his appearance had even been set.

He climbed up the poorly lit stairway carrying the heavy army surplus duffel bag on his back. The drive from California had taken almost two weeks. He had to avoid the interstate highways and the patrolling police, so he had been forced to use the old highways and less-traveled side roads. He was careful, and it had been slow going. The car was stolen, and although he had changed license plates, he didn't want to push his good luck, which was running hot, very hot.

He tapped lightly at the paint-chipped, worn wooden surface of the apartment door. He had long ago lost his key. There was no answer, but he could hear the muffled sound of snoring inside.

He was tired and impatient, so his rapping grew louder and more insistent.

The snoring stopped, and he could hear whispers inside. "Who is that?"

He recognized Flash Johnson's voice.

"Flash, it's me, Larry. Let me in."

There was a pause, then the door opened a few inches. There were no lights on inside the apartment. Two eyes peered out at him.

Then the door was flung wide open. "Goddamn, if it ain't," Flash said loudly. "Shit, man, we thought you was dead."

"Keep your voice down and help me with this."

A light went on inside the apartment. Flash was completely naked, his long, thin body sleek except for knobby elbows and knees. He helped Larry Gormley lug the heavy bag into the room, then closed the door.

Thelma Sturdevant stood in the middle of the room, blinking her eyes in sleepy confusion. She too was naked but apparently not conscious of it. "Larry?" she asked, wondering if she was having another drug-related hallucination.

"Yeah, it's me, honey."

She walked slowly forward and then threw both her arms around him. "I missed you," she said, her stale breath making him draw back.

"I'll bet you did. Go get some clothes on."

Alice Mary Brennan came out of her bedroom, her lumpy body wrapped in a worn, faded robe. She too blinked at him, trying to come awake.

Al Martin came in from the kitchen, where he kept a cot. Scratching his thick beard with one hand, his other hand held up a pair of wrinkled trousers.

"Glad to see me?" Larry Gormley asked. He felt the fatigue lifting now that he had reached safety. He grinned at them, displaying the dimples and college-boy freshness that had always made him so popular. His blond hair had been cut short but was nicely styled. He was tanned and lean.

"Where in the hell have you been?" Alice Mary's voice whined angrily. "They convicted Johnson and Hagen, and they're going to execute them. Just where the hell have you been while all this has been happening?" Her words became harsh and loud.

"Things have been hot here, Larry," Martin said. "I think you owe us an explanation."

Flash Johnson said nothing. He grinned guiltily as he struggled to get his trousers over his thin legs. Thelma had covered herself with a sheet. After all, Thelma had been Larry Gormley's girl. Flash tried to determine if Gormley might really be sore. He had his razor in his trouser pocket, just in case.

Gormley looked at them. "Things have been 'hot,' huh?" His voice was full of disdain. "How hot? Have you done anything, or have you just sat around waiting for the cops to come jamming in here? Is that your definition of hot? Well, maybe I'm wrong about you people. Did you get any operating money? Did you get any weapons?"

"Don't give us that . . . that . . ." Alice Mary could still not bring herself to say shit. "We have been waiting for you. You were only supposed to be gone a week or so, but it's been months!"

He laughed. "Some rebels! God, you people need a keeper, not a leader. I'll show you what I've been doing." He unzipped the duffel bag. "You need weapons, right? I mean all armies have to have weapons. Try this for size."

He dipped into the duffel bag and pulled out a German machine pistol; a glistening black weapon with a long ammunition clip hanging down in front of the trigger guard.

"Damn!" Al Martin said reverently.

"And this." Gormley pulled out a British-made Sten gun, a tubelike automatic weapon. He laid it on the floor and then gently dropped loaded clips next to the weapon.

There wasn't a sound in the apartment.

"Now these." Gormley began taking pistols from within the bag and laying them on the floor. "And the best prize of all," he announced proudly. Tipping the bag on its side, he rolled out a dozen army hand grenades.

"Jesus, Mary, and Joseph!" Alice Mary exclaimed.

"Well, what do you think of my California trip now?" Gormley asked quietly.

Their eyes were riveted on the weapons arrayed at their feet.

"My God," Al Martin said in awe, "we'll be invincible."

Flash Johnson felt nervous just looking at all the deadly hardware. He preferred a nice chrome-plated revolver or a dependable switchblade knife. They were weapons he was familiar with and liked. The stuff on the floor spelled real danger. He swallowed to help his suddenly dry mouth.

Gormley pulled out an old cigar box from the duffel bag. He opened it, taking out rolls of money and tossing them playfully at the others. "About eight thousand dollars, give or take a few expenses." He stood up, his eyes suddenly hard. "Now, you tell me, just what the hell have you people done for the cause?"

executive judge's problem

"GOOD night, Judge." His law clerk waved a cheery fare-well from the office door.

"See you tomorrow," Judge Powell smiled up at her.

Ted Hemmings, one of the policemen assigned to his courtroom, came in. "Can I give you a lift home, Judge?"

"No, thank you, Ted. I brought my car down today."

"Want me to hang around until you're ready to leave?"

The judge shook his head. "That won't be necessary, Ted. You go on. I'll be here for a while."

The policeman frowned. "It can get a little rough down here at night, Judge. I'd be happy to stick around if you want."

Judge Clyde Powell leaned back in his chair. He was touched by the officer's concern. "This is Wednesday, Ted," he said. "I happen to know you bowl tonight." He chuckled. "Of course, I might be doing your team a favor if I kept you away, but there really is no need. I'm parked in the judge's lot beneath the building, and there is a guard on duty. I'm a big boy now, I'll make it. You go ahead and win a trophy tonight. I'll see you tomorrow."

The big officer grinned and shrugged. "Okay, if you want to be difficult. I'll see you tomorrow." He was gen-uinely fond of the tall black judge. They had been to-gether now for a number of years.

"Tomorrow," Judge Powell said.

After the officer left, the courtroom was silent. Judge Powell tried to return his full attention to the yellow pad in front of him. On the pad were the figures for the cases heard by the court for the preceding month. He had also recorded the number of persons in jail awaiting trial. The totals were alarming. The jail population was building up sharply, while the rate of cases disposed of showed no increase at all. They were losing the battle.

He stood up and stretched, easing the ache in his back. He was sixty-one years old and people kept telling him that he was still young, but he didn't feel young.

Since the death of his wife he had become acutely aware of the advance of age. Life seemed to be quite empty, one day being very much like another. He made a special effort to try to fill up his hours. There were always political meetings to attend, and his friends had been lavish in their invitations, but it was never the same.

His son, George, was in Washington, a government lawyer. His daughter was in Seattle with her doctor husband. Now all that was left of their family was the annual visit, usually by him, and somehow they seemed to have lost that special closeness they enjoyed when his wife was alive. He sighed aloud, realizing he was depressed. He had read up on what happens to surviving spouses, and he was painfully passing through each stage. He would recover, but even the books made the stark point: It would never ever be the same.

The other judges had elected him executive judge. After the death of his wife he was grateful for the extra work. Now running the criminal court had become a challenge. The mass of cases threatened to engulf them all, but none of the others seemed to care.

Judge Powell looked out at the traffic flowing below his office. Everyone was in a hurry, everyone had a place to go. He envied them.

He forced himself to the figures. The monthly meeting of all the judges was scheduled for tomorrow, and he hoped he could marshal enough facts to inspire the other judges to work harder, to apply themselves to the very real problem of the growing mountain of cases. Also, tomorrow's meeting marked an anniversary. It would be his first year as executive judge. They would hold the annual election for that post. He didn't have to worry about losing, because no one else wanted the job. Unless he was prepared to protest strongly, he would be reelected. It was just as well; he needed the extra tasks to occupy his mind and fill his empty hours. And he liked to think the court needed his careful management and mature judgment.

He took out his pen and began to break the figures of cases heard into two columns, jury and nonjury. He forgot his own loneliness as he concentrated on the work before him.

the assistant prosecutor

EMERALDS Mulligan was not Irish. He was a well-fleshed black lawyer who favored expensive but loud clothes and who had received his name because of the large emerald rings he wore, two on each hand. The glistening green stones were laid in heavy gold settings. Emeralds had been mugged once and had a finger broken as the thieves struggled to get his rings off, but the experience had not affected his taste. He immediately replaced the rings as soon as the splint had been removed.

So that such a nuisance would never again have to be endured, Emeralds had defended two hoodlums free but with the provision that they find and punish the thieves.

He didn't need cops. The two avengers gave full service. The junkies who had been so bold as to rob the distinguished Emeralds Mulligan had their arms, both arms, broken—slowly. The word soon spread on the street, and Mulligan and his emerald rings were forever safe.

He was a good trial lawyer. Perhaps a bit loud in his delivery but shrewd in judging what a jury might buy. However, his real skill lay in negotiating pleas—called plea bargaining by the press, but known as copping a plea among the less literary set who frequented the criminal court.

Emeralds Mulligan was the lawyer used by Goldfadden Bonds, an establishment that provided bail money at a suitable rental; and being the biggest bonding office, they in turn provided Mulligan with enough clients for a thriving and hectic criminal law practice. He split his fee with the bondsman but used the bond office as his headquarters, thereby saving a considerable sum in overhead expenses.

Mulligan had weathered the wild disorder of the morning case call: the presiding judge's hassle with the attorneys assembled for the day's trials. He had maneuvered until he was assigned to a courtroom he considered reasonably favorable.

Mulligan first considered the judge. The choice often depended on the kind of case he had. Judge Woldanski was death on reduced pleas, even if the prosecutor recommended it. He had wiggled his way successfully against assignment to her courtroom. On the rare occasion when he couldn't avoid it and was assigned to her, Mulligan went to trial. Most of the other regular criminal court lawyers also disdained pleas before Old Lady Woldanski, preferring to take their chances with a jury.

He also considered the assistant prosecutor assigned to a courtroom. He would have to get official sanction if a plea was to be offered. He knew each man well and studied his basic personality, noting each lawyer's particular likes and dislikes. Bribes only invited jail, at least where most of them were concerned. However, other favors, completely legal, were remembered. Mulligan had a mental catalog of each trial man the prosecutor's office employed, and he made it his business to find out which man was assigned to each judge each month.

He had been assigned to old Cannonball O'Brien's courtroom. Cannonball, he knew, was not averse to settling a few legal matters for money, but he only dealt with a "club" of trusted legal cronies, mostly Irish, and Mulligan knew, despite his name, that he was the wrong color to get into O'Brien's "club." But the old man was not a hardnose and would usually go along with anything recommended by the prosecutor assigned to him.

Ace Gilbert was the assistant prosecutor working Judge O'Brien's courtroom. Emeralds liked Gilbert. He was a young man who never seemed to take himself or the world too seriously. And the experienced black attorney knew that Gilbert was amused by him but respected his abilities, so the two of them hit it off very well. Gilbert wouldn't take a "dive" on a case, but he was reasonable and would listen to a well-reasoned approach.

Emeralds Mulligan walked into the courtroom, booming a greeting to everyone there by name. He had a cigar for the clerk and a leering wink for the judge's young female court reporter. It was a loud but pleasing entrance, and he had perfected it as an actor might perfect a winning stage performance.

He extended his jeweled hand to Ace Gilbert and pumped the young man's hand vigorously. "Well, baby, you and me got some work to do today. We sure do! Frankly, my man, I am prepared to whip your white ass all over this here courtroom. The state is wrong, and I feel strong . . . whoeee!"

Gilbert grinned. "Whatcha got, Emeralds?"

"The fascist blue devils have gone and done wrong this time, and no lie. They have accused my client, Mr. Washington T. Brown, of criminally assaulting his beloved girl friend with intent to commit great bodily harm." That charge carried a ten-year sentence, and with his client's record, Brown stood to do most of it.

"Anybody hurt?" Gilbert asked. The detective in charge of the case hadn't come up to the courtroom yet, so Gilbert had no knowledge of the details of the crime.

"Cut his girl friend a wee bit," Emeralds grinned. " 'Bout fifty or sixty stitches' worth."

Gilbert whistled.

"Just a lover's quarrel, you understand, that's all, just a short misunderstanding."

"Sounds like a little more misunderstanding and the lady might have been killed," Gilbert said. "Is she going to prosecute?"

"Yeah, she's pissed off 'cause he's got another woman. That's what started the whole thing in the first place. You know how these women can get."

"Tell me, how do you plan to whip my ass with a case like that?"

Mulligan laughed. "Shit, the defendant got carved too. Not as many stitches, but she was coming at him like a flashing propeller. Self-defense, my man, self-defense, pure and simple."

"He got cut?"

"Both arms. Trying to ward her off, you know."

"Got a record?"

"Yeah, long one, but most of the convictions were all for gambling, except for one long stretch for car theft. Washington T. Brown is not a violent man, no sir."

"Jury?"

"I asked for one. Of course, if you was to offer me, say, simple assault, I might persuade Brown to go for that."

Gilbert laughed. "Not with that many stitches, even with possible self-defense. Hell, if he was really trying to defend himself, I don't mind if the jury lets him go."

The negotiations had begun.

"That's exactly what it was, self-defense. My man will testify that the lady—scorned, you know—came at him with her little knife and he had to use his blade to escape from being skinned alive." Emeralds paused, shaking his head. "Of course, she says just about the opposite thing. She claims—and I shall prove that she lies—that Brown tried to rape her, and when she resisted, he pulled out his knife and went to work. She will say—all lies, you understand—that she managed to get a few licks in with her trusty pigsticker but that it didn't do any good."

"Sounds like I've a pretty good case, Emeralds, at least if what you say is accurate."

"Hey, Ace, have I ever lied to you?"

Gilbert shrugged. "Oh, maybe you've colored a few things now and then, but no, you've never lied to me."

"Right! When I say something, you can hang your hat on it, man. That's the case. It could go either way, Ace, what with them both carved up."

"Maybe."

"How about aggravated assault? That's only a year. Brown ain't really a bad guy. He'll serve time, and everybody will be satisfied."

"I don't know. You know the office policy on serious injury. It wouldn't look too good, you've got to admit that."

"Sure it would, Ace. Hell, you never know what a jury might do. This way the state gets its pound of flesh, and Brown does a little time to remind him to pick up only unarmed girls from now on."

Gilbert shook his head. "No, I don't think I can go for aggravated." He thought for a moment, as if weighing his next words carefully. "I might go for felonious assault, but only maybe."

"Christ, Ace, that's four years. With Brown's record, he'll get most of that."

"Best I can do, Emeralds, and I have to check that first with the officers in charge. I'll go for that only if they approve. I don't want any more hassles with the cops, at least not over this kind of case anyway."

Emeralds pretended disappointment, but inwardly he was elated. He had hoped for just that offer. He knew his client, who was court wise, would be delighted.

"I don't know, Ace. Maybe. I'll have to check with Brown. After all, he's the one who has to do the time."

"Well, it still depends on the cops," Gilbert said. "Oh, here they come now. I'll ask them and let you know."

The tall prosecutor made his way to the pair of detectives who had just escorted the prisoner up to the courtroom. Emeralds Mulligan knew them both, old-timers and lazy as hell. They would go for anything, just to have the morning free. He knew they'd put on a show for the prosecutor, pretending they were disturbed about the proposed plea, but in the end they would "reluctantly" come around and agree.

Even considering time off for good behavior, Emeralds Mulligan had saved his client at least four years in prison. That was well worth the fee on anybody's scale of things.

Mulligan watched Ace Gilbert talking earnestly to the cops. He liked Gilbert. Most of the criminal trial lawyers did. Emeralds knew that Gilbert didn't like plea bargaining. Gilbert would rather try the case than negotiate a reduced charge. That in itself marked him as different. Only the very good ones preferred battle to compromise, and Gilbert was one of those. But it was all part of the business, the good old American criminal justice system. Emeralds hoped that Gilbert would make the adjustment, that he wouldn't go sour and quit, like so many others. The court needed good men like Ace Gilbert.

Emeralds smiled as he watched Gilbert come walking back, his long form slightly stooped. From the assistant prosecutor's slightly disgusted expression, Mulligan knew he had a deal.

an informal meeting

Justice James "The King" Tingle had carefully planned out his strategy. The political training he had received in the state senate and in Congress had not been wasted. He knew exactly what to do. If everything went well, he could expect pleasant editorials, freedom from debt, and the gratitude of Chief Justice Buckington—which might come in very handy sometime in the future.

Tingle had eaten a snack at the Alpha Restaurant, one of his favorite places in the state capital, chosen not only because of the food but also because the oversized chairs easily accommodated his large bulk. He was comfortable there. He found the chairs in fewer and fewer restaurants fit as he continued his unstinted life-style.

The two-hour drive down from the state capital had been pleasant enough. His big new Continental, a gift from the taxpayers, hummed along. He had listened to the FM radio as the sun set in his rearview mirror. The trip was not tiring, and it gave his stomach a chance to digest the food consumed.

There was no hurry. He had called earlier in the day and set a late hour for the meeting. The King hated to rush.

It had been a temptation to put off the meeting. There were several women in the city who would have been glad to see him. However, he resisted, and this time he did put business first.

He swung the large car up the exit ramp, leaving the interstate and turning into the nearly deserted city streets. Even though he had been born there, he had never liked the city; it had no soul, and had become just a cage that trapped people in it by means of invisible economic fences. It mattered little if you were white or black; if you had no money, the city was your cage, and you could never get out.

He turned left on Palmer Avenue, a narrow concrete ribbon running through the sheer cliffs of darkened office buildings. Tingle drove several blocks and then pulled into Largen's parking lot. Largen's was one of the few downtown places still open at night. Their success was due to a large budget spent for security. They protected their patrons. The parking attendant and two armed guards greeted him as he stepped out of the big car.

"Hey, Justice Tingle!" One of the guards called him by name. "It's been a while. Nice to have you back."

Tingle grinned and handed the man an expensive cigar. The guard was almost as big as himself and a shade more black. "Here you go, my man. It's nice to be remembered."

"Thanks, Judge." The man was delighted. Tingle pushed his way through the club doors.

The place was about half full. A three-piece combo played easy music for several slow-dancing couples who were circling one another on the small dance floor. The bar was almost completely filled. As Tingle walked in, a small, wiry man with a huge moustache slid off a bar stool and came forward, almost at a run.

"Am I glad to see you," the small man said, grasping his hand. "I've been sitting around here so long that I've started to get a buzz on. Another drink and I wouldn't know what we might be talking about."

The King beamed down at the little man. Even cold sober, Tingle doubted that Judge Milton Harbor, moustache and all, would ever fully understand what anyone was talking about. Intelligence was not Judge Harbor's strong point.

"I'm extremely flattered to be called by a justice of the supreme court," Milton Harbor said, his moustache twitching with pleasure. "Something must really be up."

The hulking supreme court jurist put his large arm around the small man's shoulders as they followed a waiter toward a secluded table. "Something is indeed up, Milton," Tingle said, grinning, exposing his large and perfect teeth. "Something very big, something that will be very important to you personally." He could feel the small man shiver with pleasure. He patted his shoulder and released him as the waiter indicated their seats. "Have you had dinner?" Tingle asked.

"Yes," Harbor said, sounding almost guilty about the admission.

"You wouldn't mind if I ate in front of you, would you?"

"Certainly not!"

Tingle gestured to the waiter, who came hurrying over. "I'll be having a bite for dinner. Bring me the prime rib, rare, and baked potato. Thousand Island on the salad." He winked up at the waiter. "Tell the chef that the King is here tonight and to make everything in king-size portions. Okay?"

"You bet, Judge."

"What are you drinking, Milton?" Tingle asked.

"I think I've had enough."

"There's no such thing as enough, Milton. What are you drinking?"

"A banana daiquiri."

Tingle tried not to make a face. Maybe Milton was queer in addition to being stupid. It was strictly a lady's drink as far as the King was concerned.

"Bring the judge here a banana daiquiri." He hated even to say it. "And I'll have a double shot of Scotch with water."

The waiter hurried away.

Tingle studied the anxious face of Milton Harbor, judge of the criminal court. Harbor's father had been a famous local judge, but the son was only a very pale replica of the father, although the name had been strong enough to get him elected. He had married money, and his burning ambition was to rise above "the Zoo" into the more socially acceptable civil courts. This ambition was blocked because his stupidity kept coming to the surface. No governor would take the risk of promoting him, and although his political name ensured reelection, it was not strong enough to promote him to the higher place he sought.

"Milton, as you may know, we in the supreme court keep an eye out for bright and energetic judges. You can tell a lot from the kind of trials a man conducts, sort of get a flavor of the man from his decisions and orders, you know what I mean?"

Milton Harbor's large brown eyes seemed about to pop out from their sockets.

"We get an idea of what's going on . . ."

Tingle was interrupted by the return of the waiter. The man grinned as he began to deal out the burden he carried on his tray. "I brought the salad and the bread right away, Judge," he said. "I figured you'd be hungry." Then he delivered the drinks, putting the yellow concoction in front of Milton Harbor last of all.

"Looks good," Tingle said, ripping his fork into the salad after shoving the linen napkin into the ridge of his collar. He plunged a healthy portion of salad into his mouth, rolling his eyes in pleasure. The sound of his large jaw crunching lettuce rose even above the soft dance music. Tingle washed it down with a gulp of Scotch. "Damn, that's better."

He ripped a roll in two, covered it with butter then took it in one bite. "Sure you won't have something?" he asked, the words almost lost in the chewing.

Milton Harbor looked away and shook his head.

"Milton," Tingle continued, as he buttered the other half of the roll, "we've had our eye on you for some time. You know, Buck and I feel that a man of your talent is really being wasted on that damn criminal court."

Harbor's moustache twitched at an ever-increasing rate. His large eyes began to blink in excitement. Tingle was amused at the effect he was having.

"I think we can be of some help in assisting you to a higher bench, perhaps the court of appeals. That is, if you'd like that?"

If he'd like it! It was his life's ambition. Without noticing, Judge Harbor bolted down the entire daiquiri as if it were a sip of water.

"Of course that's all in the future and will take a bit of doing," Tingle went on with a studied casualness. "However, to help things along, we think you need a bit more public exposure, something really positive. Unless you'd rather not get into anything like that?"

"Oh, that would be fine, just fine," Harbor replied without any idea what he was agreeing to.

"Now, what Buck had in mind was having you take over as the executive judge for the criminal court."

Grim reality popped Harbor's balloon of hope. He knew most of the other judges disliked him and thought him incompetent. They would never elect him. "Judge Powell is the executive judge," he said sadly. "The meeting is tomorrow. I'd never have enough time to campaign." He knew that even if he campaigned for the next hundred years, he could never unseat the popular Powell. He wished he had another daiquiri.

"Now, Milton, there are a few problems down here in the criminal court that need immediate attention. You boys have an overcrowded docket. The newspapers are on your back, alleging that none of the judges put in sufficient hours. In other words, Milton, there has come a time for a new hand at the helm."

"But Clyde Powell . . ."

Tingle waved away the protest. "I like Clyde. Why, I've known that man since I was a boy. I think of him as a father, Milton, I really do. But Clyde is getting old, and this problem needs the energy of a younger man." And more to the point, Tingle thought to himself, he could never get away with a thing if Clyde Powell was watching the store. With Harbor, it would be an entirely different matter.

The prime rib arrived, brimming with blood just the way he liked it. There were two baked potatoes instead of just one, and both were smothered in a mound of sour cream. Tingle attacked it all with relish.

"Now, Buck and I are prepared to take certain steps, Milton," he said, talking with his mouth full, "but I have to be sure that I'll have full cooperation, you understand?"

"Well, you certainly know that I would do anything the supreme court asked of me," Milton said. "I feel that as a judge and officer of the court I should carry out any duties assigned to me. And I would be prepared to carry them out to the letter."

"Even if things got a little rough?"

"I don't understand."

"You might end up being a bit unpopular with your fellow judges, at least for a while anyway."

"If popularity is the price to be paid for serving the court, then I am prepared to pay it." His words were brave, but Harbor knew that his fellow judges barely tolerated him anyway, so that price was cheap.

"Okay, I like your attitude," Tingle said. "Here's what Buck wants done." He kept using Buckington's name because he knew it would have a special impact on Harbor, like mentioning God to a priest. "As you know, the supreme court has superintending control over all state courts, right?"

"Yes." The word was so intense it was almost a hiss.

Tingle rammed another piece of meat into his mouth and ground away at it. "Buck has ordered me to take over the criminal court. However, the way I see it, the only real way to be effective is to name a new executive judge whom we know we can trust." He paused to swallow. "We need not only a man we can trust but a man capable of carrying out some new ideas I have for cleaning up your docket. Would you be willing to serve?"

Harbor started to tremble. He could almost see the golden stair leading him out of "the Zoo." "Oh, yes, Justice Tingle, I would be delighted to serve."

"Okay." Tingle finished off half a potato in one gulp. "I'll call a press conference for tomorrow morning, say about eleven o'clock. I'll announce that the supreme court has appointed you as the new executive judge, and then I'll spring a few of my ideas on the press. Sound all right?"

"Perfect, but shouldn't I know what those ideas are?"

"You will, Milton, you will. But tomorrow let me answer the questions. Just look wise, and I'll take care of the rest."

"What about the other judges?"

"We'll meet with them tomorrow night. It's the regular monthly meeting anyway, right?"

"They'll be angry."

"Look, the supreme court has absolute power to take over the court and name whomever we wish. The judges can't do a damned thing about that, it's the law. Anyway, don't you worry about them being angry. I'll take care of that."

"What about Judge Powell?" Harbor asked, his voice almost a whisper. "Don't you think you should tell him what you plan to do?"

Tingle grinned as he sopped up the juice on his plate with a roll. "Milton, there's one big lesson to learn in life. If you got to make an omelet, you have to break a few eggs. Dig?"

the probation officer

FRANCIS Xavier Conroy pulled his new Ford compact up onto the cracked concrete apron leading to the private parking lot. He got out and unlocked the big padlock, sliding the heavy chain barricade until it lay flat upon the ground. Getting back in his car, he drove over it, then stopped and rechained the entrance. He sought out a parking space near the rear of the empty lot.

As usual, his was the first car. The lot was leased by himself and several other court workers. It was just an empty space between two ancient buildings, a place where a structure had once stood. Now it was topped by rough cinders, but the private lot was the envy of many at criminal court. The few members of this exclusive club saved a great deal of money, since the parking rates charged by the nearby lots were high and rising all the time.

A big gray rat stopped nuzzling a decaying mound of garbage and eyed Frank Conroy as he walked down the alley. The rat showed no fear, only curiosity. Conroy had become used to the rats, although he still made it a policy always to walk down the center of the alley.

The rising sun had caught the clouds high above and tinted them a fiery pink. Conroy could only see a narrow slice of sky as he walked between the buildings, but the clouds were a touch of beauty and a contrast to the filth and decay of the alleyway.

He experienced just a small headache, nothing more. He knew it would pass by the afternoon and he would feel fine again. Experience was a wonderful thing.

The back door to the Criminal Court Building was unlocked, and Conroy nodded to the guard lounging against the marble wall. The bored guard acknowledged the greeting with a shrug.

Conroy took the automatic elevator to the third floor and unlocked the door to the probation department. The place reeked of the strong cleaning solutions used by the night maintenance crew. He signed the attendance book, noting the time of arrival and his destination. He relocked the door and left, this time taking the elevator to the basement.

The basement corridor was bathed in stark light from overhead fluorescent fixtures. He listened to the echo of his own footsteps as he strode toward the "Tank."

Even before he reached the turn in the corridor, he

could smell them. He wondered if they were getting worse lately or if, like an experienced jungle guide, his senses were developing beyond those of normal men.

As he rounded the corner, he was dismayed to see that Sergeant Bellardo was on early duty. Bellardo's disdain was almost physical. Conroy knew that the police officer was a devout Catholic and an usher at Saint Dominic's. They had been friends until Bellardo found out that Francis Xavier Conroy was an ex-priest—a "failed priest," as the policeman put it. From that point on, their friendship was over. To Conroy, Bellardo's hostility was not an unknown reaction. Even those Catholics who weren't as militant as Bellardo were often uncomfortable in his presence. One of his co-workers, Michael Polarski, inevitably reverted to addressing him as "Father" if they carried on a conversation for more than a few minutes.

"How many this morning?" he asked Bellardo, making an effort to be cheerful.

The swarthy sergeant's upper lip curled into a sneer as he looked at the probation officer. "Forty-five." He snapped off the answer with such anger that a young policeman working with him turned around to see who was receiving the sharp end of the sergeant's well-known temper.

"Where are the records?" Conroy asked.

Bellardo nodded at the metal desk near the cell entrance.

Conroy was pleased as he picked up the sheets of criminal records. Forty-five was really low. It was a bonus. Usually they had to process twice or three times as many in the drunk tank. The morning would pass quickly.

He thumbed through the arrest records. Most of the men in the tank were old customers. The stench was especially bad this morning. The rank smell of vomit, excretion, urine, and sweat dominated the strongest industrial cleaner. He would soon become accustomed to the odor, although every morning it was still as offensive as the first time he had been assigned the duty, at least for the first few minutes. It was his steady job now, a convenient place to put an ex-priest, he supposed, and he found a strange satisfaction in the work.

Conroy stepped to the cell door and looked at the men through the bars. A few were standing, but most sat and a few lay on the tiled floor, noisily snoring. They had all pulled away from a splotch of vomit, leaving that part of the floor unoccupied.

He took the first record and called out the name. "Baylor, John E.!"

The familiar form uncurled slowly from the floor, got up, and shuffled across the floor to the bars. His chin was covered with a dark stubble. His face was so tan that his skin resembled worn leather. He walked with a stoop, his clothes bagging on his thin form. He grinned, exposing yellowed teeth.

"Hi, Mr. Conroy," he said, enveloping the probation officer in a cloud of rancid breath, combining the sour sweetness of cheap wine and the aroma of a sick stomach.

"When did you get out of the House, John?"

The grin turned sheepish. "A couple of days, almost a week."

"Went right back at it again, eh?" It was just a question without any accusation.

"You know how it is, Mr. Conroy."

"Yes, I know. You were out at the House thirty days, John. You look good, tan. You work the farm?"

"Oh, yeah, that's the best job out there. I like the farm."

"Looks like you'll have to go back."

"Jesus, Mr. Conroy, I'm all dried out and everything. There's no reason to send me back, at least right away."

"You feel up to staying on the street for a while?"

"Yeah, I feel good. You know how it is, I can pick up a few bucks delivering throwaways, maybe do a little day labor. I feel good. Doctors up at the House of Correction said I was healthy."

"Okay, John, I'll see what I can do. Do you have any money for a fine?"

"Had a twenty, but I must of drunk up ten. Got ten dollars left, though."

"Okay, you look good. I'll see if the judge will go for a ten-dollar fine. But if you show up here again this month, you'll go right back to the House. There is no way I can help that, you understand?"

"Yeah, sure. I appreciate it, Mr. Conroy." He grinned, then shuffled back to his original spot in the cell.

Conroy had quickly learned there was no point in trying to reform the veteran drunks. Just keeping them alive by sentencing them now and then to a term so that they could dry out and eat correctly was about all society could do. *Derelict* was a truly descriptive term.

The next arrest record was new. There were no prior arrests, only an old traffic violation. "Bissant, Arthur W.!" Conroy called.

A stout man in his middle fifties who had been standing against a wall came forward unsteadily. Haggard, his eyes bloodshot, he had the puffy face of an experienced drinker. The lapel of his expensive suit was torn.

This time the breath was even stronger, but whiskey was the pervading odor.

"Mr. Bissant, my name is Conroy. I am a probation officer. It's my job to interview the men charged with drunkenness and to recommend action to the trial judge. I notice you've never been arrested before?"

Bissant shook his head. "No. First time." His words were

slightly slurred. Conroy suspected that the man was still partly under the influence.

"What do you do for a living, Mr. Bissant?"

"I'm a salesman."

"What do you sell?"

"Industrial machinery."

"I understand there's a lot of money in that," Conroy said.

"Sometimes. Most of the time you just spin your wheels. It's a fast track. Lot of pressure."

"Do you have a drinking problem, Mr. Bissant?"

"I didn't think so, at least not until I ended up here. Hey, don't get me wrong, I drink, but that's part of my business. I drink a lot, but nothing like this ever happened before."

"Will you have an attorney represent you in court?"

Bissant snorted. "What the hell for? Christ, I was drunk as a lord. I'll plead guilty."

"Didn't you call anyone after you were arrested?"

The man slowly shook his head. His eyes moistened slightly as he looked at Conroy. "You think I should let my wife or one of my friends see me like this? No, I didn't call anybody."

"Okay. I suppose I can count on not seeing you down here again?"

Bissant looked him directly in the eye. "You can bet your ass on that."

"Okay, Mr. Bissant. Look, when your case is called, say you stand mute, you got that?"

"Stand mute?"

"Right, that way you aren't pleading guilty or not guilty. It's a technical thing. I'll talk to the judge. In view of the fact that you have no prior record, he may dismiss the case. Otherwise, under the circumstances, the worst that can happen to you is a fine, probably fifty dollars."

"I appreciate anything you can do."

"That's okay, part of the job. But if you can't control the drinking, I'd give serious thought to joining Alcoholics Anonymous if I were you."

"See, I finally made a big sale after a couple of dry months. I was just celebrating. Like a damned fool, I just got carried away."

"Okay, Mr. Bissant, I'll see what I can do." Conroy said it as a dismissal.

The salesman looked as if he wanted to say something more, but then turned and wavered back to his spot against the cell wall.

Conroy wrote the word *dismiss* across Bissant's record. He had forgotten his headache as he warmed to his work. It would be a good morning. He was working with Judge Perry, a man of usual pleasant disposition but with an occasional burst of violent temper. If Judge Perry was in a good mood, everything would go very well indeed.

The formal proceedings in the courtroom seemed to fulfill Frank Conroy's need for daily ritual, and he sometimes even experienced an almost spiritual feeling there, even though he no longer believed in spiritual things.

chapter three

the world liberation army

THE World Liberation Army was no longer quartered above the porno bookstore. Larry Gormley, in addition to successfully robbing banks, had taken a short course in California from experts in the most efficient manner for terrorists to live and work. The knowledge had been distilled from Irish, Arab, Italian, and German terrorist gangs and their collective experiences over a number of years.

Having all the operational money they needed, the procedures were being carried out quickly but carefully. Both Alice Mary Brennan and Thelma Sturdevant had purchased new wardrobes. Gone were the patched jeans and ragged shirts, and in their place were stylish dresses and tailored casual slacks. Despite protests from Alice Mary, the girls' long hair had been cut into short, business-girl modes. They looked like two career women devoted to the American ideal of hard work and healthy living.

With one exception, the men had been made over in similar fashion. Al Martin's full beard had been shaved off, leaving only a thin, neat moustache. Gone were his wrinkled work shirts and baggy trousers. Martin's thin frame looked good in quality, conservative clothing. Larry Gormley, his blond hair already styled, also dressed the role of a fashionable young salesman.

The exception was Flash Johnson, who insisted on keeping his outdated tight pant suits and his wide brim hat. There was no way he could be persuaded to give up the mystique of his gaudy necklaces and glistening cheap rings.

Instead of relocating in a rundown part of the city, Larry Gormley had rented two apartments in a modern complex devoted to young or middle-aged people without children. It was integrated, but the high rents ensured that the integration was only racial and not economic. The place had a common swimming pool and tennis courts. The manager of the complex, who believed the two women were secretaries and the three men carpet salesmen, even helped them rent new furniture for both units. It was the kind of apartment complex where the tenants never got to know one another beyond a nod or an occasional "Good morning." The underground called such places "safe houses," because no one would ever think of looking for terrorists in such nice, civilized settings.

They purchased two small cars, several years old but

respectable and in good condition, Flash Johnson still insisted on driving his old Cadillac.

The guns, ammunition, and explosives had been divided between the two apartments, one on the first floor and the other, just above it, on the second floor. Upon the installation of telephones plus the purchase of a police radio scanner, the headquarters became operational.

Everything went so well that even Flash Johnson began to think they might turn into an efficient team. Gormley kept them busy, teaching them the lessons he had learned on the coast. They engaged in mock plans and exercises. And he trained and drilled them in the use of their new weapons.

The World Liberation Army was ready to hit.

the burglar

"WATCH that fuckin' bus!" Gus Simes yelled. Eddy Bradshaw jerked the wheel, swinging their panel truck, just missing the big square rear of the big yellow vehicle.

"You worry too much, Gus," Eddy said, grinning, his cigarette popping up and down as he talked. "You got to loosen up, man. We're supposed to be cool, remember. 'The nerve of a burglar,' that's what they say, Gus. So you and me got to have cool nerves, or we'll end up giving the profession a bad name." He laughed.

"I'm cool," Gus Simes protested, "it's just your goddamned driving that's making me nuts. Jesus, the way you hot-rod this thing, it's like sending a signal to any passing scout car."

"So what? We're on the way to a job, we ain't got nothing in the truck. Worst thing we can get is a ticket, right?"

"Yeah, but you drive like a maniac coming back too. I don't ever want to go back to the joint. I'd hate like hell to end up there just because of you cowboying around in this goddamned truck."

The smile left Eddy Bradshaw's face. "I'm never going back there, Gus, never."

"Then just watch your fuckin' speed."

Even the mere thought of prison caused Gus Simes to feel anxious. He had been a successful burglar for ten years before his first conviction and imprisonment. His second conviction, resulting in a long jail term, came through the testimony of a fence who had been promised immunity. Gus Simes had been out of the joint for three months. The old "delivery truck" burglary gig was working well. The fence was as trustworthy as there was in that line of business, and they had been making good money, without taking great risks. The prospect of having to leave it all behind and be locked away again was unthinkable.

They pulled into the suburban street where the houses were well kept. This time Eddy Bradshaw drove slowly. Both men were clean-shaven with neat haircuts. Both were dressed in matching blue coveralls. They knew which house they wanted, they had been watching the place, along with other likely prospects, for weeks. The family had gone on vacation and had taken their dog along.

Simes worried about Bradshaw. His size and strength were a great help in carting out the stolen property, but the man was becoming erratic lately, careless. Theirs was a daylight operation, and a man had to keep his wits together to pull off these bold open jobs. They had to look as if they belonged.

Eddy pulled the delivery truck into the driveway. Gus

hopped out and opened the back of the panel truck, carrying out two huge tool cases. The cases were empty, but he pretended they were heavy. Eddy had his lockpick concealed between papers held on a clipboard. He made a show of checking the address, then moved to the door. It was an easy lock, and Gus had taught him to be an expert in the pick's use. If anyone was watching them enter, it all went by so fast that one would have to presume the two men had a key.

From the moment they entered the front door, the race was on. Gus had taught Eddy what to do. Both men scrambled through the house, grabbing obvious items of value and searching for places of concealment.

Gus Simes found a jewelry box between the mattress and springs of the bed in the main bedroom. Most of it was junk—he had a good eye for jewelry—but there were a few pieces of value, including a large diamond in an antique-ring setting. The rings and the other jewels went into the bag.

They worked silently, piling the loot into the toolboxes. They were racing against the clock. Ten minutes was all they could safely allow. They had to complete the job in that time, taking no more than five minutes to load and drive away. They would have to be gone before nosy neighbors even got through discussing the deliverymen at the house of the vacationing family.

Most of the appliances were used and of little value. However, the color television was new and had an attached video recorder, which further enhanced its value. The two men took the now-filled toolboxes out to the truck, then returned for the television set.

Although they were well within the time limits they had set for themselves, they did not foresee the actions of the lady who lived next door. She had read about panel truck burglaries. She was a close friend of the vacationers and had promised to watch their house. She knew that no delivery or work had been scheduled. At almost the same time Eddy Bradshaw had opened the front door, the woman was dialing the police emergency number. The call was routed through the dispatcher, but the car assigned to that sector was just completing work at a minor traffic accident. There was a few minutes' delay in their response, but they came on, driving without flashing lights or siren.

Eddy Bradshaw was at the bottom of the front steps taking the full weight of the television set when Gus Simes saw the scout car pull into the street.

"Cops," he said, his voice hardly above a whisper. "They're coming down the street. Act natural. We're just a couple of repairmen picking up the set to fix it. Be calm."

"Are you nuts?" Bradshaw let the expensive set fall. He turned and began to run.

The officers saw Bradshaw run. The car roared into life.

Eddy Bradshaw had blown their only chance to talk their way out. Escape was the only route left. Simes turned and ran back into the house, racing through the rooms to the back door. The owners had installed several locks and chains, holding the door fast against invasion. Gus Simes fumbled with the locks with both hands, cursing his own slowness. He managed to get off the last chain and stepped out onto a small back porch. He heard a muffled sound down the street. It sounded like a shot. The backyard was unfamiliar to him. Since it hadn't entered into their original plans, they had failed to look it over.

A round aboveground swimming pool dominated most of the space. All four sides of the yard were enclosed by an eight-foot steel Cyclone fence. It would not be difficult to climb, but he knew time was running out.

Gus Simes sprinted to the rear of the yard, leaping up and grabbing the wire. His shoe tips found holds in the steel webbing, and he thrust himself up.

"Hold it, asshole!" The voice came from behind him, and there was excitement and anger in it. He froze against the fence.

"Let yourself down slow and keep your hands up where I can see them."

He did as he was told.

"Turn around and walk over here slowly. Keep your hands up."

Simes turned and faced a veteran police officer, his face flushed and taut, who leveled a big revolver at him with both hands. The muzzle was thrust through the steel wire of a side gate. Simes, his mind numbed, walked slowly toward the policeman.

The policeman ordered him to stop when he came up to the gate. "Okay, asshole, open this gate," the policeman commanded.

"There's a lock on it."

"I can see that, shithead. You're a burglar, open the fucking thing!"

"Hey, you got it all wrong. We were delivering a television. My partner's got a nonsupport warrant out for him. You guys scared him, that's all."

The policeman cocked back the hammer of the revolver. "Open it!" The hard threat in the voice drained Gus Simes of any hope of trying to talk his way out. They had him cold for burglary. It would be daytime, so he would probably get three to five years, considering his past record. Bitterness filled him.

"My pick is in my pocket," he said to the cop. The policeman seemed still excited and angry, an unusual reaction for an arresting officer under these circumstances.

"Which pocket?" the officer snarled.

"Right."

"Reach in and take it out slow. If it even starts to look like a knife or gun, this Magnum will take your head off."

"I believe it." Simes very slowly extracted the pick from his pocket. He held it up for the officer's inspection.

The policeman, never lowering the gun, stepped back. "Open the lock."

Gus shrugged. The padlock was easy, it snapped open in his hand.

"Okay," the cop said, "slowly open the gate and step out here."

Gus Simes felt the awful crush of total defeat. Three years in prison would be very, very long years. It didn't seem fair; everything had been going so well.

The policeman made Gus Simes lean against the side of the house as he searched him roughly. The handcuffs felt cold as they were snapped on his wrists held behind him. The cop jerked up on the cuffs, sending a sharp pain through Simes's arms and shoulders.

"Christ, take it easy, will you! God, we didn't hurt anybody."

"Shut up." The officer shoved Gus Simes toward the street.

"Okay, so you made a burglary bust," Simes protested, "don't be so damned sore about it."

A younger uniformed officer came up to them. "Shall I go inside?" he asked. He looked pale and shaken, his eyes wide with emotion.

"No," said the older man. "We'll wait for a backup unit."

"There's nobody inside," Simes said.

"I told you to shut up!"

"Hell, I'll shut up, but aren't you guys supposed to read me my rights or something?"

"Homicide will do that."

"Homicide?" Gus Simes almost yelled the word. "Hey, we didn't kill anybody!"

"My partner shot the man who was working with you. He's dead," the older policeman said, his voice strained. "Any death caused during the course of a felony is first-degree murder in this state, asshole. You have finally bought the big ticket."

"I didn't kill anybody. What the hell are you talking about?"

The older man's face relaxed a bit. "That's the law. You were committing a felony, burglary, and a man died during the commission. It doesn't matter that you didn't actually kill him, the law still holds you responsible."

Suddenly Gus Simes realized the cop was right. They had talked about that law in prison. He felt nothing for Eddy Bradshaw; the fool shouldn't have run. But this time Gus Simes knew he would never get out. He would end up like the toothless old men he had seen others brutalize in the prison yard. He felt faint. The policeman grabbed his arm and steadied him.

"Really fucked yourself up this time, eh?" For the first time the man sounded almost friendly.

the assistant prosecutor

HE hated the waiting. When he had first come on the staff, it had been exciting, like waiting for the results of an election after a heated campaign, a real drama, but now it was merely mind numbing. There was nothing to do. Sometimes the jury took minutes to decide a case, other times they might spend hours or even days before coming up with a verdict. Ace Gilbert really didn't care what a jury did anymore. In the beginning it had seemed so important to win, to be the cutting edge of society, the sword of justice sweeping down to protect the people. Now the passion was gone. He still did a workmanlike job of prosecuting cases, he could still muster the fire and fury when needed, but it was done like an actor merely performing a role. He really didn't care anymore—and the cases were all beginning to seem alike. He couldn't hardly remember what case he had tried last or what the defendant had looked like.

It riled him that he had to be there. It wasn't legally necessary that he be present when the jury came in with their verdict. His job as prosecuting attorney was all done. But this judge insisted that the assistant prosecutor be right where he could find him, in case the jury asked for additional instructions. Ace Gilbert couldn't even leave the courtroom, except to get a quick cup of coffee in the lobby, and even then he had to leave word where he was going. It was boring, but he had to wait it out with the others.

The office also preferred that the assistant prosecutor assigned to a courtroom wait until the verdict came in, although it wasn't an absolute rule. It kept the judges honest—they were less likely to try to slip something in if the prosecutor was around to watch. Ace Gilbert was assigned to old Cannonball O'Brien, who was, at least where jury trials were concerned, usually straight. Cannonball did have the court's docket clerk in his pocket, who could occasionally steer "special" cases to O'Brien. In those cases a "trial" was held, the jury waived, and the verdict assured—it being rendered by old Cannonball himself. O'Brien was one of the few judges who played those kinds of games, but he never tried to interfere with a jury case. So waiting for the verdict served no real purpose, which made it even more burdensome.

The uniformed court officer lounged against the closed jury room door. Fighting sleep, he looked as if his eyelids were beginning to weigh a ton.

The defendant, puffing nervously on a cigarette, sat hunched over in the prisoner's box, a wooden-railed enclosure. His lawyer sat at the counsel table engrossed in a crossword puzzle.

Gilbert wondered what was taking the jury so long; he wondered what problems they possibly could have with what should be a very easy decision. It had been a clean open-and-shut felonious assault case with eye witnesses, the injured victim, and the works. The defendant even had a criminal record for assault. Yet those twelve people had been deliberating for over two hours. Gilbert guessed that one of them was an amateur detective, a romantic who insisted on seeing something more in the evidence than was really there. One jackass like that could manufacture mountains from the smallest molehill.

Albert Charles was Gilbert's given name, but his father had called him A.C., and this had been corrupted to Ace, a name that had stuck and followed him through school and through the army. Now everyone called him Ace. Few knew or remembered his real name.

Ace—it was a name to call forth images of a slick riverboat gambler, complete with flashy clothes; a black, pencil-thin moustache; and dark, crafty eyes. But Ace Gilbert was far from that romantic conception. He had unruly sandy hair, light liquid-blue eyes, and a smooth, pale complexion and appeared much younger than thirty-five. Tall and lean to the point of being thin, he carried himself with a slight stoop, and despite his youthful appearance, he had the poise and mannerisms of a much older man.

He was relatively new as a lawyer. He'd been in the army and seen service in Vietnam; then, after the army, he had done construction work in Africa. Finally, tired of a drifting life, he had gone to law school and also married. Law school was successful, but the marriage failed. The stress of his law studies created an unbearable strain on his relationship. The challenges facing him were of no interest to his wife and they had nothing in common except sex, and even that became mechanical after a while. She left him, and divorce quickly followed. Despite the turmoil in his personal life, he had been graduated with honors.

The job with the prosecutor had been pure luck. Good jobs were hard to find for inexperienced lawyers. But he became experienced very fast in the crucible of criminal court as he was thrown into trying an endless parade of criminal cases, forced to meet and master a multitude of trial situations. Gilbert quickly became a competent workman, possessed of sharp new skills and practiced techniques. And at first he had found it all very exciting. He had hurled himself into every trial, expending his intellect and emotional fury to the fullest. But lately he had ceased to find the satisfaction he had formerly experienced.

Now he had the uncomfortable feeling that the solemn ritual of a trial was nothing more than an elaborate dance, more concerned with procedure and show than an attempt to determine the truth. The old enthusiasm was gone. He wondered if his attitude reflected just the mature outlook of a professional or whether it meant he was becoming jaded, even disillusioned. He was aware of a feeling of growing dissatisfaction in many areas of his life.

Ace Gilbert lived a quiet, measured life. He had an efficiency apartment, drove a small-size Buick, played golf and tennis, and swam. There had been a procession of women, but no lasting relationship. He wondered if the failed marriage had caused him to become wary or whether he had lost the capacity to feel deeply about a woman. At the moment there was no one, although he was strongly attracted to Kathleen Ann Mulloy, a court probation officer. She was cute and seemed to bubble with life. He had tried to date her several times, without success. This puzzled him. Ordinarily he had no problem with women, at least not in the initial stage, but Kathleen failed to show even minimal interest. That alone made her something of a challenge.

He was thinking about Kathleen Mulloy when the short rap from the other side of the jury room door resounded through the near-empty courtroom like a shot.

The jury paraded out single file. They stood in front of the judge's bench, and their foreman, a stern-faced woman, delivered the guilty verdict.

"Good job, Ace," one of the court officers whispered. "You won another one."

"What else could they have done, under the circumstances?" Gilbert replied with a shrug. He remembered a time when a courtroom victory was a thrill. He was pleased that the jury had finally done the right thing, but he felt no thrill. He walked slowly from the courtroom.

Ace Gilbert wondered if he was really cut out for this kind of work.

the burglar

THE sheriff had divided up his cramped jail space according to the possible problems posed by the prisoners. Traffic offenders and small-time crooks awaiting court or prison were kept on the first floor; they had the most to lose by causing trouble. The second floor was devoted to women prisoners who were charged with crimes ranging from murder to prostitution, with most of them being just prostitutes. The third and fourth floor held the men awaiting trial or transport to prison for serious felonies. The fifth floor was reserved for insane prisoners or prisoners who pretended to be insane or who otherwise posed a threat to the sheriff's peace of mind. The sixth floor was considered the most dangerous floor. Here the men held for murder awaited their fates. The place dripped with guards, but the inmates had more room than the other jail prisoners, with just two men to each cell and a large day room with a piano and a battered television. The television was on most of the time, but no one ever played the piano.

Hagen and Johnson posed the biggest threat of all. Local celebrities and considered dangerous, with dangerous friends, they had been kept away from the other prisoners until one of their lawyers complained and cited a recent case where such action was considered cruel and unusual punishment and prohibited by the Constitution. Reluctantly they were put in with the other men. The sheriff was holding Hagen and Johnson only until their motion for a new trial had been heard. Then he could ship them off to the newly built death house at the state prison. He would have charge of them for only a month or two, much to his relief.

Hagen paid little attention to the other men in the day room. He kept to himself, stone-faced and distant. Jesse Johnson, on the other hand, talked almost constantly, arguing loudly with the other prisoners and the guards. Not real disputes over important things like stolen toothbrushes or selection of television programs, but arguments about political philosophy. He couldn't stop recruiting, even among these doomed men, trying to enlist new members in the World Liberation Army.

Murderers' Row was the one place where Gus Simes had never done time, and it was the one place where he never expected to end up. He was not a violent man. But despite that he was locked in with the others; wife killers, robbers who had murdered, hit men, and the famous Hagen and Johnson.

Simes was an old "con" and made friends easily. He protested his dislike for institutional life, but he was used to it and knew its ways. Johnson had become the natural leader in their little group, and therefore, Simes made it his business to become the black man's friend, since it always paid to be allied with the powerful in jail. It was protection against robbery and rape. So Simes pretended to believe the garbage that Johnson spewed forth, and the black man was convinced that he had a new convert to the World Liberation Army and its goal of world revolution.

Simes's lawyer, a young public defender with too many cases to handle, was unsure that he could work out a deal with the prosecutor. He told Simes that while he doubted that a jury would give him the death sentence, it was always a possibility because of his record as a burglar. That prognosis was not reassuring, not to a nice, harmless second-story man who had never done any physical harm to anyone.

Gus Simes had always done his time easy, that is, he had never tried to escape or even think about escape. He had just accepted his fate and tried to stay out of trouble so that he would look good when parole time came up. There would be no parole board now, not for first-degree murder. The young lawyer had assured him that they would charge him with first-degree murder even if he didn't pull the trigger. Now the only question was plea bargaining on the basis of getting a life sentence rather than risk a jury and execution. Gus shivered at the thought of his grim future and for the first time began to think of escape.

Johnson came up, expending nervous energy by puffing irritably at a cigarette. "World is just plain fucked up, ya know that?"

Gus nodded, his eyes appraising the speaker.

"It's ready for revolution, baby, a real, honest-to-God revolution. People ain't goin' to take no more of this government shit, ya understan'?"

"Yeah." Simes tried to sound enthusiastic.

"Pretty soon this whole fuckin' thing goin' to blow up. The people goin' to take over, and we goin' to lead them, you understan' me?"

Simes met Johnson's excited eyes. "Look, I agree with you, Field Marshal." He had found that the man demanded the title as the price of friendship. It took a bit of practice to get used to, but it was an easy price tag. "I agree with everything you're saying. But the revolution won't come in time to help us. Hagen and you are going to the gas chamber, and I'll probably be right behind you. There just isn't enough time."

Johnson exhaled noisily. "Ain't goin' to no gas chamber," he said, dropping his voice to a near whisper. "They ain't goin' to do me or Hagen, you can count on that!"

Simes looked around before speaking. He wanted to be sure no one could hear them. In a practiced way, he spoke out of the side of his mouth, making words without the appearance of speaking. "Escape?"

Johnson looked at him, a half smile on his lips. "I never said that." He paused for a moment before continuing. "But whatever happens, are you going to be with us, brother?"

Simes thought of the old men at prison, also of the new gas chamber. "I'm with you, Field Marshal," he rasped, "I'm with you all the way."

the judges' monthly meeting

THE judges' meeting was proceeding just as King Tingle had thought it would. He had planned things down to the last detail, even the seating. He had broken up the expected troublemakers—there would be no double-teaming in this game.

Although there were strident objections, they met in Harbor's courtroom, since he was the new executive judge —now a fact, despite some grumbling by some of the judges.

Tingle listened to the angry words, the heated outcries against what was happening in the criminal court. He had usurped Harbor's bench and sat looming over the others like some dark angel sitting in final judgment. He was accustomed to this kind of political infighting and relished it. He had cut his political teeth in shouting, swearing party caucus and the jammed riotlike conditions of contested conventions. He knew all the dirty moves and tactics, knowledge acquired after years of confrontations while serving as a state senator and a congressman. He knew the political animal was predictable, more so than any other. Tingle knew every player and could foresee every move. He presided over this stormy session, contented and sure of himself despite the shouting and name calling. Justice James Tingle was enjoying himself.

Milton Harbor, white-faced, slouched down in his seat at the counsel table trying to hide from the rage of his colleagues. Tingle was thankful that he had decided to chair the meeting rather than let Harbor do it. These rough and clever judges would have torn a half-wit like Harbor apart.

State law provided for only ten judges of the criminal court for a city of over two million. The number was inadequate by half, but the state legislature and the county commissioners weren't anxious to spend more money on enlarging courts, even if that was the only sensible answer to a growing problem. The ten slots were filled by nine men and one woman. This was the first monthly meeting in years when all ten judges had attended.

Cannonball O'Brien was on his feet and stalking up and down in front of the other judges, spewing forth his displeasure at the high-handed tactics of the supreme court. He solemnly decried the treatment of the distinguished jurist, Clyde Powell, in his unceremonial and illegal purge from the post of executive judge. Tingle listened, his face grave, but he was really amused. He knew that the only thing on O'Brien's mind was protecting his man, the docket clerk. O'Brien did a thriving business when the clerk arranged for certain cases to find their way before old Cannonball, the "fighting liberal."

Tingle watched the faces of the other judges as O'Brien roared. As usual, Clyde Powell showed no emotion, his face a placid ebony mask. Tingle knew the quick intelligence behind that mild mask. Powell was a man to be feared. Judge Stewart Richards was another danger. Richards, a black man with white cottonlike hair, sat quietly, his eyes closed and his hands clasped across his round stomach. He had a habit of seeming to slip off to sleep, but while others might think Stewart Richards was sleeping, Tingle knew he was hearing every word.

The other two black judges posed no problem. Luther Perry was straight, and a good student of the law, but he was naïve. Tingle knew he would be able to handle Luther Perry easily. A bottle was the way to Judge

Marcus Young. The distinguished former trial lawyer had slowly slipped into alcoholism. Protected by his staff and a press who remembered his former greatness, he was sloshed by noontime. Tingle knew he could count on Young's vote if things got heavy. The man was hanging on by his fingertips and knew it. He wouldn't do anything that might risk shaking his precarious hold. Young would be easy to control.

Old John Sloan's bushy gray eyebrows twitched continually as his piercing, hawklike eyes followed the action. Tingle knew that Sloan was crooked, but he was a careful man, and Tingle appreciated a careful man. Sloan would also be easily handled as soon as he knew he would be able to continue to get his piece of the pie.

A few years back Carol Woldanski would have meant trouble. She was stern and unyielding, and criminals called her "The Polish Peril." If anyone was found guilty, they could expect the maximum sentence from Carol. But the old girl had become hard of hearing lately, and her memory was going. In her late sixties, Carol Woldanski was showing some of the early signs of senility. Tingle heard that sometimes she sat staring at the courtroom wall, her face grim, her mind an obvious blank. She would be no threat.

Even Cannonball O'Brien wouldn't cause any real trouble. The man was all wind and bluster. As soon as he could, Tingle planned to drop a hint to O'Brien that the judge would still have some selection power over cases to be assigned. That would silence O'Brien's voice of opposition.

Two judges who were capable of causing problems were Herbert Abrams and Michael "Mickey" Noonan. Both were wily political animals, street smart and quick. Jewish and Irish—it was a bad combination if both turned against you.

Abrams had at first only quietly observed the meeting, but then he had risen to speak his own careful opposition to the "takeover" by the supreme court. Tingle knew that Abrams was a bit vain and a womanizer, but these were the only chinks in his armor. He was honest and he was smart, a bad combination as far as Tingle was concerned.

Mickey Noonan had also taken the floor briefly, counseling quiet but firm protest to the supreme court. He was the youngest judge; his handsome, fleshy Irish face held a special appeal for the voters; and everyone recognized that judge of the criminal court was only the first step on Mickey Noonan's political ladder. He had a reputation for honesty, though not for diligence. He greeted long hours in the courtroom with something less than enthusiasm. He preferred to be out, using his witty charm on groups and meetings. There were few votes to be earned during the daily grind in the criminal court.

Tingle knew he would have to keep a sharp eye on Noonan and Abrams and on Powell and Richards. He knew they were laying back now waiting for the right time, the right opportunity. They were smart. But he felt he was even smarter, and he would see that they would be given no opportunity to strike out at either him or his plan.

The meeting was long, and most of the judges appeared tired, especially the older members of the court. Tingle had let them vent their venom, he had let them get it all out of their systems. Now as Cannonball O'Brien rambled on calling for something close to armed revolt, the judges were all talked out and ready to quit.

Tingle stood up, knowing that his great height and width was intimidating. "I have listened to everything you have said." He kept his voice soft and friendly. "I think I can speak for the rest of the supreme court when I say we anticipated most of your objections when we decided on this move."

He looked at Mickey Noonan. "You know, it's just natural, everyone is resistant to change, even judges. It's just human nature, and despite our robes and pomp, we are just as human as anybody else. Believe me, the justices of the supreme court were reluctant to change things, but something had to be done."

Tingle sought the dark, intelligent eyes of Herbert Abrams. "There are people in that jail who have been waiting over a year to go to trial." He raised his voice. "It isn't your fault, we know that. But the fact remains that prisoners are being held for many months before their cases are heard. And may I remind you that both the state and federal constitutions provide for a speedy trial in criminal cases. A year is not 'speedy.' We cannot allow this to go on. We have tried to get help from the legislature, the governor, and even other judges, but nothing has worked. We have our backs to the wall." Now he sighted on Clyde Powell's quiet face. "We may have to start reversing criminal convictions on that ground alone— that the defendant did not get the speedy justice called for in the Constitution."

" 'Speedy,' shit!" O'Brien growled. "What about the long time your own—"

Tingle held up one of his huge hands. "I afforded you the courtesy of listening when you were speaking, Judge O'Brien. I ask only for the same courtesy." He waited. O'Brien sneered but kept quiet.

"So something has to give, right? Either we respond to the crisis—and let me assure you that this situation is indeed a crisis—or this court will be disbanded by the legislature as unworkable."

"Bullshit," O'Brien snapped.

It was time to play the trump card, the card that would defeat all opposition. Tingle slowly shook his head. "I'm afraid the discontinuance of this court is a real possibility. On behalf of the supreme court, I tried to lobby the legislature to get more judges for you. You will remember that I spent a good number of years there as a state senator. What the leadership of both the lower house and the senate told me was alarming."

He had their complete attention now.

"As you know, this is the only separate criminal court in the state. Criminal cases elsewhere are handled by circuit or district courts. I was told by the leadership that this court is regarded as a 'mess' and that the legislature is in a mood to do away with this court and enlarge the county circuit court to handle the criminal cases." He paused. "There are also some political reasons for such a course of action."

"Such as what?" Carol Woldanski demanded, suddenly interested. She had three more years to put in on the criminal court bench before qualifying for a full retirement pension.

"Black folks like me is the reason, simple as that," Tingle said. That part was true enough. "The city has a large black population. There are four black judges sitting here now. If they do away with this city-based court and make it a countywide function, the black voters in this city will lose their numerical ability to elect black judges. The white vote predominates countywide. So that's what some people would like to see, a court made up of only white judges. Oh, the legislative leadership gave a lot of lip service to other reasons behind disbanding this court, but the racial basis is the real one. But even you white judges have your political power bases in the city and not the county, so such a move could mean that you all might lose your jobs."

Tingle was pleased, he had even caught O'Brien's rapt interest. O'Brien could never hope to control the docket in circuit court, even if elected. Tingle watched the belligerence drain from the man.

"Look, for a number of reasons, we are all in this together. Admittedly, it is a 'crash' program, and admittedly a lot of people will feel that justice hasn't been served, but we have to take steps, or others will take drastic steps for us."

Tingle held up his hands like a minister about to bestow a blessing. "All that is asked is that you try this program for a while. Milton Harbor will be handling the paperwork, and I'll be trying to smooth out the rough spots. Everyone will have to work, but I know I can count on all of you to do that. I think success will justify what we have to do, and I know that success will preserve this court and its judgeships.

"The hour is late and we can end up talking about this all night." He smiled and continued in a firm voice. "But it won't do any good, so let's adjourn. I'll be working with you daily. Try it, you might like the way things are going. If not, we'll hold another meeting one month from today. At that meeting all gripes will be heard and suggestions received. Now let's adjourn. I'll handle the press."

"What is this, some kind of gag rule?" O'Brien growled.

Tingle quit smiling. "At this moment you people are not enjoying the best reputation for case production. If any of you publicly protest without giving this a try, I think you can expect to have your protest backfire on you very seriously. Believe me, I have no wish to 'gag' any of you, but I know the press and I think that at the moment I am in the best position to handle things. It would be unseemly for a group of jurists, such as ourselves, to appear to be snarling and snapping over a proposal to get more work out. Think it over."

He waited. "Any objections to me being the spokesman?"

They were silent, except for Milton Harbor, who popped up from his chair like a schoolboy. "I think it would be a super idea," he said.

Tingle smiled. Harbor would be a very useful idiot.

the probation officer

FRANK Conroy stood in the witness box, where he was close to the judge and could communicate by a whisper without interfering with the parade of defendants being tried.

The drunks had been formed up in a line, single file. Each shuffled forward when his name was called. The line was comparatively short, and it was moving quickly.

"*People* versus *Harrison*," the court clerk called.

A gaunt man, his thin face a gray mask, shuffled forward from the line and stood in front of the judge. He did not look up. He held both hands tightly before him to conceal the trembling. The young uniformed arresting officer came up and stood next to the defendant.

"How do you plead, guilty or not guilty?" The clerk's nasal voice was mechanical and disinterested.

"Guilty," the man mumbled.

"What happened, Officer?" Judge Perry asked. He was signing warrants and had not looked up. Neither the judge nor the man he was about to sentence had yet seen each other.

"While on duty last night," the young officer began,

sounding interested in what he was doing, "I observed the defendant here, later identified as Thomas Harrison, sleeping in a doorway at 1300 Clinton Street. I woke him up and detected the strong odor of alcohol on his breath. He couldn't walk without help. I arrested him as being drunk in a public place and conveyed him to the First Precinct." The officer's testimony had been given in a sure, loud voice, just the way he had been taught in the academy.

Frank Conroy leaned closer to the judge. "Harrison looks pretty bad," he said. "I think he needs some time to dry out. Better give him thirty days in the House of Correction. If he's left on the street in his condition, he'll be dead in a couple of weeks."

"Probably better for him," the judge said, his attention still on the papers he was signing.

"Harrison is one of our regular customers, Judge. About the only thing we can do for him is keep him alive."

The judge scowled. "That costs the taxpayers money, but you're probably right." He had never looked at the defendant. "Thirty days," he said in a loud voice.

A court officer led the wobbling Harrison back toward the holding cell. The last man in the drunk line stepped up.

"*People* versus *Bissant*."

It was the middle-aged salesman in the torn suit. He stepped up quickly, looking physically better than he had in the basement drunk tank.

"How do you plead," intoned the clerk, "guilty or not guilty?"

Bissant looked up at Frank Conroy as if for assurance that he was really doing the right thing.

"Stand mute," he said.

"Enter a plea of not guilty," the judge said automatically. The arresting officer came up and stood next to Bis-

sant. He quickly put in his testimony, his flat voice recit-
ing the facts of the incident and the arrest. It was nothing
more than the run-of-the-mill case of a loud drunk disturb-
ing the other patrons in a bar.

The judge scowled. He was young, but the scowl was
becoming his permanent expression. "Any damage or
injury?"

The officer shook his head. "No."

"Well, what do you have to say?" the judge asked the
defendant.

Frank Conroy hurriedly whispered in the judge's ear.
Although the scowl remained unchanged, the judge nodded
in agreement.

"In view of your past good record I am going to dismiss
this case. But God help you if I ever see you back here
again."

Bissant nodded his gratitude to both Conroy and the
judge. He hurried away as the court officers began to line
up the prostitutes.

Working Early Sessions had one side benefit: Usually
the probation officer assigned to that duty was through
early in the day. It was understood that the unpleasant
task of dealing with a jail full of drunks, plus the trauma
of talking to an endless stream of prostitutes, thieves, and
derelicts, deserved some special consideration. Thus, it was
an unwritten rule that as soon as Early Sessions was
through and the paperwork completed, the rest of the
day was free.

For most people that would have mattered, but Francis
X. Conroy found little satisfaction in his free afternoons.
At first he had enjoyed them, but soon just trying to fill
up the time without an early visit to a bar became a problem. He looked forward to the release liquor gave him,
but he disciplined himself so as not to start too early.
Handling alcohol was all a matter of pace, he had decided.

Lately, with the good weather, he had taken long walks through the business district of the city, a detached spectator enjoying the people, reviewing the varied parade of humanity passing by. But the novelty soon wore off, however, and he had begun going back to the office. At least at the office he could find people to talk to, people who shared common interests, and people with whom he could feel a sense of ease, at least for a few minutes.

He talked to Harry Salter. Salter had just made a home visit where the inhabitants had been just this side of hell dwellers, and the sights, sounds, and smells had shaken the young probation officer. He needed someone to talk to, and Frank Conroy was a good listener.

After the demon of memory had been exorcised, Harry Salter had gone home, hurrying to his wife and family, leaving Frank Conroy alone in the large office, or almost alone. Kathleen Ann Mulloy was at her desk at the far end of the long office, her typewriter rattling as she waded through a stack of reports.

Kathleen Mulloy worked late many evenings. She was in her late twenties and had been a policewoman. She had earned a degree in sociology, and civil service had picked her up as a probation officer. Her days were taken up with sordid stories of beaten wives and battered children, of psychotic mothers and drunken fathers, of the whole miserable kaleidoscope of the underbelly of society. She worked hard, interviewed defendants, their families, friends, and employers; and then reduced it all to a short, precise statement giving a complete picture to a sentencing judge so that he could determine whether a man or woman might be a good risk for probation or whether prison was the only answer. She dealt, as they all did, in human lives.

A pretty woman, with soft reddish hair and full lips, she had the pale, milky complexion of an Irish beauty. Her large blue eyes and good figure had attracted a number of men around the criminal court, including lawyers, policemen, and other probation officers. And she had attracted one judge.

Like everything else in the probation department, nothing was ever entirely a secret. She had tried valiantly to hide her relationship with the judge, but the entire office knew about it. And those who were her friends worried about her.

Frank Conroy was her friend. He walked over to where she was working. He suspected that most of her activity was just for show, just make-work designed to kill time until His Honor called. She seemed nervous, almost anxious.

"Kathleen, you'll have calluses on those beautiful fingers if you keep this up."

She stopped and looked up, irritated until she saw who it was.

Conroy grinned. "Be fair, now, my dear, is there an opening for promotion coming up around here? Such diligent efforts must have some sinister motive besides mere service to the community."

She smiled weakly. "I'm bucking for your job, Frank." She sat back and hunched her shoulders to release the tension of typing.

He laughed. "Perhaps I can invite you out for a drink, then I can explain about some of the more unattractive aspects of what I do."

"Such as the drunks?"

"Lovely people, once you get to know them."

"Frank, I don't know how you can stand it day after day. Especially the smells." She made a face to reflect her distaste.

"As Ben Jonson once said, my dear, the term is *stink*. You and I smell, with our noses, you see. Thus, the poor drunks stink, and I smell."

She laughed. "Well, that's show business, Frank." Kathleen reached into her large leather purse and extracted a pack of cigarettes, offering them to Conroy.

He smiled and shook his head. She quickly lit one, nervously exhaling a stream of smoke.

Conroy continued. "Actually you get used to the drunks. It's just a matter of forming the right attitude, or at least that's what I keep telling myself."

She shook her head. "Yeech! Your job is safe from me."

"Well, how about that drink anyway?"

She inhaled, holding the smoke for a moment. "I'm expecting a telephone call," she said quietly without further explanation.

"Well, some other time, then." He paused, noting her anxiety. "Is everything all right, Kathleen?"

"How do you mean that?" Her tone of voice suddenly turned defensive.

He smiled easily. "Now, you should know me better than that. I'm not some old busybody trying to push my way into someone else's life. But I am concerned for your welfare, you understand?"

"I'm fine," she said quickly. "I'm a big girl. I can take care of myself."

"Indeed you can, Kathleen. But even big girls can be hurt. I know without having to be told that none of this is any of my business, but as a friend I would like to tell you to keep your emotional guard up, eh? In other words, be careful. Feelings can get us all into some pretty deep water sometimes."

She looked offended for a moment, but then she leaned back and studied him. "You really can't throw away that Roman collar, can you, Frank?"

"It's gone forever, Kathleen."

"I'm seeing a married man, Frank. Does that shock you?"

"No."

"No wonder they threw you out of the Church."

He shook his head. He didn't like to discuss the subject, but he supposed he had opened the door to her inquiries. "I wasn't thrown out, my dear. I left of my own free will."

"But you still worry after nice little Irish Catholic girls like me."

"Only as a friend."

"Not as a priest of God?"

Frank Conroy felt suddenly uncomfortable. It was never easy convincing people, especially Catholics, that his past was just that—his past. "Look, Kathleen, believe two things, if you will. First, I'm a pal of yours and available if you need a shoulder to cry on sometimes. Second, I don't believe in God."

"Really?"

"Really what? About being a pal or there being no God?"

"You really mean it, about God?"

"You can bet on it."

Her eyes were troubled. "What happened, Frank? I mean, are you bitter about it?"

He laughed. "No, not in the least. I'm not bitter at all. I lost my faith. It was a slow process, nothing dramatic. One day I woke up to the hard reality that for me at least the idea of God simply did not wash."

The telephone rang at her desk. She jumped as if caught doing something wrong. She snatched up the receiver.

"Yes," she said quietly. She listened for a moment. "Yes, that will be fine. I'll meet you there in about twenty minutes." She paused. "Of course." Then she hung up.

Frank noticed that her cheeks colored slightly as her eyes met his.

"Well, folly or not, Frank, I'm off. But I thank you for your concern."

"Like I said, be careful."

She jumped up, ran her hand through her hair, then grabbed her purse. "I'll see you tomorrow." She almost ran down the row of desks as she hurried out of the echoing office.

Frank Conroy waited awhile after she had gone. If she was meeting the judge in the building, or near it, he didn't want to blunder along and embarrass her. Waiting was tough, because he suddenly needed a drink very badly.

Perhaps Kathleen was right, Conroy reflected. Maybe residuals of that long-worn Roman collar did remain. He had to admit that he never felt entirely comfortable in his new role. He had a career, a life of his own now. He knew he should be primarily concerned with his own problems. Still, he couldn't help worrying about others, people like the drunks or fellow workers like Kathleen Mulloy. Maybe it was just the force of a lifetime habit. Whatever it was, he wished he could rid himself of it.

Finally sufficient time had elapsed. He locked his desk and closed the office. The elevator whisked him to street level, and he walked briskly along the avenue toward the beckoning of the Spartan Bar. He always began at the Spartan.

He thought about the young woman. And he thought about her lover, the Honorable Michael Noonan. Mickey Noonan: pillar of the community and the church; married and the father of five; a rising political star; a laughing, charming Irishman; and, as far as Francis X. Conroy was concerned, a rotten, cheating son of a bitch. But, he reminded himself as he had these black thoughts, no one was perfect, especially himself.

The delicious odor of whiskey filled his nostrils as he walked through the worn door of the Spartan Bar.

the information desk

RED Mehan swung back and forth on his swivel chair, his eyes watching the people in the lobby, his head bobbing to a silent rhythm of his own. A young uniformed officer listened to him. The young policeman, waiting to testify in Early Sessions court, was sipping coffee and killing time.

"Justice is a funny thing, if you think about it. Down here it's like a fuckin' raffle. Everything depends on who you get as a judge. I mean, whether you did it or not has very little to do with it. No, I mean it. Look, suppose you get caught passing bad checks, right? Okay, if you go before Judge Woldanski, you'll get the maximum sentence. She hates check passers. But if you end up before old Marcus Young, you'll get probation. No shit. Old Marcus, he believes that check passing is an illness and won't send anybody charged with that to jail. So where's the justice? If fate tosses you into Woldanski, you'll do heavy time. If you go to Young, you walk out of this place free as a bird. See, that's the reason these lawyers are always trying to figure out a way to pick the judge. They call it judge shopping. You can understand why they do it. Shit, the facts of the case don't mean anything. It's who you get as judge that's important.

"Same thing with sex cases. Take old Cannonball O'Brien. That fucker would sell anybody out for a nickel usually, but bring a sex case before him and it's the kiss of death. It's the one thing he won't fix. See, if you arrest some senile old shit who's been running his hand up little

girls' dresses, he'll get twenty years from Cannonball for carnal knowledge. But you take the same dirty old man before Judge Luther Perry and he'll get probation if he promises to seek psychiatric care. Same case, only one judge salts the old fuck away for what amounts to a life sentence while the other judge lets him go. Funny, eh?

"All those guys got their own little hang-ups and preju-dices, see? So if you know whether a judge is easy or hard on the kind of case you've got, then you know what to do.

"What they ought to do is eliminate the judges entirely. Just run the court like Las Vegas. See, you could have one big fuckin' roulette wheel here in the lobby. Every de-fendant gets a number; like number seventeen means five years, twelve means life and seven means complete free-dom, like that, see? Then you spin the wheel, and your luck depends on what number comes up.

"Of course, no one ever listens to anything practical, they just keep doin' what they been doin' since time began. There just ain't no place for us innovators.

"Hey, see that woman that just came in? The tall broad, nicely dressed. Distinguished, huh? Looks like a judge's wife, right? Nope! That's old Rocking Chair Martha. Best goddamned madam in the city. Keeps getting busted lately. I hear the bellboys turn her in—she's bad for their business.

"Look, that's the law of the jungle. You got to look out for yourself. And baby, all these people here are tough jungle animals, every damned last one of them."

2

preparation

chapter four

the world liberation army

FLASH Johnson was the last to arrive. It irritated Larry Gormley that Johnson persisted in resisting his authority. It was symbolic, but being late and failure to complete minor assignments plus grumbling about the lack of revolutionary progress were Johnson's means to annoy the leader of the World Liberation Army. The others were being welded into an efficient team, and they were enthusiastic despite the lack of plans for firm action. Gormley sensed, however, that he had to reveal his plan quickly, or their enthusiasm would fade, and they would soon follow Johnson's lead.

They had been completely changed from a ragged bunch of misfits. Even Thelma Sturdevant had moderated her use of drugs, and her eyes had lost their vacant quality. And she had returned to permanently share Gormley's bed, as she had before he had gone to California. Gormley suspected that this was another reason for Flash Johnson's obvious resentment.

Al Martin idly stroked his moustache. He was beginning to look more like a banker or accountant daily. He liked the conservative suits Gormley had ordered for him. And he kept them neat without being told. Alice Mary Brennan looked less frumpy, but even the best-tailored clothes failed to completely conceal her lumpy figure.

Gormley wondered if the five of them could really pull it off. There was only one way to find out.

"What do you see as the primary objectives of this organization?" Gormley asked.

They were sitting around the kitchen table. They glanced at each other before Alice Mary Brennan began a reply in the stylized tone of a memorized recitation. "To free the men and women of the working class, to break the chains of capitalism that bind them, we . . ."

"I said primary objections, Alice Mary. Those are long-term goals."

"The primary thing is to get my brother and Hagen the hell out of jail, at least that's what you all said you'd do." Flash Johnson sneered. " 'Course, I expect some things are changed now."

Gormley felt the skin at the corners of his mouth tighten. They would need Flash Johnson for now, but there would come a time when they wouldn't need him, and then Gormley would settle matters.

"Flash is right," he said evenly, concealing his anger. "Hagen and Johnson are officers of this organization, but more than that, they have become a symbol of the World Liberation Army. If we do nothing to help them, people will think we are just impotent crackpots. So one of our primary objectives is to get them out of jail."

"Aw, shit," Flash said, "how you goin' do that? You got a magic wand or something?"

"Maybe," Gormley replied, ignoring the challenge. "The other primary objection is the execution of Judge Abrams. Johnson announced to the world that we would kill the man. The newspapers made a lot out of it, so we have to take care of that piece of business."

"What good will that do?" Alice Mary asked. "Another just like him will be appointed. It's the system we have to change."

"That will come in time," Gormley said. "But now we have to take dramatic action in order to build this little group into a respected national organization. We must carry out our threats. If we don't, people and groups who might otherwise give support won't have anything to do with us."

"Well, what do you propose, Larry?" Al Martin asked.

"We all watched this morning's television news, right?"

Most nodded their assent.

"What do you recall about the program that might be important to us?"

"They tried a revolution in Bolivia," Thelma Sturdevant said, as if showing off for a teacher.

Gormley shook his head. "That revolution was put down. Probably badly organized, from the sound of it." He smiled to reassure Thelma anyway. "The important local item of interest was the judges' meeting last night."

"That criminal court thing with King Tingle talkin'?" Flash asked.

"That's it."

"Big fuckin' deal, man! What the hell good is that goin' to do us?"

Gormley did not smile this time. "The point of the whole thing is that they schedule monthly judges' meetings. In other words, every damn judge of the criminal court is in one room on one night of the month. And with probably few, if any, guards. Does that give you any ideas?"

"Bomb the fuckers?" Flash asked.

"No. That wouldn't get your brother out of jail."

"Sure would kill that hebe judge that sent him there, though," Flash grinned.

"We'll get to him in due time. We have one month to plan and practice what we are going to do."

Al Martin frowned. "And that is?"

"We are going to take that entire bunch of judges hostage. We'll use them to bring Johnson and Hagen to us."

"Be more like we'll end up with them, not the other way around," Flash grumbled.

Gormley's voice was cold and commanding. "Look, we will have every damned judge of the criminal court in our hands plus one supreme court justice. Every one of those judges has a block of voters interested in him, otherwise he wouldn't be there. The authorities couldn't risk getting tough. We would really have them by the short hairs."

"So what happens even if they do spring Hagen and Johnson? We have them, but they have us too," Al Martin said.

"Not really. We have important hostages. We demand money and an airplane."

"That's been done before, Larry. Most never get away with it." Alice Mary shook her head.

Gormley sighed. He decided he would have to tell them

everything in order to sell them on the plan. "Look, if we have all those judges as hostages, we may have to kill one or two of them to show that we mean business. They'll send Hagen and Johnson to us, believe me. Once we have them, then we ask for the plane, and not just an airliner but a B-52 bomber."

"Aw, shit, man," Flash said, "they ain't never goin' to give us no big bomber. That's crazy."

"We're not asking for bombs, just the bomber. Hell, they don't even have to worry about a civilian crew, they can use military pilots. Besides, the bomber is our ticket out of here and into Africa."

They all watched him, surprise written on each face, including Flash Johnson's.

"When I was in California, I found out that Colonel Fasid of Samwand will give asylum to anyone who can bring in a war plane or anything else he can use in his African army."

"Isn't he nuts?" Martin asked. "Christ, I've read the newspaper stories about him. I don't think you can take him at his word."

"Samwand is the unofficial capital of all terrorist groups, did you know that?" Gormley asked. "Since it became a country and since Fasid took it over, Samwand has become a safe refuge for anyone who can raise hell with the Western countries. That's all Fasid really cares about. He wants a strong army to beat hell out of his neighbors, but he enjoys throwing a scare into the whole political setup over there. He'll be grateful for the bomber, believe me."

"Oh, man, I don't think I like this at all," Flash moaned. "That colonel dude may be black, but I don't think I wants to trust him. You know, missionaries ain't the only ones who end up in the cook pots over there."

"Right now Fasid's support, his money and guns, come from the allies of the terrorist groups. He knows it, and they know it. If he gets tough, there goes his power, and he is the one who ends up in the cook pot." Gormley smiled. "I think we'll be safe enough."

"Why should those people support us?" Martin asked.

"Right now there isn't a reason in the world. We are just seven people. They have no reason to be interested. But when we pull this off, we will be famous. If things go right, we shall stand the United States right on its ear. These people respect ability and nerve. This will earn us a reputation. Then we can sit in their councils and actually become an effective part of a worldwide movement."

"And you think this will do it?"

"Remember the Red Brigades in Italy and Aldo Moro?" Gormley replied. "Christ, until that happened, the Red Brigades were branded as just a collection of student nuts. But after they kidnaped Moro, killed his bodyguards, and then left his body in that car on that street in Rome, the Red Brigades were suddenly a powerful force, a force to be reckoned with. By the way, the people who planned and carried out that Moro thing are in Samwand right now."

"How do you know that?" Flash asked.

"Sources. The same ones who helped provide our guns and grenades. Does that answer your question?"

Johnson nodded reluctantly.

"Suppose they move Hagen and Johnson to state prison? Won't that ruin things?" Martin asked.

Gormley pursed his lips thoughtfully. "No, not really. It would just take more time to get them back, that's all. Besides, I think with the motion for a new trial and the other legal steps necessary, they'll be in the city jail at least until the next judges' meeting.

"Well, we have to do something," Alice Mary said. "We just can't sit here forever." She paused, looking around the table at the others. "I'm for trying it."

Martin fingered his moustache. "You honestly think we can pull this off, Larry?"

"I'm convinced of it."

Martin nodded. "Okay, let's do it, then."

"How about you, Thelma?" Gormley asked.

She smiled a lover's smile. "If you say so, Larry, it's okay with me."

Gormley and the others looked at Flash Johnson. He sat back in his chair, his eyes fixed on the ceiling. "A lot of folks goin' to get killed," he said to no one in particular.

"At least Judge Abrams." Gormley's quiet statement showed an icy determination.

The thin black man's eyes flicked around at the others, his lips curled into a half-smile, half-sneer. "To tell you the truth, I think the whole thing ain't worth shit. We'll probably get our asses shot off. But because of my brother, I'll go along with it for now."

Gormley smiled, sliding his hand into his coat pocket, his fingers seeking the butt of his revolver. "It's in or out, Flash. You can't have it both ways. Which is it?" Gormley's finger wrapped around the trigger.

Flash Johnson had no idea he was in any danger. "Shit, whole lot of people goin' get killed, but I'll go along with it."

"There'll be no backing out," Gormley said quietly.

Flash met his eyes. "I won't be backing out, man. I said I was in, and that means I am in!"

Gormley relaxed. "Good. Okay, let's get down to work. We have to do some preliminary planning." He smiled at the others. "If we're careful, we'll have an international reputation written in blood. No one will forget the World Liberation Army."

the assistant prosecutor

ACE Gilbert, like many thin people, often had to remind himself to eat. Occasionally he went on food binges, stuffing himself with bags of fast-food hamburgers or frying up mounds of bacon and eggs. But except for those rare occurrences, he never really thought about food. He ate only to obtain fuel for his body.

The Athens Lunch Room occupied a strategic corner at the junction of the criminal court, the jail, and the city's medical complex. Its worn counters, stools, tables, and chairs attracted a strange mix of human beings, a combination found in no other place. Just as an African water hole attracts both predator and prey, the Athens was an oasis for all people. Doctors, some still in their green operating-room outfits, nurses, and orderlies sat together with bandaged patients. Cops munched greasy hamburgers next to tables of recently bailed-out robbers. Judges and prosecutors mingled with prostitutes and defense lawyers. In any other place they would all be highly nervous in such company, but the Athens was neutral territory, and no one paid any attention to his neighbor.

Ace Gilbert liked the Athens. It had a distinctive atmosphere, a friendly, warm place where the men and women who dealt in bodies or lives could relax for a few moments. And the coffee was good.

As always, the place was jammed at lunchtime. All the counter stools were filled. He searched the tables and booths to see if he could spot a friendly face and an empty seat.

In a booth at the rear of the restaurant he saw a man

wave to him. Recognizing Emanuel Gonzales, the probation officer whom everyone called Speedy, Gilbert worked his way through the packed tables toward the back of the restaurant.

Gonzales grinned, his dark face providing a vivid contrast to his large white teeth. "Com'on, Gringo, we make room for you." He slid over, making space.

Wriggling past a stout prostitute who was sitting at a nearby table with her ample backside partially blocking the aisle, Gilbert eased his long form into the narrow space in the booth.

He was startled to see that Gonzales was not alone. The two women had been hidden from view by the booth partition. They sat across the table. Kathleen Mulloy looked beautiful, her soft red hair catching the reflected ceiling light. She sat next to Boom-Boom Douglas, also a probation officer. Boom-Boom had earned that name because of her provocative walk.

"Well, the champion of the people," Boom-Boom said in greeting, amused that he had eyes only for Kathleen Mulloy.

Ace grinned. It was a great opportunity. The beautiful redhead couldn't avoid him in the confines of the small both. "How are you both?"

"I'm fine, Ace," Boom-Boom said. "Whatcha up to in court? If you're handling a good sex case, I'll come and watch. A good rape always makes me feel better."

"Watching or experiencing?" Gonzales leered at the willowy probation officer.

"Watching is second best," she said. "Helps the imagination, though. You ever rape anyone, Speedy?"

"You mean in addition to my sister?" He pronounced it *sees-tar.*

Kathleen Mulloy laughed. Ace admired her perfect teeth and inviting lips.

Boom-Boom snorted. "Aw, you wouldn't know how.

What about you, Ace? What kind of man are you, a lover or a fighter?"

Kathleen dropped her eyes as he looked at her. "I hate to fight," he said. "I favor persuasion over force."

"Oh, a little force helps sometimes," Boom-Boom said. "I remember this sailor, you know, when I was a kid. Well, he was home on leave—"

"Was he on the *Nina* or the *Santa Maria?*" Gonzales interrupted.

"Goddamned wetback. If your mother couldn't swim, you wouldn't be here right now."

Gilbert paid little attention to their mock verbal battle. It was the usual criminal court talk, full of racial and sexual jests and slurs. It was always a contest to see who could think up the grossest insult. It reflected the world they dealt with daily—often both sickening and shocking. The rough humor seemed to mirror their working lives.

"How have you been, Kathleen?" he asked, ignoring the other two.

"Just fine, Ace," she said, her clear blue eyes meeting his. As before, he sensed an interest there. Maybe not invitation, but at least interest. But each time he had asked her out, she had politely refused. He knew she was single, and if she had a boyfriend, he thought she would tell him, that seemed only fair. But all he received were gentle turndowns with no real explanation. It was puzzling. She was more than merely attractive, she was a classic Irish beauty with an air of pleasing innocence. He wondered if it wasn't this aura of innocence that was the most attractive quality of all, something that challenged the most primitive of male desires—to be the protector. Whatever it was, he wanted her.

He had only eaten a bite or two of his hamburger when Kathleen finished her lunch, said something about pressing office work, and excused herself.

"Are you going back to the court building?" Gilbert asked.

"Yes."

"I'll come along," he said quickly, allowing her no time for a refusal. He left the still warring couple in the booth and followed Kathleen Mulloy toward the cashier. She was paying her bill by the time he had worked his way through the crowded restaurant.

She moved with purpose. He had to trot a few steps to catch up with her.

"Kathleen, I have tickets for that new musical at the Tyrone Theater. It's for Thursday night. I was wondering if you'd like to go with me?"

She looked up at him. She seemed to hesitate for a moment before answering. "Thanks, Ace," she said, "but I'm afraid I'm busy Thursday. I hear it's a good production. I'm sure you'll enjoy it." She sounded honestly disappointed.

"I'd like it better if you were there with me."

"What a nice thing to say. Well, I have to go to work now. See you." She ducked into the probation office, leaving him standing in the hall.

Safe inside the office, she wondered at her own conflicting feelings. There could be no one for her but Mickey Noonan. Still, the tall, quiet prosecutor, his manner reminiscent, in a way, of Gary Cooper, was damned attractive. And she knew that Ace Gilbert really liked her, which made having to refuse even more painful. She had been tempted for a moment. She never went anywhere anymore. It was obvious that she and Mickey couldn't be seen together in public, and she accepted that. But she did miss the fun of being with other people, of parties and shows. It was the price she had to pay.

Kathleen wondered why Ace Gilbert should make her feel guilty. She loved Mickey Noonan. Mickey was dark, dashing, and wit and charm seemed to exude from him like an inner light. He had become the center of her existence. Their moments together were treasured like rare diamonds. She assured herself that she had no regrets.

Still, she felt bad that she had refused Ace Gilbert without being able to tell him the real reason. She supposed that was also part of the price she had to pay.

honorable clyde powell

CLYDE Powell felt exhausted. The other judges had tried to make him into a martyr, to use him as a foil to defeat the purposes of the supreme court. It had taken all his energy and wile to escape that crown of thorns. He was not about to let them make him the symbol of resistance. Not that he wasn't angry. Judge Clyde Powell was seething inside. But after long years of practice it was relatively easy for him to conceal his emotions. And the anger had quickly passed, though not the dismay.

There was no question that the criminal court needed something to move the mountain of cases that threatened to crush that institution. He did not quarrel with the intentions, only the means. He knew James Tingle better than if he had been the man's parent, and he also knew the dark side of the man's nature.

It somehow always surprised him to find his apartment empty when he returned at night. Powell had read that the loss of a spouse was one of the most traumatic events in life, but he had not expected that the recovery period would take so long.

He wondered if it would be wiser to move from the apartment, to start life again in a home not so filled with memories. Each room seemed to carry its own shock of loss. Yet he loved the large, rambling apartment, and although it was painful, he felt a sense of communication with his wife. He wondered if others had so difficult a time, but then he and his wife had been married so long and had always been so close.

He had only a sandwich at lunch, and that had long ago worn off, but he did not feel hungry, at least not for food. He did have a hunger to talk to someone, to discuss the day's events. But there was no one to listen, and he sometimes felt as though the emotions that boiled within him might spill over without an adequate vent.

He went to the kitchen and poured a glass of white wine, adding an ice cube. It was expensive wine, and the ice was an insult, but he was in no mood to wait for the wine to chill.

He removed his suit coat and took the drink into the living room. Kicking off his shoes, he relaxed in his favorite chair. He sipped the wine and looked out the window at the city below. It had been good to him, this city, these people. As a boy he had known poverty and hard work. As a young black lawyer he had endured insults and discrimination until the tide finally began to turn. It has been a hard road, but no harder, he mused, than the road traversed by many in a country that could elevate a former shoeshine boy to the position of judge. He felt strongly that he owed the people and the city something for that honor.

Powell studied the wineglass and thought about the first time he had encountered James Tingle. Tingle had been very young, very skinny, and very tall, an intense young law student trying to find work as a legal clerk. They had hired him, even though the firm really didn't need a clerk. But the partners knew that the young man wouldn't stand a chance with the white firms, not in those days. So he had come to work as a clerk. And after passing the bar examination Tingle had stayed on as an eager young lawyer.

Clyde Powell had recognized in the young man a sharp intelligence and the seeds of burning ambition. He had introduced Tingle to influential politicians in the black community, and Tingle had taken it from there. Powell had had great hopes for him when Tingle had been elected to the state senate, the second black man ever to serve in that body.

It began then, he supposed, Tingle's desire and need for the flash and excitement of the so-called high life. At first James Tingle had been the voice of conscience in the senate, but that soon changed as he learned the real game and the use of power. It was then that he started to put on weight, and it was then that his private life-style began to earn him the name of the King. Everything was done on a grand scale: clothing, cars, liquor, and women. And after his election to Congress his wild living became even more renowned.

Clyde Powell remembered Tingle's entrance at Powell's own swearing-in ceremony. Powell had taken pains to see that everything connected with his oath-taking as a judge would be dignified. The governor had come down from the capital to do the honors. But both he and the governor had to take a backseat when the flamboyant Tingle arrived, late as usual, and came striding through the auditorium waving and calling to politicians in the crowd. Tingle had stomped up onto the stage, disrupting the proceedings as he lifted Powell off his feet in a rough bear hug. Without invitation, Tingle had then made a short but enthusiastic speech about his old mentor. The whole thing had the ring of a circus to it, but Powell had endured the show. After all, Tingle was a congressman, and the sentiments he expressed, if loud, did seem genuine and sincere.

And then Tingle had been elected to the state's highest court, the first black man to serve on the bench of the supreme court. But instead of bringing honor, Tingle had become just a caricature—a loud, raucous man completely controlled by base appetites. Powell had heard the whispers about gambling and women trouble. He considered Tingle a disgrace.

Now this man had control of his court and the hundreds of cases that poured into it daily. If handled correctly, such complete control could be a great boon to justice, but if a man wanted to make money—big money—and had no scruples, then Tingle was in an ideal situation.

Clyde Powell sipped his wine and watched the city, just as he planned to carefully watch the activities of his former protégé, James "The King" Tingle.

the burglar

GUS SIMES had been escorted from the court's bullpen into the courtroom of Judge Milton Harbor. He could hardly see the small judge, whose head just barely seemed to come up over the bench. But he could see the frowning eyes peering over a large moustache. The judge's expression made Simes shudder. Harbor had the reputation of being a mental lightweight. The prisoners handicapped the criminal court judges the way racetrack men handicapped horses. Also Harbor had a reputation for being mean, erratic at times, but always mean.

This was to be the examination only, so the worse the

judge could do was to bind him over for trial. Still, he felt sweat bead on his forehead as he was led to a place behind his lawyer.

His lawyer, pale and appearing underfed, glanced up at his client. Simes took a seat behind him. The young man half-turned in his chair. He looked at Simes.

"Simes? Gus Simes, right?"

"Yeah, of course."

"I'm sorry, I see so many. Okay, now do you understand what's happening today?"

Simes shrugged. He was no virgin when it came to the criminal process. "Sure."

His public-defender lawyer proceeded as if Simes had answered in the negative. "In this state there is no indictment by grand jury. Therefore, in order that the court can determine that the state is acting in a fair manner and that the defendant will not be put to the trouble of defending himself on a trumped-up charge, it holds a preliminary hearing. This is called an examination."

"I know."

The lawyer bristled. "Listen to me," he said. "I don't want you complaining later that you didn't know what was happening."

"Look, I've been—"

"The examination," the lawyer said, cutting him off, "is to determine if a crime was in fact committed and also if there is probable cause to believe that the defendant committed it. That's all the state has to show. If they can show the crime—in this case, murder—then they must show the existence of probable cause, in the legal sense, that you are responsible for that crime. Do you understand that?"

"Look, this isn't my first time in court. I understand the whole thing. Can't we make a deal with the prosecutor?"

The young lawyer sighed. "I tried, but so far nothing.

Maybe after this examination they won't feel so cocky. We'll see what we can do, Chime."

"That's Simes, Gus Simes."

"Whatever."

The case was called, and in a whisper his lawyer informed him that the defense did not need to present evidence, only the prosecutor, a fact Gus Simes was well acquainted with.

Simes sat back and listened to the procession of witnesses: the relatives who had identified the body of his late partner, followed by the medical examiner who told how he had cut him up and weighed everything carefully. The cause of death was a gunshot wound. Simes's lawyer had no questions.

Then the two police officers who had answered the burglary call testified. The testimony was straightforward and truthful, even Simes had to admit that. They just told what happened. The younger officer who had done the shooting still seemed affected by it. His testimony was given in a tense monologue. Both officers identified Gus Simes.

The young lawyer from the public defender's office just asked a few questions, establishing very firmly that Gus Simes had been unarmed and that he had actually not shot anyone. Simes glanced up at the judge during this testimony. Harbor's expression showed no sign of interest.

Afterward his lawyer and the prosecutor made lengthy arguments to the judge about the law of murder. The prosecutor seemed sure of himself and the law he was spouting. Simes's lawyer appeared to be just going through the motions. Still, Simes knew that there was a new crash program in the court, so there was some hope that a deal could be made.

As Simes had expected, the judge bound him over for trial on the charge of first-degree murder. The judge walked off the bench, and Simes watched anxiously as his lawyer talked to the prosecutor. He could not hear what they were saying.

Both attorneys were somber young men, intense in their discussion. Finally the talk was finished, and his lawyer came walking back across the courtroom. Gus Simes hoped for a break. Second-degree murder would be just fine; they didn't execute people for that. Even manslaughter was a possibility. Simes prayed that he would get lucky.

"What did he say?" he asked his lawyer.

"He said he is going to burn your ass."

The lawyer collected his briefcase, nodded to Simes, and then walked away. Gus Simes sat fixed in his chair, stunned and shocked.

the hotel

As usual their lovemaking had been frantic, almost an athletic event, leaving both of their bodies glistening with perspiration. Kathleen Ann Mulloy lay back on the cool pillows feeling fulfilled and satisfied. She looked at Mickey Noonan. His hair was mussed, but it didn't spoil the attractiveness of his handsome Irish face. His features were broad and strong, but his pale-blue eyes were soft and gentle. Although slightly overweight, he was heavily muscled, and his thick body was smooth and exciting to her.

"Want a cigarette?" she asked.

"Couldn't lift it. I'm pooped."

"Was it good?" She always wondered if she really satisfied his ardor.

He looked over at her and grinned. "What do you think?" She made no reply, but leaned over and took a cigarette from the pack on the side table. She inhaled deeply and lay back. For the first time she noticed the soft music. It was an expensive hotel, which provided everything including stereo and FM radio.

She studied the ceiling and reflected. She remembered what she used to think of other women who became involved with married men. But it had started so innocently. She had admired Judge Michael Noonan and had found him handsome and fascinating. She had been flattered that he had seemed interested in her and in her work as a probation officer. There had never been any decision on her part, no plan to lure the husband of another woman. It had all been so natural. They had been drawn to each other and had become lovers before she even fully realized all the implications. It had been exciting, a sudden, explosive adventure. Drawn so swiftly into the swirl of their relationship, she had asked no questions, sought no answers. But recently Kathleen Mulloy had begun to wonder about some things.

She knew it was dangerous water, but her curiosity could no longer be contained. "Mickey," she asked. "Is it the same with your wife?"

"What?"

"Sex. Is it the same with her as it is with me?"

He rolled over and looked at her. She was relieved that there was no anger in his eyes. "What brings that up?" His eyes only reflected amusement.

"We've never talked about it," she said.

"No, we haven't. Do you really want to?"

She blew out a stream of smoke. "If you don't want to, it's okay with me."

He sat up, pulling a sheet over his legs. "I don't mind, Kathy, but I don't think it's wise."

"Why not?" She was alarmed, worried that perhaps she had intruded into an area where he felt she had no right.

"Look, I'm married. Unhappy, but married. There are a multitude of reasons why I must stay married." He paused and looked over at her. "I've told you all this before. The situation hasn't changed. I know you must wonder about my relationship with my wife. That's only natural."

She waited.

He reached across her to get at the pack of cigarettes. The touch of his body seemed to set her aflame. She instantly regretted having started the conversation.

He inhaled before speaking. "*Frosty*—I think that's the word that best describes the relationship between my wife and myself. As far as sex is concerned, my wife has always been a very inhibited person. Sex to her is something dirty to be done in the dark, if at all." He paused, studying the smoke. It was all a lie, but he knew that it was what she wanted to hear, and besides, it was none of her business. "We don't have sex anymore," he said, sounding somewhat sad. He knew that if he told her that he and his wife had made love the very night before, she would be crushed. Although if she had had half a brain, she wouldn't even have had to ask.

"She must be very lonely," Kathleen said, almost to herself.

Noonan fell back into the pillow. "Hell, no! Christ, she has the children and she is active in about two dozen church things. She has a full life. She likes being the wife of a judge, even if she doesn't particularly like the judge." Again he gave his voice just a hint of resigned sadness, just the right touch. "Besides," he said, again reaching across her to put out his cigarette, "you are the best piece of ass this side of the Mississippi. No one could ever be as good as you." His hands sought her breasts. His mouth was warm and insistent as he kissed her naked shoulders. She put out her cigarette and gave herself to him.

courtroom no. 1—honorable milton harbor, presiding

JAMES Tingle disliked working with Milton Harbor. The primping little fool had a dozen mannerisms that irritated like fingernails on a blackboard, and he knew he would have to be closeted with Harbor every working day. It was an awful fate, but one that was unavoidable. Harbor was his patsy. Everything Tingle did was completely unofficial, at least on the record. Judge Milton Harbor, on the other hand, was the executive judge, and everything was signed only by him. It was perfect. The man might be irritating, but he was stupid, and stupidity was a great virtue, at least in a patsy.

By the second day Tingle had established the routine. He sat with Harbor behind a large executive desk in the chambers of the executive judge. A long line of attorneys waited outside, each man clutching a file. It was bargain basement day in criminal court.

The first attorney was ushered in by the court officer. "Good morning, Mr. Justice," he beamed at Tingle. "Good morning, Your Honor," he said in a slightly less deferential tone to Harbor.

"Whatcha got?" Tingle asked.

"Embezzlement," the attorney replied. He was an old-timer with a whiskey nose and a beer belly. His skin had the patchy red gloss of a heavy drinker.

"How much?" Tingle asked.

"Pardon me?" The lawyer looked puzzled.

"How much do they allege he took?" Tingle replied, spelling it out.

"Oh! They claim he took six thousand dollars."

Harbor felt he had to take an active part. "Why isn't this a federal prosecution?"

The attorney smiled, showing a multitude of lead fillings in his yellowed teeth. "He took the money from a state-chartered credit union. They don't have any connection with federal law. They didn't even have depositors' insurance, so it's just a state bust."

"Can he make restitution?" Tingle asked.

"Most, but not all. His mother can come up with a couple grand. He hasn't got a pot to piss in."

"Criminal record?" Tingle asked, leafing through the file, looking for a record printout.

"Couple of traffic things, speeding, but nothing else."

"Okay," Tingle said, making up his mind. "How about simple larceny? Just a misdemeanor. We'll put him on probation. You have his old lady pay in what she can, and he can make payments of five or ten bucks a week until it's all paid off."

"It's really paid off now, Mr. Justice. He was bonded. The insurance company took care of it."

Tingle shrugged his massive shoulders. "Fuck the insurance company. I'm not going to be a collection agent for them. We'll make it simple larceny and give him a twenty-five-dollar fine, no jail or probation. How's that?"

"Jesus." The attorney almost squeaked the word in surprise. "That's one hell of a break. I appreciate it." Suddenly he stopped, and a worried frown replaced a look of elation. "I don't think the cops will go along . . ."

"The police will do what we tell them," Tingle said

firmly. He paused and then continued in a more conversational tone. "The crush of cases here dictates that the police, attorneys, and judges all cooperate. Everyone understands that this is a crisis."

"Well, maybe," the lawyer said skeptically. "But you'll have to tell them, they'll never believe me."

Tingle grinned. The man obviously had a bad reputation with the police; probably he had cut one corner too many on cases to help pay for his drinking.

"Now, don't you worry about a thing, Counsel." Tingle assumed his most solemn and sincere expression, speaking in a deep, authoritative voice. "We have designed a form to take care of any questions. In other words, we give it to you in writing. Judge Harbor, will you please fill in a form and sign it for this gentleman?"

Harbor dutifully began to scribble the agreement on a form taken from a stack in front of him.

"This is a formal order of the court," Tingle continued. "It will cover almost all situations. Judge Harbor will just fill in the name, file number, and disposition. In this matter the reduced charge and the sentence will be set down. Judge Harbor himself will sign the order."

The attorney's red face twisted with agitation. "But the cops," he said. "Jesus, Mr. Justice, they'll want some kind of say in this."

"And they have it." Tingle smiled. "This order will go to the clerk's office, where it will be reviewed by an assistant prosecutor. If the policemen in charge of a case have any complaints, they can make them to that prosecutor. And if the prosecutor thinks the complaints may be justified, he will bring the matter before Judge Harbor and myself. We will then reexamine the entire case. This usually takes place at the end of the day." Tingle had invented this bit of procedure to offset any complaints. It appeared to be fair and evenhanded. It wasn't, but that's how it would look. It would take care of any critics.

"In other words, I won't know if I've got a deal until tonight?"

"There is no 'deal' here," Judge Harbor snarled, his moustache twitching above his small lips. "I resent your implication, Counselor!"

Tingle sighed to himself. Harbor was a monumental pain in the ass, but unfortunately he was a necessary pain. "I'm sure counsel intended no implication at all," he said soothingly, putting his large hand on Harbor's shoulder to emphasize his sincerity. "He has to tell his client what he may expect, that's all."

Without waiting for Harbor to reply, Tingle looked up at the lawyer. "You can check with the clerk at four o'clock. There might be a line, but the clerk will let you know then if anything's changed."

"Thank you, Your Honor." The man almost bowed his way out, as if in the presence of royalty.

"I didn't like his attitude. It was . . . well . . . snotty," Harbor persisted.

"These lawyers are used to a different system, Milton. It will take a while for them to adjust their thinking. For years around here it's been tough getting a plea reduced; now it's suddenly easy. They all think they smell a rat, that's all. Once they get used to this new procedure, everything will run smoothly enough."

"I just didn't like his attitude . . ."

"We better hurry along, Milton." Tingle's voice took on a stern, commanding quality. "If we move along, we can get the job done. As I figure it, we can only spend three minutes on each case, and that's all. It's just mathematics. If we can't turn them out that fast, we won't make a significant dent in the backlog. Remember, we have over six thousand cases to dispose of. We must move them along, Milton." Tingle forced himself to remain civil.

"I appreciate the problem," Harbor said petulantly, "but I really think there should be more safeguards. After all, if the lawyers aren't telling the truth and we haven't heard from the police, I don't think we can arrive at a proper decision."

"The prosecutor assigned to the clerk's office will handle any cases where the attorneys may have misrepresented the facts. That's a big safeguard. So far, Milton, no one has had a complaint about the process."

"Still, I think . . ."

Tingle's great hand raised up like a stop sign, and Harbor shut his mouth. The hand was larger than Harbor's head.

"Milton." Tingle's voice was gentle, almost a whisper. "Buck says it has to be done this way. We have to produce. You haven't forgotten about the court of appeals, have you? Buck is watching to see how you do."

Like a dog on a leash, thought Tingle to himself as he watched the small man jerk perceptibly at the mention of the chief justice.

"Well," Harbor said quickly, "I didn't mean that we shouldn't move the cases. I was just expressing concern . . . oh, well, forget it."

"No problem." Tingle patted Harbor on the back. "Bring the next case in," he said to the uniformed court officer at the door.

Both judges recognized the next attorney. Balding and wide-shouldered, the man's large eyes peered through thick glasses. His expression was set, determined like a fighter just before the bell. He was well known in the courts and generally considered to be the leading murder defense lawyer in the city.

"Mr. Justice," the man said, shaking hands with Tingle. He ignored Harbor.

Tingle smiled. "A pleasure, Mr. Ambrose. We don't see enough of you up at the supreme court. We always enjoy your presentations. Have a seat."

The lawyer sat on the edge of a chair facing both jurists. His manner was alert but tense, suggesting a wary animal about to leap to the attack.

"Mind if I smoke?" he asked.

"Well, I—" Harbor started to speak, but he was cut off.

"Feel free," Tingle said, glad for an excuse. Harbor disliked smoking. "I'll join you. Care for a cigar?" He offered one of his special big cigars to the lawyer.

"No, thank you. A cigarette will do fine."

"What do you have, Mr. Ambrose?" Tingle was casual but respectful, his manner much different with this attorney. A man had to be careful with a lawyer like Carl Ambrose.

"First-degree murder."

"What's the story?" Tingle lit the cigar, emitting clouds of thick smoke, most of which enshrouded Judge Harbor.

Ambrose took a file from his briefcase. He adjusted the thick glasses pushing the frame back over the bridge of his nose. "My client, Harold Revelle, is accused of shooting and killing a taxi driver. The police allege that the cabbie was shot resisting a holdup. They have a witness who saw a struggle and can identify my client as firing the fatal shot. My client denies the robbery and says that the cabdriver tried to cheat him. There was an argument, and during the ensuing fight the cabby was shot. My client claims the gun belonged to the cabdriver."

"Any proof of that?" Tingle asked.

"None."

"How about past convictions?"

The attorney inhaled the cigarette deeply before answering. As he spoke, smoke poured from his mouth and nose. "He has a rather bad record: car theft and robbery.

He was convicted of unarmed robbery and, later, of armed robbery. He was out of prison a month before the shooting took place."

"That doesn't sound so good," Tingle commented.

Carl Ambrose nodded. "Perhaps. But if we go to trial," he said with quiet confidence, "the jury may believe my client's story that he was acting only in self-defense."

"With that record?" Harbor interjected.

The attorney's cool eyes glanced over at Harbor for the first time. "I don't plan to put him on the stand. They can't bring out his record unless he testifies." The disgust in his voice made the words sound like an answer to an idiot who should have known better than to propose the question. "He told his story about acting in self-defense to the detectives. They'll have to relate that at the trial."

"You'll lose," Harbor said, irritated at the lawyer's obvious attitude toward him.

Tingle leaned back in his chair, eyeing his cigar as if he had never seen it before. "Mr. Ambrose, I'm the first one to admit that you have a certain way with juries. Still . . ."

The attorney allowed himself a faint, cold smile. "I'll grant you the case isn't the best from the viewpoint of the defense, but I've won cases much more difficult than this one, as I'm sure you're both aware."

Tingle nodded. "Perhaps. Would you consider a plea?"

"Manslaughter," the attorney said without a moment's hesitation.

Tingle laughed. "This isn't Christmas, and I'm not Santa Claus, Mr. Ambrose. I was thinking of second-degree murder. That would be quite a break, under the circumstances."

"Perhaps, but he could draw a long prison term under that. The sentencing judge could give him forty or fifty years," Ambrose said.

"Suppose he got a life sentence?"

The lawyer's eyes showed a flicker of interest. "Straight life?"

Tingle nodded. "Straight life. That means he would be eligible for parole in ten years. If he kept his nose clean in prison, there's no way the parole board could deny him, at least under present law."

The lawyer ground out his cigarette in the large desktop ashtray. "I think my client would agree to that. Of course, he would have to have some assurance that his sentence would be straight life."

"No problem," Tingle said. "We'll give it to you in writing. We'll issue an order accepting the plea to second-degree murder with a statement in the order that the sentence will be life in prison."

"In writing?"

Tingle smiled. "Court order, no less. Judge Harbor will issue it. The case will remain with him. He'll impose the sentence after the presentence report."

"There's liable to be trouble on this one," the lawyer said. "The homicide detectives believe my client has killed a number of cabbies. They can't prove it, but the method of operation was the same in all cases. I think you may draw some heat by reducing the plea. I thought I should warn you, in all fairness."

"I appreciate it," Tingle said. "I'll be ready if anything comes up, Mr. Ambrose. However, the public doesn't know the difference between a life sentence and a sentence for a term of years. If the police should object to a man receiving a life sentence, the public will think they are crazy. I doubt anyone will make waves on this."

"You know best." The lawyer nodded.

"Make out the order," Tingle said to Harbor.

The small judge looked as if he might protest. It was a murder case, and the lawyer's warning had been plain enough even for him. There was political danger in signing the order.

"Come on, Milton," Tingle said gently. "Remember, we have to keep these cases moving. We are fighting time."

Harbor signed, remembering the promise of a higher bench. That was really all that was important anyway. He handed a carbon copy to the lawyer, keeping the original for the court file.

"Thank you," Ambrose said as he left; however, the words were addressed only to Tingle.

Harbor's face reflected his anger. "Really, I think we should have at least consulted with—"

"Get the next case," Tingle said to the officer at the door. Then he turned to Harbor. "We're moving cases, Milton. Believe me, when this is all done, you can expect nothing but applause and glowing editorials. You'll be a hero, man, a real hero." And I'll be rich, Tingle thought to himself. He knew that the word would spread quickly on the street: King Tingle had complete command of the criminal court. The offers would start coming in soon.

"Good morning!" The next lawyer was a young woman, short but with a good figure. She almost seemed to bounce into the office. She had carefully accentuated her best features with makeup and hairstyle to highlight an otherwise plain face. Although she was a militant feminist, she was not above using her feminine charms for all they were worth if the situation demanded.

Tingle stood up, his huge form rising like a mountain. Milton Harbor remained seated, his moustache twitching with impatience.

"I'm Francey Monroe," she said brightly. "I represent a man charged with passing bad checks."

Tingle eased his bulk back into his chair. "How much paper did he hang?"

She grinned at him. "Twelve checks. They total about five hundred dollars."

"Any record?" Tingle asked.

"Convicted twice, both bad-check charges."

"Restitution?"

She shook her head. "He doesn't have a dime. Wrote the checks for food money."

Tingle liked her; but then, he liked most women. "How about attempted uttering and publishing?" he said. "Uttering and publishing carries fourteen years. Attempt is half, so the most he can do is seven years. I suspect an understanding judge might only give him a year. Probably have to give him some time, what with that record and all those people holding bad paper."

"That sounds great to me."

"Then we'll lower the charge and send the case to Judge Noonan," Tingle said. The girl met his appraising gaze without flinching. "We have to spread the goodies around a bit." He smiled. "This way Judge Noonan gets an easy plea and credit for a case. Judge Harbor will sign a form telling Judge Noonan that we've agreed to the lesser charge. You'll have to take the sentence up with Judge Noonan, but I understand he has a soft spot for pretty women, so you should do all right."

"Thank you. My client will be delighted, by the way."

Harbor wrote out the order as Tingle boldly looked her over. "You get much criminal business?"

"Not too much. I do mostly workmen's compensation. But I get over to criminal court every so often."

Harbor handed her the paper.

"Nice doing business with you, Ms. Monroe," Tingle said.

"Call me Francey," she replied, her eyes conveying subtle invitation. "And it has been my pleasure."

She walked out swinging her hips.

"Should be more women lawyers," Tingle said, mostly to himself. Then he raised his voice and spoke to the court officer. "Show the next customer in," he said.

chapter five

the world liberation army

"IT should be easy, man. From what I could find out, there ain't nothin' more than just token security for them judges' meetings. They all meet in the executive judge's courtroom; that's on the second floor. For those court people it ain't no big deal. They don't attach no great importance to it, if you see what I mean." Flash Johnson lounged on the apartment sofa, enjoying being the center of attention.

"Are you sure no one became suspicious because of your questions?" Larry Gormley feared that Flash Johnson might give their plan away. He had developed an active dislike for the cocky Negro and distrusted the man's abilities.

Flash's black face reflected his arrogance. "Hey, man, I was down among my people. I mean, I didn't just walk up to anybody and tell them we was planning to blow away the judges. Shit, I'm no fool, I don't want to get my black ass shot off. I was cool. I talked a bit to this one, a bit to that one. Just rappin', ya know, cool and easy. No one suspects anything." He smirked, obviously pleased with his own performance.

"What about your brother?" Thelma Sturdevant asked. "Did you get to see him?"

Flash frowned. "Man, that was a rough scene. I made out a visitor's pass application. You do that in that public main room of the jail. I gave it to one of them turnkeys, and as soon as he sees who I am, the whole place is ass-deep in cops. They searched me and then spent about half an hour questioning hell out of me. I was lucky I left my knife and smoke things at home. They would have really busted my ass if they found me with weed and a switchblade."

"Well, did you finally see him?" Gormley demanded.

"Yeah, I finally got to see him. They got a fancy deal up there where you go into a little booth and look through glass at the person you want to talk to. I had a microphone in front of me, and so did Jesse. It was strange, ya know, looking through the glass at him and talking like we was on the radio or something."

"Jesus, you probably were," Al Martin said. "They probably monitored every word."

"And you think I didn't know that, Al! Shit, man, I got a few brains."

"Okay, what was the conversation?" Gormley asked.

Flash sat up and stretched. "I just talked to him 'bout family things. I told him Cousin Larry was back in town and that maybe he'd see old Cousin Larry if everything went okay. I said we heard on the news that there was goin' to be a judges' meeting soon, and maybe if they all got together, he might get a new trial. I think he understood what I was tryin' to tell him."

"The cops are liable to check out that cousin business," Gormley said.

"Then they better do a lot of checking," Flash snorted. "Man, I'll bet I got maybe a hundred cousins, or something near that." He laughed. "Gots to be one of them is named Larry."

"They may have followed you from jail," Martin said.

Flash shook his head. "No way. After seeing Jesse, I went over to see my mamma and tol' her everything was all right with him. Didn't see no cops. But I went over to the neighborhood poolroom and shot a couple of games. After that I waited a bit, then drove on over here. Nobody followed me."

"And you're sure about the judges' meeting and the guards?" Gormley asked.

"Unless they change the way they been doin' it, I'm sure. You'll have maybe one or two cops at the back entrance to the court building and at the most one or two more in the executive judge's courtroom. That's it. And most of them court dudes is just worn-out old coppers who have found a soft job. They ain't exactly no candidates for a SWAT team, if you see what I mean?"

"When do they hold the meetings?"

"Usually right after court closes—about five o'clock. Mostly the meetings don't take more than an hour."

"We'll have to get by those officers at the rear entrance," Martin said. "That could be a problem."

Gormley shook his head. "Maybe not. Suppose we went in during regular court hours and just stayed over? Do you think we'd run into trouble, Flash?"

The thin black man shrugged. "Don't see how. There's always somebody hanging around at that time. As long as you look like you belong, no one's goin' to bother you."

Gormley nodded. "Then that's what we'll do. During the day of the meeting each of us will enter the building and wait until it closes. We'll be in, and we won't have to worry about getting by the guards on the first floor, only the ones in the courtroom."

"How do we get the weapons in?" Martin asked.

"That's easy," Gormley replied. "You, Alice Mary, and myself will pose as lawyers. We'll carry briefcases, big ones like the cases they carry exhibits in. And we can load up Thelma's big purse. Between the briefcases and the purse we can get everything in that we'll need."

"I can carry a briefcase," Flash said.

Gormley laughed. "No offense, Flash, but unless you get a different hairstyle and clothes, you sure don't look much like a lawyer."

It hit the others funny, and everyone laughed.

Except Flash Johnson.

Gormley noted the black man's expression. The resentment was deep. Flash Johnson would have to go, Gormley decided. It was now only a question of when.

"We have some time to work all this out," Gormley said. "We need plenty of drill. I want everyone to know exactly what to do and when and where to do it. If we carry this off, the whole world will know and respect us. But if we miss, we'll just be so much dead meat. So, planning is everything, right?"

Flash Johnson began to formulate some plans of his own. He did not intend to end up as "dead meat."

"It should be a night to remember," Gormley said, his voice brimming with enthusiasm.

the probation officer

No one else seemed affected by the death. It had come suddenly, without any warning, but they had all shrugged it off as just another passing incident in the working day.

Frank Conroy had talked to the old man in the holding tank in the early morning. He looked bad, his wrinkled skin ashen, but he was an old, familiar customer and he seldom looked any better. He had only a few yellowed teeth remaining and he sprayed spittle when he talked. His mind was still sharp despite the years of alcohol abuse, and he tried earnestly to convince Conroy that he would be all right back on the street. But the probation officer thought otherwise and recommended a thirty-day drying-out period to the judge.

The old man had a name—Francis P. Garrity—not unlike Conroy's. Garrity's record as a drunk and vagrant was multipaged. He had shuffled off to the bullpen after sentencing to await the bus ride with the other prisoners to the county work farm. Then it happened. Garrity made an odd sound, the other prisoners said, fell to the tile floor, and began shaking. It was not unusual in drunks. Most of the other men just moved away from the jerking limbs, presuming it to be the onset of delirium tremens. But it wasn't. Francis Garrity was dying. His body shook violently, and his eyes bulged as his being fought against death. He vomited and soiled himself simultaneously and then lay still, his stench filling the barred room.

The officers unlocked the cell door and rushed in, but Francis P. Garrity was already dead.

Conroy had been attracted to the cell by the commotion,

although it was only momentary. The business in the courtroom never stopped, the misdemeanor cases rolled along
uninterrupted even when the men from the county morgue
removed the body in a canvas bag. A court officer mopped
up the mess in the cell. Everything continued as if nothing
had happened.

Frank Conroy could not shake a feeling of dread. A
man had died, and no one even acknowledged it. They
cleaned up, that was all. It was as if Francis P. Garrity
had never existed, as if he were meaningless, no longer a
memory in the world of the flesh or even the spirit.

Frank Conroy struggled to put the death out of his mind
but without success. In the late afternoon he noticed his
hands shaking slightly. He tried to think of things to do,
something to occupy his time and mind, so that it wouldn't
happen again. He did not want to get drunk again. He did
not wish to end up like old Garrity.

The sense of depression grew. He had tried to finish
some of his probation reports, but he found he couldn't
concentrate on the files. The paperwork wouldn't fill the
void.

He dialed the medical examiner's office and identified
himself. The attendant looked up the case record. No
known relatives, no known friends. An autopsy had already
been performed. The cause of death was coronary occlu-
sion with a finding of long-established heart disease. What
was left after the autopsy would be held for the mandatory
thirty days, and then the remains would be buried in a
pauper's grave without ceremony or service. It happened
all the time.

Conroy knew why he had made the call. He had hoped
the old man had a relative, just someone who might have
shed a tear or had a memory, but there was nobody. He
realized that Francis Garrity probably lived the typical
disruptive life of an alcoholic and had long ago driven

away relatives and friends, but even so, his death had seemed so cold and so very lonely.

He tried walking. The weather threatened rain, but no drops fell. He strode along, swinging his arms, inhaling deeply, hoping the exercise would drive out the devils building inside him. But it did not work. Somehow he knew it would not work.

His apartment drew him like a magnet. He knew why he wanted to go there and dreaded the impulses that seemed to control him. It was almost like physical pain. He needed relief: relief from a hostile world where men were animals, a world without promise or illusion, a place heartless and cruel.

He needed a drink, a strong one.

His apartment was comfortable but spartan. He preferred it that way. His stereo was expensive, and his record collection extensive. He liked all kinds of music, from the classics to country-and-western.

Conroy went to the compact kitchen and opened the cupboard. The bottles were as varied as his record collection. Vodkas, imported gins, and whiskeys of all kinds. Most of the bottles had been sampled, some were almost empty. He reached in and drew out an unopened fifth of expensive Kentucky bourbon, 100 proof. He needed a powerful drink.

The amber liquid spilled into the tumbler until it was half full. He had not meant to pour so much. He debated for a brief moment pouring some into another glass for later, but he knew he wouldn't do that, that he really wanted all that whiskey, that he needed it. He dropped in two ice cubes and then filled the glass with a dash of tap water.

Walking back into the living room, he kicked off his shoes, sat in his big recliner chair, and sipped the whiskey. The very first taste seemed to restore a sense of peace within him. He knew he shouldn't continue drinking, that his mental frame of mind made it dangerous to go on, but he continued to sip.

Frank Conroy stared at the stereo. It would be pleasant to listen to soothing music, something to ease his mind. But he knew what he was going to play.

After the last time, he had sworn he would break that damned worn record. It made him almost physically sick just to look at it, at least when he was sober. He had stuck it up in the closet, behind his hats. Out of the way, hidden, but still there.

He sipped the whiskey and let the thoughts come. There was no God, of that he was sure. No God would have let Mrs. Garrity's fine boy die such an ignominious death. No God would have let poor Francis Garrity get into that deplorable state in the first place. No God would allow men and women to debase themselves and others the way Frank Conroy saw it happen. Just animals, thinking animals, no more, no less. He shivered and drank the rest of his drink.

He experienced a pleasant fuzziness as he padded back to the kitchen for a refill.

"You're going to do it again, you fucking drunk," he said softly. "You're no better than the men in the tank. You and Garrity are one of a kind, Franky, my boy."

He drank deeply and then turned for the closet door. The record jacket was torn. He pulled the record from it with a desire to smash the damn thing. But he couldn't. Playing that record again would be an agony. He knew that.

He placed the recording on the turntable and turned the set on. Then he carefully lowered the player arm to a particular spot on the record.

He staggered slightly as he walked to the chair and sat down.

The music gently filled the room. The familiar music of the old Latin Mass pulsated softly. It was the Requiem Mass—the High Mass for the Dead. A true Requiem, the music and the Latin words beseeched God to forgive and forgo justice for mercy. It begged and pleaded for the dead one's soul.

Frank Conroy drank and listened. As it began, his mind, trained as a priest's, translated the Latin as the priest in the recording chanted the ancient and chilling "Dies irae, dies illa."

"Dies irae, dies illa," sang the voice.

Day of wrath, O Day of mourning.

"Solvet saeclum in favilla."

Lo, the world in ashes burning.

"Teste David cum Sibylla."

Seer and Sibyl gave the warning.

Glass in his hand, Frank Conroy began to sing along softly with the music.

His mind was a blank. He was drunk. His voice began to take on more authority, he was no longer conscious of the record. He was doing what he had done years before, chanting the Mass for the Dead.

Frank Conroy sang the Latin, his voice moving beautifully along each passage, tears streaming down his flushed cheeks. At the time when the name of the departed was to be mentioned, he sang the name of Francis Garrity without even realizing that he had done it.

the information desk

SPEEDY Gonzales always liked to spend a few minutes with Red Mehan every day. It was a nice break in the workday. Red did all the talking. He could be amusing, and once in a while he came up with a good story or a choice piece of gossip.

"*Speedy, you guys in the probation department probably know more about this than me, but have you ever noticed that crime is divided up for the rich and the poor?*

"*Naw, I don't mean that justice depends on how much money you got, nothing like that, although that don't hurt neither. What I mean is there are laws for rich people and laws for poor people.*

"*See, if you're a poor man there's a whole list of no-nos. I mean you can't be drunk, you can't beat up on your old lady, you can't steal from the local grocery store. Things like that. Those are acts that only poor people do usually. I ain't saying that occasionally a rich guy don't take a poke at his old lady, but, hell, she ain't going to swear out no warrant. Just isn't done in them circles, you know. Nope, assault charges are only for the poor. It curbs their expected action, see?*

"*Now, the rich, they don't get off by any means. Hell, things are just adjusted for their status. Take embezzlement. That's a rich man's crime. You ain't going to find no fuckin' pimp charged with embezzling his girl's money. No way! That's what he does, but that charge don't apply to him. It's only for bank presidents, controllers, and cashiers.*

"Antitrust charges, income tax evasion—those are rich people's crimes. I mean, society expects them to do them things, right? So they set up rules.

"And God help the poor son of a bitch who commits a crime belonging to the other class. Especially the rich people. Suppose some bank president swipes a pack of cigars from some cut-rate drugstore. Holy shit, it's front-page news! I mean, they really go after the son of a bitch. He'll lose his job, his old lady will divorce him as soon as it's possible, and his kids won't speak to him anymore. He's a common thief, right? He crossed the line and committed one of their *crimes. Society will crucify him.*

"Same with the poor man. Of course, he don't have as many shots at the good stuff. But suppose he embezzles welfare money from the government. Hell, half the contractors doing business with the Defense Department rip it off for millions more than their contracts call for, but let the poor sucker try to squeeze a few bucks out of welfare and they'll slam his ass into jail, and for a long time too. I mean, he can swipe things at the grocery, shoot somebody, or knock the old lady's teeth out, and they'll give him probation. Those crimes are consistent with his class. But let the poor bugger step into the fancy-type crimes and he'll end up hanging off that cross too.

"No, I ain't no Communist, but that's just the way it is. There is one set of laws for the rich and another for the poor. Both are run as fair as possible, I suppose, but they are different.

"You know, sometimes I wish I was rich. That way I could swat the old lady and not get thrown in the clink."

the burglar

GUS Simes sat on a bench in the common room and watched the other prisoners. All murderers, they really seemed not much different from any of the prisoners with whom he had done time. There were the usual flare-ups, but nothing more than with any other group of confined men. Jail was jail, the same for murderers as for burglars. There was a quickness to anger among these men, but even that could be explained away by the terrible pressure they were all under. The death penalty hung over them all. Certainly that grim prospect was never far from his own thoughts. He imagined it was the same for the others.

He tried to shake the fear, to free his mind so that he could figure a way out. There had to be some solution.

The legality of the state's new death penalty was currently being challenged. It was all up to the state's supreme court. Like the other prisoners, Simes now closely followed every legal step as the convicted murderer Harold Hawkins fought against being the first man to be executed under the new death law. Their lives rode with Hawkins. If Hawkins could somehow legally beat the execution law, they would all be free from that ultimate fate. But if Hawkins failed . . . Simes hated even to think about that.

Simes watched Johnson. The black man had changed. He seemed quiet, almost contented. He refused to share the source of his new mental attitude with Simes, but it was obvious that something he considered good was going to happen. Hagen knew. Hagen had been withdrawn, but now he too seemed relaxed and even entered into conversations within the cell block. Something was in the wind. They had promised to include him. Simes knew that most jailbreaks usually resulted in death for the principals, but it would be good to be part of their plans anyway. He might find out something useful, something he could use to bargain with the authorities for his life.

Ever-present anxiety gripped Simes. It was unfair. He had not killed anyone, yet here he was, awaiting trial for first-degree murder. His nights had turned into endless nightmares that always began with that walk to the glassed-in cubicle, then the hiss as the gas pellets sizzled in the acid, and the choking smell of the deadly gas. He always awoke shaking and sweat soaked. Every night it was the same dream, every night the same fears.

Maybe Hawkins could beat the death law. Then there would be hope.

He watched Hagen playing gin rummy with another prisoner. The man's eyes were concentrated on the cards. He seemed to be without nerves, as if he had forgotten the fate that awaited them all. Simes looked around at the men in the dayroom. They were all going to die unless the courts overturned Hawkins's sentence. But Hagen and Johnson seemed unconcerned.

Gus Simes was more than concerned, he was goddamned scared.

the offer

To know Harlee Simmon was to know evil. The tall black man seemed to exude evil like some after-shave lotion liberally used. His luminous black skin and great height were genetic gifts from his African forebears, giants who roamed the great plains. Although almost seven feet tall, he had an easy grace, an almost snakelike quality.

This fluid movement plus his highly charged temperament, so reminiscent of a thoroughbred racer, led to his nickname Racehorse. That became his "street" name, known in every dark and dangerous alley in the city's turbulent inner city. Racehorse had almost forgotten his given name. His golden Jaguar had *Racehorse* stenciled in small red lettering at the top of each door. It was a powerful warning to potential thieves. Hard-eyed men might be tempted to steal such a handsome and expensive car but would draw quickly away when they saw that dreaded name.

Racehorse had risen to power and wealth by climbing a difficult and deadly ladder. He had learned his trade at the feet of some of the city's most vicious gangsters, serving them in capacities from runner to hired killer. It was this last talent that brought him the most renown, and by that skill he had managed to acquire a large chunk of the "black" rackets by the simple device of eliminating all the competitors.

He was successful in a number of areas: He was a pimp with a stable of beautiful women who provided him a large and regular income. He ran two small after-hours gambling places that catered to big-money players. The take there was good, but his main source of money was import.

Racehorse purchased and brought in his merchandise from overseas—from Europe, China, Mexico, or any other place where they grew poppies or processed heroin. It was a business of often fatal rivalry, and the risks were high. Huge amounts of cash kept the drug tubes pumping. Death from hijackers, other dealers, or a crazed junky was always a possibility. But for Racehorse the profit justified that risk.

The other risk was jail.

Racehorse lived in a house decorated in rich velvets and

costly tapestries. He employed his own chef. There wasn't anything in the way of creature comforts that he denied himself. He had grown accustomed to the finest liquors, women, and food. Jail, for him, would be a disaster.

But the police had him this time, and they had him good —possession and sale of heroin—a solid case without loopholes. Racehorse, like any good businessman, knew the law as it applied to his enterprise, and he knew that when his lawyer told him that the best he could get was twenty years, he was not joking. The narcotics squad had played a clever game on him, and he had fallen for it. The police had him on film, tape, all backed up by eye-witnesses.

His lawyer was as respectable as Racehorse was un-savory. Racehorse knew it paid dividends to employ only good professionals. His lawyer had been a judge but had left the bench to go into practice and make money. He had been a former director of the local bar association and was a visible patron for the more important city-sponsored charities. Being a patron provided protective respectability. Like Racehorse, he was tall and black and had a certain grace of his own. He did not like his client but found nothing objectionable about his client's money. It was a compromise that Racehorse fully understood. It was a matter of business.

The Hollywood, a high-priced nightclub with mostly black trade, was considered neutral territory. Criminals and civic figures could attend the club without notice. Policemen, who also patronized the place, were careful to keep a blind eye and not to notice some of the more notorious guests. The Hollywood was strictly legal; the owners kept a stern eye on the customers so that their reputation remained spotless, thereby ensuring good busi-ness and no police problems.

Resplendent in a multicolored silk outfit, Racehorse

entered the club, his face a stiff, almost hostile mask. Two of his very best women clung to his arms. As he had requested, he was escorted to a table at the very back of the club, far away from the excellent jazz quintet that was playing on a stage behind the bar.

When he reached the table, Racehorse spoke to the girls. "You ladies get up to the bar," he said softly, his voice just audible above the music. "I don't want you to hustle your ass, you understand, just be by the bar for a while. No tricks tonight. I'll send for you when I've completed some business."

One of the girls started to protest, but one icy look from Racehorse silenced her. Racehorse took his seat and waited. He lit an imported cigar as the waiter put a double Scotch in front of him and then scurried away.

His lawyer eased his way through the crush of tables near the bandstand, came up to the table, and sat down.

"You called." Racehorse's tone was impatient.

Horace Ridley, the former judge, did not reply directly. He looked over the crowd. "This is a good spot. They can't bug this table, not with that swinging band up there. They wouldn't pick up a thing except the music."

Racehorse drew in on his long cigar before speaking. "Why should bugging make any difference?" His sleek black features gave no hint of feeling or interest.

"There's a possibility we can get you off on that heroin charge."

Racehorse's eyes flickered for a moment, then became stony again. "Go on," he said.

"I can't promise anything yet, but I think I can arrange to have you plead guilty to habitual use."

"I don't touch that stuff, man, I just sell it."

"I know that," Ridley said. "But conviction as a first-time user carries only three months at a rehabilitation center. If we can plead you to that charge, it will cost you only three months."

"I'll bet that's not all it'll cost."

The attorney looked at him, a slight smile playing at the corners of his mouth. "Getting you that plea ranks with raising the dead. The man who can set up the action wants two hundred thousand in cash, payable before anything takes place."

Racehorse sneered. "I'm not a charity. I need insurance."

"Can't do it, not this time."

"Why not, man? I'm not about to hand over that kind of money without a damned good guaranty."

Ridley sighed. "My fee will be one hundred thousand. Don't jive me. I know you have the money. For the price of a miracle it is most reasonable. Think about it."

Racehorse tipped the cigar ash into an ashtray on the table. "You got a lot of nerve, Ridley, you know that? Jesus, I practically support you now. Why the hell should I lay out an extra hundred grand to you, just to take a lousy plea?"

Ridley's eyes were steady. "It's my connection that gets you that plea," he said quietly. "The man who is going to take care of things will deal only with me. He trusts my discretion."

Racehorse sipped his drink. "So I just hand over three hundred thousand and sit back and see what happens?"

"That's about it."

Racehorse studied the ice cubes in his glass. He had planned to jump bail and head for South America. He had recognized that he was abandoning a gold mine, but the alternative was twenty years in prison. He thought he had no choice. Now he was being offered the chance to escape the felony charge and serve only three months in some junky hospital. His business could withstand his absence for three months. No one would make any moves knowing they would have to face him shortly. The price, under the circumstances, was cheap. Still, he never quite trusted Ridley, or anyone else for that matter.

"Sounds like a fuckin' fairy tale to me, man," he said.

Ridley never changed expression. "The cash has to be laundered. I don't want to get any marked narcotics squad bills. And the man who will take care of the case wants clean money, and in small bills."

"Shit, what if this is a scam? I end up in the joint for twenty years, and you have three hundred thousand big ones. Not my kind of deal. Too much risk."

Ridley shrugged. "Suit yourself. We go to trial in two weeks. We don't have a damned prayer, and you know it."

Racehorse sighed. "Yeah." This time his voice lost some of its hostility. "Who's gonna take care of the plea?"

"I'm not at liberty to say."

Racehorse laughed. "Shit, Ridley, you think I don't know that the King is sitting up in the criminal court and settin' up deals? It's Tingle, ain't it? You got a supreme court dude in your pocket?"

Ridley's face was as masklike as his client's. "Doesn't make any difference if it's a supreme court justice or a janitor, so long as the job gets done, does it?"

Racehorse nodded. "It'll take me a week to get you your 'clean' money."

"The sooner the better. You never know when something like this might go sour." Ridley stood up. Without saying good-bye, he again worked his way through the tables, leaving Racehorse by himself.

Racehorse drew deeply on the cigar. The hint of a smile played on his smooth face. He knew he would never have enjoyed South America.

little chester

ABRAHAM Gallente wheezed as he climbed the second flight of stairs. The place stunk of cabbage, cooking odors, and urine. Paint had peeled away from the ancient walls. A naked bulb cast just enough light to allow him barely to see the steps.

It was familiar territory to Gallente. He stopped at the head of the stairs and wiped his sweaty brow with his imported linen handkerchief. It took him a minute to catch his breath. He was in his fifties and overweight, but he did this kind of work better than anyone he could hire.

The old apartment door had long ago lost its number, leaving only a faded outline of the numerals. Music came from within. Gallente rapped sharply. A chain rattled as the door opened and an eye from within inspected him.

"Come on, will ya," Gallente's raspy voice conveyed his irritation.

The door closed, the chain dropped, then a thin black man in a dirty T-shirt and wrinkled trousers opened it wide, his smile exhibiting missing teeth. "Hey, Bad Abe, baby! It's good to see ya!"

Gallente walked past him. "Where's Eddy?" he asked.

"Back in the kitchen, playin' poker. Ya want me to get him?"

"I'll go back there." The small living room was jammed with black men and women. A cheap stereo blared forth a pounding rhythm and a large woman gyrated to the music, rolling her large hips as if they were oversized bowling balls. The air was blue with pungent marijuana smoke.

Gallente recognized several customers and nodded his acceptance of their greeting. He moved through the crowd into the narrow hall leading to the kitchen in the rear of the apartment.

He noticed a naked couple writhing in a frantic act of love as he passed an open bedroom door. They were oblivious to him.

The usual game was going on at the round kitchen table. Dollar bills were piled high in the center. The air in the kitchen was equally blue with smoke, but this was the choking aroma of cheap cigars. Eddy Henry, the owner and operator of this "blind pig," held his cards closely against his chest, his fat black face a death mask.

"Raise." One of the players shoved several bills toward the center.

Another player cursed and threw down his hand. Two others, including Eddy Henry, matched the bet. "Call," one of them said.

"Aces over fives." The man spread the cards before him. "Fuck!"

"That's a whole lot of money for just two pair," Eddy Henry said, grinning now, his hand still concealing his cards. The man who had showed his hand seemed to sag.

"But it's good enough to beat me." Eddy threw his cards down. He reached into the pot and extracted several bills, placing them under a green cloth at his side. " 'Bout right?"

"Yeah," the other player agreed, allowing that Eddy had collected his percentage fairly, his share for running the game. The green felt piece was called a cut cloth, and all the players knew that a percentage of each pot always went to the house, even when the "house" himself was a player.

Eddy looked up and smiled. "Say, hey, it's my main man, Bad Abe Gallente! Wanta join in, Abe?"

"Not tonight, Eddy. Can I see you for a minute?"

The fat Negro nodded to a tall youth who was standing by the kitchen sink. "Sit in here. I don't want you playing, just take what's due out of the pots till I get back."

The youth nodded and took the vacated seat.

"Come on out on my veranda, Abe." Eddy Henry led him out onto a rickety porch overlooking the darkened yard below. He closed the door. A dog barked endlessly in the quiet night, and a faraway argument could be heard.

"Looks like this porch ain't safe," Gallente said.

"Stronger than it looks. I wouldn't jump up and down, though. What's up? We don't get to see you much anymore."

"Busy as shit," Gallente said. "Working like a son of a bitch and not makin' any money. Stinking business."

"Ah, come on, Abe," the other man laughed, "don't hand out that shit. You're a fuckin' millionaire. You should retire and enjoy your money."

Gallente's chuckle was without humor. "I have been married four times. Each one of those bitches stole me blind. Gotta work."

"If you say so." Henry's voice betrayed his disbelief. "It looks like you're doing all right."

Henry shrugged. "Not bad. Got a couple of new whores. Sell some pot, but liquor and gambling are still the biggest things up here. Have to grease a few palms, but I get by. The trick is in staying small. They never really go after a small operator. The guys who get into trouble are the ones who get carried away and try to expand. It draws flies, ya know."

Gallente nodded in agreement. "You know Little Chester?"

"The B and E man?"

"The same."

"I know him."

"The little fucker didn't show up for his trial this morning. They issued a bench warrant and forfeited his bond, the one I put up."

"How much bond?" Eddy Henry asked.

"Ten thousand."

Eddy whistled. "Shit, you really took a bath."

"I can't afford no ten-thousand-dollar baths, Eddy. I'm lookin' for that little shit, and I'll find him."

Eddy's shiny face caught the light reflected from the kitchen window. "What's the deal?"

"Two hundred if I get him."

The black man shook his head. "Everything costs more nowadays, Abe. You know that. If you're hanging for ten G's, I figure Chester is worth at least five hundred."

Gallente swore under his breath.

"Don't get sore, Abe, it's just a matter of business."

"Okay. Five hundred, but only after I get him."

Henry smiled. "Now, that's the generous Bad Abe Gallente we all know and love. You want me to send some people to go get him?"

"Just tell me where he's at. I'll get him myself."

Henry chuckled. "You ain't gettin' no younger, Abe. Still, if you're up to it, he's most probably over at his lady friend's place. She is one of the girls working out of here, but you probably already knew that, or you wouldn't be here, right?"

"Right."

Henry gave Gallente the address. "Chester don't wear no gun that I know of," the black man said, "but he's got a knife, and I understan's he's good with it."

"Thanks. If I get him, I'll send the money over."

Henry smiled and patted the other man's shoulder. "I know you will. There's not another bondsman in this city that's got your reputation for honesty, Abe. I trust you."

Gallente pushed his way out of the blind pig and walked

down the stairs to the street. His driver, Elmo Halstead, sat behind the wheel of Gallente's big Lincoln.

Gallente climbed in and repeated the address he had been given. Halstead, his battered black face illuminated by the dashboard lights, pulled the car out from the parking space in front of the darkened houses and sped across the city.

"You want me to come along, boss?" Halstead asked when they arrived at the apartment house. He had been a good heavyweight fighter in his prime and he now served as Gallente's right-hand man.

"Yeah," Gallente grunted as he checked his equipment. The big .38 was tucked into his waist holster, and the small ankle gun was strapped against his leg. He slipped the handcuffs into his left coat pocket and the blackjack into his right. The lockpick was also in that pocket.

The two men climbed out and walked to the apartment door. The entrance was cluttered with broken glass, paper, and garbage.

Gallente stooped over the outside-door lock and went to work with the pick. Halstead stood in front of him, shielding him from street view.

Abe Gallente had started out as a street collector for a loan shark. He had drifted through a number of businesses, all on the fringe of the law: car repossession, which required a knowledge of locks; manager of a small loan company; and, finally, with the help of a few friends, bail bondsman.

He had been a bondsman for fifteen years. The defendants paid him ten percent of the bond if they wanted their freedom. That percentage was never returned, no matter what the outcome of the trial. And it was only a paper transaction with the courts. Gallente signed as a representative of a surety company. No actual money went to the court unless someone jumped his bond. That was serious, that cost real money. Then the bondsman had to pay in the full amount of the bond to the court. And the only way he could ever get it back was to bring in the defendant.

He was good at bringing in skippers. He kept up a large street network, not only to trace errant customers but also as promoters for his bonding company. It had worked very successfully. They called him Bad Abe because he was the "gentlest" of the bondsmen in town.

The lock sprang open, and Gallente and Halstead slipped into the musty interior of the building. They quietly climbed the stairs to the second-floor apartment.

Again Gallente was puffing. Eddy Henry had been right, he was getting too old. And he had enough money to retire comfortably. Still, he liked what he did. It was exciting.

Gallente listened at the apartment door. There was no sound and no light under the door. He nodded to Halstead, who flipped a small flashlight beam on the door lock. It snapped open easily with a sharp click. He twisted the doorknob, but the door swung open only a few inches, stopped by a chain inside. Gallente shrugged, took out his blackjack, and stepped back.

Halstead kicked his powerful leg at the door, ripping the chain and lock away. The door swung and smashed against the wall. Two heads appeared from beneath a ragged blanket spread over the bed in the center of the room.

Halstead's flashlight found the wide-eyed face of Little Chester as Gallente rushed in and smashed the blackjack against the man's temple. Chester slumped back on the bed. The woman, naked, tried frantically to escape from the bed, kicking furiously at the bedclothes.

Halstead reached over and gripped her bare shoulder. "Take it easy, girl," he said softly. "We ain't here to hurt anybody. Just collecting Chester for the police, understand?"

She sagged and sat still.

Gallente was sweating as he pulled Chester's inert form from the bed and handcuffed the thin arms behind the man's naked back.

"Where's his clothes?" Gallente asked the girl.

She nodded at a chair.

Gallente slipped trousers over the pipestem legs, first extracting a long switchblade knife from a pocket. Halstead picked up the man's shoes and shirt.

"Just sit tight, girl," Halstead said. "We're leaving now."

"What about my door?" the girl moaned.

"I'll tell Eddy to have it fixed," Abe told her.

They drove the reviving Chester to the nearest police station. He was still groggy from the blow and kept sighing softly.

Gallente had his driver wait as he walked the barefoot, handcuffed man into the precinct house.

"Hey, Abe, how ya doing?" the desk sergeant called as he walked in. "Who ya got?"

"One of my customers, Chester Roberts. They call him Little Chester. He's a burglar. Trial was this morning. He didn't show up."

"So you went out and got him."

"Right."

"I guess you'll want a receipt for the prisoner."

"If I want to get my money back, I'll need it."

The sergeant wrote out a small form. "Jesus, you're good at this kind of thing, Abe. The city ought to consider hiring you."

Bad Abe smiled, accepted the receipt from the policeman, and walked out to the Lincoln. He lit a cigar and looked up at the clear night sky. There was a lot of satisfaction in being a bondsman.

the assistant prosecutor

JUDGE Clyde Powell sat alone in his chambers sipping the coffee Ted Hemmings had brought him and scanning the morning newspaper. Unlike most of the judges, Powell habitually arrived early. He enjoyed the quiet and the chance to spend a few tranquil moments before the busy day began.

The prosecutor liked to rotate his trial men, so each month Powell was assigned a new assistant prosecutor. This time he had drawn Ace Gilbert, and Powell was pleased. Gilbert was very good at his job. Although the tall young man had lost much of his early enthusiasm, the fire had been replaced by finesse.

Gilbert was an interesting young man. Powell had made it his business to find out about him. Ace Gilbert had quite a war record. He had enlisted in the army and had risen through the ranks to lieutenant. He had put in two tours of service in Vietnam and had been decorated a number of times, including two Purple Hearts. He had been an honest-to-God combat soldier. But he didn't look like it. His easy manner and relaxed air seemed at odds with his past history. Also, Powell had noticed, Gilbert avoided talking about the war and his army experiences.

Powell sipped the last of the coffee. Soon the cases would start coming up. The new system had Tingle and Harbor acting as a combined presiding judge, taking pleas and assigning cases. The cases were being spread around so that each judge would have a high case production figure, even if all the basic decisions had already been made by Tingle.

His clerk knocked and then stuck his head in the door. "Judge, the prosecutor would like to see you."

Powell threw the cardboard cup into the wastebasket. "Send him in."

Ace Gilbert came in carrying a file. He looked concerned. "Judge, take a look at this," he said, handing the file to Powell.

"Sit down, Ace." Powell took the court file. It was a new case, apparently the first assigned to him for the day. One of the new forms had been attached to the folder. It bore Harbor's scrawled signature. Glancing at it, Powell immediately saw what was troubling the prosecutor.

"This gives you a problem?" he asked Gilbert.

The young man's face, usually bland, was suddenly animated. "Damned right it gives me a problem. The original charge is armed robbery, Judge. That's an offense that carries a life sentence. Tingle and Harbor have reduced the charge to simple assault, a misdemeanor. The most he can get is ninety days."

"I'm quite familiar with the penalties," Judge Powell said quietly. "You are the prosecutor, Ace. You can object."

Gilbert grimaced. "I just called my office." His voice carried an edge of anger. "I talked to the chief assistant. He doesn't like this business any more than I do, but he told me the office policy is to go along with Tingle, at least for now."

"So you can't object, then."

Gilbert grinned. "You know, I've been getting a little fed up with prosecuting anyway. To hell with the office. I'm going to object to the reduction as being against the interests of justice."

"Maybe there's a good reason to reduce the charge," Powell said. "Sometimes some of the elements of a crime may be difficult to prove."

Gilbert shook his head. "I just looked at the detective's

write-up. They got this bird cold. He knocked over a liquor store, got nailed running away, and confessed. The store owner identifies him. You can't do better than that, Judge."

"First offense?" Powell asked.

"No, not at all. This guy was busted once before for armed robbery. He got a break then. They reduced it to unarmed robbery. He did two years. He has a couple of other minor convictions as well."

Powell sighed. It was all part of a pattern. Tingle was unplugging the docket by letting the guilty either go completely free or receive a wrist-tapping sentence. The judges were supposed to look the other way and go along with his program while he emptied the jail, and probably lined his own pockets.

"If I grant your motion, Ace, do you know what will happen?"

Gilbert shook his head.

"According to the new rules, if a judge disagrees with Judge Harbor's signed order, the case is returned to him. So, if I rule that the charge cannot be reduced, the case goes back to Tingle and Harbor. They will send it to another courtroom where the judge and the prosecutor aren't so particular."

"So there's really nothing you can do." Gilbert shook his head slowly. "Jesus, what a hell of a system." His voice carried the disgust he felt.

"Of course, if I keep the case here, I'll give the man the full ninety days. At least that's something."

Gilbert snorted. "I think I'll look into being an armed robber. It pays better than prosecuting, and there's very little risk anymore. I'd call it a growth business."

Powell smiled. "Don't be bitter, Ace. These things happen in the law sometimes. There is a public outcry against the jammed jails and the long wait until trial. A proper outcry, by the way. So for the moment, Tingle and his plan look very good. That's why your office won't oppose him. It would be political suicide. Tingle is on the side of the angels, at least for now."

"But this sort of thing," Gilbert gestured at the file, "is a gross miscarriage of justice."

The young man was right. "Tingle would say that the state is saved a trial, the docket is reduced, and the guilty defendant punished. He would say this is an emergency situation and requires emergency measures. That sounds pretty good, doesn't it?"

"Sure it sounds good, but it's a lot of crap."

Powell chuckled. "Ah, youth. It's a difficult world, Ace. Right now the press and public are buying that 'crap' you speak of. How would you propose we stop it?"

"Take it up with the supreme court."

Powell got up, took off his suit coat, and donned the judicial robe. "The supreme court sent Tingle down here. He is the supreme court at the moment. So there goes your appeal."

"The federal courts?"

"Come on, Ace. They wouldn't touch this with a ten-foot pole. Besides, they have no jurisdiction."

Gilbert stood up. "You could oppose it. You and the other judges."

Powell zipped up the front of the robe. "Yes, quite right. Except that at the moment few would risk the political consequences."

"What could they do to you?"

"Well, to begin with, any judge opposing the plan without giving it a chance to work would be branded as a lazy obstructionist. In my case, at my age, I rather imagine there would be a few hints that I was jealous or perhaps a touch senile. James Tingle, though he's a supreme court justice, is an experienced street fighter, Ace. A judge opposing him would feel the lash. He'd get the trials, the contested cases that Tingle didn't adjust. The other judges would be turning out dozens of cases a day, while the rebel judge would be lucky to get out one or two juries a week. Then, just by using the production statistics, they would prove that the rebel was a lazy incompetent who couldn't carry his fair share." Powell laughed, but there was no humor in it. "It's a very rough world."

"So nothing will be done about any of this." Gilbert was thoroughly disgusted now.

"Oh, some of us are old street fighters too, Ace. In these matters you have to pick your place and time. Everyone makes mistakes, even supreme court justices."

Gilbert said nothing, but he obviously doubted that there would ever be an opposition. The look in his eyes made Powell feel cheap.

The judge adjusted the full sleeves on his robe. "Well, Ace, let's go to work, shall we?"

Gilbert shrugged. "If that's what you call it."

The policemen, the defense attorney, and the defendant were all assembled when they entered the courtroom.

Powell took the bench as the clerk called the robbery-armed case.

The defense attorney made the usual statement, withdrawing the plea of guilty to robbery armed and offering the plea to the charge of simple assault.

"Mr. Prosecutor," Powell said to Gilbert, "do you object to the court accepting the reduced plea?"

Gilbert stood up straight. He was very tall when he stood without his customary slouch. "The people object, Your Honor," he said, his voice defiant. "The offered plea is a travesty. Justice wouldn't be served, it would be raped."

Powell looked at him. The young man was risking his job. If he went along with the prosecutor, he would show his hand too early to Tingle. He would lose considerable advantage. Tingle would respond. His case count would drop, and he would get only the sticky cases, the long ones, the cases that would eat up time and make him the least productive judge in the building. He would be putting his neck out, putting it right where Tingle would like to have it. It was too early to make a fight of it. Still, despite it all, he had taken an oath to see that justice was done. He studied the determined face of Ace Gilbert for a moment.

Powell spoke in a soft voice. "The court finds that the offered plea has no justification. The offer to plead to the reduced charge is therefore denied."

Powell was pleased at Gilbert's startled expression. At least the young man would know there were a few men still interested in justice. Perhaps that might ease some of the apparent disillusionment. Perhaps not.

"Judge," the defense attorney protested, "we have a written order from Judge Harbor—"

Powell cut him off with a wave of his hand. "Then you had better take the matter up with Judge Harbor."

The attorney shook his head. He was a court veteran and he fully understood the implications. He looked up at Powell. "I'm very sorry, Judge," he said. "You know I wouldn't be the one to . . . to . . ."

"I know," Powell said. "Don't worry about it. Take the case back to Judge Harbor."

The explosion wouldn't be long in coming. He could expect a visit from King Tingle. The battle had been joined. Powell wished it could have come at a better time. All the odds favored Tingle.

Then he looked at Ace Gilbert, who was grinning up at him. The expression in the young man's eyes made it all worthwhile, odds or no odds.

chapter six

the world liberation army

GORMLEY called a dress rehearsal, a dry run. The purpose was to discover any kinks in their plan. Everyone would execute his or her part just as if it were the real thing, although this time they would carry no explosives or guns.

Flash Johnson had provided all the building layout information. He was to be their scout, the first one to enter the criminal court. It was an easy assignment. He was just to lounge around the lobby and alert the others if something looked suspicious.

Although it was just a rehearsal and he had been in the court many times, Flash Johnson felt real fear. After entering the building he fought against an impulse to get the hell out. His pulse seemed almost audible, and his palms were wet, but he tried to look calm and at ease.

Flash was dressed for his part. He had on his "going to court" clothes: a pearl-white silk shirt, open at the neck, black satinlike trousers and vest with white trim, topped with a wide-brim black hat. His outfit may have been dated, but he knew a number of "bloods" who still favored the once stylish mode of dress.

Everything in the lobby looked normal. The redheaded cop was at his post in the information desk, as usual. And, as usual, he was talking a blue streak to anyone who would listen. The blind man was at his candy and coffee stand, peering up sightlessly at the ceiling while he felt the change in his hand to determine what denomination of coin he had been given.

The usual collection of lawyers, policemen, and defendants milled about, some just standing and watching as he was, others busily talking or arguing. It was a noisy place, the marble walls acting like reflectors bouncing sound back into the busy space and enlarging the volume.

A tall Negro dressed in a skin-tight suit approached him. Flash's heart beat even faster.

"Hey, brother," the man's breath was heavy with alcohol, "you got a light?"

Flash pulled out a pack of matches. His trembling hands made it difficult to strike the match. The other man noticed.

"Shit, man, what they got you on?" The match finally burst into flame. The man lit his cigarette, holding Flash's wrist to steady it. "Man, you all ought to get out of here and get you'self a couple of drinks. That whiskey's good stuff to steady the nerves." He grinned at Flash and winked.

"Besides, ain't nothin' to worry about. The way King Tingle is running this place, don't hardly nobody go to jail anymore anyway, dig?"

Flash nodded. "Yeah."

"Now, you take it cool, ya hear?" The man walked away, his body smoothly moving in easy rhythm to a tune only he could hear.

Flash tried to quiet his nerves. Christ, if he was this nervous now, he knew he'd never be able to make it on the actual day. He felt shaky and nauseous.

Thelma Sturdevant came in first. She was well dressed and carried a large purse. She stopped and looked around the lobby. She knew where she was to go. The third floor had a public ladies' room. On the real day she was to duck in there and wait until closing time. But today she was just to go to the third floor, look around, scout the ladies' room, and then leave. Today she carried no guns or grenades in her purse.

Thelma's eyes rested on Flash for a moment, giving him a chance to signal if something was wrong. He ignored her. She turned and walked quickly toward the elevators. Flash had to admire Thelma. She looked entirely relaxed, as if she were right at home and doing nothing unusual. She didn't show any of the anxiety he felt.

As planned, a few minutes passed, and then Alice Mary Brennan entered. She wore a tweed suit over her ample body, and her horn-rimmed glasses gave her stern features even more fierceness. She carried a large briefcase snug under her arm. She could have been a woman lawyer, a social worker, or a probation officer. The important thing was that she looked as if she belonged.

Flash watched her stump up the marble staircase to the second floor. That's where the action would all take place. The television crews would be assembled in the hall and the judges all tucked away nicely in the executive judge's courtroom. Alice Mary was just passing from sight when Al Martin came in.

Martin's hair had been trimmed, his bushy beard shaved to a pencil-thin moustache. His suit fitted his thin body perfectly. He walked in, stalled for a moment at the information board, looked at the redheaded officer, then glanced over at Flash. There was no signal, so Martin turned and hurried up the stairs to the second floor.

Timing—Flash could almost hear Gormley counting the seconds—it was all timing. With the exception of Thelma, everyone was in a position to draw a weapon and protect and support the others in case something went wrong—like an infantry squad advancing, Gormley had told them.

Larry Gormley sauntered in through the revolving doors. He looked relaxed to the point of boredom. Swinging his briefcase easily, he walked across the lobby as if he didn't have a care in the world. He looked over at Flash, looking through him, and then he too slowly climbed the stairs.

They were all in now. It was his turn. Gormley had decided that having too many people going up the staircase might attract attention. Flash was to use the elevator. Trying to walk with his usual strutting stride, Flash felt his long legs wobble as he propelled himself toward the elevators. Jesus, he thought to himself, there's no way I can get through this when it's the real thing.

Several lawyers and a fat woman pushed into the elevator with him. Flash pushed the button for the second floor. His heart was pounding. The doors shut, and the elevator rose slowly, or so it seemed to him. The doors opened, and he stepped out.

Martin and Gormley stood together talking. They looked like two lawyers discussing a case. Alice Mary sat on a long wooden bench in the hallway as if waiting for someone. Thelma came walking down the staircase, stepping carefully because of her high heels. It had all been timed perfectly. It worked.

Two detectives and a man reading a newspaper were the only other people on the floor.

Gormley and Martin stepped into the executive judge's courtroom. It was part of the test. They were unchallenged. Alice Mary looked at her watch impatiently, got up, and walked back down the stairs.

"Sir, what's the time?"

Flash jumped at the sound of Thelma's voice. She was right at his elbow as planned. That way he would have easy access to her weapon-filled purse when the time came.

"Four . . . four thirty," he stuttered.

"That late? Thank you." Thelma walked away and pushed the Down button for the elevator.

It was ending. The exercise was almost over. They still had to be assured that the courthouse would remain open past four thirty, that their continued presence would cause no problems.

Flash walked down the stairs. He was tempted to run, to fly right through the beckoning revolving doors. But he stopped as he had been told to do. Several other people stood in the lobby. The blind man was locking up his concession stand.

The redheaded officer got up and let himself out of the information booth. He hobbled along on obviously painful legs. He was heading straight for Flash Johnson. The black man shoved his hands deep into his pockets to keep from showing the pronounced trembling.

"Waiting for somebody?" the redhead asked.

"My lawyer." Flash barely got the words out.

"Well, okay, but they lock this place up at five thirty. Everybody has to be out by then, unless they're still in court of course."

"Yeah, I understand."

The officer looked at him. "It's the rules, you know. No offense."

"Yeah, rules is rules. I'll be gone, don't worry." Flash felt the sweat popping out on his forehead.

"Good night to you, now," the redhead said as he shuffled painfully away.

Flash knew his armpits were soaked. And it was his best shirt, too. To hell with it, he thought, I'm goin' to get the fuck out of here.

Just then Martin and Gormley came hurrying down the staircase, their faces bathed in triumphant smiles.

It had worked. The plan was operational, Flash could see it in their faces.

They hurried out the door.

Flash made himself wait the agreed-upon time, then he, too, burst through the revolving doors to the freedom of the street.

The exercise might have proven to the others that they could carry it off, but to Flash Johnson it revealed that he could not stand the suspense nor the danger. If they actually went ahead with their madness, he would not be part of it.

He couldn't tell them that, but he had made up his mind. Jesse would just have to accept whatever fate awaited him. Flash Johnson knew he could not face what he felt would be certain death.

He breathed deeply as he walked down the outside stairs. It was good to breath, to be free.

There were a few advantages to being a coward, he decided—like staying alive.

justice tingle

HE awoke to the raspy sound of nasal snoring. The woman who had last night looked so soft and attractive now looked like a corpse, her jaw slack and mouth hanging open, one large breast exposed. The sheet covered the rest of her large body.

He tried to swallow away the taste of cotton in his mouth, but the dryness just made him cough. His head pounded. He forced himself to sit up. Feeling dizzy, he waited for a moment for the sensation to pass. There were liquor bottles on the floor, but his stomach turned at even the thought of another drink.

But he didn't regret it. It had been a proper celebration: good food, lots of liquor, and a passionate woman. That spell of breathlessness and sweating had passed quickly, just a reminder that someday he would have to curb his appetites a bit. That someday could wait. He had deserved a celebration.

Justice James Tingle stood up and walked slowly and carefully to the bathroom. He quietly closed the door and switched on the light. His puffy, haggard face stared back at him in the mirror. Despite how he felt, he managed to smile at his own reflection.

"Hungover, but happy," he mumbled to himself.

He ran the shower and stepped in, allowing the hot water to steam his body back to life. He had made it. The gambling debts were all paid off, every last cent, plus a modest amount left over. That in itself was a mighty accomplishment. He was free, his own man again. And just one case had done it, just one slipped in among the thousands. No one would ever notice it.

He turned the faucet to cold and shivered as icy water splashed over his bulk. He was fully awake now. He turned off the water and toweled briskly.

It was all succeeding beyond even his wildest hopes. He had three more similar cases lined up—all with discreet and trustworthy lawyers—and he would then be a wealthy man. One more month would do it.

The press had been carefully nurtured. He had spent much of his time with reporters and columnists, and they gobbled up the figures he fed them. It made news: six thousand cases disposed of in one month, compared with the usual two thousand—triple production without any increase in judges. *Budget savings, efficiency*—those words were repeated in every story written about the reform program in criminal court. And the glowing editorial in the morning newspaper yesterday had been the cherry on top. It compared the court turnaround with the parting of the Red Sea—not a bad comparison, Tingle thought.

The editorial had come at just the right time, too. Tingle knew that some of the judges were considering doing more than just grumbling. He was surprised they had been so docile this long. A parade of criminals were streaming through their courts and back into the street. The "reform" program would reduce the numbers for a while, but the repeaters would soon fill the jail and the docket again. It would be only a short-term miracle.

Knowing this, Tingle had played down his own role, fashioning a public stance as just an "advisor" to the real mover, Judge Milton Harbor. When the shit hit the fan, old Milton would be holding the bag. And he didn't have the brains to see that an elaborate "frame" was being hammered together around his weasellike face.

Tingle dressed quietly so as not to awaken the woman.

It was unlikely, as she had enough alcohol in her to pickle a cow. Still, he wanted to avoid any additional contact. The celebration was over.

He softly closed the apartment door and took the elevator to the street. He walked a block to the hotel restaurant. Food and lots of it would make him feel perky again. He enjoyed a half-dozen eggs and double rashers of bacon and potatoes. The busboy kept the hot coffee flowing. He was feeling better by the minute.

It would be another long day of wheeling and dealing. It had been an inspiration to have Harbor sign all the orders. Any one of those released under those orders might murder a woman or child someday, and the newspapers would go after the man who signed the order that released such a beast back on the street. They would have forgotten the big push to clear the docket, they would have forgotten their own editorials, and Harbor would end up crucified. But only Harbor. Tingle smiled as he sipped his coffee.

Tonight he would sleep alone. A good night's sleep was just what he needed. Tomorrow he would be "up" for the monthly judges' meeting. Rebellion was forming, but between newspaper coverage and the irresistible force of the production figures, he had sufficient ammunition to crush any uprising. And if not, the rebels would be sacrificed to an angry public, exposed as lazy public servants more interested in their own comfort than in justice. Most of the smart judges knew he held those kinds of cards. Still, it would be a stormy meeting, and he was determined to be at his best.

Tingle left a tip worthy of a king. He could afford to do so now.

a touch of power

MICKEY Noonan knew the real function of the Downtown Athletic Club. It had a pool, gym, and showers, but they were seldom used; it was "athletic" in name only. The most prestigious of the local clubs, its principal purpose was to serve as a gathering place for the businessmen and financiers who actually made the city and its commerce flow. It reeked of wealth in understated but expensive furnishings. There was a feeling about it, as if its members were titled aristocrats shielded by the castlelike club from annoyance by a filthy and noisy populace. It was a feeling never expressed but generally shared by the men who belonged. It remained a man's club despite the prevailing feminist winds. The men who belonged made the law, and they saw to it that judges understood that the "club" was indeed above the regulations imposed on the general public.

Judge Noonan was escorted to a small private dining room in the rear of the building. These rooms were secluded sanctuaries where gentlemen could discuss the most delicate business matters without fear of being overheard. Only the oldest and most trusted of the waiters served these rooms, and even then most conversation ceased until the waiter had withdrawn. It was that kind of place.

His invitation had come from Thaddeus Murch, the president and founder of Murch Savings and Loan. Murch was a steely-eyed financier who served on a number of boards for some of the city's largest and most influential business concerns.

Noonan was surprised to see that Murch was not alone.

He recognized the other two men. Calvin Todd was the head of Selman and Todd, the giant advertising firm. Todd, like Murch, was in his sixties, tall, and elegant. The other man, Thomas Hardy Pratt, could buy and sell both of them. He presided over a conglomerate that controlled businesses from banking to construction. Pratt was the moving force behind the city's new civic center, a billion-dollar monument of glass and steel. It was Pratt's personal stamp on the city, a hallmark of his ownership.

They exchanged pleasantries. Noonan had met Todd and Murch before, but it was the first time he had encountered the legendary Thomas Hardy Pratt. Pratt was heavy, his portly figure encased in an ill-fitting, cheap suit. His much-worn tie was slightly askew. But there was something about his bearing and manner that proclaimed he was not a man to be trifled with. Both Todd and Murch showed him absolute deference as the luncheon went on.

Mickey Noonan had not risen from poverty. His father had been a successful contractor, and while not a millionaire, he had been able to shower Mickey with most of life's blessings, including a good education at an Ivy League school. So Mickey Noonan felt at ease with men like Murch, Todd, and Pratt.

"We were discussing the crash program at criminal court before you came in," Todd said, sipping his water. None of them had ordered drinks.

"It's an interesting experiment," Noonan said, careful not to commit himself.

"It gives the criminal a free ticket." Pratt's voice was wheezy but full of authority. "It looks good on paper, but all it does is let the criminal element out of jail for the time being. A paper tiger," he growled.

"Some say that," Noonan said.

"What are your views, Judge?" Murch casually buttered part of a hard roll. Noonan sensed it was an important question and perhaps the reason he had been invited. Something was up.

He thought for a moment before answering. "As Mr. Pratt says, basically it is just a device to clear the jails and the docket. Those who do go to jail get much lesser terms than ordinary. They wouldn't plead otherwise. The figures do look very good as far as cases decided and reduction of docket, but it really is just a first-aid remedy." He paused for effect. "However, the other side of that coin is the cost of any other kind of solution. Prior to this crash program a man could be in jail for a year before his case came to trial. The criminal court was never enlarged as the city grew and the crime statistics soared. You know, it is a little like playing football with only four men against eleven. It was becoming quite overwhelming."

No reaction showed on the expressionless faces of the three men. Noonan decided to go on, no matter what the consequences. "The only real answer to the problem is more judges," he said. "Plus more staff and more efficient professional court administration. Right now each judge runs his court anyway he wishes. But more judges and more court personnel cost money. I doubt if the voters would stand for more taxation just to bring criminals to justice more quickly.

"I think this crash program, as odious as it is, serves a purpose. It does buy some time. Perhaps we can reorganize and meet the challenge when the cases come flooding back again. And they will be back, I'm afraid."

"How soon?" Pratt asked.

"Do you mean how soon will things get to a crisis stage again?"

"Precisely."

Noonan thought. "Well, given the time for arrest, investigation, and that sort of thing, the numbers should start to climb again about six months after the crash program ends. That's an educated guess."

Pratt said nothing but attacked the veal set before him.

"How long will the crash program go on?" Murch asked.

"That's hard to say. I have talked to Justice Tingle about it. Basically he believes he'll be back in the Capitol in another couple of months. So, based on the rate the docket is dropping and presuming that it continues, I would guess the program will last another three or four months. Some of the judges are quite disturbed about it now. I can't see it lasting much longer than that."

The older men exchanged glances.

"That would make it a year, give or take, before things got bad again, right?" Pratt asked.

"About that. That's a guess, remember. But I think the time frame wouldn't be too far off from that."

Noonan was neglecting his food. Something was definitely in the air.

Pratt pushed his plate aside and wiped his mouth with a napkin. "I hear good things about you," he said to Noonan, in a tone one might use with a servant. "These men and others tell me you are a level-headed man who understands business and the needs of a community."

"I try," Noonan replied.

Pratt did not seem interested in anything Noonan might say. He appeared to be concerned only with his own words. "The municipal elections are next year. Mayor Wright will not seek reelection."

"I've heard nothing . . ."

Pratt waved his hand impatiently. "Look, when I say the man isn't running, he isn't running." He looked over at Todd and Murch. "Isn't that right?"

They quickly nodded their agreement.

"Wright has made some basic mistakes," Pratt continued. "He's a good man as far as that goes, but he won't be able to win against a strong black contender. And there is going to be an all-out campaign by a black."

"The council president?"

Pratt nodded. "He's the one. He can beat Wright. It is as simple as that. Noonan, I have a big investment in this city. These men"—he indicated Murch and Todd—"also have a substantial investment to protect. We need to have friends, strong friends in city hall."

"That's understandable."

"Right. Now, it's not that I won't do business with a black man. I will, and I do often. But they have to be men whom I feel I can trust. The council president has been opposed to most of my interests since the day he was first elected. Of course, part of that is sheer politics, but I think he really believes much of what he says, and that, sir, is drivel for the most part."

Noonan said nothing.

"We need a candidate for mayor who can win next year, a man we know and can trust, a level-headed man who knows that business has to prosper in order to provide jobs and income for the city's people. We believe you are that man."

"Well, I'm flattered, but—"

Irritably Pratt waved him down again. "I'll be frank, Noonan. We can supply you with more than enough money to do the job. Todd here can provide media experts to run a winning political campaign. In other words, we can almost guarantee your election as mayor."

"I like what I'm doing." Noonan was too much of a politician to jump at the first offer.

"You're a good judge," Pratt said. "We know that. But being a criminal court judge isn't exactly a great springboard to other things. If that's your personal horizon, then I am surprised at your lack of ambition."

"Being mayor isn't exactly a long-term proposition," Noonan replied, this time employing a harsher tone. "The population is shifting. If they don't elect a black man this time, they will the next. Those are the facts of life. What you're offering is a one-term office. No matter what kind of a job I might do as mayor, I'll be turned out in all probability."

Pratt looked at him with new interest. "We have a black man of great promise, a vice-president of one of my banks, as a matter of fact. We plan to run him for city council. As mayor you can see to it that he is given sufficient public exposure to become your natural successor. You're right, a white can only win once more."

"Being a one-shot mayor isn't my idea of a magnificient ambition, if I may say so," Noonan added. "Why should I give up a job I like just to put in four turbulent years that are bound to end in defeat?"

Pratt nodded. "How about the United States Senate? Does that interest you?"

Noonan laughed. "Sure."

"That's where we'll put you if you do this for us, Noonan."

"That's easily said."

Pratt shifted his bulk in his chair. "Harry McClure is the senior senator now, right?"

"Yes."

"Harry will be over seventy when he comes up for re-election. He won't run again."

Noonan frowned. "Senator McClure can be assured of reelection if he runs. Why should he not?"

Pratt looked Noonan directly in the eye. "McClure is my man, you understand? His health isn't what it should be. Another term would be too risky. He won't run." Pratt's words carried complete conviction.

Noonan nodded. He was impressed.

"Governor Whistler is my man also," Pratt continued. "He has a problem, did you know that?"

"You mean his drinking?"

"It is a big problem. He has a good staff, and they can

handle state government, but Whistler wouldn't last two minutes in Washington before he'd disgrace himself. In any event, if Whistler is still in office after your term as mayor, Senator McClure will resign for reasons of health, and the governor will appoint you."

"And if Governor Whistler has been defeated?"

Pratt growled the answer. "We'll back you fully for election to the Senate if Whistler isn't around to appoint you."

Noonan thought for a moment. "I don't want to appear unappreciative, gentlemen. I'm flattered and honored by your interest, believe me. But I have a large family to support, and I'm afraid I'm in no position to gamble. As a politician I can assure you that things change. You're asking me to make a considerable change in my career. I have your assurance, but nothing more. I trust you, of course. I know your reputations. However, you must admit that if I asked you to make a major business commitment based only upon my verbal assurance, you'd probably turn me down."

"Don't trust us, eh?" Pratt snapped. Before Noonan could respond, Pratt continued. "That's as it should be, Noonan. I can't stand a fathead, and I like a man who can see things as they are. Here's what I propose. I want you to resign as judge in about two or three months. I don't want you to get smeared with any of the crap that this crash program is sure to throw up. Prior to your resignation, the senior partner of Cross, Warbler will offer you a full partnership. Part of that offer will be an advance of one hundred thousand dollars and a five-year contract as part of the inducement to get you to resign the bench. Of course, you'll be expected to be our candidate for mayor. If defeated, you will remain as a full partner of that law firm with double your judicial pay. If something goes wrong, you are completely protected. How does that sound?"

Noonan smiled. The old man had held those cards until forced to play them. "That's agreeable, gentlemen."

Pratt looked at the other two, who nodded their assent. "We are also in agreement. Next year you will be elected mayor. Five years from now you will become a Senator of the United States. You can count on that, Noonan."

"It's quite something to think about."

"Of course, and we fully expect that we shall be able to count on you," Pratt added.

"I understand." Noonan smiled. "You won't have any regrets, gentlemen, let me assure you."

"Fine," Pratt said, standing. "Now, if you'll excuse me, I have an engagement." He extended his hand to Noonan. "Judge, then mayor and Senator. Maybe more, eh? You can never tell."

Noonan felt the power in the fat man's grip.

"Oh, one more thing," Pratt said. "If you've any skeletons in the closet, get rid of them."

"Pardon me?"

The older man's eyes were cold. "If you happen to have a girl friend or anything of that sort, get rid of her. We aren't playing games, Noonan. This is for big stakes."

They knew about Kathleen Mulloy. He hoped the surprise didn't show on his face.

"I want you projected as the perfect family man, the ideal husband and father, that sort of thing," Pratt said. "We can't afford to have the opposition trot out a weeping mistress at the last minute."

"There'll be no skeletons," Noonan said quietly. "I can assure you of that."

"You're a smart young man," Pratt said, smiling for the first time, although his eyes were still icy. "It'll be a pleasure doing business with you."

Murch and Todd also excused themselves, leaving Noonan alone with his coffee. He sat quietly, digesting all that had transpired. It was his golden opportunity, a chance he had only dreamed about, and now suddenly it lay within reach. He knew what they wanted, and he knew he could deliver it. Nothing crooked. These men were too big and too rich for petty graft. Influence, that's what they needed, official oil to keep their enterprises perking along. He could handle that.

The United States Senate, even perhaps . . . he shook his head. One thing at a time. He felt the thrill of all gamblers when they hit the jackpot. With the help of these wealthy and powerful men he could become a political comet lighting up the nation's skies. He knew it was really going to happen.

They had obviously screened him carefully, finding out about Kathleen Ann. Well, it was only a reasonable thing to ask—a man would have to be a fool to trade a brief affair for the chance of a dream career. Kathleen Mulloy was already in the past, as far as he was concerned. He would have to handle it carefully, of course. Just dumping her could cause waves. But it would have to be done as quickly as possible. She had always had a guilt thing about his wife and children, and that would prove very useful.

Mickey Noonan smiled as he envisioned telling Kathleen that his conscience had propelled him back to church and family. That was something she would understand. She would think him noble.

He wondered if he could get away with laying her just once more but decided against it. Business first.

"U.S. Senator Noonan," he whispered aloud. It sounded great, even when whispered.

the probation officer

THE crash program affected everyone connected with the court. The probation department had been caught in such an avalanche of work that no one could adequately discharge his or her duty. Their efforts now were mostly for show. There was no time for home visits, no time for in-depth investigations. And all the probation officers knew that their recommendations for jail were being ignored by the judges except in the most flagrant cases.

The law required a probation report in each criminal case, so everyone on the staff was pressed into double duty just to meet the bare bones of legal necessity. The younger officers liked it for the overtime meant more money. The older ones resented the long hours and having to do their own typing. Tension rose as tempers became strained.

Even Frank Conroy had been drafted. He still had the responsibility of the drunk tank in the morning, but the luxury of free afternoons had gone. Like the others, he was busy all day, running from jail interviews to typing short, inadequate reports. The usual six-page report had shrunk to a half-page paragraph, which sounded the same in all the cases.

After his last episode Frank Conroy had been watching his drinking. He rationed his liquor, being careful not to let it become his answer to emotional stress. While in the priesthood, he had seen many a man slip slowly into an alcoholic womb, letting liquor ease the pain of life. He still used it, but he was more careful now.

It had been a long day. To Conroy it seemed as if only

the drunks were going to jail. After disposing of his aromatic crew in the morning Conroy had spent the day in the jail interviewing a multitude of convicted felons, taking down their life stories, accepting their statements as if they were true, which, he knew, most weren't.

But it didn't matter anymore. The stories were just something to put down on the report. They could have been in another language, no one would have noticed. He disliked the jail. Even though he knew he could get out, a primitive fear lurked beneath his consciousness that maybe somehow, when the time came, they would keep him along with the others. It was always a relief to get back out on the street.

There was a hint of rain in the humid air. It promised to rinse the littered streets, and that in itself would be welcome. He walked slowly, realizing for the first time that he was hungry in addition to being tired. His briefcase contained dozens of handwritten notes. They would have to be typed and ready for tomorrow's sentencings. Typed, he hoped, by one of the clerks, if he could find one; if not, by himself.

Conroy decided to check back at the office before having a quick dinner, just in case he could get a typist. The office was full, unusual even considering the crash program. However, the crew was made up of probation officers. There were no clerks.

"Oh, Frank," Harry DuMont, the chief deputy probation officer, called to him. "Can I see you for a minute?"

Conroy laid his notes on his desk and walked into the little cubbyhole DuMont called an office.

"What's up, Harry?"

Harry DuMont was a younger man, with not much experience but loaded with college degrees. "Frank, you can do me a favor, if you will."

"Depends." Conroy knew DuMont had a reputation for ducking work and avoiding unpleasant assignments.

"Mr. Kingston is in Indianapolis."

Kingston was their boss. He was a speaker at a seminar in Indiana. "I know."

"Well, tomorrow night I have to give a talk at the university. Sort of a recruitment thing, you know."

"So?"

"Ah, Justice Tingle called awhile ago. He wants somebody from our office at the monthly judges' meeting tomorrow night."

"What the hell for?"

"Oh, just a public relations thing. He wants a report to the judges on the probation department's work for the last month. Figures, Frank, just figures. You know, how many first offenders, how many on probation, how many went to jail."

"So what's the favor?"

"The boss is away, and I can't make it, so I wonder if you could show up there and give the report? I'll have all the figures prepared."

"Nothing to it, right, Harry?"

"Exactly." The other man beamed.

"Except that hardly anyone went to jail last month. They might be looking for someone to skin for that, and you think it might be us, so you don't want to go."

"Look, Conroy, it was just a request, not an order."

"Oh, Christ, Harry, show a little class, will you? These people are nothing to be frightened of. If you made it your business to get to know the judges, you wouldn't have to—"

"I wasn't looking for a lecture." DuMont's voice was angry.

Conroy sighed. "Okay, no lecture. Get the figures for me, and I'll show up there and give them to them."

"If it wasn't for my previous appointment . . ." DuMont's voice trailed off.

"I understand. Don't sweat it, Harry. I'll take care of it. Anything else?"

DuMont looked sheepish but relieved. "No, that was all. I appreciate it, Frank."

"Sure. I'm going out to get a bite to eat. Want to come?"

"No, thanks, Frank, I'd love to, but I have other plans."

"Okay." Conroy left DuMont and headed for the elevators. He spotted Kathleen Ann Mulloy waiting for an elevator. She didn't look well, white-faced with puffy eyes.

"Hi," Conroy said. "You come here often?"

She jumped at the sound of his voice. "Frank, I didn't see you."

"I'm just going out for a bite. Care to join me?"

She shook her head, then reconsidered. "Where?"

"Probably the Hellas Café. Lamb sandwich, rice, and a shot of Greek brandy.

She smiled weakly. "I don't feel like eating, but the brandy sounds like a good idea."

Conroy looked away from her. He didn't want to stare. It was obvious that her eyes were red from crying. "This extra work getting to you, Kathleen?"

She shook her head. "No. Just life in general, I guess."

The empty elevator arrived. They stepped aboard.

"My, it sounds like you have an advanced case of the blues. Not a hormone thing, I trust?" He said it lightly.

"Wish it was."

"Your mother died. Am I close?"

"About four years ago. Not even warm."

"Father is back in the insane asylum?"

She laughed despite herself. "No. Although he's never been too far away from that, I think."

"Ah ha! Then you have heart troubles, a myocardial infarction of the amour muscle, how's that?"

They got off at street level and walked to the night door. "You're a great doctor, Frank. That's a pretty good diagnosis."

"Come on, kid, a couple of brandies will loosen your

tongue. You can tell me anything. Just remember that I'm
one of the biggest gossips around, okay?"

"Okay."

They walked along the street.

"He decided to go back to the wife and kiddies, is that
it?"

She whirled. "Was it that obvious?"

He shook his head. "This 'Zoo' of ours is just one big
unhappy family, kid. Everybody knows everybody else's
agony. You're well rid of him."

"You don't know him, Frank." Her voice was distant.

"I know him. I know a thousand like him. When this
all wears off, you'll see him for the self-centered creature
he really is. Your heart is broken now, Kathleen, but later
you'll thank God it was ended."

"I thought you didn't believe in God?"

"It's just an expression, honey, that's all. Anyway, you've
escaped."

"He did it for his children, Frank."

Frank Conroy looked at her. She meant it. Jesus, women
seemed to be born without brains sometimes. Creatures
existing on emotions and not intellect. "Sure, and that
makes him a great guy in your eyes, right? I wish I could
do that to people—make them love my lies. Hell, he may
even believe it himself."

"Frank, please!"

Even in the street light he could see her eyes brimming.
"Hey, I'm out of the business. I forget every so often, you
know. No more sermons, my dear. I'll ply you with liquor
and see if I can't replace him. How's that?"

"No one can ever replace him, Frank."

"Yeah. I know. Come on, here's the Hellas and the
medicine to help the hurt get smaller."

the supreme court

CHIEF Justice Buckington stood at his office window surveying the green expanse of the well-kept capitol lawn. It was a pleasant sight, like a college campus, but without the throngs of students. He was taking a quiet moment to prepare himself. As chief justice it was his duty, and prerogative, to release the supreme court decisions to the press and public. He usually kept to a schedule, releasing a flock of decisions at regular intervals. Sometimes he held back a decision because of high public interest. The single release guaranteed a flurry of stories, and that high-impact publicity promoted the court—and him. It was not unpleasant to see one's name in the newspapers.

Based on the facts, the *Harold Hawkins* matter had been a very simple case. Hawkins was nothing in himself, really. It was the imposition of the death penalty that gave him a measure of importance. Buckington had never seen Hawkins, nor did he care to.

The man had been convicted by a jury of the premeditated murder of his wife. Hate plus insurance money had been the motive. It had not been the usual fatal domestic quarrel. Hawkins had planned it carefully, but not carefully enough. The second jury, as required by the new statute, had authorized the death penalty, which Judge Walters in Reed City pronounced with glee. Walters was a stern, mean son of a bitch, and Buckington knew that the old man loved the idea of sending someone to the gas chamber.

There had been an appeal to the state's court of appeals.

A three-judge panel had upheld the law and the sentence. Then the case came to the supreme court. Since it was a capital case, calling for either life or execution, the court was required to hear it.

It came on in due course. First, the long briefs—statements of fact, law, and argument—were submitted by the defendant's lawyer, the prosecutor, and a committee opposed to the death penalty. Oral argument followed several months later, a boring affair despite the drama of the subject matter. Each side had an hour. The defense attorney's argument had been a long recital of the history of capital punishment delivered in a monotone as he dissected the meaning of legal cases relied upon to keep his client from inhaling the deadly gas. The county prosecutor assigned to the case seemed stagestruck in front of the nine justices. He mumbled through his short speech, his voice quaking when the justices asked a few questions. The attorney for the committee opposed to the death penalty had launched into a political speech, but they had cut him short with sharp questions. It had all been very dull.

As usual one of the justices was selected by Buckington to write the first draft of a proposed opinion. The other justices were not barred from writing their own, but with the press of business it had become the practice to spread the cases around that way. The designated justice turned the matter over to his law clerks, who did the actual work of reading cases and citing law. The first draft was roughly written and decided in favor of the state on the original verdict and sentence.

The draft was passed around. Some justices made suggested changes, but seven agreed with the decision, at least to the extent they did not want to go to the trouble of writing a separate opinion. Buckington was opposed to capital punishment, a popular stance with the liberals who supported him. He had his clerk write a stinging opinion dissenting violently from the main decision. This too was passed around. Justice Tingle, before leaving for the city, had agreed with Buckington's dissenting opinion, but he was the only one. Thus, in the case of *Hawkins* versus *the People*, there would be two opinions entered into the law books: the majority and ruling decision spelling death for Hawkins and Buckington's dissent, which wouldn't do Hawkins one bit of good.

The typed final decisions with signatures were lying on top of Buckington's desk. He decided that this morning would be an excellent day to release the opinions. He usually waited until the printer had run them off, but this time he decided to release typed drafts. The news had been slow lately, and this would grab headlines.

Buckington picked up the decisions and walked out to his secretary. "Mrs. Waltham, please make a dozen . . . no, maybe two dozen copies of these decisions in the *Hawkins* case. Then call the Capitol newsroom and tell them I'm holding a brief press conference at eleven about the case. Don't tell them what we've decided. They'll try to get that from you, you know."

"They haven't yet," she smiled. A mousy woman, but efficient in her own dreary way.

Buckington walked back into his office and sat down in the huge chair behind his neat desk. Hawkins was a dead man, that was certain. Oh, his lawyers would try to have the U.S. Supreme Court hear the matter, but that court had just blessed an almost identical statute in Oklahoma. There was no chance that the justices in Washington would reverse themselves. There was nothing unusual legally in the *Hawkins* case.

Chief Justice Buckington idly wondered how Hawkins would take the news. It would be dreadful to know that you were going to die on a certain date. And the manner— sitting there in that glass room with people watching—that grossly offended Buckington's sense of dignity.

Although not stated in his dissenting opinion, that lack of dignity was the real reason Buck Buckington opposed capital punishment. The taking of a life did not offend him. It was an ancient punishment, honored in its tradition. However, the manner of execution was repulsive. The fact that the condemned's life was snuffed out by rope, electricity, or gas made no difference. The horror of having others watch one's death agonies was the thing that bothered him.

If the state legislature had provided death by drinking hemlock, and in seclusion, Buckington would have had no objections. That would be the gentlemanly way.

He began to formulate his thoughts for the press conference. He would keep it brief, accentuating the ruling position of the court and only reluctantly allowing them to draw him out on his own dissent. It should make good copy. He was pleased with himself.

With the good news coming out of his ordered takeover in the criminal court plus his own good sense of timing in releasing decisions, he felt that the name Buckington would soon become a household word.

the assistant prosecutor

HAVING drawn Justice Tingle's wrath, Judge Powell's court became one of the few working courts. It got jury cases. For most of the other judges the monthly court business had become a production line of guilty pleas, adjusted down from the original charges, and a procession of sentencing.

Ace Gilbert, for one, was happy to be doing some real work. For many of his fellow trial attorneys on the prosecutor's staff, however, it had been like a vacation, just sitting around drinking coffee and exchanging stories with the defense attorneys who escorted their clients before the bar—and usually out the door. The defense lawyers were universally happy. It was like an early Christmas, lots of fast pleas and lots of fast fees, as Emeralds Mulligan had told him. Emeralds was in seventh heaven, running from courtroom to courtroom, making nice but short speeches and pushing ever more cash into already bulging pockets. Emeralds told the other attorneys it was like being on a winning streak in Vegas, only here you just couldn't lose.

But there was an occasional loser. Chester Roberts, known by family, friends, and police as Little Chester, was a loser. If he had shown up for his original trial date, he would have partaken in the bonanza of pleas being lavished on the others. But he had forfeited much more than mere consideration.

Because of many reasons—booze being the main one— Little Chester had jumped bail, and the bondsman had to hunt him down. Even with Justice Tingle running the criminal court, Chester's actions constituted a crime that called for punishment. If the customers got the idea they could just walk away, the whole legal structure would collapse: no jobs for judges or juries, no fees for attorneys, and, down the line of priorities, no punishment for wrongdoers.

Therefore, there would be no deal for Little Chester. He had broken an unspoken commandment. He had threatened the court system. He would be suitably punished as an example to all. He was not allowed to plead to a lesser charge. The main indictment for breaking and entering a dwelling in the nighttime with the intent to commit a felony stood. And that carried fifteen years maximum. Since Chester had a long record, he could count on a minimum of ten years. It was a heavy hit, especially in view of the easy sentences being received by other burglars, who were more diligent about showing up for their trials.

Little Chester had no money, just the clothes on his back and a lump where Bad Abe Gallente's sap had hit him. He petitioned the court for appointed counsel. The court had two options. It could have Little Chester's case assigned to the public defender's office, where an attorney working on salary would defend him, or, if the public defender's office was especially busy—as it was now during the crash program—the court could appoint a private lawyer, who would work at an hourly rate. If a trial ran two or three days, it could add up. Since Little Chester had no choice but to appeal to a jury—hoping somehow that justice would miscarry—it would be a multiday trial and worth a few dollars.

None of the regulars wanted to waste precious hours at trial when they could run dozens of cases through the system in the same time, so a new lawyer was appointed, a young woman.

Ginger Steiner received a notice that she had been appointed to defend one Chester Roberts. It was her third criminal trial, and she was excited about it until she interviewed Little Chester in the jail. Ginger knew then that even a combination of Clarence Darrow and Daniel Webster could never get Little Chester off. But he wouldn't plead guilty. She would have to take the case to trial. She had tried only one jury case, so she looked forward to increasing her experience, win or lose.

A jury trial would also provide an acceptable vent for her acting ability. Almost thirty, Ginger Steiner had trained to be an actress. Her original college degree had been in drama with an English minor. In New York she had been in some off-Broadway plays and had lived the hectic life of a fledgling actress, finally abandoning the stage for marriage. Marriage had been a disaster. Her husband, handsome as a Greek sculpture, revealed himself to be just an arrested adolescent looking for a mother. Ginger was too young to play mothers' roles, so divorce resulted.

Admission to the city law school followed. Her grades were good, and she was graduated with honors. The law practice was not yet completely successful, but the partners were making ends meet—just. Ginger still retained much of the flair of a New York actress, affecting a breezy and sophisticated manner. Men were attracted to her. Her copper hair, green eyes, and almost Oriental face marked her as a beauty in any league. She was lean, her dance training having left her with a healthy, athletic body. She had moved through a series of love affairs, none with the passion or commitment she wanted—still it was a good time of life, and she enjoyed living it.

She liked Judge Clyde Powell instantly. His twinkling eyes betrayed a sense of humor concealed by his expressionless face. His gray hair set off his black skin handsomely, and his intelligence was immediately evident. He had been very kind to her, knowing that she was new to criminal court.

Even the jury seemed in good spirits. This was one of the few cases being tried, and they seemed delighted to be working.

But of most interest to her was the assistant prosecutor, whom they called Ace. He certainly knew his business. At first he did not respond to her and was almost condescending. Because he had so much more court experience, he tended to treat her like a student. But when she began to cut into his witnesses with sharp cross-examination, he changed quickly. He became a competitor and was, she sensed, suddenly interested in her as a person, and as a woman.

During the course of the trial she had made discreet inquiries and discovered that the sandy-haired prosecutor was also divorced. And since competition seemed to arouse such a keen response in him, she really laid it on. She made him work. She used every trial tactic she had ever read about. Having a losing case, she was completely free to experiment. And although Ace Gilbert expertly continued to weave a snug web of evidence around Little Chester, she sensed that the jury felt warm toward her and was entertained by the developing battle between the two lawyers.

She didn't dare put her client on the stand, not with his record. And there were absolutely no witnesses who could testify to his good character. Little Chester had offered the names of his parole officer and one of the guards at the prison, but she had to assure him that while they might say he was a prince among men, the fact of who they were and how they met him would sink what little chance he had.

They battled for two full days. They were proving to be an even match for each other, her technique matching his experience. But finally Gilbert finished the prosecution's case.

Ginger Steiner had no case for Little Chester. She could offer no testimony on behalf of her client. She made the usual motion for dismissal as soon as Ace Gilbert announced that the people's case was complete.

Judge Powell politely listened to her argument as she stretched the facts a bit to try to beg a dismissal. Gilbert heatedly objected several times during her remarks. She knew that Judge Powell could cruelly cut her down with a few sharp-tongued remarks, but he was courtesy itself. He did, of course, deny her motion for dismissal or directed verdict.

Ginger Steiner then reluctantly rested her case.

It was nearly the close of court hours, so Judge Powell recessed the case for the night. He told both lawyers to be prepared to argue to the jury in the morning. Following their summations, he would then instruct the jury in the applicable law. Then the case would be in the jury's hands for decision.

Clyde Powell wanted the rest of the afternoon free. He planned to meet with several of the judges. The monthly judges' meeting was scheduled tomorrow, and he hoped that he and the others could come to some agreement on the proper strategy to contain King Tingle and restore a commonsense approach to the court's problems. Tomorrow would be an important day.

Ginger Steiner bid good-bye to Little Chester as the officer led him away. She packed up her briefcase, aware that the lanky prosecutor was watching her, and hesitated a moment, hoping that he would perhaps invite her out for a drink. But he said nothing.

As she walked out of the courtroom, Ginger Steiner decided she would have to do something about that man. If competition excited Mr. Ace Gilbert, she would give it to him. She would put on a dramatic production for the jury tomorrow. She hoped it would impress them, but it was the prosecutor she really wanted to impress. He was a definite challenge.

She, too, considered the coming day important.

the burglar

THE news of the *Hawkins* decision hit the cell block like an explosion. At first there were loud discussions, heated and indignant. Then the men began to quiet down. Most were withdrawn, lost in their own thoughts. But the tension had started to build.

By noon there had been two fistfights, quickly quelled by the guards. The prisoners were realizing that now the terrible walk to the glass box would be a certainty. Gus Simes reacted by becoming nauseous.

The news affected them all, except for Hagen and Johnson. It was as if they hadn't heard of the *Hawkins* result. Relaxed and smiling, they played a quiet game of gin rummy as if they hadn't a care in the world. Despite his stomach problems Simes walked over and sat down with them, not saying anything, just watching the game.

"Shit, man, why'd you throw down a nine? You just picked up a nine two draws ago." Johnson's voice, as always, was loud.

"Wait and see. Wait and see." Hagen smiled contentedly.

"Hey, what do you think of that *Hawkins* thing?" Simes asked.

Johnson pulled a card from the deck and studied it. "Goin' to be a lot of empty fuckin' bunks around here. Right, Hagen?"

The other man laughed but said nothing.

"Maybe the Supreme Court will—"

"Oh, man," Johnson interjected, "those fat asses in Washington don't care what happens here. Jesus, you know the score, same as everybody else, Gus. They okayed the same law in Oklahoma, so they're goin' to let this one stand, sure as shit, you'll see."

He was right. Gus knew the truth—they all did. But that made him wonder even more why these two men were so much at ease.

"Things are getting pretty tense up here," he said quietly.

"Gin!" Hagen laughed and slapped down his cards, drawing a curse from Johnson. Hagen made a note on a piece of paper and then shuffled the cards. "If you gettin' worried, Simes," he said, "relax. I'm goin' to start teachin' a course that should help out."

"What kind of course?"

Hagen grinned. "How to hold your breath." Then he roared with laughter. "Shit, I bet the whole place will sign up for that one."

Johnson was chuckling as he picked up his cards. "You worry too much, Gus," he said in a low voice, something unusual for him.

"My God, how can you not worry?"

"You're with us, man. You don't have to sweat it. Somethin' good is about to happen."

"What?" Simes asked, his voice a whisper.

"Mind your business, Gus." Hagen's voice was cold. "Just mind your business and wait. Things will work out."

Simes started to speak.

"And don't ask questions, understand?" Hagen's eyes were like little steel agates. It seemed to Simes that he saw death looking out at him.

"Yeah, sure," he stammered. "Say, thanks, fellas. I'm with you, you know that."

"We won't forget you, Gus," Johnson said, picking a card from the deck. "Just don't push your luck, dig?"

"Sure, don't worry." Simes forced himself to sit with

them. It would look better, and they wouldn't become suspicious.

"I wonder what that kid lawyer of mine thinks," Simes said, as if just making conversation. "I mean, hell, I didn't kill anybody myself, you know. Maybe there's something in that *Hawkins* case that lets people like me out."

Johnson looked over at him. "You still fussin' about that. You're in, man, same as the rest of us. But, what the hell, if you got a doubt, send for the shyster."

"Yeah, that's a good idea," Simes said. "It wouldn't hurt to ask."

"You won't need it," Johnson said. "But if it makes you feel better—"

"Gin!" Hagen again slapped down his cards in glee.

Simes slipped away and walked to the bars nearest the guard. "Hey, Mr. Dufflow."

The guard, who was reading a paperback book, looked up. "Yeah?"

"Could you give my lawyer a call? Tell him I got to talk to him right away?"

The guard laughed. "You know, Gus, everybody in here has asked to see his lawyer today. You don't think that *Hawkins* case has anything to do with it, do you?"

Gus tried to smile. "It might," he said weakly.

"Well, what the hell, I'll give him a call for you. Can't hurt."

"I appreciate it."

Gus walked to a deserted part of the cell block. Johnson and Hagen were going to break out and soon. If he told his lawyer and alerted the authorities, they might be grateful enough to drop the request for the death penalty. That was all he wanted, just to be free of the threat of the gas chamber. The roof of his mouth seemed dry. Hagen and Johnson would kill him if they even suspected he was going to give them away. It was a dangerous risk, but then the gas chamber seemed a sure thing.

He hoped the harried young lawyer had enough smarts to handle the thing right. Jesus, he thought to himself, if only I had enough money to afford a real lawyer.

another informal meeting

JUDGE Herb Abrams stepped off the elevator and walked down the rear corridor to Judge Powell's courtroom.

The courtroom was empty except for Ace Gilbert, who was packing away tools marked with the red evidence tag into a large leather case.

"Hey, Ace, how are you?" Abrams strolled over. He always liked Gilbert. He liked all lawyers who did a competent job. "What are you doing?"

Ace Gilbert nodded. "Packing away a set of burglary tools. Public service doesn't pay enough, Judge, so I have taken up a sideline."

Abrams chuckled. "You're too damned tall to be a burglar, Ace. That's a job for fast little compact guys like myself. So I'd stick to prosecuting, if I were you." He picked up a steel jimmy bar and hefted it. "Good tool."

"Yeah, belongs to a real professional. We have a jury case going on. I'm earning my pay too. The defense attorney really comes on."

Abrams handed back the jimmy. "Who is he?"

"It's a she. Ginger Steiner, and she's damned good. Unfortunately."

"Don't know her. A jury, eh?"

"I'll bet this is the only jury trial in the whole building. Gilbert nodded.

"They're really doing a job on Judge Powell."

"So I understand."

Abrams sighed. "Damned shame too. Everywhere else they are moving cases as if the defendants were at a fire drill. It's getting pretty bad."

Before Gilbert could reply, they were joined by Judge Stewart Richards, who greeted them both.

"Mickey Noonan coming?" Abrams asked.

"No," Richards replied. "He said he didn't have time."

"Aw, Christ," Abrams snapped. "He's spending all his time fooling around with that bimbo of his."

Richards smiled slightly. "Bimbo? Apparently I haven't been tuned in on the latest gossip. Do I know her?"

"Oh, sure," Abrams replied. "She's that cute kid in the probation department. Oh, what the hell is her name . . . Kathleen Ann something."

"Mulloy?" Ace Gilbert asked.

"Yeah, that's her." As Abrams spoke, he remembered he had heard that the prosecutor was also interested in the girl. He regretted his indiscretion. "Well, I'm not sure, actually," he mumbled.

"Enough of judges' love lives," Richards said, "let's get on with the main business." He smiled at Gilbert. "See you later, Ace."

Abrams quickly followed Richards to Judge Powell's chambers.

Gilbert remained where he was. He was surprised that he felt no resentment. Kathleen Ann Mulloy had probably been overpowered by the famous charm of Judge Mickey Noonan. And he felt only a twinge of jealousy. Things like that happened. And at least it explained why she wouldn't go out with him, and why she couldn't tell him. She was such a nice girl. He hoped things would work out for her. Probably he would have felt more regret or have had a stronger reaction if it weren't for Ginger Steiner. Whereas Kathleen was quiet and vulnerable, Ginger was assertive, with a quick intelligence, and she challenged him. It was the challenge that made her so damned exciting.

Ace Gilbert packed up the evidence case and left the courtroom.

In Judge Powell's chambers there was an atmosphere of frustration.

"If Noonan isn't coming," Abrams said, "that probably means we can't count on him."

Powell nodded. "He's looking to his political future. He doesn't want to make war with Tingle, not unless he can win."

"What about Luther Perry?" Richards asked.

"We can't count on Luther either," Powell said. "I talked to him. I don't think Luther really understands what is going on. He's honest but he wants to give Tingle's plan a chance to work. I know him. After a few months he'll come around, but until then he won't join any opposition."

Richards puffed on his pipe. "I think you have counted noses, Clyde. Give us the rundown."

Powell nodded. "It's bad. Obviously Milton Harbor is one hundred percent behind Tingle. O'Brien and Sloan are up to their old tricks, I understand, so they are all in favor of Tingle." He paused, his face quite somber. "Tingle has scared the hell out of Marcus Young. He has threatened to have charges brought against him for his drinking. Same thing with Carol Woldanski. She's close to pension, and Tingle has threatened to ask for a disability commission hearing. Carol wouldn't even peep."

"Plays rough," Abrams said.

Powell nodded. "James Tingle has always played rough."

"So that leaves just the three of us," Richards said.

Powell nodded. "Just three out of ten."

There was a silence.

"For the moment he's got us. There isn't a damned thing we can do," Abrams said. "Even if all three of us yell our heads off, the press will be on his side, at least for now. We'll look bad and make him look good."

"Justice—just think of all the crimes in history that have been committed in that name," Richards said. "But we really have a duty to do something. Just sitting here and saying how bad things are isn't discharging our obligation as judges."

Abrams shrugged. "I can't argue with you. Tingle's throwing open the gates. Christ, murderers are going out. Rapists, robbers, all back out onto the streets." He paused. "But we should be practical. Let's recognize our duty, but let's wait until we can do something effective about it."

"Like when?" Powell asked.

"Look, Tingle is playing fast and loose. It's only a matter of time until he makes a mistake, a big one. Then is the time we stand up and shout."

Powell shook his head. "Then you think we should hang back until a more opportune time?"

Abrams nodded.

"There's a lot in what he says, Clyde," Richards said. "Look, if he and I join with you in refusing to take pleas, we'll get some of that special Tingle mud splashed all over us. In fact, if I were you, I'd back off for a bit. Make it seem like you'll go along. Just for a while. Then, like Herb says, when that mistake happens, we'll nail Tingle. Anything else is impracticable."

Powell nodded. "Well, I can't argue with your logic.

But I can't go along with it either. Someone has to put all this on record. I'm already in as a rebel, so I'm going to stay in. Maybe we can force a mistake."

"He'll do everything in his power to ruin you, Clyde," Abrams said.

Powell smiled sadly. "Well, what is to be will be. But my daddy used to have a saying that covers the situation."

Abrams looked interested. "What's that?"

"The hawk only gets the rabbit that runs," Powell replied.

"What the hell does that mean?" Abrams asked.

Powell sighed. "If you show fear, your enemies will see that and really come after you."

"So you're going to persist in needling Tingle?" Abrams said, his voice showing his opinion of that course.

"I'm afraid so," Powell said. "Anyway, we'll see what happens at the judges' meeting tomorrow night."

"Are you going to speak?" Richards asked.

"I might," Powell said softly, "I just might."

the world liberation army

THEY had been at it for hours. Flash Johnson looked around at the haggard faces. The fatigue showed on everyone except Larry Gormley. The table was spread with hand-drawn maps of the court and several printed maps of Africa. Gormley really believed they would make it. The power of his personal conviction carried the others along. They had all become fanatical believers in success.

Each man and woman had been extensively drilled in the use of the weapons. They had taken them apart, cleaned them, and dry-fired them. Each of them knew everything about the grenades and explosives. They had become experts with the equipment. And Gormley had coached them on the operations, tossing quick problems at them, demanding solutions, making them combat-ready, prepared for anything.

Flash had drilled along with the others. But it was just for show. He had no intention of showing up in that courthouse tomorrow. Tomorrow would be death for everyone in the room, and probably for Jesse and Hagen too—but not for him. Flash was just going along until the right time came, and then he would take off.

He looked at his watch. It was past midnight. "Hey, we got anything to drink in this place?" He asked the question, knowing that Gormley had forbidden liquor and drugs.

"No." Al Martin's voice was tired.

"Man, this is heavy stuff. I'm goin' to pop across town for a quick drink. I needs a little something to sleep." He paused and looked around. "Y'all invited." He forced a toothy grin, trying to look loose and relaxed.

"No drinking," Gormley said quietly. "We'll have to be sharp for tomorrow. Once we pull this off, we can really throw a party, but no drinking tonight."

"Shit, man, I ain't goin' to get drunk or nothin', just have a few belts. I gots to loosen up, this is all pretty hairy stuff."

"Flash," Gormley said, getting up and stretching, "let's talk in the next room, okay?"

Flash Johnson pushed back the kitchen chair and followed Gormley into the apartment's living room. Al Martin followed behind.

"Sit down, Flash," Gormley said.

"Hey, man, I've been sittin' so long my tailbone feels bent."

"Sit down," Gormley repeated, but with a smile. "That chair is soft."

Flash glanced over at Martin, whose thin face looked taut and solemn. This was serious. He sat.

"For some time now, Flash, I have had the idea that you really haven't been too wild about what we plan to pull off tomorrow."

"Hey, man, at first I thought the whole thing was impossible, but now I'm with you all the way. Yeah. I'll admit I thought the idea was weird, but I'm ready to go now." Flash sensed danger. He was slouched down in the soft chair. His only weapon, his knife, was deep in a trouser pocket, almost unreachable. "I'm with you guys, honest to God," he said quickly. "Shit, it's my brother we're trying to save, right?"

Gormley nodded. "That's right, Flash. But this is more important than just releasing your brother. We are going to make a statement tomorrow, a statement that will be heard worldwide. People like ourselves all over the world will be thrilled and cheered by what we do. They will draw strength and encouragement from us."

"I know that, Larry." He looked at Gormley. "Shit, all I wanted to do was get a lousy drink!"

Gormley's eyes never left him. "Maybe. Maybe that's all you wanted, Flash, just a drink. But maybe you figured to bug out, perhaps even go to the police."

"Aw, man, why you think I'd do that?"

"You're yellow, Flash. That's why."

The black man snarled and tried to push out of the soft chair. He stopped immediately as both Gormley and Martin pulled revolvers. Flash exhaled audibly as he stared down the barrel of Gormley's gun, only inches away from his face.

"You're yellow, Flash," Gormley repeated. "Hell, anyone could see it. You were shaking like a rabbit when we went through that rehearsal at court."

Flash's face was trembling at the corners of his mouth. "So I was nervous. Shit, I'll admit that. That's no big deal. I just got a little shaky, but I did my part. Man, I did my job."

"That was when there was no danger, but there'll be danger tomorrow night, Flash, lots of it. I don't think we can count on you then."

"You can count on me," Flash protested, trying to sound tough. "You all need me. I know that courthouse. I'll be able to spot trouble. That's what I do, isn't it, watch out for trouble?"

Gormley shook his head. "I get this funny idea that you'll see 'trouble' no matter what happens, Flash. Even if everything is all right, you'll scrub the thing. You don't have the nerve for it. From what I saw the other night, I don't think you've even got the guts to show up."

Flash growled. "Listen, I got guts. What the fuck are you talkin' about! I was the one who went into the jail to see my brother. I was the one who cased the court, talkin' to people, seein' how things run. I'm the only one who took any risks. So don't go sayin' I ain't got nerve, man. I've proved what I can do!"

"Words, Flash, just words," Gormley said softly. "We have all seen that you've lost your nerve. That right, Al?"

Martin's thin face was white and grim. "That's right," he said quickly. "Gormley's right. We've all seen you coming apart on this thing."

Flash looked from Martin to Gormley. "Okay, so I was scared. But I'll be ready for tomorrow, you'll see."

"We can't take that risk," Gormley said, his voice soft, almost friendly. "And we all need our sleep, so we can't waste the night standing guard over you. Besides, tomorrow you'd be all alone in that courthouse. You could do something to blow the whistle on us even if you didn't mean to. I'm really sorry about this, Flash."

Flash Johnson recognized mortal danger. His street

instincts went to work. "You guys are kidding, right? I mean, you sound like you're going to off me right here and now. Shit, you all gots nothin' to worry about old Flash." He sat up gradually, getting his legs ready. "Besides, Jesse would be really pissed—" He made a swipe for Gormley's gun but it was pulled out of reach, and he missed.

Al Martin hit him along the side of his temple with the butt of his pistol. Martin wasn't a powerful man, so Flash didn't lose consciousness; the blow just hurt his head. He tried to shift his position so that he could get at the knife in his pocket.

Both men pinned his arms against the chair. Gormley forced all his weight against the struggling figure as he shoved his revolver hard into Flash's chest.

The sound of the shot, although muffled, made both women jump. They had expected it, but as with a child overinflating a balloon, knowing what would happen did not lessen the shock of the noise.

Al Martin stepped out into the kitchen, his face white.

"Is he dead?" Thelma asked.

Martin lit a cigarette, puffing at it nervously. "Yes."

Back in the other room Larry Gormley stared at the body. He had never seen anyone die before. The odor of gunpowder seemed almost overwhelming. He felt a wave of nausea, and he realized his hands were shaking. It wasn't like the books. The reality of death had unnerved him. Panic seized him. He wanted to run, to get away, to deny what he had done. He felt tears welling in his eyes.

If the others should see him reacting as he was, all was lost, he knew that. They would only follow him if they knew he was strong. If he transmitted his fright and panic to them, it would all be over.

Larry Gormley forced himself to look away from the corpse. He inhaled deeply and willed his stomach to obey his intellect. When he was young, he had bitten the inside of his cheek to control the show of emotion. The pain always stopped laughter or tears. He bit the cheek hard, his head jerking. Quickly he wiped his eyes with his handkerchief.

It was no more than "buck fever," the shock any hunter feels at first, he assured himself. All revolutionaries must have felt the same the first time they had been forced to kill.

Breathing more evenly now, Gormley lit a cigarette, satisfied that at least his hands had stopped shaking. He was afraid to look at Flash's body. The panic was still there, although he was getting the telltale signs under control. He had never expected to experience such a reaction. It shocked him. Fear—he thought he had long ago laid fear to rest. He remembered the terrors of his childhood, but he had conquered those terrible feelings. It was ironic. He had executed Flash because he thought the man might turn coward; now he wondered about himself. He knew he had to put on a show for the others.

They stared at him as he stepped into the kitchen.

He looked at them. "That had to be done," he said, keeping his voice low and calm. "He was a danger to the operation."

They silently nodded their agreement.

Gormley forced himself to walk casually to the kitchen table. He began to gather up the maps.

"What will we do with him?" Alice Mary asked, her voice almost a whisper.

Gormley was acutely conscious of another wave of nausea. "We'll use the other apartment tonight. There won't be any odor for a while, and by the time they find him, we will be safe in Africa."

They seemed stunned.

"Come on, goddamn it," Gormley said. "Let's get the hell upstairs. We'll need all the rest we can get. God knows when we will get the chance to sleep again." He had the maps and strode quickly toward the apartment door, carefully keeping his eyes away from the body in the chair. He bit the inside of his cheek again.

They followed him silently. As soon as he was out of the apartment, Larry Gormley felt immense relief. He raced up the flight of stairs, grateful for the chance to breathe deeply without having to explain.

He was in control again. "Tomorrow will be a great day," he said as they entered the other apartment. "What happened tonight should prove to each of us that we are determined and that we will succeed." The shock of fear was being replaced by exhilaration. "Tomorrow we will be famous."

He could see that his rising enthusiasm was infecting them. "Tonight we are just nameless people. Tomorrow each of us will be known all around the world."

Al Martin grinned, and Thelma nodded. Only Alice Mary still showed shock.

Gormley was pleased with himself and proud of his control. He had never shown them his fear. They would still follow him, and tomorrow *would* be a great day.

But that night Larry Gormley could not sleep. He tried to think of the plan, to keep his mind occupied with the court, but he kept seeing the eyes of Flash Johnson at the moment of death.

the information desk

ONE of the jurors sipped his coffee while he leaned against the rail of the information desk. Red Mehan was a character, a real character. The juror told his family every night about him and the other strange people in criminal court, but he knew they thought he was making it all up. Although it was the end of the working day, Red Mehan seemed as fresh as if it were just the beginning.

"Ya know, this so-called crash program is a lot of shit. Goddamn, you ought to see the stream of slime that pours in and out of here all day long. I see it all here. This is a good spot to see everything interesting.

"The lawyers bring in their scumbag clients, plead them guilty to anything they want, then waltz them right out onto the streets. Fuck, I haven't seen so many happy faces since I was a kid at Christmas. And when you come to think of it, they got a big black Santa Claus upstairs giving out lollipops to every thief and stickup man in the city.

"It's hard to believe, but yesterday a young lawyer stops by here. He tells me he has this client who shot a friend, fatally, you know. Anyway, they got this guy on second-degree murder. Shit, the kid lawyer comes down here, and Tingle goes for manslaughter and the sentence is—hang on to your hat—one year probation and a two-hundred-dollar fine. Honest to God! No fix either, just the normal course of business. I ain't ever seen anything like this.

"But you know, it all boils down to money. Nobody

wants to shell out any more taxes, see? They want all these crazy bastards put away and safe streets, but they ain't about to spend one extra cent for more prisons or more cops, no way.

"So there you are. You got crime and lots of criminals but not enough jails or enough cops or even enough of these crazy judges, so what do you do?

"It sounds nuts, even to me, but they just started letting everybody go. Saves money, looks good on paper, and nobody is howling. If it works, don't fuck with it, ain't that the old rule?

"Ya know, I've been around long enough to remember how it was in the old days. Jesus, they had enough cops to do the job. I mean, if someone got killed, the precinct dicks and the homicide boys came down like gangbusters. They worked every witness, looked under every rock. They had the people and the time. Damn, nowadays unless somebody comes into the station and confesses, they ain't interested. They don't have the time or people to do even a half-assed job.

"And it's the same down here in the courts. They used to have savvy old prosecutors in those days. Lawyers didn't have it so good then, and a steady job was a big thing. They really had competent men then. You either did a good job or you got your ass fired. Now all they get is bright-eyed kids out of law school. I mean, they seen Perry Mason on the tube, right? And they figure they know how it's done. Meanwhile they get their dumb asses wiped by the real operators around here. Then when these young guys get smart enough to do a good job, they quit, go into trial work, and make a real buck for themselves.

"And take the judges. It's hard to get good ones. Most sharp lawyers can make more on the outside. What do they need with a judgeship? Oh, now and then you get a few good ones. But somebody said this is the age of medi-

ocrity, right? The salaries here can't match the big money in law practice, so you generally get a lot of lightweights, a bunch of hacks just putting in time toward a pension. You sure don't get the guys with brains anymore, at least not as a rule.

"Same with the cops. I guess it's the same all over. The system sort of rewards mediocrity. You know the old saying: You only get what you pay for. Well, that applies to justice the same as apples. You buy cheap apples, you get lousy apples, right? You buy cheap justice, you get lousy justice.

"No, I ain't no philosopher, I just watch what goes on, that's all. You watch and you learn. And I been doin' a lot of watching around this 'Zoo' for a long time brother, a long, long time."

3

the
sequence

chapter seven

5:30 a.m.

FRANCIS Xavier Conroy studied his face in the bathroom mirror. The drinking, he decided, was beginning to show, especially in the mornings. His eyes were bloodshot, his skin puffy and sallow. He held out his hands. At least tremors had not yet begun.

He felt better than usual. He had managed to ration the liquor and had not become roaring drunk, only happy, or as happy as he was capable.

Conroy switched on the radio. The voice of the morning disc jockey was full of cuteness and overenthusiasm. Conroy put up with it only because the news was next. He shaved as he listened to the account of the previous day's happenings—the usual procession of conspiracies and war threats, a recital of murder and mayhem. Even the stock market and weather reports were dismal.

Conroy slipped into the shower and let the stinging water wash away the feelings of despair and uselessness he was experiencing. He knew he had to make a determined effort to raise his spirits, or he was in for another self-destructive drinking bout. He toweled off briskly, hoping he could find some promise in the coming day.

It would be difficult. Awaiting him was the agony of the men in the drunk tank, a long day of work, and then the report to the judges' meeting in the evening. He consoled himself with the thought that he would be too busy to start drinking too early, even if the depression did not lift.

8:15 a.m.

"COME on, Simes," the guard called. "Your lawyer is here to see you."

Simes, who had spent a restless night full of bad dreams, forced himself to walk casually after the guard. He had to be careful to do nothing to excite suspicion in Hagen or Johnson.

The young lawyer waited in the interview cell, a pane

of glass separating them with microphones for communication.

"Look, Simes, make this fast. I have to be in court in fifteen minutes."

Gus Simes swallowed. Everything was pressure. "Listen, what will that *Harold Hawkins* decision do as far as I'm concerned?"

The lawyer shrugged. "That's what I thought you wanted to talk about. It doesn't do a thing for you. If you're convicted of first-degree murder, it can mean the death penalty."

"Even if I didn't do the actual killing?"

"Nothing's changed. Like I told you before, that doesn't make any difference legally. Now, it might with a jury, you never know. But under the law you face the same thing Hawkins faces."

"The gas chamber."

"Right." The lawyer shifted and looked at his wristwatch. "I have to be going."

"Wait a minute," Simes's voice was an urgent whisper. "If I came up with something, I mean something really big, would they go for a deal? All I want is a life term, no death penalty. That's all I'd ask."

The lawyer looked skeptical. "What could you come up with?"

"If I had something, something that could save a few lives, for instance, would they deal?"

"I suppose so. It would have to be pretty good, though."

Simes could feel his palms sweating. He never trusted the microphones. He knew he could be talking into a tape recorder, or worse, to a guard who might tip off Hagen or Johnson. But there was no other way.

"You know that I'm in the same cell block as Hagen and Johnson, right?"

214   ■   WILLIAM J. COUGHLIN

"I didn't know, but I suppose that makes sense. They usually keep the murderers together." The lawyer smiled weakly. "I mean, the men accused of murder. So?"

"So Hagen and Johnson have become very buddy-buddy with me. I even joined their screwball outfit to get information."

"The World Liberation Army?"

"Yeah."

The lawyer smiled. "You're right about them being screwballs."

"I know," Simes agreed, "but they're dangerous."

"Go on."

Gus Simes almost pressed his face to the glass, he was so intense about this, his only chance for survival. "They're planning something. A breakout."

"When?"

"I don't know. But as far as I can tell, it's sometime soon. They're relaxed as hell. Not even that *Hawkins* thing bothered them."

"Did they tell you what they planned to do?"

"No. They just told me I'd be a part of it."

The lawyer sneered. "That's not even a good try, Simes. I'd be a fool if I went to the sheriff with that story—my client noticed Hagen and Johnson are relaxed and suspects a break. You'll have to come up with something better than that."

"But they aren't going to tell me."

The lawyer stood up. "See what you can do. If anything changes, and I don't mean in your imagination, let me know. I have to go to court now."

Simes was led back to the cell block. He felt condemned, lost.

"How'd it go, man?" Johnson asked as Simes walked by without seeing him.

"Huh?"

"Your lawyer? Did he offer any hope?"

Simes shook his head.

"Gus, don't you worry. You're with us, and we'll do more for you than a regiment of lawyers."

"Like when?" Simes asked out of desperation.

"You'll know that when it happens." Johnson stood and patted Simes on the back.

Simes watched the black man walk over to Hagen, who was reading a magazine. Hagen and Johnson clasped hands and grinned at each other, obviously excited.

Gus Simes sensed that whatever it was, it would happen today. But who would believe him?

He would have to stay close to Hagen and Johnson and hope he could get information, the kind that would save him from the death house.

And if he didn't, maybe going out with Johnson and Hagen wouldn't be such a bad idea after all.

Simes was a desperate man.

8:50 a.m.

CLYDE Powell greeted Cannonball O'Brien as they climbed out of their cars in the judges' parking lot under the court building.

"Well, Judge, I haven't had much time to talk to you since we've been under the new system," Powell said. "How have things been going?"

Cannonball adjusted his coat over his protruding stomach. "This whole thing sucks, Clyde. I have had my ass run right off this past month. I don't know about your people, but my staff is bitching about the long hours. Morale isn't very high around here, I'd say."

"Are you going to bring that up at tonight's meeting?" Powell asked.

O'Brien, who usually responded with bombast, looked thoughtful for a moment. "You know, I can't stand that fucking Tingle running my courtroom, but I have to admit he is getting the job done. It's a pain, and I'd do things a lot differently, but I think I'll let it ride for a while before I speak out against it. You know—give 'em enough rope and let them hang themselves."

Powell smiled slightly. "No problems with the docket?"

O'Brien shook his head. "Oh, there were some at first, but I had it out with Tingle, and we got the rough edges honed down. It's working well enough now."

Powell nodded. Obviously Tingle had agreed to let Cannonball play his old games with the docket, and that had satisfied the feisty judge. He had been right, Tingle had O'Brien in his pocket.

Still, there were others.

9:05 a.m.

THE expressway was clogged. According to the radio, a steel truck had overturned, blocking two lanes. It would make him an hour late at least, but even this failed to irritate Mickey Noonan.

Locked in a solid river of cars, he sat back and relaxed.

He smiled to himself. They couldn't start without him. At other times he might have found this forced idleness a cause for rage, but now it gave him some time for private reflection.

His life, he decided, was like traveling on a freeway. His career, like his car, moved along with traffic, capable of great speed but contained by others. And once in a while he hit a backup like the present road condition. But that never lasted long, and he was always released to roar again toward his objective.

His career would soon take off like a high-powered race car. He felt a thrill of anticipation.

It was a good feeling. Even his family had sensed the change. He was spending much more time at home now. A spotless background was part of the deal. It was all image. A man, if rich enough, could hire image makers and buy the office of senator or governor. No experience was needed, just money and know-how. And the money and know-how were going to be supplied for him. He knew the price, and he was willing to pay it. Favors, influence, it was all part of the political mosaic.

He thought of Kathleen Ann Mulloy. She was a nice kid, he had to admit that, but certainly not worth losing what he had been promised. Anyway, she was a good-looking woman and would soon find a replacement. He fancied that any replacement for him would suffer by comparison.

9:15 a.m.

JUSTICE Tingle smiled at the lineup of lawyers waiting outside Judge Harbor's chambers. They grinned and nodded, happy participants in bargain day. Tingle strode into the chambers and found Harbor seated behind his desk, clothed in his judicial robe.

"Good morning, Milton," Tingle greeted him. "Sorry to be late, but Judge Sloan buttonholed me on the way up."

Harbor looked relieved that he had arrived.

"How we doing?" Tingle asked, taking his seat next to Harbor.

"We haven't started."

Tingle arched an eyebrow. "This is a fast track, Milt. Can't waste time."

"I didn't want to start until you came," Harbor said almost in a whisper.

"I'm flattered, Milton, but you're the one running the show here. I'm just an advisor. Pretty soon I'll be back up at the supreme court." Tingle saw the look of fear in Harbor's eyes. The man was out of his depth and knew it. "Of course, I don't expect you'll be wasting your talents in criminal court very long." Tingle winked, and Harbor relaxed.

"What did Judge Sloan want?" Harbor asked. "Is it about tonight's meeting?"

Tingle lit a cigar, allowing the acrid smoke to swirl about Harbor's distressed features. He loved watching his discomfort. The pompous little ass was really getting on his nerves. "He expressed the thought that the court was doing too much work. I think that's the main complaint we'll hear tonight." Actually, old Sloan had said just the opposite. He was, in his half-senile way, enthusiastic about the program. Tingle figured the old crook was making more money than he was. Sloan knew a bonanza when he saw one, and Tingle was sure the old judge was doing a land office business on the side.

"I'm worried about tonight," Harbor said, coughing nervously.

"Don't worry, Milt. We got these guys right in our pocket. Wait until you see the afternoon paper."

Harbor looked up at him like a dog to his master.

Tingle grinned. "I spent the better part of the evening with Mike Talbot, the managing editor over there. Shit, I fed him facts and figures like slop to a hungry hog. Damn, he couldn't get enough. By the way, I pointed out that you were the chief man behind the program. Mike says we'll have a front-page story on how effective our program is and an editorial—he said he would write it personally—about the miracle taking place in criminal court. How's that?"

For a moment Tingle was afraid Harbor was going to cry. His eyes watered with joy.

"So you see, Milt, by the time the afternoon paper hits the stands, the judges who are looking to do in our little program will have had their nuts cut clean off. Not bad, eh?"

Harbor swallowed. "I'm pleased, James." He coughed on the blue cigar smoke. "I am really pleased."

"Good!" Tingle slapped him on the back, almost banging the small man's head on the desk. "Then let's get to work, shall we? We have to live up to all those stories." He called to the court officer. "Send in the first case."

10:15 a.m.

GINGER Steiner knew she had a losing case. More important, her client, Chester Roberts, knew it. The small black man seemed to accept his fate with good grace. He understood that all of his troubles were self-made, not only the burglary itself but the failure to show up for the first court appearance. It meant a number of years in prison, but he accepted it. It was like being in a traffic accident and having your leg broken. There was nothing much you could do about it, the leg was broken and that was that. He felt the same way about the prospect of jail; there was nothing much he could do about that either.

Although Little Chester had accepted the ultimate outcome, Ginger Steiner had not and was determined to give the case her very best shot. She had three very good reasons to do so. First, she felt a responsibility to Chester Roberts, to give him the very best defense possible under the circumstances. Secondly, she needed the court experience, and this trial would provide a rehearsal vehicle to try out various techniques of persuasion. She wished to perfect her skills. A need to impress the assistant prosecutor was her third, and perhaps most important, reason.

The tall, sandy-haired prosecutor fascinated her. No man had stirred her so in a long time, and she wondered why. Ginger Steiner admired good attorneys, and Ace Gilbert certainly knew his job. But he had begun the trial with an almost jaded attitude, as if he no longer really cared about the outcome. Just a competent workman doing a competent job, no more, no less. But when she had prodded him, he had responded, getting better, putting more of himself in view as she made him work. There was real power in him, and she was bringing it out. Perhaps he was the sort of man who needed a certain kind of woman, a woman who had the intelligence and ability to challenge his talent into full explosive bloom. She warmed to that prospect. She knew that her tactics had aroused his interest. If challenge was the key to unlocking the fiery instincts inside Mr. Ace Gilbert, Ginger Steiner was determined to provide it in full.

Before the arguments started, Judge Powell handled a few sentences. The jury was waiting in the jury room. Soon they would file out. Ginger Steiner felt a rising excitement, just as she had when she had been on the stage. It was like waiting for the curtain to go up. Some actors were terrified, their nerves causing them untold agonies as they waited for their moment to go on. But Ginger had been the other kind, the performer who loved center stage, who trembled too, but with the anticipation of giving a great performance, a performance that would bring the house down. She felt like that now as she waited.

The prosecutor would argue first. She presumed that Ace Gilbert's presentation to the jury would be as complete and logical as had been his presentation of the evidence. He would be intellectual, but his summation would be done without spending much emotional energy.

She would play off that cold logic. It would be her chance to star. She knew she lacked Gilbert's expertise and experience, and the facts of her case were terrible. Still, she would give that jury and Mr. Gilbert a performance they would never forget.

The excitement of anticipation gripped her.

11:00 a.m.

ALTHOUGH there hadn't been as many drunks as usual, they had been even more odious, making up in stench for what they lacked in numbers. Frank Conroy was glad to get away from them. He knew that none of their fragrance actually lingered on him, but it always seemed that way. He stopped for a cigarette, letting the smoke wash into his nostrils.

Depression's iron fingers kept grasping for his mind. He knew the signs and the feelings. It could only end up in another bout with the bottle.

The main office of the probation department was a hub of activity. Every typewriter was being used, some by experienced typists, others by two-finger, hunt-and-peck people. The reports had to get out somehow.

So many telephones were being used that the office looked like a bookie parlor at race time. Telephoning had replaced home visits during the crash program.

Kermit Blackburn was using the telephone at Conroy's desk. He nodded but made no effort to get up.

"Yeah, that's right, Mrs. Schrieber, Kermit Blackburn of the probation department. It's about your son, Eddie."

He looked at Conroy and made a disgusted grimace. "No, Eddie isn't into any new trouble, Mrs. Schrieber. It's the old trouble I'm talking about. You know he was convicted of molesting a minor last week, right?"

Blackburn sighed as he listened to the reply. "I know he pleaded guilty, lady. But that's the same thing as a conviction. Look, I need some information about Eddie for our report."

Frank Conroy perched on the desk and lit another cigarette.

"Okay, lady," Blackburn said into the phone, "I have Eddie's record in front of me. He's nineteen years old, and this is his third conviction for sex offenses." Blackburn's lips pulled back in a snarl. "Yes, I know they were all girls, Mrs. Schrieber. But they were all little girls, girls under the age of sixteen. That's a crime, you understand?

"What do you mean, Eddie's a good boy!" The words were almost shouted into the telephone, then Blackburn continued in a calmer voice. "Okay, to you he's a good boy. Look, let's get to the questions, okay? Does he keep late hours?" Blackburn started down a list of prepared questions. The answers would form the bulk of his report.

There was an almost visible sense of frustration in the office. No one could do his or her job properly. But an attempt had to be made to satisfy the law. It was no more than a sham, but, Conroy supposed, a necessary sham under the circumstances.

Kathleen Ann Mulloy sat in front of her typewriter, staring at it. Conroy walked over.

"How's it going? You look like you ran out of lies."

She was startled. "Oh, Frank," she said, looking up. "How are you?"

He sat on the edge of her desk. She had been crying again. Her puffy red eyes told the story.

"I asked how you were doing?"

"Harried, like all the rest." She forced a smile.

"That's work. How about other things? Are you keeping your chin up?"

She looked away, her lip trembling slightly. "I'm not doing too well, Frank." Her words were no more than a whisper.

He studied her. The dark rings under her eyes were only partially concealed by makeup. Frank Conroy had spent his life, clerical and lay, making judgments on people, estimating their emotional reserves, their inner strengths. Kathleen did not look good. He felt he would have to do something.

"I wonder if you might give me a hand, Kathleen. I hate to ask, I know you're busy, but this could be important."

She looked at him.

"Harry DuMont stuck me with making the report for our office at that judges' meeting tonight. The man is afraid of the black robes, so I got handed the duty. Considering what's been happening here during this crash business, I may be in for some rough sledding. Do you think you could give me a hand with preparing the report? And go with me to the meeting, just for moral support?"

Her eyes widened. "I couldn't, Frank!"

"I know you're busy."

She shook her head, looking around to make sure no one could hear them. "He'll be there, Frank. I couldn't face him, really."

Conroy's voice was kind, but firm. "You'll have to deal with it eventually, Kathleen. It's like pulling adhesive tape off delicate skin. The quicker the better—it hurts less that way."

"I really don't think I . . ."

His voice was just above a whisper, audible only to her. "Life goes on, Kathleen. You can't let this thing ruin your life. Face up to it. The shock of seeing him isn't going to kill you. Maybe you'll start to see him for what he really is, just another flawed human being, just another kind of jerk. He certainly isn't the romantic hero that you've built him into being. You just need a touch of Old Man Reality—he's a great doctor. And the sooner the better."

She stared up at him, indecision written on her anxious features.

"I'll even buy you dinner afterward," Conroy grinned. "You know, you can really help me out on that report, if you will?"

She seemed lost in thought for a moment, then she looked up at him again. "Always the healer, aren't you? Okay, but if I skip out in the middle of that meeting, promise me that you'll understand."

"You won't skip." He smiled. "You have more courage than you think."

12:10 p.m.

THELMA Sturdevant had fixed tuna fish sandwiches. Despite his thin frame, Al Martin was always hungry. He gulped down a sandwich before the others had even touched theirs.

They were all in the women's apartment. No one wanted to admit he or she was squeamish about being in the same apartment with Flash Johnson's corpse downstairs, but Gormley knew and kept them away from there.

And he kept them busy.

They were tense, but Gormley felt that was a good thing. Like the sharp edge of a razor, they were honed and ready to do their job.

Gormley munched his food. He watched Martin quickly dispose of a second sandwich and Alice Mary Brennan, her square face grim, toying with hers. His eyes switched to Thelma Sturdevant. She had surprised him. She had come full circle. From a vacant-eyed girl tripping out on drugs she had progressed to a competent, efficient human machine. She carried out all orders quickly and without question.

"Let's finish lunch and run through the whole thing again," Gormley said.

"Must we?" Alice Mary asked. "I think we must all know everything backward by now. We've certainly gone over it enough."

"I want to run over the plan and the maps once more. Then we'll be ready. When we're done this time, we'll burn everything in the incinerator—notes, plans, maps, the whole works."

"Why?" Martin inquired, talking with his mouth full. "By the time they discover this place, everything will be all over, and we'll be on our way."

"Some of the maps are marked. And some of the notes tell where we're going. I don't want them to know that."

"Okay," Martin said. "That's reasonable. But let me finish lunch first."

12:25 p.m.

GINGER Steiner had surprised him. He already knew she was intelligent, that had been obvious during the trial. But he had never guessed at her polished style and ability when it came to argument. Ace Gilbert had seldom heard a better closing argument, and he had heard some of the best.

There was no way she could win the case, so he had just walked through his opening argument to the jury. He kept it short, feeling that the jury would appreciate brevity.

But he hadn't counted on her dramatic ability. Starting softly, she began what was really a lot of nonsense, but as she got going, the force of her personality and presentation made that nonsense sound plausible. The jury had been caught up in her enthusiasm. He had seen it in their faces. She was damned good. Even her client, Little Chester, perked up after she had made her argument to the jury.

Her speech was like a challenge. He arose to make his final argument. The prosecutor always had the last "say," since the state's burden of proof—guilt beyond a reasonable doubt—was so difficult. He made an attempt to match her enthusiasm, but he failed. He had the facts and the law on his side, but he could find nothing in the case that stimulated him or, he feared, the jury. His closing argument, he knew, lacked equal punch.

He looked at her as he returned to his seat after thanking the jury for their attention. Her eyes held an amused twinkle, as if she had played an immense trick on him and was enjoying it very much.

She was truly a beautiful woman. He had known that when he first saw her. She had intellect and personality to match her physical attractions. He was keenly aware of her.

Judge Powell smiled at the jury. "I see that it's lunchtime, ladies and gentlemen. I think we'll wait until after we've eaten before I give you my instructions as to the law in this case. I know it's a great temptation, but please don't discuss the case among yourselves or with anyone else. You'll have plenty of time for that when you come back here." Judge Powell glanced at his watch. "We'll recess until two o'clock sharp. Thank you."

The clerk rapped the gavel, and everyone stood as the judge left the bench. Little Chester was led away to the cell, and the jury filed out of the courtroom under the stern eye of the uniformed court officer.

Ginger Steiner stood up and brushed her hair back, allowing herself the luxury of relaxation. She knew he was watching her.

"You're pretty good," Gilbert said.

She turned and smiled as if she was seeing him for the first time. "Well, thank you." She put her note pad into her briefcase. "You're very good yourself, Mr. Gilbert."

"Not today, I'm afraid. Anyway, from now on I'm going to beware of pretty women with brains. A dangerous combination."

"A nice compliment, Mr. Gilbert," she said.

"Call me Ace, everyone else does."

Her eyes twinkled. "So I understand. Does that have any significance?"

He laughed. "Not much, I'm afraid. How about lunch, or do you have plans?"

Ginger Steiner looked pensive. "I really should go back to the office."

He started to speak, but she cut him off. "But a working girl has to eat. Where did you have in mind?"

1:10 p.m.

"JESUS, Horace, you should try these oysters, they're damned delicious." Justice Tingle slurped a mound of oysters from his fork.

Horace Ridley, former trial judge and distinguished lawyer, was appalled at Tingle's table manners. The man attacked food as if he were starving. Ridley, being black, felt that black professionals should conduct themselves with great dignity. He found his associations with the earthy Tingle distasteful—but profitable.

"Hey, Eddie," Tingle called loudly to their waiter. "Trot out another mess of those oysters."

Horace Ridley felt embarrassed and kept his eyes on the plate of broiled pickerel before him.

"You know, Horace, I really got those bastards off their ass and working over there." Tingle rammed half a roll into his mouth. "Hell, for a lot of them it's the first time they've put in a full day in years."

"I hear there's a lot of grumbling among the judges," Ridley said quietly.

"Hah!" Tingle's snort seemed to echo in the quiet restaurant. "Wait till you see this afternoon's paper. They do everything but nominate me for sainthood."

"Maybe. But a few of those judges have standing. They could give you trouble."

"Trouble, shit," Tingle said in a lower voice. "You're thinking about Clyde Powell. He's a fox, but I got this thing snowballing so that anyone who gets in its way will get crushed. I hope Clyde won't get in the way, I really do."

Ridley said nothing, just toyed with his water glass.

"This isn't forever, you know," Tingle went on, now almost in a whisper. "Christ, I'm knocking down that backlog, and in a few months I'll go back to the supreme court. Then Clyde and the rest of them can do what they want."

"What about Harbor?"

Tingle smiled. "The man is an idiot. I don't mean that he's just a little dull, either. I mean that little shit must have a borderline IQ. He can't do a thing for himself. He follows me around like a dog. When I leave, those others—Sloan, O'Brien, and the rest—will have him for breakfast."

"And the court's docket will pile up again."

"Probably."

"So what will it all accomplish?"

Tingle's face grew solemn. He sipped from his third bourbon. "Well, for one thing, counselor, it's making both of us rich." His voice was low, almost inaudible. "And it sets me up as a miracle worker. Politically, that ain't bad."

"And when the whole thing collapses?"

Tingle motioned to the waiter to bring him another drink and more food. "When it collapses, Milton Harbor will be ruined, in all likelihood. I will reluctantly come down again and take 'control' of the court. We can do this all over again. I like being a hero, especially a rich one."

Ridley shook his head. "You really understand the system."

Tingle smiled. "After all my years in politics, if I didn't, they should toss me out on my ass, right?"

The waiter brought another plate of oysters and another bourbon.

Tingle grinned. "You are paying for all of this, right, Horace?"

"It's deductible," the attorney said.

"So it's a business luncheon, then?"

Ridley lit a cigarette. "Yes, it's business. I have a client who is charged with conspiracy to gamble."

"Conspiracy's no big deal. Five years, tops."

Ridley inhaled deeply on his cigarette. "My client is on federal probation now. Any conviction will be a violation of that probation. He could serve both a state term and a federal term. There are other people interested. The feeling is that he might become too talkative if he faces all those years."

"Who is it?" Tingle asked.

"William Berman."

"You mean Blinkey Berman, the gambler?"

"That's the man."

"And you want the whole thing kicked, no lesser charge?"

"That's it. Any conviction would activate the federal probation charge."

Tingle wiped his mouth with the linen napkin and burped, causing Ridley to wince.

"Damned good oysters," Tingle said in way of explanation. "Look, that's awfully risky. If we take a lesser charge like we did with your man Racehorse, no one can really throw too many stones. You know—justice is served, the man did do time for the offense—that same old shit. But just dismissing a case can draw flies."

"There's a lot of money in it."

"How much? And don't try to low-ball me, Horace. Give me the top figure."

Ridley crushed out his cigarette. "Two hundred and fifty thousand."

"God," Tingle said, "that's my split?"

"Right."

Tingle thought for a moment. "How come his friends don't have Blinkey Berman erased? It's a hell of a lot cheaper."

"They believe he has left some information to be given to the authorities if he is . . . ah . . . erased."

"Smart fella."

"Seems so."

"Counselor, do you know of any persuasive legal reason that the court can dismiss this case?"

"The main witness is a coconspirator. She is being held as a material witness under the statute, although she wishes to be released."

Tingle played with his drink. "If she was released, bad things could happen. That witness might be killed or just disappear."

"She would probably disappear," Ridley said evenly. "As I said, a great amount of money is involved. Without their main witness, the prosecution's case would collapse."

"What's the name of this witness?"

"Cindy Farber. She's Blinkey Berman's lady love."

Tingle nodded. "I suppose a writ of habeas corpus might be slipped through. That would get her out of the jug. But if there's going to be big trouble, the deal is off. You can tell your friends that."

"They'll understand. There shouldn't be any trouble at all. The witness plans to marry Berman. A wife, of course, can't testify against her husband."

"The payment to be handled the same as with Race-horse?"

"If that suits you?"

Tingle grinned. "That suits me very well, very well indeed." He raised his glass, his eyes sparkling with good humor. "Here's to reform."

Ridley did not raise his glass in response. "You don't seem worried about the judges' meeting tonight."

"Hey!" Tingle grinned. "I'm too old a cat to be raped by a bunch of kittens like that. No sir, there's goin' to be no trouble, no way." He chuckled. "Can't have trouble if I expect to take care of good friends like yourself, can I?"

Ridley was glad the lunch was coming to an end. "I hope things go the way you plan."

"Oh, they will, Horace, they will. They don't call me the King for nothing."

1:35 p.m.

"OH, God! Not the fuckin' flower show again!" Eddy Milton, the chief of Channel 12's Mobile Unit protested. "Jesus, nothing moves over there, no broads, no gimmicks, just a bunch of pansies and old women sniffin' at the flowers. What the hell kind of a story do you expect us to shoot over there?"

Chuck Barry, the station's news and assignment editor shrugged. "Just pan over the flowers. We'll do a voice-over later if we use the footage."

Milton shook his head. "And this judges' meeting, what the hell do you expect there? We won't even be allowed into the meeting? We use film, remember? We need something that moves or talks."

Barry controlled rising anger, remembering that Eddy Milton was an extremely competent and imaginative television cameraman. The assignments were, he had to admit, frustrating. "Look, just set up in the hallway in criminal court. Maybe do a few interviews. We probably won't use the footage anyway. The other stations are covering the meeting, so we'll go along just to play safe. You never know."

Milton grimaced. "Jesus, what a dull fuckin' town! Nothing ever happens here."

"Maybe one of the old ladies at the flower show will moon you."

"If one does, it will be the most excitement we'll see." Milton turned and stalked out of the newsroom.

"Have a nice day," Barry called after him, knowing that it would irritate him. But the cameraman was right, it was a very dull day. They would have to do a lot of talking about the flower show tonight on the eleven o'clock news just to use up the time.

2:25 p.m.

ACE Gilbert always admired the way Judge Powell instructed a jury. He did it as a kindly teacher, explaining the laws in a simple way, letting the jury know exactly what each part of the law meant in relation to the facts in the case before it.

Some judges used the instructions to put their own stamp on the case. Like actors, they used facial expressions and voice tones to convey their own opinion of the evidence. It was unfair. Such tactics never showed in the typed transcript of a case on review. Some juries resented the intrusion by the judge into their province, and then the judicial antics backfired. But sometimes a judge's manipulation of the instructions robbed the defense of an impartial trial.

Clyde Powell never let the jury know what he thought. He just explained the law. He was always courteous and fair to both sides.

"In order to constitute a breaking," Powell's voice was gentle, "it is sufficient if the building or place be closed by the owner, his agents, or employees so that it would be necessary to use force, however slight, to gain access to the interior." Powell smiled slightly. "For example, the pushing open of a closed door, the opening of a screen door, the removing of a screen, or the raising of a window sash have all been held to constitute a breaking. If any force at all is necessary to effect an entrance into a building, through any place of ingress, usual or unusual, whether open, partly open, or closed, such entrance is a breaking sufficient in law to constitute burglary."

Powell leaned forward to explain further. "It is sufficient to establish an entering of the premises if, as a result of any breaking as I have defined it, any portion of the defendant's body was introduced into the building. As they used to say in law school, an example is a person raising a closed window and sticking his hand in. That would be a breaking and an entering."

Judge Powell continued, his voice containing sufficient animation to keep the jury's interest, unlike many judges who read the instructions in a dull monotone, which had the effect of a sleeping pill for everyone in the court.

Ace Gilbert was acutely aware of the presence of Ginger Steiner, seated across the counsel table. Occasionally he glanced over at her. She was politely intent upon Judge

Powell's remarks. Her profile was almost Egyptian. It reminded him of sculptures of Egyptian queens he had seen in museums. She was a beautiful woman.

He wondered what she thought of him. They had agreed not to discuss the case, and it had been a wonderfully flirtatious lunch. She was so enthusiastic about being a lawyer. He could remember being that way once. Talking to her reawakened those feelings. She seemed interested in him, but then she had told him that she had once been an actress. If she was acting, she was very good indeed.

She caught him looking at her, and he quickly looked away. Ginger Steiner felt a rush of pleasure. She was genuinely intrigued by this complicated man they called Ace. Things were going very well.

Judge Powell began to define "reasonable doubt" to the jury.

3:00 p.m.

LARRY Gormley had checked through both apartments twice. He had searched every drawer and closet. Outside of Flash Johnson's corpse, now stiffened grotesquely, nothing else remained that might tell the authorities anything about them. Although he avoided looking at the body, there was no recurrence of the previous evening's panic.

He had collected all notes, papers, maps, and other similar material. Not trusting the others to do it, he took the filled basket to the incinerator himself. Most people just opened the steel door in the hall and dumped their trash.

But Larry Gormley lit each paper separately and waited until it flamed fully before allowing it to drop down the shaft.

Finished finally, he closed the steel door and walked back to the apartment.

They were waiting for him. Each was dressed as they had planned. The weapons and explosives were already checked and in their assigned receptacles. Everything was ready.

Gormley looked at the others. They were tense, but not overly so. They were trained to the edge he wanted.

"Tonight, we will make history," he said softly. "Let's go."

They preceded him, then he closed the apartment door for the last time.

3:30 p.m.

As soon as he finished instructing the jury, Judge Powell retired to his chambers to read the newspaper editorial once more. It was quite a triumph for the King. The editorial read as if Tingle himself had written it. Perhaps he had. There seemed no end to the power of James Tingle. With the backing of the press and the public, he appeared to be impregnable to attack.

Only Clyde Powell was prepared to make a fight now.

It might not be politically smart, but he believed it was the right thing to do.

Powell had to admit there was wisdom in Richards's advice. If he seemed to go along with Tingle's program, he would be left alone. But if not, Tingle would attack. Clyde Powell knew just what the King would do. It wouldn't be direct. First would come the subtle suggestion that old Judge Powell was bitter about losing the post of executive judge. And then Tingle would hint that perhaps age had caught up with Judge Powell. He would be leading the pack to tear Clyde Powell to pieces.

Still, someone had to do something. He would make a fight of it, win or lose.

3:45 p.m.

GUS Simes had not been able to finish lunch, even though the food had looked good for a change. He was too upset to eat.

Danger—that word seemed to echo through all his thoughts. If he failed to find out Hagen and Johnson's plans, he would end up in the gas chamber. On the other hand, if he tried too hard to discover their purpose, there was an equally good chance that Hagen or Johnson would finish him off much more quickly. Still, he had to try. *Danger*—it was a fitting description of his situation.

Johnson had become more tense as the day wore on. Simes walked up and shared a cigarette with him. It was Gus's last cigarette, so the sacrifice was more than a mere courtesy.

"Man," Simes said, "you keep telling me that I'm an officer in your army, but I really don't know what the hell's going on. Hagen just laughs when I try to talk to him. And you give me nothing but political philosophy. If we're going to pull something off, I better know just what you guys expect of me."

"Just hang in there." Johnson spoke softly.

Simes forced himself to look directly into Johnson's eyes. "I'm going to have to do something myself," Simes said, whispering. "I got to get the hell out of here. I didn't kill anybody, but they are going to burn me anyway. I can't count on you people. I've been around, I know all about jails. I'll make my own damned plans to get out of here."

"You're goin' out, Gus. Just cool it."

Simes was determined to goad Johnson into revealing what was going to happen. "You guys are nothing but hot air, you know that? I really thought a lot of you and Hagen. I had respect, man, I really bought those ideas you told me about. But I can see it's all fairy-tale stuff. There ain't no 'army,' and you guys are going to death row just the same as me. It's all been just a bunch of crap!"

"Ain't no bullshit!" Johnson's eyes narrowed in anger.

Despite being frightened, Simes persisted. "What is it, then? Nothing, that's what. You guys got nothing going."

Johnson's facial muscles rippled with suppressed rage. "Don't push it."

Somehow Simes found the courage to continue. "I'm going out by myself. I don't need you or your fairy tales."

Johnson grabbed the front of Simes's shirt and pulled him roughly forward, bringing Simes's ear next to his lips. "Listen, asshole, it's tonight." The words came out in a hiss. "You dig? Now keep your shit together and your mouth shut."

"Tonight?" Simes whispered.

"Yeah."

"How you going to . . . I mean, what's going to happen?"

"You'll know that when it happens. You'll have duties then. But for now keep loose and shut up." Johnson released him and walked away.

Simes's heart was beating wildly. His cigarette had burned down almost to his fingertips. To push for more information would certainly be fatal. But perhaps he had enough now. He fought to control his fright and excitement.

Simes waited until Johnson had lain down in his cell and Hagen was playing cards with another prisoner. He idly moved to the front of the cell block.

The guard was seated close by. He looked up. "Hey, Simes, what's with you?"

"Call my lawyer, will you? It's important." Simes spoke in practiced convict fashion, his words audible to the guard alone.

"You just saw him this morning."

"I know, but this is important."

"Christ, if it isn't one thing, it's another. I'll call him if I get a chance."

"Please!" The whispered word carried all of Simes's desperation.

The guard sighed. "Okay, I'll call when I go on break. Christ, you'd think you people were star athletes or rock stars or something—all the time ask, ask, ask."

4:00 p.m.

WHEN the guard's telephone call came into the public defender's office, Simes's assigned lawyer wasn't there. A message was put in his box.

His lawyer was in the prosecutor's office discussing another case with the head of that office's Homicide Trial Division.

The matter settled, the young public defender was about to go when he thought about Gus Simes.

"Say, while I got you," he said to the prosecutor, "I have another murder case coming up for trial."

"Which one?"

"Gus Simes."

"I don't recall . . ."

"He and his partner were doing a daylight burglary at an unoccupied house when the police came up. The partner was killed trying to escape. Simes was bound over for first-degree murder."

"So?"

"I know that he's technically guilty, but he really didn't kill anyone. He's not the type. How about second-degree murder?"

The prosecutor thought for a moment and then threw up his hands. "Oh, why not. Christ, the court's letting everybody go anyway. Hell, they'd probably give him manslaughter or double parking. Sure, I'll settle for second-degree. Will your man go for it?"

"Like a burglar."

They both laughed.

4:10 p.m.

Larry Gormley walked leisurely into the Criminal Court Building. He looked like any of the attorneys hurrying about or lounging in the halls. He wore a three-piece suit, the vest concealing a pistol tucked in his waistband, his coat open so that the bulge of the revolver could not be seen.

In his briefcase he had the British Sten gun, its metal stock folded against the barrel, several full clips, and two hand grenades. Gormley held the case firmly under his arm.

He was taking Flash's duties: watching for trouble and directing the initial part of the plan.

Everything seemed normal. People came and went. There was the usual collection of lawyers, witnesses, policemen, and hangers-on. The redheaded cop in the information booth was busily talking to a young uniformed patrolman.

Thelma Sturdevant entered the building. Her weapon-laden purse was slung over her shoulder. She glanced at Gormley. He did nothing, gave no signal. Everything was going well. She turned and walked calmly toward the back of the building and the bank of elevators.

Gormley felt the rising throb of excitement. It had started.

4:20 p.m.

JUDGE Powell returned from a short conference with Mickey Noonan. He had read the man correctly. Noonan wanted no part of a fight with Tingle. He wearily admitted that the program destroyed the basis for any justice, but like Abrams and Richards, he cautioned that now was not the time to oppose Justice Tingle. Rather than being depressed, Powell felt a sense of growing determination. It was a matter of principle. Sometimes winning wasn't everything.

He was amused to see Ace Gilbert perched on the counsel table talking earnestly to the good-looking woman attorney. He had watched Ginger Steiner stalk her prey the last few days, and Ace Gilbert had been completely unaware that he was her target. The judge wondered if these wonderful insights were always saved for old age when they were of no help.

"Has the jury reached a verdict?" he asked his court clerk.

"No, sir, not yet. Ted says you can hear them arguing through the door. Shall we let them go home for the night, Judge?"

Powell shook his head. "No, we'll keep them at it a bit longer."

The judge walked over to where the two attorneys were talking. They were engrossed in each other and were startled when he came up.

"Please sit," he said, smiling. "Miss Steiner, it looks like the jury isn't near a decision. I thought we'd keep them awhile. Sometimes that helps, you know. However, I don't wish to inconvenience you. You can leave. If they come in with a question or a verdict, we can call your office."

"Thank you, Your Honor," Ginger said. "But I'd prefer to stay around a bit."

"There will be people here tonight," Powell said. "We are having our monthly judges' meeting in the executive judge's courtroom just down the hall. That shouldn't take too long. We should be out by six o'clock or seven. If the jury hasn't reached a verdict by then, I'll send them home for the night. Is that agreeable?"

"Certainly, Your Honor," Ginger Steiner replied.

"That's fine." Ace Gilbert looked pleased at having an excuse to spend more time with his opponent. "Is it okay if we wait here, Judge?"

"Absolutely. Like they used to say in the service— smoke 'em if you got 'em. Just blow away the smoke if the jury comes in. Keeps up appearances, you know."

"Will my client get dinner?"

Powell laughed. "My dear, perhaps the jury will free him, and in that case he will have to pay for his own meal. But if not, I'll make sure that he gets a sandwich if he has to go back to jail tonight."

"Thank you, Judge," she said.

"You're quite welcome. By the way, I'm right next door, Ace, so if the jury comes in, have one of my officers come into the meeting and get me. I'll take the verdict and then go back."

"Sure, Judge. Will the side door to Judge Harbor's courtroom be unlocked?"

"Oh, yes," he chuckled. "We aren't the college of cardinals. The doors are never locked. Our meetings are usually so dull that no one in his right mind would want to intrude, believe me."

"Maybe it won't be so dull tonight," Gilbert said.

Powell chuckled again. "I think I can guarantee that, Ace. There'll be fireworks, but I'm afraid they won't last long. I'm going to have a few things to say that may make me a bit unpopular around these parts, but I think I'll be alone. One-man wars don't take too much time, so I expect I'll see you two shortly."

Judge Powell left the two young people and began to run over again what he planned to say at the meeting. They wouldn't like it, but it was going to be said.

4:35 p.m.

CHANNEL 12's was the last crew to arrive. The other stations had already run their electric lines, set up their lights, and positioned themselves in the second-floor hallway

The Criminal Court Building layout was simple and easily covered. Each floor above street level contained two large courtrooms, one at each end of the building. A wide public hallway extended between the courtrooms, an elevator bank on one side and offices on the other. A second—and much narrower—hallway ran behind the elevator bank. It was for the private use of court personnel. It, too, connected both courtrooms.

A palatial marble staircase lead to the second floor and was located near Judge Harbor's end of the public hallway. Because of the width and length of the public hall all the crews had plenty of space to work without getting in one another's way.

The private hallway behind the elevators contained only a holding cell and a small private elevator, both located near Harbor's courtroom also. That corridor was of no interest to the newsmen, and besides, cameras weren't allowed in that area.

Eddy Milton directed the crew as they quickly set up the television camera and the lights. They were bored and anxious to call it a day. The flower show had been a washout; a huge hall full of garish floral arrangements but no people. They had duly taken pictures. Milton had their reporter lie in a bank of flowers for a gag. The place had had the overwhelming aroma of a funeral home anyway.

"How's it going, Eddy?" The crew chief for the IBC outlet walked over.

"Slow as shit. Bad day for news." Milton looked down at the IBC camera set up near the entrance to Judge Harbor's courtroom. "That a new talker you got?"

"Yeah, another pretty face for the eleven o'clock news. Jesus, in these rating wars they keep changing these guys like light bulbs. You come to work and there is a new talking face, all mouth and no brains."

"How's this new guy?"

"Not bad. Not smart, but a decent sort, you know."

"You're lucky."

The other crew chief nodded and wandered away.

Eddy Milton lit a cigarette. "I don't know why the hell they sent us here," he said to the audio man. "Nothing is going to happen except those assholes will spend all night patting each other on the back. Damn, but I hate politicians."

4:45 p.m.

ALICE Mary Brennan came through the door. She strode purposefully across the nearly empty lobby, her large purse and briefcase slung on each side of her like saddlebags. Her stern face defied interference. She looked like an angry high school principal on the way to give hell to an errant student. She stomped up the marble staircase.

Larry Gormley wanted a cigarette, but he also wanted his hands free, just in case, so he did not smoke. He was tense now, ready for action. He wished Al Martin would hurry.

Almost as if he had willed it, Martin came through the doors. He was the picture of a successful attorney carrying a large and obviously heavy evidence case. Martin's face was strained as he struggled with its weight. He did his best to hide his discomfort and tried to walk in a casual manner. At the stairway he put the case down and looked over at Gormley. Gormley stared back, giving no signal. Al Martin again gripped the case, lifted it, and started up the stairs.

Gormley watched him go. He took a deep breath and held it to calm his racing pulse. It was his turn. He walked along, listening to the click of his heels against the tile of the lobby floor. Then he, too, began climbing the wide staircase.

4:50 p.m.

JUDGE Herb Abrams felt relaxed. It promised to be an exciting evening. It had been a long campaign and now, at last, Sylvia Cohen was to meet him later for dinner. Dr. Cohen was in Cleveland at a conference. Sylvia had been most emphatic that only dinner was involved. But they both knew better than that. It was just a "for the record" statement, just part of the game. He thought of her cool loveliness and almost shuddered with pleasure.

The judges' meeting would be a nuisance. He would have ducked out, but he had promised Clyde Powell he would be there. Abrams didn't like Tingle's crash program any more than Powell did, but he knew that opposition at this time was political suicide. Still, Clyde was a friend, and a promise was a promise.

He stood up and stretched, feeling the exhilarating sense of life pulsating through every part of his body. It was a beautiful feeling. Abrams slipped into his suit coat and left for the meeting.

4:55 p.m.

KATHLEEN Ann Mulloy was white-faced, her lips compressed, her hands trembling slightly. It had seemed such a good idea when he had proposed it. It had made sense. She had to confront the problem, or it would overwhelm her. Noonan would be there, and she had to face him sometime—it was like lancing a boil.

Watching her, Frank Conroy had realized he had not anticipated the depth of pain it would cause the girl. He wondered if he had gone that one step too far. There was a danger in meddling with other people's emotions. Still he felt his decision had been correct. It was a case of kill or cure. He hoped it would result in a cure.

Conroy and Kathleen emerged from the elevator on the second floor. The television cameras and lights had been set up and the crews were standing around in the hall talking. Conroy was aware of two lawyers who were also in the hall. But he didn't recognize either man: a thin man with a pencil-thin moustache and a tall, well-built blonde who hugged a bulging briefcase.

Down the hall a thick-set woman watched through horned-rimmed glasses, her stern face grim. Conroy wondered who she was. If she was an attorney, God help the other side.

He held open the courtroom door, allowing Kathleen to enter. The executive judge's courtroom was no different from the others in the building. It was equally as large, with the same rows of spectators' benches. Most of the judges had already arrived. They were gathered around the two large counsel tables or were perched in the jury box. They looked different without their robes. Those black mantles had an aura of authority; they were a uniform of rank and power. Without them they looked like what they were: a collection of middle-aged and older men and one thin, mean old lady.

Mickey Noonan lounged in one of the chairs in the back row of the jury box. He didn't even raise an eyebrow when he saw Kathleen Mulloy. His expression never changed. Conroy disliked the man, not because of any lingering Catholic morality, but rather because he despised people who used other people and then discarded them without thought or pity. Mickey Noonan was that kind of man. Conroy hoped he could convince Kathleen that she had escaped destruction, for that was all the Noonans of this world ultimately offered. They were only users.

Judge Abrams hurried in through the side door, smiling and nodding to his colleagues.

Conroy and Kathleen took a seat in the first spectator row. Harold McNary, the chief assistant prosecutor, was there, sitting with Cletus Gillespie, the deputy chief of corrections. Conroy presumed they, too, would be called upon for reports of the month's progress.

Judge Milton Harbor came walking in, white-faced but in his robe—as a kind of defense against the people arrayed before him. Rather than joining the group of judges, he walked up to the bench and took his accustomed seat, looking down on the others.

The huge form of Supreme Court Justice James Tingle loomed in the doorway. He was loud and profane as he walked across the front of the courtroom, greeting some of the judges by name, playfully insulting a few, and ignoring others. He stepped up and took a seat in the witness chair, looking out at the judges. A wide, triumphant grin split his black face.

"Well, I see we're all here," he said jovially. "That's damned nice of everybody to be here on time. I appreciate it, and I know Judge Harbor does. Now, I know you all have important engagements this evening, so we'll get right to business."

chapter eight

THELMA Sturdevant walked down the staircase to the second floor. She felt little emotion. She just concentrated on doing what Larry had instructed her to do. The top of her purse was snapped open. She had her hand inside, gripping one of the pistols.

The television crews were set up in the hallway. She had expected them.

Alice Mary saw Thelma and started toward the court-

room door. Larry Gormley and Al Martin, talking together, also strolled toward the door. Thelma hurried to
carry out her part. The purse was heavy, the strap cut
into her shoulder, but she hardly noticed.

She opened the courtroom door and stepped in. There
was no policeman at the door, although there was a uniformed officer standing near the front of the court. She
saw a big black man sitting in the witness chair talking to
the others.

Thelma proceeded toward the front of the courtroom,
sensing that Alice Mary had come in behind her. She
could hear the heavy tread of the other woman's steps
behind her.

Thelma walked past the few people sitting in the front
spectator's row and started out into the courtroom proper.
She didn't look but she knew that Larry and Al were
already in the courtroom.

It was going just as they had planned.

Tingle felt in complete command of the meeting. The
faces of the judges were all turned toward him, some hostile and some expectant. "I know you all read the story
and editorial in today's paper. We have really turned
this court around during this past month, and the credit
doesn't belong to Milt Harbor or myself. It belongs to all
of you. You have pitched in and done one hell of a job,
and you have every right to be proud of your accom-
plishments."

He noticed that this bit of flattery drew a few faint
smiles from some of their stonelike faces. "As to tonight's
informal agenda," he continued, "I thought we would
have some brief reports from departments and offices
working with us: the prosecutor's office, the corrections
department, and our own probation office. They, too, have
been slugging it out in the trenches, and their hard work

has contributed greatly to our success. After the reports we'll excuse them and the court officer and have a brief executive session where we can really let our hair down, so to speak."

As an attractive blond woman in an expensive business suit entered the rear door of the courtroom, carrying a large purse, Tingle supposed she must be part of the probation department's representation. They had a lot of good-looking women working in that office, he thought.

"Before we start," Tingle said, "I would like to give you a few of our own case production figures. They are really outstanding." He stopped briefly as a heavy-set woman came into the room. She looked like a parole officer. "As you recall," Tingle continued, "the reason I was sent down here was because of the huge backlog of cases. That was only a month ago, although we have all been working so hard that I know it seems as if more than a mere month has gone by." At that point two well-dressed young men carrying briefcases came in the back door. They looked like lawyers. The two women had passed the delegations seated in the spectator rows and had now entered the court proper.

"Folks, I'm very sorry," Tingle said amiably, "but this isn't a public meeting. This is the monthly meeting of the criminal court judges, and we—"

The pretty woman pulled a pistol and leveled it at the uniformed court officer as the woman in the horn-rimmed glasses strode to the middle of the courtroom. She pulled a hand grenade from her purse. With her other hand she calmly pulled the pin, holding the grenade firmly to compress the safety lever.

The two men in the back moved swiftly. The blond man produced a short, snubby machine gun and snapped a long clip into it, holding the barrel pointed at the judges. The man with the moustache took out a pistol. He turned to face the rear door, obviously prepared to shoot anyone who entered.

"Don't even breathe," the pretty girl said to the uniformed officer, whose hands slowly rose toward the ceiling.

"Sit still," the blond man with the machine gun commanded as he walked forward. "Don't any one of you move. Do you all understand that?"

"What the hell is this?" Tingle demanded, his voice filled with rage.

"What does it look like?" the blond man said, smiling. "You are hostages."

"Now look, goddamn it—" Tingle began.

The machine gun's muzzle swung until it was pointing directly at Tingle's large stomach. "I told you to be quiet," the blond man said firmly. "We are the World Liberation Army. I think you've heard of us."

Judge Herb Abrams went cold with fear.

"This woman," the blond man indicated the heavy-set woman, "has a live antipersonnel grenade in her hand. If anyone gets heroic and something happens, that grenade will fall. The shrapnel will kill everyone within thirty yards. We are all in that range, so if you try anything, prepare to die. We are prepared to die."

The pretty woman took the officer's pistol and put it into her purse.

"Young man, we are all reasonable people," Tingle said, speaking very softly. "You can be assured that none of us will do anything to hurt you. However—"

The muzzle came his way. "*However* won't do!" the blond man snarled. "This isn't some kind of student demonstration. You'll do exactly what you are told." He looked around at the other judges. "First, I'm going to search each of you. Starting with you," he said to Harbor, who was almost out of sight beneath the bench.

Tingle hoped that Harbor wouldn't do anything idiotic.

Each bench had bulletproof steel built inside the knee hole so that if trouble came, the judge could drop down to safety. If Harbor tried to duck, Tingle felt these crazies might just spray bullets at the rest of them.

"Stand up, Milton!" Tingle commanded. "Now walk down front to where this young man can search you. Do it now."

The blond man raised a quizzical eyebrow, but Harbor obeyed. Tingle became slightly less tense.

"Keep your hands where I can see them," the blond man commanded Harbor. "And get that damned robe off."

Harbor quickly did as he was told.

The woman with the grenade now held a pistol in her other hand. The two women covered everyone while Larry Gormley searched each person carefully. Three of the judges and the chief assistant prosecutor had been carrying pistols. The weapons were confiscated. As each person was searched, he was directed to take a seat in the jury box. Soon all fourteen seats were filled—Tingle, the ten criminal court judges, the court officer, the prosecutor, and the corrections chief. Gormley pulled two chairs over in front of the box and faced them the same way as the other seats. Frank Conroy and Kathleen Mulloy took their places on these chairs. Gormley had searched Kathleen and Judge Woldanski in the same rough but efficient manner he had used with the men, running one hand over their bodies while keeping the muzzle of the machine gun pressed against them with the other.

Finally it was done. Gormley looked at the big black man. "You're Tingle, right?" he asked.

"I'm James Tingle."

"Okay, Tingle, you're the ranking man around here. So you'll do the talking to the authorities for us."

Tingle kept a placid face. "That depends, son."

The blond men stared at him. "I don't know if you

quite appreciate this situation or not. The probabilities are that we are all going to die. We are prepared for this, but I doubt that you people are. Unless this thing is handled absolutely correctly, there are going to be a lot of dead bodies in this courtroom." Gormley dropped his voice, speaking in an almost friendly manner. "As you can see, we have a number of weapons. But probably more importantly we have explosives. That single grenade there could wipe us all out. But we have enough to blow this entire building up. So please believe me when I tell you this is no bluff."

"I believe you, son," Tingle said quietly. The others were frozen into silence, except Cannonball O'Brien, who continually muttered under his breath.

Gormley glared at Tingle. "I would appreciate you not calling me 'son.' I don't call you 'boy.' "

"But I'm afraid I don't know your name," Tingle said evenly.

"My name is Larry. The woman with the grenade is Alice Mary. The other woman is Thelma, and the man at the rear door is Al."

"Thank you, Larry," Tingle said, "that is a help. Now, I presume there is something you people want?"

"That's right," Gormley said. "First, we want our brothers, Johnson and Hagen, to join us here."

The mention of those names caused Judge Abrams to feel another icy chill of fear.

"But they have been convicted of murder and are locked up," Tingle said softly, smiling.

"That's where you come in, Tingle. You will arrange for their release and have them brought to us here."

"Then what?" Tingle asked.

"First things first," Gormley replied firmly.

"Say, I have a heart condition." Judge Sloan spoke up, knowing that what he said was a lie. He was in perfect health. "I'm an old man. You people don't need me here. My medicine is upstairs, and I'm not feeling well."

Gormley shook his head. "Look, if you're going to die, you're going to die. We're all in this together, friend. A heart condition is something we can't do anything about." He looked at the others. "That goes for everybody. Get this through your heads. You are hostages who are, I presume, of some value to this community. So, you see, we can't give up anything so valuable."

Judge Abrams was seated in the second row of the jury box. His mind was working fast. There had to be a way out, especially for him. If they brought Johnson and Hagen back from jail, he didn't stand a chance. He tried to remain calm.

Frank Conroy was consumed with anguish at having brought Kathleen Mulloy into this. The young blond named Larry was right, he thought. Some of them would die. Kathleen certainly had a lot to thank him for. Conroy felt sick.

"Tingle," Gormley commanded. "I want you to come down here. Do it slowly."

"At my size there's no other way," Tingle said, surprised at his own sense of calm.

"We'll go into the office, and you can call and get Johnson and Hagen over here."

"All right, Larry." Tingle moved slowly, conscious that the muzzle of the machine gun moved with him. He walked ahead of Gormley into Harbor's office.

"Whom would you like me to call, Larry?"

"I'll leave that to you. The governor, the mayor, the chief of police, whoever has the authority to get those men over here. You pick him."

"All right." Tingle sat at Harbor's desk.

"Keep your hands where I can see them," Gormley commanded.

"Don't worry," Tingle said, forcing a smile. He knew the man called Larry was right. Matters would have to be handled just right or they would all die.

He dialed the mayor's private number and prayed that he would still be in his office. Gormley picked up an extension phone, holding the machine gun in one hand.

The secretary answered. She knew Tingle's voice and switched the call to the mayor.

"Hey, King," the mayor greeted him, "how you doing? I've been reading all this great stuff about you. Senator, governor? Where you going, Jim?"

"Frank." Tingle spoke slowly and evenly. "I'm afraid I'm in trouble. Please have your secretary pick up her extension and take down this conversation."

"You kidding?" the mayor asked.

"I'm afraid not," Tingle said quietly.

"Just a minute." There was a dull sound as the telephone was put on hold. Then, after a long minute, the mayor came back on the line. "Mary's all set, Jim. Go on, what's the problem?"

"I am in the executive judge's courtroom here at criminal court." Tingle spoke slowly and precisely so that the girl would have no trouble taking it down. "All the criminal court judges are here, and the chief assistant prosecutor, the deputy chief of corrections, two people from the probation department, and one uniformed officer." Tingle forced his attention away from the muzzle of the machine gun pointed directly at his sweating face. "There are four people here with guns . . ."

"No details about us!" Gormley hissed.

"These people also have explosives. One of them is standing in the middle of the courtroom with a live grenade. The pin is out, and she is holding it in her hand. Do you understand?"

"Oh, Jesus!" The mayor's response was a whisper.

Tingle continued. "We are completely at their mercy.

The officer has been disarmed. So far no one has been hurt, but things are pretty desperate."

"What do they want, Jim?" the mayor asked, his voice tense but businesslike.

"Apparently a number of things, but their first request is rather simple."

"Go on."

"They want the prisoners Johnson and Hagen released and brought up here to join them."

"That's not so simple. Those two have been convicted of murder."

Tingle's calmness was beginning to desert him. "These people claim they are part of the World Liberation Army. They want Johnson and Hagen up here."

"Tell them the answer is no."

Tingle felt a shiver of fear. "Don't say that so fast, Frank. We are in a hell of a spot up here."

"You know the way things are played, Jim," the mayor said, sensing that a terrorist was probably listening in. "It's public policy not to give in to these people. If you do, the sky is the limit."

"Think it over, Frank. These people are serious."

"We'll see."

Tingle's patience came to an end. "Look, goddamn it, Frank, these people are going to start killing. You damned well better get those two prisoners over here. If you're worried about responsibility, I'll take it. I'll order their appearance before me as a justice of the supreme court."

"Take it easy, Jim."

"Take it easy—hell. You're not here, Frank, and I am," Tingle snapped. "I know what I'm talking about. You get those two over here now!"

There was a pause. "Well . . . ah . . . let's keep this thing open-ended, Jim. I'll have to check this out. We'll keep this line open, okay?"

"What do you mean, open?"

"We won't hang up. Mary will man this end. That way we'll always have a line of communication. Will that be agreeable to the people holding you?"

Gormley looked at Tingle and nodded.

"Yes, that's agreeable," Tingle said.

Gormley spoke. "Tell him he has ten minutes to get Hagen and Johnson here. The jail is just across the street. He can have them sent right over."

"He said—" Tingle began.

"I heard him," the mayor snapped. "I'll check, Jim. I'll be back with you."

Tingle could feel his heart pounding. "They mean it, Frank."

"Don't worry, I'll check back." Tingle heard the mayor lay the receiver down. There were muted noises and voices at the other end of the line. Tingle looked at the blond gunman. He felt a chill of terror as Gormley calmly looked at his wristwatch to note the time.

5:35 p.m.

THE mayor used the direct police line. The chief of police said nothing as he listened to the mayor's secretary read back the conversation she had taken down over the extension phone.

"Well?" the mayor demanded. "What the hell do we do now?" He was using the secretary's office so that he couldn't be overheard on the live telephone in his own ornate office.

The police chief spoke with assuring authority. "We have a contingency plan for this kind of thing. We'll call in the cruisers and the patrol cars designated for emergency response. They'll get to the scene first. Then we'll bring in our special squad, trained snipers and other experts. Remember, you watched some of their training?"

"How long will all this take?"

"The cruisers and scout cars will start converging as soon as I call. It'll take a half hour or so to get the first elements of the special squad up to the courthouse."

"You heard what they said about the ten-minute limit?"

The chief paused. "Commander Blake did a special study on how to handle terrorists. His information was based on reported worldwide experience."

"So?"

"You wait them out. Encourage them to talk. We have special people trained just for that. But you wait them out. It can take days, but they usually cave in."

"Is that what you recommend—officially?" the mayor demanded.

Again there was a pause. "Yes."

"What about Hagen and Johnson?"

"Leave them right where they are, Mr. Mayor, under lock and key."

The mayor nervously lit a cigarette. It bobbed up and down as he talked. "Listen, you had better be right. They have every damned criminal court judge up there plus the only black on the supreme court. If they get killed, your ass will be grass." He paused. "And, by the way, so will mine."

"I'm giving it to you right from the manual, Mr. Mayor. We stay on top of these things."

"All right," the mayor sighed. "Get going and round up your squads and teams on the double. By the way, you take charge of this thing yourself, I don't want any half-assed captain running this. And stay where I can talk to you instantly, understand?"

"Yes sir."

"What does your manual say I should tell these people? They've given me a deadline."

The chief answered without hesitation. "Just tell them you're working on it. Tell them there's a lot of paper-work involved."

"Oh, shit, they'll never believe that!"

"It will stall them," the chief said firmly. "I'll contact communications and get back to you."

"Make it quick!"

"Right."

5:45 p.m.

THERE was no clock in Harbor's office, and Tingle fought the urge to look at his watch. Sweat was pouring from him.

"Do you mind if I smoke a cigar?" he asked the blond gunman.

"Yes."

Tingle shrugged. He wanted the relief of a smoke, but it was no time to protest.

The gunman looked at his watch, his face expressionless.

Outside in the courtroom everyone was quiet. Judge Carol Woldanski had a nervous cough and every few seconds would issue a compressed little chirp. It was the only sound except for audible and nervous breathing.

Clyde Powell sat in the front row of the jury box. The first shock and fright had begun to leave him, and he now tried to assess the potential of the young terrorists guarding them. The pretty girl called Thelma possessed the coolness of a robot. She gave no sign of being tense or nervous. She kept her pistol steady, her eyes emotionless, like a bored store clerk waiting on a customer. The other woman showed strain. Sweat beaded on her forehead. Of course, she held the live grenade. Powell hoped she had a firm grip.

The young man standing guard at the rear door betrayed his anxiety by his stance, crouched like a spring, as if expecting an attacker to burst through the courtroom's door at any minute.

Powell hoped they had cleared the jury and attorneys out of his courtroom. He prayed that at least they would be safe from danger.

In the distance he heard the howl of multiple sirens. Tingle heard the sirens too. So did the young gunman. Gormley glanced at his watch. "Nine minutes gone," he said softly.

Tingle snatched up the telephone receiver from the desk. "Hey, Frank," he called.

There was a pause, then the mayor came on the line. "I'm here, Jim."

"They say nine minutes have gone by. Where's Hagen and Johnson?"

Gormley had picked up the extension telephone, again keeping the machine gun pointed at Tingle.

"It's taking time, Jim. Jesus, the sheriff won't give them up without a court order. We're working on it, but it will take time. Tell those people that."

Gormley shrugged. "Thirty seconds to go," he said.

"Listen," Tingle snapped, "they're not buying that shit, and neither am I, Frank. You get those two people over here right now!" Panic seized Tingle as the blond gunman stood up.

"Wait! You heard him," Tingle pleaded with Gormley. "They're on their way. It will take time, that's all."

"Tell him to stay by the telephone," Gormley replied as he stepped to the office doorway. "Go ahead, Thelma." His voice was calm, but the words were unmistakably an order.

"Oh, Jesus," Tingle whispered to himself. He could feel himself trembling.

Thelma Sturdevant had been coached on exactly what to do. She had seen his picture in the newspapers, so she recognized him. "Judge Abrams," she said, looking directly at him.

"Yes?" Abrams kept his voice calm.

"Step down here, please." Thelma's voice was almost cheerful.

"Why?"

"Please step down, or I shall have to shoot you," she said quietly.

Abrams felt his legs quiver as he stood up. He climbed past the others in the back row and then stepped down, stopping directly in front of the girl.

"You are Herbert Abrams, the judge who pronounced sentence on Field Marshal Johnson and General Hagen?"

"Two men with those names did appear before me," he said, surprised at his own coolness.

The blond man stood in the office doorway, his gun pointed in, presumably at Justice Tingle. Abrams knew he would be cut down by that man's machine gun if he tried a dash to the side door. He could not make it past both women and the machine gun. That route of escape was barred.

"We, the World Liberation Army," the girl began to speak in a singsong voice, mouthing an obviously rehearsed speech, "have found you guilty of crimes against humanity, and the penalty will now be carried out." She raised her pistol until it was pointed directly at his head.

Instinctively Abrams ducked. The pistol noise exploded as she missed. The sound gave Abrams extra strength. All the tennis paid off as he burst past the two women, hurdled the first row of spectator benches, and then dashed for the rear door.

Al Martin, who had expected danger only from without, was frozen with surprise as Abrams sprinted toward him.

"Get him, Al!" Gormley shouted.

Martin swung his pistol around, firing at the figure who was coming so fast. The first shot went wide, missing Abrams, who was almost to the doors. The second shot also missed.

Judge Abrams hit the exit like a runner breaking tape, the doors flew apart as he burst through. He saw all the camera crewmen staring at him and heard additional pistol shots as he leaped for the stairway. He landed on his feet halfway down the stairs, but his legs gave under him, and he crashed hard into the marble landing. He had no thought of pain or injury, just escape. Like a maddened land crab, he frantically scurried on hands and knees, then bumped down the rest of the stairs on his stomach, ignoring the jarring, still conscious only of danger and driven on by his terror. When he reached the lobby, he tried to stand but couldn't. Abrams saw that his left foot was twisted at an odd angle. He touched the ankle and felt the swelling. It was broken. Breathing in short sobs, he took a quick inventory of the rest of his body. There were no bullet holes. They had missed him. He ignored the throbbing pain of the ankle and crawled quickly toward the blind man's empty stand, something he could hide behind in case they came after him.

Al Martin had followed Abrams only a few steps into the hallway. Now he noticed the television crews, who were staring at him in shock. Martin lifted the pistol and fired one shot into the ceiling as he retreated to the courtroom. Everyone dived for the floor. Martin, breathing heavily, pulled the large doors shut. He resumed his stance, taking a second pistol from his waist and pointing it at the closed doors.

"What happened?" Gormley called from the entrance doorway.

"I think I got him, Larry," Martin said, his voice trembling. "I shot at him, and he fell down the stairway. I'm pretty sure I got him." Martin wasn't at all sure, but he didn't want to admit it. "I think I hit him in the head. I'm not sure—things were moving pretty fast."

"You think?" The words were an accusation by Gormley.

"I'm pretty sure, Larry. For Christ's sake, I couldn't take the time to go look. That hallway is full of people. But I'm pretty sure Abrams is dead."

Tingle heard the words and started to get up from the desk.

"Sit!" Gormley snarled. Tingle eased back into the chair. He was drenched with perspiration.

A mixture of angry and frightened sounds came from the hostages inside the courtroom.

"Be quiet!" Gormley snapped the words from his position in the doorway. There was a new nervous quality to his voice, which made his words even more threatening. Suddenly the muttering in the courtroom stopped, and everything was quiet. Tingle was aware of the pungent odor of gun smoke.

Once again Larry Gormley had to fight against panic. Things were beginning to go wrong. Even if Abrams had been killed, and that was doubtful, it should have happened as they had planned—an execution in the courtroom. Then the authorities would know they were dealing with efficient and ruthless people. Gormley wished Hagen and Johnson were with him. They would provide the needed strength and determination. He took a deep breath to calm himself. He had to keep control. At this point it was all up to him.

Tingle noticed that the corners of Gormley's mouth were now tense and taut. Gormley looked directly at him and spoke in a low, hostile voice. "Okay, tell your man that he has another ten minutes. If they're not here by then, he'll have another dead judge in the hall. Tell him!"

"Frank." Tingle's mouth was so dry he could hardly talk.

"I'm here."

"They just killed Herb Abrams."

"What!"

Tingle found he was having trouble breathing. He tried to calm himself. "These people just shot Herb Abrams to death," he said dully. "They gunned him down out in the hallway."

"Oh, God!"

"Frank, they say you have another ten minutes to get Hagen and Johnson over here. If you don't, there'll be another judge dead in the hallway." He paused, trying to control himself and his thoughts. "They are going to kill one of us every ten minutes until those prisoners get up here."

"Oh, my God!"

"Frank, cut out the 'God' shit and get busy. You just got a man killed. Now move your ass and get those two men over here."

Gormley moved back into the room and picked up the extension.

The mayor's voice trembled. "Jim, they say it's the wrong thing to do—"

"Wrong thing!" Tingle shouted. "Listen, you dumb ass-hole, if you get us all killed because of some lunatic police department policy, the people will run you out of office. Shit, they'll run you out of the state—can you get that through your fuckin' head?!"

"Easy, Jim," the mayor's voice was barely audible. "Tell them I'll have the prisoners sent over right away."

For the first time Gormley spoke directly to the mayor. "Have Hagen and Johnson sent up by the public elevator. Have them walk in alone through the hall doors to this courtroom. Got that?"

"I have it." Now the mayor's voice shook with anger.

"If you screw it up, I'll kill everyone here. Do you understand that?"

"I understand," the mayor said.

"He means it, Frank," Tingle urged. "No tricks, just get those men here, right?"

"Right."

Gormley looked at his watch. "Tell him he has ten minutes, starting now."

"I heard him," the mayor said. "Stay by the telephone."

Tingle felt himself shaking. "Look, Larry," he said softly. "I'll admit it, all this has scared the shit out of me. I need a drink, but I'd settle for a cigar. Is that too much to ask?"

Gormley studied the heavy black man. Sweat poured down his ebony face, which was taking on a grayish shade. "Okay, but don't blow any of that smoke my way. I don't like it."

"Don't worry." Tingle's big hands trembled as he extracted a cigar from his coat pocket. The cigar would help his breathing, clear his lungs, and steady him. He lit the tip, fanning the smoke away with his large hand as sweat cascaded down his back.

5:55 p.m.

ABRAMS saw them coming. It was, he decided, the most marvelous sight he had ever seen, and that included many beautiful women. The policemen came in cautiously. They wore riot helmets and flak jackets, and some carried shotguns. Two policemen attended to Abrams while the others moved carefully up the staircase.

The television crews were pinned down. The closed door to Harbor's courtroom posed a threat that barred retreat to the stairwell.

"You people," a uniformed sergeant whispered to the frightened newsmen, "move over here and down the stairs. We'll cover you. Leave your equipment."

A few began to move, the rest hesitated, their eyes on the door.

"Move it, damn it," the policeman commanded.

Other officers positioned themselves at the lip of the top stair, their weapons pointed at the closed courtroom doors.

The men of the camera crews moved all at once, bumping into each other as they raced for the safety of the stairway. They rushed past the officers lying on the stairs, past the waiting guns.

The wide hallway, littered with the camera and light fixtures, was completely deserted. Everything was deathly quiet.

5:58 p.m.

IN Judge Powell's courtroom Ginger Steiner was perched on the counsel table exhibiting her good-looking legs to Ace Gilbert, who lounged back in a chair thoroughly enjoying himself. He had heard what he thought might be muffled gunshots but dismissed that as improbable. A car backfiring most likely. He paid little attention. He was enchanted by Ginger Steiner and her amusing stories of her days as an actress.

6:00 p.m.

GUS Simes was a picture of utter dejection as he sat by himself in the dayroom. The prisoners had switched from the news program to watch old television reruns. No one there liked listening to the news because it reminded all of them that there existed a life outside of their cells, a world where people moved freely. The news was contact with the real world and was therefore painful. The reruns were fantasy and escape.

The corridor outside the cell block was suddenly filled with stern-faced policemen. They were heavily armed, some in flak jackets. A quick conversation was held between the jail guards and a policeman with a lot of gold braid on his cap.

The guards looked worried as they listened to the ranking officer, who kept his voice low but talked very earnestly. The group was joined by a tall man in a business suit. Simes recognized him as the county sheriff—the head of the jail. He spoke firmly to the guards.

The head guard turned and walked to the cell door. "Okay, Johnson and Hagen," he called, "come on. You're coming out."

Johnson strutted forward, a superior smile on his face. Hagen, grinning, followed him.

"What's up, man?" Johnson asked, as the guard unlocked the cell door.

"Never mind," the guard snapped.

"Oh ho! This shit might be some kind of trick. Unless we knows, we ain't goin'. Right, Hagen?"

Hagen also sensed that they had the upper hand. "That's right. You guys could be taking us down to the street to shoot us. Jesus, you sure got enough guns."

The policeman with the braid spoke. "Some of your people have taken hostages in the Criminal Court Building. We are taking you to them."

"Just like that?" Johnson asked.

The top policeman's face registered no emotion. His voice was calm and even. "They tried to kill one judge. They say they will kill another if we don't get you over there."

Johnson snapped his fingers in delight. "Don't let's keep the brothers waiting." He and Hagen began to move through the open cell door, then Johnson stopped. "Oh, yeah, we're taking my man Simes with us." He grinned. "You don't mind, do you?"

The policeman showed no reaction. "They asked only for you two. We'll talk about Simes later."

"No, we talk now!" Johnson bellowed. "Time's runnin', man. Either Simes comes too, or we don't go."

"All right," the policeman said.

"Come on, Gus!" Johnson laughed. "I told you we were walking out of here."

Gus Simes hesitated. If only his lawyer had called him back. Now all chance for a deal had gone. Going with Hagen and Johnson was dangerous, but now it was the only hope that he had. "I'm coming." He hurried to catch up to them, his eyes on the policemen and their guns.

"Let's go, Gold Hat," Johnson commanded in an imperial voice.

The policeman's face remained stiff, although his eyes narrowed slightly. "This way," he said, leading the prisoners toward the jail's rear elevator.

"Which judge did they try to waste?" Johnson asked as they all boarded the elevator's steel cage.

"Abrams," the policeman said. "But he's alive."

Hagen grimaced. "They fucked it up," he said in disgust.

Johnson grinned. "They just need a little inspired leadership, that's all. Abrams don't mean shit, man. We're stepping out, and that's what's important."

6:05 p.m.

"NINE minutes gone," Gormley said, his eyes fixed on Tingle's sweating face.

Tingle's cigar was clamped between his teeth. He extracted it and picked up the telephone. Gormley picked up the extension.

"Frank!" The name was almost an inaudible croak of agony. Tingle swallowed and repeated. "Frank?"

There was a pause, and then the mayor came on the line. "I'm here, Jim." He sounded tired.

"Nine minutes gone," Tingle said, having difficulty breathing.

"They should be there by now, honest to God!" The mayor's voice now sounded frantic. "Put that guy on I talked to before."

"I'm here," Gormley said quietly.

"Listen, I'm not kidding you or trying to stall. Hagen and Johnson are on their way, honest to God. Now, please don't kill anyone. They'll be there in just another minute or two."

"Ten minutes, that was the deal." Gormley sounded completely calm. "You have thirty seconds left." He paused. "Twenty seconds."

"Come on, for Christ's sake, man, give us a break, will you!" The mayor was screaming into the phone.

Inside, Gormley was anything but calm. Things seemed to be getting away from him. The plan wasn't working out, and he had no alternative plan. He had been so sure everything would work. He was frightened.

"Five seconds," Gormley said. He felt like an actor playing a part, just speaking lines. It didn't seem real somehow.

Tingle listened to the telephone, it sounded to him as if the mayor was crying.

Gormley desperately wished that Hagen and Johnson were with him. They had the nerve to pull it off. They had the strength. He would be all right if only Hagen and Johnson would come. He felt the warning wave of nausea.

"Okay, Thelma," Gormley called out to the courtroom. The words were spoken almost softly but they were obviously a command.

Thelma moved closer to the jury box. She felt ashamed that Abrams had escaped her. She was determined that it would not happen again.

"You!" She pointed her pistol at Cannonball O'Brien.

He pretended that she was talking to someone else.

"You," she repeated. "Stand up or I'll shoot you right there!"

Judge Richards and Judge Young, who sat on either side of O'Brien, involuntarily drew away from him.

"Stand up," she hissed dangerously.

Cannonball O'Brien wobbled as he stood, his florid face jerking uncontrollably.

"Somebody is coming," Al Martin called from his post at the rear of the courtroom. He kept his pistol leveled at the door.

"Hey in there!" A voice called from the outside. "Don't shoot. It's me and Hagen!"

"Any cops with you?" Martin called back.

"No cops. Just a pal of ours from murderer's row."

"Come in," Martin said, tensing. "But one at a time."

Johnson walked through the door as if he owned the place. "Hey, baby," he shouted, "this is cool!"

Martin waved him to one side. Next was Hagen, a crooked grin stretched across his face. He gave a clenched-fist salute to Gormley, who now stood in the office doorway.

Gus Simes followed, his face white, his eyes darting around the courtroom, taking it all in.

"Who is this guy?" Martin asked, his pistol pointed at Simes's chest.

"He's Gus Simes. Was busted for murder," Johnson replied easily. "I recruited him in jail. He's one of us, so you can relax, Al."

Cannonball O'Brien fell back into his chair. He had involuntarily wet himself. Silent tears rolled down his red cheeks.

Larry Gormley felt an intense feeling of relief. He had been closer to the edge than he had suspected. But now it would be all right. Johnson and Hagen had come. The plan was working. The nightmare sensation passed. He felt exhilaration and a surge of confidence. Once again he felt powerful and ready for all challenges.

"Hey, Larry, this is really all right, brother!" Johnson strode across the courtroom and hugged Gormley's shoulders. "Man, I knew we could count on you." He saw Tingle seated at the desk in the office. "Who is this dude?"

Gormley had regained full control, but he was careful not to show his relief. He was running the operation again, and he meant to keep it that way. His face betrayed no emotion. "This is Tingle," he said simply. "Supreme court justice."

Johnson giggled and did a little dance step. "Oh, shit, you bagged old King Tingle himself. Oh, ain't that fuckin' sweet! Damn, but this is going to turn into a fine little party."

Johnson looked around. "Where's Flash?"

Gormley had expected the question. He gripped his gun tighter. "We had to execute him."

"What?" Johnson's eyes narrowed dangerously.

"He was going to turn us in to the police." Gormley replied as if that was a proven fact.

Johnson hesitated a moment, his expression grim. He shook his head. "Well, that's too bad but it's his own damned fault. He should have known better." Johnson smiled, showing no resentment. "To tell the truth, I always was a little suspicious of Flash myself, brother or no brother."

Gormley relaxed. Everything was working out. They were a team, a powerful, unstoppable team.

"Jim! Jim!" The mayor's voice was filled with fear as it echoed through the telephone. "Is everything all right?"

Tingle wondered about his breathing problem. He couldn't quite seem to get his breath. And his damned arm felt numb too. "Yeah, they got Johnson and Hagen. They just came in. Just in time too. They were going to shoot O'Brien."

"Oh, sweet Jesus," the mayor said.

"Who is he talking to?" Johnson asked.

"The mayor," Gormley replied.

Johnson giggled again. "My, my, but don't we have nice friends."

Gormley's expression remained stonelike. "Tingle, now that you have the mayor on the phone, you can tell him our other demands."

"And what are they?" Tingle asked.

"We want three million dollars in cash. Then we want a B-52 bomber with two pilots and a navigator."

"Hey, come on," Tingle said, "be reasonable, for God's sake."

"That's what we want, nothing less," Gormley said. "He has two hours to get the money up here. He has three hours to get the airplane. We start killing people again in two hours." He looked at his watch. "The time starts to run from now."

Tingle felt odd; the pressure on his chest was a definite sensation now. "He says—"

"I heard him," the mayor snapped. "Tell him it's impossible."

Tingle was annoyed at his shortness of breath. It was beginning to interfere with his ability to talk. "Impossible or not, Frank, that's what they want." Tingle's voice was tired, and his words came slowly.

Gormley spoke into the extension phone. "You have exactly two hours to get that money here. You have three hours to arrange for the bomber. Fully fueled, by the way. We are not going to negotiate with you. If you fail to comply by the deadline, we will again start executing hostages." Gormley was conscious of Tingle's labored breathing. He looked at him. Tingle's dark face was blotchy.

"Another thing," Gormley continued. "The police department has an armored car. We have seen pictures of it in the papers. I want it parked in front of the Criminal Court Building. Leave the armored panels up so that we can see that no one is inside. Leave the keys. We'll use that vehicle when we leave here, but I want it out front now."

"Look, whoever you are, the damned banks are closed. Even if they weren't, they are not about to just hand over their depositors' money because I ask them to do it."

"They'd better," Gormley replied, "or there's going to be a whole lot of dead people up here."

The threat had its effect. The mayor paused before speaking again. "Even if I could get the money, the government isn't going to hand over a bomber."

"You never know if you don't ask," Gormley said. "Time is running, you'd better get going." Gormley watched as Tingle loosened his collar. Sweat was soaking through the black man's suit. "My name is Gormley," he said into the telephone. Tingle looked very bad. "From now on you'll be dealing with me."

"Gormley," the mayor said, his voice softening. "I have some people here who would like to talk to you. Just talk, nothing more."

"I will talk only to you."

A new voice came over the telephone. "Come on, now, Gormley, what harm can come from just talking over the telephone?" The voice belonged to a policeman trained in the psychology of dealing with terrorists.

"I will talk only with the mayor," Gormley said quietly but firmly. He took the receiver away from his ear. The new voice rambled on, but the words were indistinct.

Tingle still had the telephone. "This is Justice Tingle.

The man isn't listening to you, so put the mayor back on the wire." He took a deep breath. "Now!"

"I'm here, Jim."

"Do what . . . they tell . . . you." It was hard to get out the words. There didn't seem to be enough air in the room.

"Are you all right?" The mayor almost whispered the question, as if that would somehow limit the conversation to just the two of them.

"I'm not feeling . . . well. Do what they . . . tell you, Frank." It felt as if he were choking. "Please!" He managed to get the word out.

"Okay, put Gormley back on." The mayor sounded defeated.

Tingle nodded to the blond gunman. Gormley placed the receiver next to his ear.

"Gormley," the mayor's voice was strained with anger, "you win. I'll be the one talking from now on. Now, what the hell are you people doing to Jim Tingle?" The words snapped out in icy hate.

Gormley's expression never changed. He watched as the big black man squirmed in the chair, his hands clamped over his chest. "We ain't doing anything to him," he said in a conversational tone, "but it looks to me as if he is having a heart attack."

"Then, for Christ's sake, let him go!"

"Just as soon as we have the money and the airplane." Gormley's tone barred any further negotiation as far as Tingle was concerned.

"Oh, God." The mayor sounded desperate.

"Time is running. You had better start moving." Gormley's words were almost gentle.

6:15 p.m.

OFFICER Ted Hemmings leaned against the closed jury room door. His feet hurt. Inside, the jury had been quiet some time. He hoped that their silence signaled agreement and a verdict. Officer Hemmings wanted to go home.

Like most of the officers assigned to criminal court, Ted Hemmings was a used-up patrol cop. The court job was coveted by policemen. It represented a quiet pasture where a man could pleasantly pass the rest of his duty until pension time. The job offered regular hours, usually, and the requirements did not strain a man physically.

High blood pressure under stress had been the finding of the department doctor when Hemmings had passed out on the job. He had been getting dizzy spells and headaches after tough shifts. The blood pressure might have been a ticket out for a disability, but Ted Hemmings wanted to stay as a cop, to get in his twenty-five years and retire. The retirement benefits were good, and a man could get another job. But on disability benefits they cut you off as soon as you went to work for anyone else. He had asked for the transfer to court duty and had used all his contacts to swing it. It had paid off. For the past five years he had been assigned to criminal court. He had less than a year to go until the pension.

While waiting for the jury, Ted Hemmings had idly observed the flirtation between Ace Gilbert and the woman lawyer. It still amazed him, even after five years in the courts, how well lawyers got along when the legal battles were over. He had seen them come to near fistfights in the courtroom, go to lunch together, then come back and scream at each other in the afternoon. Hemmings never really liked lawyers. To him they were just obstacles to good policework, schemers trying to tear apart what good cops had sweated to piece together.

Hemmings thought the woman—Jewish, judging by her name—had done a good job, although the detectives had put together a case that really nailed Little Chester. Still, she had done well with very little to work with. Being good-looking didn't hurt her either, he decided.

Maybe Ace Gilbert would knock off a piece. Hemmings hoped he would; he liked Ace. Gilbert never gave anyone any trouble, he was easy to get along with, and he did his job but never took himself seriously. Gilbert was a good man. Ted Hemmings hoped he would score with the copper-haired woman.

The knock on the jury door startled him, and he jerked erect.

He opened the door a crack. "Yeah?"

A severe-looking woman peered back at him. "We've reached a verdict," she said. She sounded excited.

"Okay," Hemmings said, "have a seat. We'll go get the judge."

The two attorneys were staring at him.

"They say they have a verdict," he explained. "I'll run down the hall and tell the judge, okay?"

He passed the judge's office at the side of the bench. "They've got a verdict," he said to the court clerk, who was sitting in the office reading a newspaper.

He started down the long, narrow private hallway. The hallway was closed to the public and concealed behind the elevator bank. The cell used to hold prisoners was located at Harbor's end of the hall, close to his side door. Across from the cell was a private elevator used for ferrying judges, court personnel, and prisoners. Ted Hemmings paused before the cell door. "They got a verdict," he said to Little Chester, who had stretched out on the long iron bench that was bolted to the wall.

Hemmings felt a bit uncomfortable at the prospect of interrupting the judges' meeting. He wondered if he should knock or just walk in. He decided that perhaps it would be best to just slip in quietly and signal to Judge Powell.

Ted Hemmings quietly opened the side door and slipped into Judge Harbor's courtroom. He saw three men in prisoner clothing standing in the center of the courtroom. Two women stood facing the jury box. All the judges were seated in the jury box.

Something was very wrong. Hemmings's mind didn't quite grasp the situation until he saw the blond man standing just inside the judge's office with a snub-nosed machine gun in his hand.

The muzzle of the machine gun swung toward Hemmings as the blond man saw him. "Don't move!" the blond man shouted, his face registering surprise.

Ted Hemmings was fifty-three, and he hadn't worked as a street cop for years, but the instincts were still there.

He quickly stepped back inside the hallway and slammed the heavy door. If he engaged in a gun battle, slugs would fly inside the courtroom and probably hit a number of the judges. And he would stand little chance against a machine gun.

Backup, he would need backup officers. Ted Hemmings turned and ran. His extra body weight seemed to slow him down so that it felt like he was running in water. He tried desperately to make his large legs pump faster. His eyes were fixed on the door to Judge Powell's courtroom. If he could make it, he would be safe. It was only a few yards away.

Gormley didn't want to open the hallway door. He was afraid the police would be outside waiting. But the others were watching. He pushed the door open and poked the gun into the opening. He could see the policeman running away down the narrow corridor. He squeezed the trigger.

The slugs caught Ted Hemmings just as he raced through the doorway. Gormley had not aimed, just sprayed in a small arc. One bullet hit Hemmings in the thigh, breaking the bone, another nicked the lobe of his ear, biting a chunk of flesh away. The other bullets ripped into the heavy wooden door of Judge Powell's courtroom, tearing it away from its hinges.

Hemmings fell, sliding into the base of the judge's bench. He pulled his pistol and snapped off a shot. His bullet cracked into the marble doorsill just above Gormley's head. Gormley pulled the door shut and retreated to the safety of Harbor's inner office.

Ace Gilbert had pulled Ginger Steiner to the floor when he heard the shots echoing in the corridor. Now he rushed to Hemmings, grabbing the injured officer and pulling him away from the menace of the open doorway. Gilbert called to the court clerk and told him to stay in the safety of the office.

"Oh, Jesus, I'm hit, Ace," Hemmings mumbled as he watched the blood well from his leg. Ace Gilbert expertly clamped down on the wound with his hand. It wasn't an artery, so Hemmings wouldn't bleed to death. Gilbert was acting on instinct, a soldier's instinct.

6:25 p.m.

LARRY Gormley pulled the heavy wooden door to the side hallway closed. He looked for a locking bolt, but there wasn't one.

"Johnson," he commanded, "get a gun out of one of those bags and cover this door."

The black man pulled a machine pistol from one of the briefcases, fumbling with a long ammunition clip until it finally snapped into place. He cocked the operating slide back, arming the weapon. He walked over to the side of Harbor's empty bench and took a position facing the side door. He was ready.

Gormley nodded his approval and went back into the office.

Larry Gormley felt shaken. He had not expected that anyone would try to take them. Obviously the policeman had entered by mistake. There had been no one in the corridor to back him up. Still, it had been an error to leave the side door unguarded. Such an error could give the police something to think about. Up until now he knew that they saw the World Liberation Army as icily efficient terrorists. But the fact that a policeman could just walk in on them, even though he had ultimately been shot, showed that they could be vulnerable. He could almost read the minds of the policemen surrounding them: If there was one gross mistake, there could always be two. It might arouse them to a real attempt to storm the courtroom. Gormley cursed softly.

Tingle was lying back in the chair gasping for breath.

The pressure in the chest had become acute pain. "I'm sick," he said simply to Gormley.

"You look it," Gormley replied.

The pain increased rapidly. Tingle felt a wave of nausea. "Get a doctor." He just managed to get the words out.

Gormley just looked at him. He silently shook his head.

The pain was unbearable. Tingle's mind was filled with a montage of thoughts. He recalled the doctor's warning about his eating and drinking habits, about his weight. He thought about his almost assured golden political future. He thought about the quarter of a million dollars that waited on Ridley's client. Then the pain smashed into a crescendo. He tried to scream as he fell to the floor, but no sound would come out.

Johnson walked into the office. He knelt down next to Tingle. Tingle's breathing was shallow and rapid, his skin ashen. "This dude's in trouble, man," Johnson said to Gormley.

"So?"

Johnson stood up and looked down at Tingle. "No skin off my ass, one way or the other, you understand, but this dude is a supreme court justice. That makes him valuable, you dig?"

"We have plenty of hostages," Gormley said, holding the phone against his chest so that the conversation wouldn't be heard at the other end.

"Yeah, that's true, but the King here is like a cherry on top of whipped cream. I'll bet most of the publicity we get will be because of him."

Gormley felt rising irritation. "What the hell do you propose?"

Johnson shrugged. "I don't know." He walked out into the courtroom. "Hey, any you people got medicine for heart problems? Looks like Tingle's got a problem."

Judge Richards, who had digitalis and nitroglycerin in pocket vials for his own condition, started to get up.

"Hey, man, get your ass back down." Johnson commanded, his eyes narrowing. "I didn't ask for no volunteers, just medicine."

"Have him swallow the white pill and put the little one under his tongue," Richards said, handing over the medicine.

Johnson went back to the office, got a small paper cup of water, and gave the medicine to Tingle. There didn't seem to be any immediate change.

"Well, if he croaks, he croaks," Johnson said, looking down.

"Get back and cover that side door." Gormley's voice was sharp with irritation.

Johnson looked at him closely as he passed. "Take it easy, man," he said softly. "This ain't no time to start losing your nerve."

"I'm not losing my nerve," Gormley snarled. "Cover the fucking door!"

Johnson shrugged and walked back to his post.

Gormley knew that Johnson was watching him. He put the telephone to his mouth.

"You there?" Gormley asked.

"Just a moment," a woman's voice replied. There was a pause before the mayor came on the phone.

"I'm trying to get the money," the mayor sounded harried.

"Good," Gormley replied. "Where's the armored car?"

"It's on the way." The mayor's voice was angry. "Look here, I can't try to get the goddamned money, talk to the Defense Department, and mind every other little goddamned detail!"

"Don't get excited." Gormley's voice was calm.

"I'm not excited," the mayor said, his voice strained. "We are doing our best here. It is tough."

"Yeah," Gormley said, "it's tough all over. By the way, we shot a cop who got too nosy."

"Oh, God!"

"You had better warn your people that we have live explosives here. Any more of that kind of crap and we'll blow everybody away. Do you understand that?"

"I understand," the mayor said. "Can I talk to Justice Tingle?"

"I'm afraid he is too sick to come to the telephone," Gormley said as he looked at Tingle.

"Let him go. You have enough blood on your hands now," the mayor pleaded.

"I'm sorry. If you want to help him, just make sure things move along quickly. The sooner we get the money and airplane, the faster you can help your friend."

"All right." The mayor's words were a sigh of frustration and defeat.

6:30 p.m.

ACE Gilbert had reacted instantly. Flipping over the heavy counsel table, he got Ginger Steiner and the wounded policeman behind it. He called to the people in the jury room to stay there. A conversation was conducted with a woman whose frightened face peered out from behind the jury room door. The bleeding officer was enough proof. The jury door was tightly shut thereafter.

Gilbert went to the rear of the courtroom and opened the back door a crack. The public hallway was empty except for deserted television equipment. A policeman in the stairwell at the far end of the hallway raised a rifle and sighted on the door. Gilbert closed it quickly and retreated.

"I don't know what the hell is going on," he said when he got back to the others. "Tell me again what you saw, Ted."

Hemmings's face was white, and pain made talking difficult, but he carefully described everything he had seen in the courtroom. A policeman was trained to be an observer, and Hemmings gave an example of his skill.

"Give me your gun, Ted."

The policeman's eyes widened in silent protest.

"I've killed more people than you've arrested, Ted. You're hit, and someone has to protect us. Give me the gun."

The policeman hesitated, then handed over the large chrome revolver.

Gilbert handled it expertly, flipping open the cylinder to check the remaining rounds. He reached over and began extracting the bullets from Hemmings's gunbelt.

Ginger watched him. Suddenly he had become a different man, no longer just a casual observer. Since the shooting, minutes before, he had lost the indifference that had seemed to be the foundation of his character. Now he was decisive, alert, and commanding.

Gilbert withdrew the spent shell in the revolver and replaced it with a live round. He snapped the cylinder back in place.

"Stay here no matter what," he said to her. "Crossing to that jury room exposes you to fire from the corridor. Just stay put. And keep pressure on Hemmings's wound."

She nodded. She had been holding a blood-soaked handkerchief against the leg of the policeman as Gilbert had instructed her to do.

He stood up.

"Please," she said, her eyes seeking his, "don't leave. Stay here."

He was looking at the open door to the corridor. It was just off the door to Powell's office. "Someone has to let the police know we're up here with a wounded man and a scared jury. Sit tight."

Ace Gilbert walked across the courtroom almost casually until he neared the corridor doorway. He could see the terrorized court clerk huddled down in a corner of the office on the other side of the corridor door. In order to reach the office, the opening to the corridor had to be crossed.

Ace Gilbert was not reflective now. There was no time to think about the similarity of this and the caves in Vietnam. There was no time for inward speculation. He was doing what he had been trained to do, a thing he had done before—often—and his total concentration was on the task at hand, nothing else.

He braced himself, then leaped across the corridor entrance, falling through the office doorway. There was no firing from the corridor. He turned and waited, listening, his pistol ready. The clerk was too frightened even to speak.

When he had jumped across the entrance, Gilbert had not seen anyone in the hall, although it was dimly lighted, so he couldn't be sure. Keeping his revolver pointed through the office door at the corridor entrance, he walked backward, feeling for the desk.

He found the telephone, picked up the receiver, and propped it between his shoulder and ear. He took his eyes off the entrance for only a moment to dial the emergency number, 911.

Keeping his voice just above a whisper, Gilbert spoke into the telephone. "My name is Gilbert," he said, speaking distinctly. He knew all calls to the 911 number were recorded, and he wanted no mistakes. "I am an assistant prosecutor, and I am in Judge Powell's courtroom on the second floor of the Criminal Court Building. We have been shot at, and we have one officer wounded. The shots came from the courtroom of the executive judge on this floor. We have a jury up here." His tone changed to command. "I want to talk to the ranking police officer on duty."

"Your name again, please?" The operator sounded bored, as if the urgency of his message had not been understood.

"Alfred Gilbert." He said it slowly, spelling the last name. "I am an assistant prosecutor."

"Please hold on," the operator said impersonally.

He waited, watching the corridor entrance. Ace Gilbert shifted his position so that he would have a better angle if he had to shoot.

"Detective Bureau, Captain Falkner." This voice sounded very excited. "Go ahead, Gilbert, give me your position and situation."

Ace Gilbert repeated what had happened and described Hemmings's wound.

"This is Detective Captain Falkner," the man repeated. "To tell you the truth, Gilbert, there isn't a hell of a lot we can do for you right now. Let me fill you in on what is happening up there." Captain Falkner told Gilbert everything the police knew about the situation in Judge Harbor's courtroom.

"If we rush them, they'll blow the place up and the judges with it," he said. "We have officers all over the place, but in order to get to you, they would have to expose themselves to fire from that damned hallway door of Harbor's. Even the back elevator in the private hall is close to Harbor's courtroom, so that route is blocked too."

"If I covered from this end, maybe some men could get here from the main hall stairway," Gilbert suggested.

"Can't," Captain Falkner said. "We're under orders not to do anything to excite these loonies, Gilbert. They are the kind who kill for no reason, so we don't want to give even the slightest excuse. Those are the mayor's orders. If it looks like the people in your courtroom might be in real danger, we might have to rethink that, but for now just sit tight and stay as far away from the action as you can." The captain's voice sounded almost hysterical.

"And if those terrorists come down here, what the hell are we supposed to do then?" Although his words were heated, Gilbert still remained calm.

"Just give 'em what they want. At least for now, Gilbert. That's the orders."

"Very brave," Gilbert said.

"Listen, asshole, this isn't my idea!" The captain exploded. "I'd blow the fuckers off the face of the earth if it was up to me, but they got the judges, one of your bosses, and a couple of other people in there as hostages. One of the female terrorists has a live grenade in her hand with the pin out. So what the hell do you suggest?" The last words were screamed into the telephone.

Gilbert wondered if the rest of the police leadership were reacting so badly. "One of my bosses?" he inquired.

"Yeah, they got your chief assistant in there. Also they got the deputy chief of corrections and a couple of probation officers, a guy named Conroy and a woman named Mulloy."

Gilbert's only sensation was a detached sadness that his friends were in such danger. He felt sorry for Kathleen Mulloy, but she was now just another component in a problem that needed solution. As in Vietnam, he was detached, almost aloof. Combat, no matter what the location, he reflected, seemed to be excellent for emotional discipline.

"What's the situation?" Gilbert asked.

"They're going to give them money and an airplane." The captain's voice mirrored his disapproval. "The mayor is busy getting the money from the banks now. I don't know how, but they're getting it together. The airplane is a different thing. They are demanding a bomber from the air force, if you can believe that." Captain Falkner paused. Gilbert wondered if he was considering the wisdom of saying too much on an open line. "Anyway, they'll work it out somehow," he said quickly. "Pretty soon these loonies will be on their way to the airport, and you people will be safe. In the meantime, sit tight and keep on this line so that we'll know if everything is okay up there."

"I'll leave the telephone on the desk," Gilbert said quietly. "You'll hear it if there's any shooting."

"Now, look, Gilbert!"

Ace Gilbert lay the telephone on the desk. He could hear squawking protests from the receiver. To hold the telephone was a distraction. He needed total concentration now.

He moved slowly toward the corridor entrance. It was very much like the caves of Vietnam again. In a way, it was almost like being home.

chapter nine

6:40 p.m.

Gus Simes had been posted by the windows in Harbor's empty jury room where he could see the front of the building. From this vantage point he observed the streets below. Now and then he caught a glimpse of armed policemen running from one spot to another. Across the street the curtains had been drawn on all the city hospital windows that faced the Criminal Court Building. On the hospital roof he saw an occasional head bob up. He presumed they were police snipers.

He felt sorry for the hostages in the courtroom. He felt sorry for the officer who had been shot. But most of all, Gus Simes felt sorry for himself. He had listened when Gormley told Johnson the plan. The whole thing was wild. If Johnson and his friends were right, they would end up free, but in some godforsaken, flea-bitten African country. It was not an appealing fate to Gus Simes. However, his only alternative was death.

The street had been blocked off so that no traffic moved, even at the intersections. Suddenly Simes heard the rumble of a powerful motor. The police armored car, looking like a miniature blue tank with large wheels, came rolling up the street. The steel panels had been raised, allowing at least some view of the inside.

"That armored car is coming!" Simes called as he watched. He heard his message relayed to Gormley, who could see for himself out the windows in the judge's office.

The armored car didn't look very big. Simes wondered how Gormley expected all of them to get to the airport in that small vehicle, considering that they would have to take hostages along as protection. He wondered suddenly if these people really intended taking him along at all.

6:42 p.m.

EVERYONE had forgotten the prisoner. Little Chester was huddled in the rear of his cell. A policeman had gone by him, saying that the jury had a verdict, then the cop came running back as if the devil was after him. Then there was shooting, lots of shooting. And then only silence.

And no one came to get him. That bothered Little Chester most of all. By now the place should be knee-deep in cops, but there was no movement. The elevator across from his cell was stationary. It was as if he had been buried away, forgotten.

The silence was strange, tomblike. He was frightened.

6:45 p.m.

HAGEN couldn't keep his eyes off the woman. She sat in a chair in front of the jury box. A man sat next to her. She was full-figured with large breasts that strained against the silk of her blouse. Her skirt outlined rounded thighs. Gormley had said it would be hours until they got the money and airplane. They were safe enough. The police wouldn't move against them so long as they had the hostages and explosives.

The sight of her excited him. He could tell she knew that he was staring at her. He was convinced that women had some inner radar system that always alerted them when a man was attracted.

He tried to remember the last time. Jesus, it had been months, very long months, since he had had a woman.

Alice Mary Brennan sat at a counsel table, still clutching a grenade. Occasionally, to relieve hand cramps, she would carefully shift the deadly load from one hand to the other.

Thelma Sturdevant looked tired. She leaned against the edge of the counsel table, supporting her pistol with both hands. It was still leveled at the assembled hostages. The hostages had become very quiet after being informed of Tingle's heart attack.

Hagen walked over to the woman seated in front of the box. "Hi," he said. He couldn't keep his eyes off her breasts.

Kathleen Mulloy did not reply or look up, although facial muscles moved beneath her skin.

He grabbed her by the back of her hair. It felt good in his hands. "I said hello, goddamn it!"

Her eyes were wide with fear.

"Leave her alone!" The man seated next to her spoke sharply.

Hagen looked at him. He was middle-aged, a little gray around the temples, not fat but overweight. Soft.

"What?" Hagen grinned at him.

"I said leave her alone." The man's voice betrayed no fear, just anger.

Hagen released the hair. "Sure, pal," he said in a friendly voice. "Didn't know she was with you."

The girl was trembling as Hagen stepped past her.

"I'm not an animal," he said to the man. "Just ask, that's all."

The man's eyes were wary.

Hagen laughed. "Relax, friend. No problem." Then he swung his right hand catching Frank Conroy hard on the temple. He crashed off his chair, landing hard on the tile floor of the courtroom.

Hagen kicked him in the groin as he struggled to get up. The man cried out in pain.

"Next time, mind your fucking business," Hagen said. He turned to the girl and again grabbed her hair roughly. "Hi!" His grinning face was only inches away from hers.

He saw her lips part in fear, and it excited him even more.

Hagen felt a hand tugging at him. He turned.

Somehow the man had struggled to his feet. "Stop it!" The words came out between clenched teeth as Frank Conroy tried to swing at Hagen.

Hagen ducked and brought his fist hard into Conroy's midsection, doubling him over. He kicked Conroy in the throat, snapping him fully erect, his face flushed with blood. Hagen snatched up a chair and swung it like a baseball bat. It caught Conroy on the shoulder, making a sickening sound and sending him skidding down in front of the far end of the jury box.

"I said mind your own fucking business, friend."

Conroy lay helpless and twitching, obviously badly injured. It pleased Hagen that the man was still conscious although unable to move. Having him listen would add to Hagen's pleasure.

He turned as quick as a cat and grabbed the girl's hair again. "Talk, bitch! I want to hear your voice."

She shook with fright and had to swallow to speak. "Please," the word was barely audible, "leave him alone."

"Is that your boyfriend, your lover?"

"Stop it," one of the elderly black men said from the jury box. "Stop this at once!" The voice was firm and commanding. Clyde Powell's face was twisted with rage and indignation.

Hagen paused, looked at the old man, then turned. "Thelma, if this old shit, or anyone else even opens his mouth, shoot him dead. You got that!"

She nodded, her cold eyes sweeping the faces of the men in the jury box. Her expression told them all that she would follow that command without question.

"All right, then," Hagen said, seeing the fear in their faces. "Hey, Johnson," he called across the courtroom, "how long since we had any ass, man?"

Johnson, over by the side door, turned. "I don't know. Six, maybe eight months."

"Too long, man," Hagen laughed, his hand locked in Kathleen Mulloy's hair.

"Go to it, man," Johnson giggled. "Shit, we got the time."

"Come on, bitch," Hagen said, pulling Kathleen out of her chair. "We're going to give these nice people a little show. Hey! Hey!" With his other hand he ripped off her blouse. "Me first, Johnson. Okay?"

The black man laughed. "Go get it, baby!"

Kathleen Mulloy was sobbing as he pulled her forward, toward the counsel table in front of the jury box. Thelma Sturdevant moved aside so that he wasn't in her line of fire. Alice Mary Brennan, a look of disgust on her features, got up and walked away into the jury room, where Gus Simes had been stationed.

Al Martin kept his eyes on the rear courtroom door, ignoring what was happening.

Gormley shrugged, disapproving but uncaring, and stepped inside the judge's office.

"Mickey!" Kathleen Mulloy shrieked in desperation as Hagen shoved her roughly onto the counsel table. Her eyes sought him out. "Mickey, please!"

Mickey Noonan looked away.

"Oh, help me, please." The words were only a whisper as Hagen, his face flushed, ripped at her skirt. Then she screamed.

Frank Conroy lay on the floor. He could only open one eye. He could not talk, his throat seemed blocked. He couldn't move or stand; he knew something was broken. All he could do was think. And that was like being condemned to hell itself.

"Please," he prayed. "Help her."

The girl's cries and sounds seemed to echo in the courtroom.

Conroy writhed in pain. "I am your priest," he called

silently. "I am a priest like Melchizedek. God, I call on you to help that girl!"

Hagen's rising giggle was obscene.

Frank Conroy's clenched teeth were exposed as his face twisted in the agony of being unable to do anything. His very being seemed on fire. "Damn you, I know you are there," he screamed inside himself. "Damn you, damn you! You exist, you are! Now, damn you—help that girl!"

Through his one eye he saw Ace Gilbert, gun in hand, slip in through the side door. To Conroy he was the avenging angel. Even before the shooting started, Frank Conroy knew that his desperate prayer had been answered.

6:50 p.m.

LITTLE Chester's world had lost all meaning. There was no logical explanation for the things that happened.

Some woman was screaming.

The prosecutor who had tried his case came gliding by the cell door, a revolver in his hand and wearing no shoes. He was moving quickly but quietly. He glanced in at Little Chester and held a finger to his lips to indicate silence. He passed out of sight.

Then Chester heard the gunshots.

6:51 p.m.

IT was her screams that did it.

Gilbert knew the police would do nothing, that had been explained to him as official policy. There was no bond between himself and the girl. Once he had been fond of her, but that was over. Still, something had to be done.

The situation wasn't much different than the caves. It would be the same here, just instinct, no time for thought, mind and body united into a killing machine. And if you died, it was because this was the time and the place for dying.

He had slipped off his shoes so that his approach would be silent. Six shots, that was all he had, and there wouldn't be time to reload, but he was good with a pistol and experienced.

He had gestured to the prisoner in the corridor cell to be quiet.

She had been calling for Judge Noonan, her voice a scream, as Gilbert had carefully and silently twisted the doorknob. In one swift motion he had slid the door open partway and slipped into the courtroom.

A black man in prisoner clothes had a machine pistol in his hands. He was only a few feet away, but he was turned, watching something. Gilbert shot him through the head. He was aware that the black man was falling as he swung the pistol.

The judges sat in the jury box like a grotesque frozen painting. A blond woman with a pistol in her hand was turning toward him. Gilbert noted that she did not have a grenade.

Another man in prisoner clothes was struggling with a woman on the counsel table. Gilbert did not look at the woman. The man was rising, his face dazed by surprise. His trousers were half off.

Gilbert's bullet caught him in the face. He stumbled back. Gilbert fired again, without care for the judges directly behind the man. There was no time for thought in combat, only action. The second bullet hit the man in the chest, finishing him.

The woman near the jury box hesitated, her eyes on the two fallen men.

Gilbert sensed movement inside the judge's office and at the rear of the courtroom. The woman with the pistol had crouched down behind the table. She fired without aim, the bullets going wild. But slugs were cracking into the marble frame of the office entrance. Gilbert turned. A man with a small moustache standing in the back of the courtroom near the entrance doors was firing.

The surprise had gone, and the odds had shifted. Gilbert dived back through the side door pulling it shut behind him. He pressed himself against the wall of the hallway as bullets from within tore through the heavy wooden doorway, exploding mists of splinters.

Ace Gilbert began to move slowly backward, his pistol aimed at the closed door. If they were experienced, he could expect a grenade. He watched the door as he backed down the long corridor. If they just opened the door a crack and rolled a grenade out, he would be killed. But if they were foolhardy enough to try to see him, he could drop the person with the explosives. It would be a short-lived victory; the blast from a dropped grenade would kill him anyway. He slid back faster, moving his stockinged feet like a dancer. He reached the safety of Powell's courtroom and slipped into the office. His eyes never left the corridor entrance as he quickly reloaded the pistol.

No sounds came from the hallway. They might be coming, also in stockinged feet.

It was a risk. A good many soldiers had died trying to peek around a corner. But it was a risk he had to take. He popped out, glanced quickly down the corridor, then drew his head back. There was no one there. For the first time he noticed that he was sucking for breath.

Ace Gilbert glanced over at the overturned counsel table. Ginger Steiner's face peered over the top. He picked up the telephone, again taking up a station inside the office where he had a clear shot at the corridor entrance. "Anyone there?" he asked quietly.

"Captain Falkner here. Is that you, Gilbert?"

"Yes," he said softly. "In a minute you'll be getting reports of gunfire in Harbor's courtroom."

"Oh, Jesus! You got any idea what happened over there?"

"I shot and killed two of the terrorists."

"You did what?" Captain Falkner screamed.

"I killed two of the terrorists," Gilbert repeated.

"You goddamned dummy, you fucking son of a bitch! What are you trying to do—get all those people there killed? Are you crazy, Gilbert?" The captain continued screaming.

"They were raping the woman probation officer. I could hear her scream," Gilbert said evenly. "I was a combat soldier with a lot of experience in this sort of thing, so I went down there. I surprised them."

"They'll start killing the judges," the policeman moaned.

"I doubt it. The judges are their only protection," Gilbert said. "Do you want to know what happened, or not?"

"Listen, I don't give a fuck what kind of soldier you

were, you understand that? You stay the fuck out of this.
This is police business. If you pull any more stunts, I'll
see that you're prosecuted, you get that?"

Gilbert felt more amusement than anger. "What for,
interfering with rape?"

"I'm not going to—"

"Listen," Gilbert's voice took on the hard edge of command. It felt natural and easy. "You are probably a mound
of fat who has spent twenty years ticketing parked cars.
You shut your mouth and get this information to whoever
is commanding the operation in this building. This is all
being recorded, Captain, and you are exhibiting some
rather strange attitudes for a policeman. Now shut up and
listen."

There was nothing but heavy breathing in response.

"I recognized the two men I shot. One was Johnson and
the other Hagen. Both are dead, I'm pretty sure of that.
I saw a blond woman, about middle twenties. She had a
gun but no grenade. I think she was guarding the judges.
I saw a man in the back of the courtroom, near the doors.
A thin man with a moustache. He had a pistol."

"What about the others? According to our information
there are three more, two men and a woman?"

"I didn't see them. I know someone was moving around
in Judge Harbor's office right next to the side door I used.
The others could have been in there or in the empty jury
room. All the hostages are sitting in the jury box."

"They just let you walk in there and shoot them up?"

"It was only a matter of a few seconds. They were
surprised. The one in the back of the courtroom reacted
first, then the blond woman. Either they were too excited
to aim or they are lousy shots."

"Jesus!"

"Bad shots or not, they were sure to hit me before I
could get both of them, so I got the hell out of there and

came back here. They fired a couple of rounds through the door, but no one came after me. At least not yet."

"Any of the judges get hit?"

"If they did, I didn't see it. I was moving pretty fast. Like I said, it was only a matter of seconds."

"Yeah." The voice had lost the sharp tone of hostility. "Look, Gilbert, I understand why you did what you did, okay? But we are playing for lives here. For God's sake, don't do it again, eh?" There was a pause. "Things are pretty tense around here, Gilbert." There was another pause. "What I'm trying to say is that I take back what I said about you. I was just upset, you know?"

"I know."

"Yeah, I guess you would." The captain paused again. "I'll get all this to the right people. Hey, hang in there, okay?"

"Right." Gilbert's eyes were riveted on the empty corridor entrance, his ears alert for sounds.

7:00 p.m.

AL Martin's bullets had almost hit Larry Gormley. He had dived to the floor when the shooting began. He lay next to Justice Tingle.

Gormley was conscious of the sudden silence, broken only by Tingle's distressed and labored breathing. Then he inhaled the pungent odor of gun smoke.

"Larry!" He heard Martin's urgent whisper, sounding more like a hiss. "Larry, are you all right?"

Gormley stood up. His legs seemed unsteady and weak. He gripped the machine gun even tighter.

"Larry, for Christ's sake . . ." Martin's voice trembled.

"I'm here," he managed to mumble. He walked slowly out of the office, his machine gun pointed directly at the closed hall door. The door seemed to have taken on a life of its own, like some imagination-created monster that posed an unthinkable threat. The wood had been splintered where bullets had torn into it. To Gormley's eyes the bullets seemed to have cut a face on the surface of the door, a frightening, savage face.

He stumbled over Johnson's body. For a moment he couldn't take his eyes off Johnson's face. The eyes were closed and the mouth open, as if in sleep, but part of his temple was missing and the blood looked like spilled paint.

Gormley looked away from Johnson's body. The woman hostage was sitting on the floor in front of the counsel table, clutching her clothing to her chest as her body jerked with silent sobs. Thelma was on the other side of the table, crouched down. Her face showed no emotion, just shock. Her mouth was slightly open, and her eyes had a dull look. Hagen's body lay near Thelma.

Simes and Alice Mary Brennan stared at him from the entrance of the empty jury room. Al Martin stood in the back of the courtroom, and even from a distance he could see the fear in the man's taut face.

The men in the jury box stared at him, their faces also showing the strain of fear.

Everybody was looking at him, and again Gormley had the sensation that it was all a dream. But the eyes of these watchers seemed like a silent accusation.

Even the man Hagen had hit with the chair was watching him. The man could not raise his head, but his eyes were riveted on Gormley.

Hagen lay on his back, his arms almost casually out-stretched. His mouth was open. The top of his face was bloody, even one of his opened eyes was filled with blood. Hagen's trousers were obscenely bunched at his knees. His nakedness seemed somehow even more shocking than the blood.

Gormley looked away from the body. He was shaking now. He desperately wanted someone to tell him what to do. He stared at the hostages.

Judge Powell saw the look in the blond gunman's face. He observed the tremors that made the short barrel of his machine gun tremble. Powell sensed that the man was at the razor's edge, much more dangerous now because of his mental condition. Powell realized that just one wrong word might turn that shaking gun into a killing machine.

"Young man," Powell began gently, "you don't want anyone else hurt. If you lay down your arms now, I'm sure that—"

Rage instantly contorted Gormley's features. He pointed the machine gun directly at Powell, holding the muzzle only inches away. "Shut up!" he screamed.

Powell remained motionless, commanding his muscles to be still so that he would show no emotion, evoke no response. He could clearly see the young man's finger on the gun's trigger. The gun was that close.

"If you give up now," Powell said quietly and evenly, "I'll do all in my power to help you."

Gormley continued to tremble, his narrowed eyes wet with emotion. Powell inhaled, expecting the worst.

"Clyde, for God's sake, keep quiet!" Judge Richards's voice was no more than a strangled whisper.

Gormley looked away from Powell and glared up at Richards. The gun muzzle swung toward the other judge. "Be quiet!" The words echoed in the quiet courtroom.

Suddenly Gormley remembered the door, that awful door that had brought such quick death. He spun around as if the door had spoken. He forgot about the judges as he covered the door with his shaking gun.

He was losing control, he knew that. Hagen and Johnson had been his courage. When they had come, he had felt safe and confident again. Now they were dead, and panic had seized him completely. He no longer worried about the others seeing it, he no longer cared what they might think. He just wanted out.

"Larry." Alice Mary Brennan's thick voice sounded strangely soothing. "Larry, what shall we do now?"

He wanted to reply, but he couldn't find words.

"Larry," she persisted, now with a bit more force. "What now?"

He watched the door. For one heart-stopping moment he thought he saw it move, but then he realized it was probably his imagination.

Gormley was dimly aware that Al Martin was coming forward from his post at the rear of the courtroom. He wanted to tell him to go back, but again he found he could not speak. His total concentration was on that side door.

"Larry," Martin asked, "are you all right?" The words were spoken in a low whisper.

Gormley said nothing.

"Come on, Larry," Martin said, gently taking his elbow.

"Get your fucking hands off me!" Gormley shouted, his face suddenly crimson with uncontrolled rage.

"All right!" Martin shouted back. "But you better pull yourself together, pal. We are in one hell of a tough spot."

Gormley forced himself to breath deeply. This was no dream, and he had to control himself. He exhaled slowly. "They'll hit us now." The words were spoken very softly. "It's just a matter of time. If one man can do it, they'll figure a squad can do it better. They'll be coming."

"What do we do?" Martin asked. They were joined by Alice Mary and Simes. Thelma resumed her post, her pistol covering the silent, frightened hostages.

Johnson's body was directly in Gormley's line of sight. He couldn't stand to look at it. "Come on in the office," he said.

Tingle had not moved. Half conscious, he lay still, his chest heaving for breath, his eyes staring vacantly ahead. Death—it seemed to Gormley that death had its icy finger pointed at all of them. Gormley tried to shake off the numbing effect of fear, to force himself to think clearly.

"We can expect an attack," he said, his voice barely audible, "either here or when we try to leave."

"They won't do that," Alice Mary protested. "They won't risk the hostages."

Gormley badly wanted a cigarette, but he was afraid his hands would shake too much even to light it. "Ask Hagen and Johnson how much value the hostages have," he muttered. "Hostages didn't save them, and they aren't going to save us. These people have made up their minds." He paused. "We won't stand a chance."

"We can do it, Larry," Alice Mary said, but her voice betrayed her own disbelief in the statement. "At least we can try," she added.

Gormley, his eyes still glued on the side door, shook his head. "We might have made it with Hagen and Johnson's help. But we'll never pull it off by ourselves."

"We can use the hostages to trade," Al Martin said. "God, we can't give up now." His tone carried his acknowledgment of defeat.

"They'll hit us," Gormley repeated. "Maybe not here, maybe at the airport, but they'll hit us. You can count on it."

"I'm prepared to die," Alice Mary Brennan said, but the words carried no real conviction.

Martin was silent for a moment. "We had better talk this over with Thelma."

Gormley shook his head. "No reason. Thelma will do what I say."

Martin nodded. He too had lost his nerve. "Look, maybe we can still bargain. We have the hostages. Maybe we can work out a deal."

Gormley looked at him. He felt the first relief from the grip of panic. Gormley desperately wanted to quit, but he didn't want to be the one who suggested it. Now it would look like Martin's idea.

"Okay," Gormley said, "I'll take a shot at it. Cover both those doors."

Martin walked out into the courtroom. He stood by the vacant judge's bench, his eyes on the closed rear doors, his gun ready. He glanced down for a moment at Johnson's body, then quickly looked away.

Alice Mary moved to the office doorway. She still held the live grenade, and her hand felt cramped, but she ignored the discomfort, covering the side door with her pistol.

Gus Simes had remained quiet, but his mind was working with the speed of a computer. He lit a cigarette. The whole situation was changing. He carefully thought about his own future.

Gormley picked up the telephone. "Anyone there?" He tried to keep his voice even and calm.

"Just a minute please," a female voice answered.

Gormley shut his eyes, trying to force himself to relax. But his heart seemed to be thumping almost audibly within his chest.

"I'm here," the mayor said at last. "I was down the hall. Look, we have almost all the money, but the airplane is—"

"Whose idea was the shooting?" Gormley's voice cracked as he spoke.

"What shooting?"

"Don't give me that shit," Gormley snapped. "We had an agreement. No tricks, remember?"

"Wait!" The mayor's panic matched Gormley's own.

"Listen, it was a mistake. The standing order is not to interfere with you. It won't happen again."

Gormley wished that he could believe the man, but he had the bodies of Hagen and Johnson as mute evidence of how much he could rely on the mayor's quick assurances.

"We have decided," Gormley spoke slowly, "that we don't have a chance to make it to the airport." He paused. "So we have agreed to blow this place up and everyone in it."

"Wait! Listen, for God's sake! Don't do that. You don't want to die. We'll do whatever you want." The mayor spoke so quickly that it was hard to understand him.

Gormley felt very tired. Just the effort of holding the phone seemed exhausting. "We have acted as an army of revolution," Gormley said softly. "All our acts have been legal acts of war."

The mayor did not reply at once. "I'm sure they were," he finally said, his voice alert but wary.

"If we surrender, we demand that we be treated as soldiers."

There was the sound of muted whispering on the other end of the line.

"Go on," the mayor said cautiously.

Gormley nodded to himself. "I want a written document stating that there shall be no criminal prosecution resulting from anything that we've done."

Again there was a pause and muted whispering.

"Okay, I can agree to that," the mayor said quickly. "I'll have whatever terms you want written up."

"No prosecution," Gormley said.

"That's right," the mayor now sounded confident. "You will be treated as prisoners of war. If you surrender and release the hostages, I will personally see to it that you are flown to whatever country you choose."

"In writing," Gormley repeated.

"All of it will be in writing," the mayor said.

"I'll check with the others," Gormley said. "Hold on." Alice Mary Brennan motioned Al Martin to return. He came back into the office. Gormley held the receiver against his chest. "I said we would surrender if we aren't prosecuted and only if we are treated as prisoners of war. They said they'll fly us to any country we choose if we give up."

"Christ, you don't believe that, do you, Larry?" Al Martin demanded.

Gormley sadly shook his head. "No." He sighed. "Oh, they'll come over with a nice legal document, but as soon as we lay down our guns, they'll charge us with everything in the book."

"Then what's the advantage?"

Gormley desperately wanted to end it. "Propaganda," he replied glibly, determined to sell them on giving up. "Look, we can raise hell in the courts. Using that document, we can speak to the issues and tell the people what's wrong with this government and this society."

"But they'll just rip the damn thing up," Alice Mary Brennan said.

Gormley stared at her for a moment. "I'll ask that they send along a lawyer for us. He can keep the document. I'll make that a part of the deal. I'll name the right lawyer so that even if they do tear it up, he'll be able to testify—"

"You people are all fuckin' nuts!" Gus Simes exploded. "As soon as we say quits, they'll jam our asses into jail, and no one will ever hear from us again."

"No," Gormley said. "We will use the First Amendment—"

Simes, his face shaking with exploding emotion, spoke quickly. "You damned loonies just might get away with it. They wink at this political shit most of the time anyway, but I am charged with first-degree murder, and if you

314 ■ William J. Coughlin

think all this has helped my chances, you got another think coming."

"We don't have a chance," Gormley said.

"Maybe you don't, maybe you do," Simes replied. "But I sure as hell don't, no matter which way you slice the cake."

"You are part of the World Liberation Army," Alice Mary Brennan said severely, "and you will obey orders!"

"Fuckin' broad," Simes said, leveling his pistol at her. "Gimme that fuckin' grenade." He held out his hand. "Now! Goddamn it!"

Gus Simes felt his heart pounding as he took the grenade. He carefully kept the safety lever compressed. The steel explosive felt slimy from the nervous sweat of Alice Brennan's hand. His own hand was clammy too.

Simes looked at Gormley. The man was white-faced and defeated. Simes felt the same way, only he had no choice. These political fools could probably talk their way into a short prison term, maybe get out altogether. It had happened before. But Simes knew that he would be treated entirely differently. He had a criminal record. He was up on murder charges. There would be no political road out for him. He really didn't know exactly what he would do, but he knew that he couldn't surrender. He had to play out the string.

Gus Simes walked into the courtroom. He slid the leather strap of the bag of explosives over his shoulder. He had his pistol in one hand, the live grenade in the other. Simes looked up at the two rows of hostages.

He turned and spoke to Gormley, who watched from the office. "If you want to surrender, that's your business," he said. "But you tell the people on the telephone that I am coming out, and I am coming out with a bag of explosives, a live grenade, and a hostage."

Gormley started to protest.

"Tell them!" Simes commanded.

He looked back at the jury box. He would need the most important hostage. Tingle was out, he couldn't even walk. And the girl hostage was a useless sobbing mess.

Simes's eyes played over the men in the jury box.

"Stand up, Harbor," he commanded.

7:08 p.m.

ACE Gilbert, still covering the corridor, moved a few steps so that he could see Ginger Steiner. She looked over the counsel table, her eyes wide with question and concern. Something was bound to happen soon. The stalemate in the other courtroom couldn't last forever.

"Stay here and keep down," Gilbert said to the court clerk, who had remained huddled against the rear of the office. The man was too frightened even to nod.

Gilbert stole a quick glance down the hallway. It was still deserted. He took a deep breath, then leaped across the corridor's opening. There was no gunfire. He kept his pistol leveled at the doorway as he walked backward to Ginger Steiner and Ted Hemmings.

Ace joined them behind the overturned counsel table. Hemmings didn't look good. His face was taking on the ashen warnings of serious shock.

"Ace, what's going on?" Ginger whispered as she gripped his arm. Her touch conveyed no panic. Her fingers seemed to signal concern and reassurance.

Ace Gilbert kept his eyes on the corridor. "Some terrorists have taken the judges hostage. The police are bargaining with them now."

"I saw you go down the hall and I heard the shots . . ." her voice trailed off.

"Did you hear the screams?"

"Yes," she replied softly.

"Well, one of the hostages is a woman probation officer named Kathleen Mulloy. They were trying to rape her. I went down there and snapped off a few shots."

"Did you hit anybody?"

He risked a glance at her. "Yes. I shot two of the terrorists."

Her grip was almost painful. "You could have been killed."

Ace Gilbert started to laugh.

"I can't see the humor," she said quietly.

"I'm soaked through," he said. "Ginger, my pulse is racing, and I'm sweating like a horse. I'm honest-to-God scared."

She looked puzzled. "I would think so."

He looked down at her. "It's a sensation I haven't felt for quite a while. It tells me something about myself."

"What?"

"I'm human."

For a moment she didn't reply, her eyes questioning. "I don't understand, Ace."

"It's pretty complicated." He still watched the doorway. "Remind me and I'll tell you about it sometime."

"I'm scared too," she said very quietly.

"Don't be," he said, putting his free arm around her shoulders. Her hair smelled good. "We're safe here. It's just a matter of time." It was a lie. The thick wooden table wouldn't protect them against bullets, nor would it stop the screaming metal fragments of an exploding grenade. They were anything but safe, but there was no reason she should know.

Hemmings was only semiconscious. Ginger had done a good job of stopping his bleeding, but he needed medical help. Hemmings groaned. Gilbert knew that the pain of a broken leg was terrible. But Hemmings was toughing it out. He admired the man's courage.

Ginger Steiner was also proving to be something very special. Gilbert knew that most women would have dissolved into tears and panic. Under the circumstances it wouldn't be an unreasonable reaction. But Ginger had displayed real nerve. She had taken care of the wounded officer without hesitation or question. She was proving herself capable and brave. She was, in his judgment, a very special person. He hugged her tightly as he kept the pistol aimed at the corridor.

"Thank you," she whispered.

7:15 p.m.

SIMES could hear Gormley talking on the telephone. They would know he was coming and they would know about the grenade, the explosives, and Harbor.

The shot-up side door posed an ominous barrier. Police might be waiting beyond, poised for a quick attack when the door opened. Gus Simes clenched his teeth. It had to be done.

"Open the door," he commanded Judge Harbor.

Harbor turned, his eyes wide with fear, his moustache twitching nervously. "Really, don't you think—"

"Open the fuckin' door!" Simes snarled.

Harbor reached a shaking hand toward the brass doorknob. He held it a moment before moving and then cautiously opened the heavy wooden door. Simes stood directly behind him, just in case. He could see down the long, narrow hallway. To his great relief it was deserted.

He poked Harbor in the back with his pistol. "Let's go," he said.

Harbor jumped and took a few quick steps to the elevator. He stopped and looked at Simes.

"Aw, for Christ's sake," Simes growled. "Push the Down button, dummy."

Obediently, the judge daintily pushed the button. Immediately they could hear the rumble of the elevator motor as it started up.

"I think you're making a mistake taking me for a hostage," Harbor said, his voice almost squeaking. "As a matter of fact, the title executive judge is really just an honorary thing. I was going to resign. I mean, I've only been executive judge for one month. Judge Powell, the black judge, the one sitting in the first row in the jury box, he was the executive judge for a long time. I think he'd probably be a better choice than—"

"Oh, Jesus!" Simes exploded. "Shut up!"

Harbor's mouth remained open but no additional words were spoken.

Gus Simes tried to watch everything at once, his head swiveling from one courtroom door to the other. Glancing into the hallway cell he saw Little Chester huddled against the rear of the cell.

"Hey, Chester," Simes said, his voice taut. "That you?"

"Yeah, Gus. Say, what the hell is going on?"

Simes's face seemed to sag. "Oh, God, you wouldn't believe it, Chester. You just wouldn't believe it."

The automatic elevator rose, and the doors opened. Simes shepherded Harbor aboard and stepped in after him.

Judge Harbor just stood there.

"Push the goddamned button for the first floor, you stupid shit!" Simes yelled.

Tears welled in Harbor's eyes as his shaking hand rose and he extended a finger to press the bottom button. The automatic doors slowly closed.

Gus Simes was quivering with fear and excitement. His hands had become slippery. The elevator gave a short jerk as it began to descend. That jerk was just enough to cause the grenade to squirt from Simes's wet grip. It made a metallic *bang* as it bounced on the steel floor of the descending car.

Both men reached for it at the same time, colliding into each other. Again, they both tried for it, sending it skidding around the car. Simes made one last desperate grab for it, but missed.

The car reached the main floor just as the grenade blew up, igniting the other explosives in the bag. The force blew out every window in the Criminal Court Building as well as windows in many of the nearby buildings. A boiling, choking smoke cloud billowed from the blown-out windows and doors of the wrecked first floor.

In the executive judge's courtroom, as smoke poured from the wrecked elevator door in the hall, Larry Gormley slowly walked past Johnson's body to the center of the courtroom. Alice Mary, Al Martin, and Thelma joined him.

Ceremoniously, Gormley set down his machine gun on the floor, stood up, and slowly raised his hands.

4

conclusion

chapter ten

the information desk

RED Mehan watched the glass workers replacing the broken panes in the lobby windows. The court was open for business, but with only three judges sitting. The public elevators had not yet been inspected, so everyone had to use the stairs. Barricades blocked entrance to the private rear hall. One of the window men took a break, bought a cup of coffee from the blind man, then walked over to the information desk, using its wooden rail as a makeshift bar. Red was glad to have an audience.

"Have ya been back there where the judges' elevator used to be? Geez, what a goddamned mess. Just a hole now, nothin' but a big fuckin' hole. The ceiling, the walls, even the fuckin' floor have all been blown apart. It will take a pretty penny to repair all that. They'll have to re-build the whole thing, and you know how things cost today.

"I understand they're going to lay out Harbor at city hall. You know, one of them public mourning things. Shit, I don't see the point in it. I mean, I would if they had a complete body, but after that blast there was nothin' left but hamburger, ya know. Christ, they couldn't identify nothin'. So what is in that casket might be Harbor, or it might be the burglar, but it's probably a mixture of both. Funny when you think about it. I mean, all those people going by the closed casket, weepin' and looking sad and maybe they're honoring that fuckin' burglar. Kinda odd, ya know?

"Of course, Harbor was no real loss. He was an idiot and he hadn't put in a full day's work since he got here.

"Naw, I ain't speaking ill of the dead; that's just a plain fact.

"The radio this morning says the governor will appoint somebody to fill Harbor's vacancy. I don't know about the process, but they keep coming up with horse's asses. It's tough, but they manage to find them somehow. The governor will have to act fast, though. This whole court was catching hell because of the backlog of cases before this happened. So they'll need all the judges they can get. That backlog was the reason why Tingle was down here from the supreme court.

"Ya know, I'll bet he never thought he would end up this way. They must have really scared the shit right out of him. You wouldn't think it of a big guy like him, but you can never tell. Heart attack. So he's laying around in an intensive care ward, all wired up and suckin' for air *through an oxygen mask. Well, that's what he gets for coming down here to 'the Zoo.'*

"*Yeah, that's what they call this place—'the Zoo.' You stick around here a few days and you'll see some real human animals. Of course, this place is almost shut down now, but on a regular day you can see sights here that you'll never see anyplace else in the world. You ought to take a day off and just hang around here. Damndest show in the world.*

"*Speaking of animals, we got an old judge here who everybody calls Honest John. Honest John Sloan. The son of a bitch is so crooked you could open the cork in a wine bottle with him.*

"*Shit, they tell me the echo of the blast hadn't died away when Honest John gets on the TV and says as senior man he's taking over the court and runnin' it just like Tingle. See, the word on the street is that Tingle was making money on the side—fixin' cases and shit like that. Anyway, old Sloan figured he had hit the mother lode. But the rest of the judges elected Judge Powell as head man. I hear old Sloan had a fit.*

"*And those terrorists. A bunch of middle-class daffies. Had the holy shit scared out of 'em, I hear. But it didn't last long. I notice from the newspapers that they are sitting over in jail making speeches and raising fuckin' hell. The Irish broad, the ex-nun—I can't think of her name— has gone on a hunger strike. Although I understand she can use it. Fat, ya know. That leader of theirs, Gormley, they tell me he won't put on any clothes, just runs around the damned cell block mother naked. Says it's a form of protest. Hell, they got him in a cell by himself. If I was them, I'd toss him into a cell full of horny lifers. He'd get his trousers on in a hurry then.*

"*I don't know what they're going to do with them. They killed one of their own people before coming down to the*

*court. Looks like a straight first-degree murder charge
against them all to me. But then you got every left-wing
lawyer this side of the Mississippi comin' into town to
defend them. They'll put on a show that will play for
years. It will be a circus. But, hell, it won't make that
much difference here at 'the Zoo'—the whole fuckin' place
is a circus to begin with. A circus with lots of animal acts.*

*"Hey, look at what is comin' through the door. See that
black dude with the big floppy hat and gold tie? See the
little bitch with him, the blond wig and tight slacks? That
ain't high society, baby, that's a pimp and one of his
women.*

"Interesting here, ain't it?"

kathleen ann mulloy

KATHLEEN Ann Mulloy lay in her hospital bed. She could
see the treetops blowing about in the light wind. It was
pleasant. The blue sky was cloudless. It was quiet in the
room. There was a television, but it went unused. Physically she was all right except for some bruises and
scratches. The doctors knew that, but they were kind, allowing her a quiet place where she could gather up the
threads of her life and find some way of mending herself.

The crying spells had stopped now. The medicine had
helped, but she knew it was really her own desire to throw
off the depression that was turning the trick.

She had not been raped. The doctors had assured her
of that. The horrible events in the courtroom at first
seemed etched in her mind for all time, but even in the

course of a few days they were already beginning to blur. She hoped that one day it would be nothing more than a dim memory.

But Kathleen could still remember the cold look in Mickey Noonan's eyes when she had begged him for help. Any feeling she might have had for him died with that uncaring stare. She felt ashamed that she had ever had anything to do with him. She pitied his wife. A man like that cared only for himself; there was no room for anyone else. But at least she had finally found that out. Frank Conroy had been her guide to the truth.

Frank Conroy—just thinking about him made her smile. He certainly had been right about Mickey Noonan. He seemed to have a sense about evaluating people that she lacked. She would be much more careful in the future.

The nurse had allowed her to walk down and visit Frank. He looked so uncomfortable propped up in the hospital bed, his arm extended from his side in a plaster cast, his face still swollen and bruised. Despite all his pain, he had been so cheerful. She realized that his attitude was out of concern for her rather than any real reflection of his physical feelings. People like Frank Conroy were rare, people who actually care what happened to others.

He had been so apologetic about bringing her to that meeting. He had wanted to help her see things in perspective and thought he had failed. But she knew that despite the danger, the experience had indeed changed her life.

Conroy had advised her to leave the probation department. She had an education and there were a number of horizons to be explored. It was good advice, and she had decided to take it. A new life, but no more affairs with flawed men. She was a grown girl now with mature judgment. Hereafter she would look beyond the facade and search for the real man beneath. There would be no more Noonans.

Kathleen closed her eyes. She felt a quiet contentment as she half-listened to the muted bustle in the busy hospital halls beyond her door.

honorable clyde powell

MILTON Harbor, in a closed casket, lay in state at city hall. Powell was told that a line of people—apparently curious —continued to trickle by the bier. A city memorial service was planned for the next day.

Clyde Powell had been asked to give the eulogy, but he deferred to the mayor. It was the kind of duty the mayor loved. The man would have made a successful evangelist.

Death had made Harbor a hero. The people needed heroes. Powell knew the mayor would do a good job in projecting that image.

James Tingle, too, had been singled out by the press for honor. King Tingle hovered between life and death in a hospital. And although Powell considered him a disgrace to the legal profession, he could not help feeling sorry for the King.

Only three judges were working in the building. The others, understandably, had taken time off to recover. But, Powell reflected, perhaps the horror they had experienced would eventually prove beneficial. He had spoken with the governor about the replacement for Harbor and the need for additional judges. For a change, the governor seemed receptive. He promised to take it up with the legislative leaders. And Chief Justice Buckington had telephoned, professing guilt at having exposed Tingle to danger. Playing on that guilt before it passed, Powell persuaded him to assign a platoon of outstate judges to the criminal court. With sufficient help the backlog would soon be whittled down.

Judge Stewart Richards came in. He was in his shirt-sleeves and he smoked a large black cigar.

"I thought you weren't supposed to smoke," Powell said as Richards pulled up a chair.

"To hell with it," Richards grunted. "If I can live through yesterday, I can live through anything. That includes an occasional cigar." He tipped the ash into a wastebasket. "Well, what's new? Are we going to get any help?"

"Buckington is sending in outstate judges, and the governor is going to ask the legislature for additional permanent judges."

Richards nodded. "You have been busy. Did the governor give you any idea whom he might appoint to Harbor's vacancy?"

"No," Powell replied, fanning away some of the thick cigar smoke, "but I suggested someone."

"Oh?"

"Young Gilbert."

"Really?"

"He's qualified, he knows criminal law, and he isn't afraid of work."

Richards scowled. "I don't know, Clyde, he's pretty young."

"We could do with a bit of youth around here."

"But I think Ace was getting fed up with this place. No use appointing someone who doesn't like the job. Maybe he doesn't give a damn anymore."

Powell peered through the smoke at the other man. "Did he look like the type of man who didn't give a damn when he walked into that hell and shot it out with those terrorists? I don't know about you, but I'll never forget it."

Richards chuckled. "Hell, you got me there, Clyde. When he walked in with that gun, he looked like Superman and the Lone Ranger all rolled into one. Damn, I was crying because of that poor girl. I was never so happy to see anyone in my life."

Powell nodded. "There's a lot more to Mr. Ace Gilbert than meets the eye. Oh, I've watched him. A lot of this crap around here turned him off. He lost some of that enthusiasm he used to have. But I think as a judge he'll get it all back. He'll have something he can do about it."

"Will the governor appoint him?"

"I think so. You know how he is. He sniffs around a lot, checks with everybody twice. Finally he does what his administrative assistant tells him to do." Powell grinned. "I talked to the administrative assistant. He read the papers. I think he'll recommend Gilbert."

"Are you going to tell Gilbert?"

Powell shook his head. "No."

"But he won't know what you did for him."

"It's better that way. I don't want him beholden to me, or anyone. We need new blood here, Stewart. A fresh start. We don't want any more Tingles."

"Think they'll send down anybody else?"

Powell frowned. "You never know. After what happened to Tingle I doubt if they could get anyone. We'll just have to be on guard."

"I wouldn't want to go through any of this again," Richards said.

Powell grinned. "With great intellects like Beaver Buckington running things, what can we possibly have to fear?"

"Oh, Lord, protect your humble servants!" Richards laughed.

"Amen."

justice james tingle

HE lay there and idly watched the slow drip from the plastic IV bottle. What little sound there was came from behind him, where the respirator motor gently pumped, forcing oxygen up through the plastic tubes placed in his nose. He was conscious of the very soft electric *bleep* that came from the monitor machines on the other side of the respirator. They had taped electrodes to each part of him, and the machines recorded each pulse, evaluating it and coding it. If anything went amiss, the machines would sound a soft alarm in the nursing station, and then he would be surrounded with a sea of faces—and stuck with a variety of needles. It had happened more than once.

Tingle, who was heavily sedated, had lost all track of time. Occasionally faces appeared. Usually nurses, and sometimes a doctor. Their words were always cheerful, always quiet. It was a place of whispers.

Tingle could remember only part of what had happened in the court, little snatches of memories, like a poorly spliced movie film. And it somehow all seemed unimportant. He presumed that was the effect of the tranquilizers.

They had provided him with the city's leading cardiologist, Dr. John Mossman.

Dr. Mossman had told him that it had been a severe heart attack but that he had a good chance of surviving it, providing he was very quiet and let nature do its healing work. The doctor had also told Tingle that if he lived, there could be no more smoking or drinking. He would have to stay on a strict diet, probably for the rest of his days. And sex would only be possible with his wife, otherwise it would be too exciting, and possibly fatal. Tingle then knew that Dr. Mossman had not read his history carefully, since Tingle was not married. No cigars, no liquor, no good food, and no women. Death did not seem such a frightful alternative. Dr. Mossman said that bypass surgery might be considered, but all that was in the future. Tingle got the impression from the unemotional Mossman that the good doctor wasn't too convinced that Tingle had a future.

He wasn't allowed newspapers or books. Reading was out. There was no television. They had even stopped visitors after Chief Justice Buckington had come in to see him. Buckington's buck-toothed face had been a pious picture of contrite guilt. He had patted Tingle's massive hand and told him not to worry, that if he were disabled, he would be able to leave the supreme court with a very nice pension. Not enormous, but enough to get by on, if one was prudent. Buckington had seemed to believe that Tingle was as good as off the supreme court. He complimented Tingle on the fine job he had done in "the Zoo." Then Buckington had told Tingle that Milton Harbor had been given a hero's burial. The chief justice had smiled, telling Tingle that the city council had had a special meeting to rename the Criminal Court Building. It was now the Harbor Hall of Justice.

It was at that point that all the monitoring machines had gone berserk. They later told Tingle that they had had to call a "cardiac arrest" emergency because his heart had stopped beating. The medical team had pounded Tingle's mammoth chest until his heart had started once again. But it had been close.

After Buckington's visit Dr. Mossman ordered no visitors.

So James "The King" Tingle lay on his back, dreamily going from sleep to consciousness and back again. He had no diversions, only his thoughts.

But his thoughts comforted him. He would make it back, physically and professionally. Tingle had faced a lifetime of challenges, and this would be just one more. The King thought about money. He had come close to real wealth. If it hadn't been for those terrorists, he would have been rich in just a matter of a few more weeks. But the past was past. At least he had paid off his gambling debts. He was back at square one, but that wasn't so bad; he had been there before. Dr. Mossman said that a positive attitude would be helpful in the healing process. It made sense. Tingle put the thoughts of lost riches out of his mind.

But they wouldn't get him off the court. Hell, he had been elected. The state constitution provided for removal of unfit judges, but it was a long process, and he would be well on the road to recovery before anyone even suggested that the removal machinery begin. They wouldn't move too fast against the state's only black supreme court justice. He would be back.

And there were always other ways of making money. If a smart man stayed alert, watched for opportunity, and seized it before it escaped him, he could grab that elusive brass ring.

Diet, surgery—whatever it took—James Tingle was determined that he would come back. Dr. Mossman had said no booze, no smoking, rich food, or women—but he hadn't said a damned thing about money.

The King would indeed return.

the assistant prosecutor

EVERYTHING had gone wrong. Preparing dinner, she had ruined the dress she had bought especially for the occasion. Then she overcooked the beef Stroganoff, making the beef tasteless and the sour cream sauce like glue.

But Ace Gilbert gave no indication that he even noticed.

Ginger Steiner even screwed up the martinis. She put in too much vermouth. She abandoned any further efforts as doomed and joined Ace Gilbert in the living room of her apartment. He was slouched down on the sofa, his long legs sticking out. With his coat off and his tie pulled loose he looked rugged and handsome.

His shoes were off, reminding her of how he had been on that day, in stockinged feet and a gun in his hand, his eyes quick and hard.

Now those same eyes looked at her, but they were soft and amused. She had discovered that his placid face actually betrayed a wide range of expressions, but you had to know him well to know what to look for. In a way he was almost Oriental in concealing his feelings, but she knew the feelings were there.

"I'm sorry about the martini," she said, watching him sip it.

"Why?"

"I put in too much vermouth. It tastes like pop. I can fix you another."

He grinned. "This is fine, Ginger. You surprise me. All this anxiety."

"It's showing?"

"A bit."

She flopped into the one big chair she owned. "I had hoped to make an impression."

"You have."

"I mean a good one. The meal was a disaster. I'm a much better cook than that, honestly."

He sipped the drink. "Tasted fine to me."

She had a difficult time remembering that this relaxed man had, but a few days ago, coolly killed two people.

She slipped off her own shoes. There was no use in keeping up any further pretense at being formal. "Ace, does it bother you?"

"What?"

"What happened the other day."

He shrugged. "I'm very popular at the office. The newspaper and TV people have had a field day. But the cops are still mad, I suppose they think I made them look bad. They say I put all the hostages in unnecessary risk. I'd do it again if it had to be done."

"That's what I mean. It doesn't seem to bother you that you . . . well . . . shot two people."

"Killed them," he corrected her. "You don't have to tiptoe around that fact, Ginger. Sure, it bothers me a little that I had to do it. Frankly, if it hadn't been for the screams, I would have stayed out of it. But something had to be done. I was in the best position, so I did it. It was necessity, not courage."

"I'd be nothing but a sobbing blob of jelly," she said. Even the conversation was going wrong. She wanted it to be light, happy, but it was turning serious and grim. Still, her curiosity burned irresistibly.

He looked at her. "I think I know what you mean," he said quietly. "Having shot two men to death, it would be only normal to show a much more intense emotional reaction."

"No, I didn't mean—"

He laughed. "The hell you didn't." He stared down at his toes. "They had caves in Vietnam." His voice was quiet, almost somber. "The Viet Cong built them. Sometimes they created regular little cities. If we found an entrance, we never knew if it was just a small hole or a system of caves. They even had crude factories built underground. One of my jobs was to go into those holes. You never knew what you might face. Some of my men were buried alive. It happened more than once."

"If it's painful for you to tell . . ."

He smiled. "A little. But if you know, you'll understand." He continued. "A pistol was the best weapon down there usually. Sometimes the caves were large, and sometimes they were just small, tight tunnels. Rifles were too big. You couldn't use explosives until you found out what was under there. It was very bad duty. Most of us were convinced we were going to die; it only became a question of when. You had to numb yourself against all emotions: love, hate, hope, and especially fear. Oddly enough, that state of mind helped." He sipped his drink. "I killed a number of people over there, Ginger."

"But they were trying to kill you."

He nodded. "Usually. Just as with the people in the court, I don't feel great about killing, but it was something that I had to do."

He finished the martini. "It was like stepping back in time for me the other day in court, a real feeling of *déjà vu.* That corridor was like the caves. All the old instincts of combat returned. No blood lust or anything like that, just the cold determination to do a job that only you could do. I really thought I would be killed. No fear, just an absence of concern, really."

Gilbert lit a cigarette. "I've thought about it since. You know, I think I did such a complete job of numbing my emotions in Nam that I have never really completely let go. I realized that when I was walking down that corridor. That's not a healthy thing, Ginger, to hold yourself in like that. Not for years anyway. Do you remember, I laughed when I said I felt fear?"

"Yes."

"I had never realized I was carrying around any residuals from the war. When I got the shakes in the courtroom, I was pleased. I was feeling something. I know it must sound weird, but I have been holding back for years without realizing it." He watched the smoke curl toward the ceiling. "That emotional blunting may account for a lot of things. Oh, I'm enthusiastic until there's danger or difficulty, and then I just go cold. I don't stop, you understand, I just don't allow myself to have feelings. That may explain what happened to my first marriage and why I feel the way I do about the law."

He inhaled deeply and slowly blew out the smoke. "But now that numbness is gone. I can experience what everyone else does. I'm alert to the problem. You know, for the first time in a long time, I am relaxed and content with myself."

He looked at her. "Does any of that make any sense?"

"Yes." She stared at him.

"I frightened you?"

She shook her head. "Oh, no, Ace, nothing like that. I just never realized how deep . . . well . . . how much danger you have had to face in your life."

He stood up. "Can I help myself?" He held his empty glass aloft.

She jumped up. "Oh, God, the perfect hostess!" She grabbed the glass from his hand and half-ran into the small kitchen.

Ace Gilbert followed her, lounging against the kitchen doorway. "What's the problem, Ginger? You're as cool as ice in a courtroom, but you're jumping around like a grass-hopper tonight."

She turned and flipped an errant strand of hair away from her eyes. "This was to have been the all-time perfect evening."

He smiled. "It is, as far as I'm concerned."

"Well, it's not, and you know it."

"Why so special in the first place?"

Ginger Steiner felt defeated. "Oh, hell, what difference does it make? I had hoped you'd think I was the greatest cook and hostess in the world, the most adorable woman you'd ever met."

"You are."

"That's nice of you, Ace, but if this evening lives up to its present course, I'm sure the ceiling will fall in."

"But why all the fuss?"

She leaned against the kitchen wall. "I was hoping to become your lover."

The grin never left his face, but she saw the change in his eyes. "Lover?"

"These are the days of women's rights." She tried to keep it light. "I'm in love with you." The words were almost inaudible. "I guess women can come right out and say it first now. It still doesn't quite feel right, though."

He never moved. His eyes were serious. "I'm not quite sure that I want a lover, Ginger," he said simply.

"Oh," she tried to laugh, "just chalk it up to hysteria."

"I believe I am in love with you too," he said, still serious. "But I'm an old-fashioned man, Ginger. I don't think I could just become a roommate, pleasant as that might be."

"I didn't mean . . ."

He shrugged. "To tell you the truth, I'm kind of in the market for a wife."

She put her arms around his neck.

Her eyes were tearing as she held him. "Jewish women make the best wives," she whispered. "They're loyal, faithful, hardworking."

"Sounds more like a Boy Scout."

She bit his neck. "I am no Boy Scout, Mr. Gilbert, which you will now find out for yourself."

the probation officer

FRANK Conroy had to be helped into the taxi by the driver. The swelling in his face had subsided, but the deep bruises remained. His broken shoulder had been set so that his arm stood straight out from his side, the arm cast held aloft by a supporting column coming up from a brace around his waist. The shoulder ached, but the cast itself was by far the greater nuisance. He could only sleep on his back, and if he turned, he jarred himself awake. And it itched.

The driver had asked him if he had been in a car accident.

"Something like that," Conroy had replied.

The taxi sped through the decaying East Side. It was his old neighborhood, but it had greatly changed.

Frank Conroy was beginning to regret setting up the appointment. He was troubled and he had thought it would help to talk to a friend. Tom Denning had been his friend since they were boys. They had entered the minor seminary together and, later, had been roommates at college. A strong bond of friendship had been formed.

As with most boyhood chums, fate had dictated they be parted. While Frank Conroy had been ordained and sent to a parish, Tom Denning had been sent to Rome for additional study.

Conroy had pursued the course of a diocesan priest with assignments to one church after another and finally appointment as pastor of a small suburban church. Tom Denning had come back from Europe but followed an administrative career in the Church, going from various administrative posts and serving eventually as secretary to the cardinal.

They saw each other only infrequently during those years—an occasional golf game or a dinner. Their professional interests and concerns were never quite the same. Father Denning had been in Rome on assignment when Frank Conroy made his decision to leave the Church.

He had avoided contact with Denning after that. The only communication had been Conroy's card when Denning had been named bishop. He had received a warm letter in reply with an invitation to visit. A long time had passed, but the telephone call Conroy made told him that the bishop's invitation was still good.

Our Lady of Sorrows hadn't changed. The big square church dominated the intersection. Conroy directed the cabbie to drive around the back to the rear entrance of the rectory. An auxiliary bishop, Denning had also been named pastor of the large parish, although Frank knew that in practice the bishop would have a good assistant pastor actually running the place.

The cabbie helped him out, and Conroy walked to the door and rang the bell. The neighborhood was quiet, and as he waited, he wondered again if this trip wouldn't prove embarrassing to both of them.

A young priest opened the door.

"Yes?"

"My name is Conroy, Frank Conroy. I believe the bishop is expecting me."

The young man's eyes were curious. "Yes, he is," he said. "Please follow me." He led the way through a hall to a comfortably furnished parlor. "Please wait here," he said, then paused before leaving. "Traffic accident?" he asked.

"Something like that," Conroy said. It saved explanation.

The young priest disappeared.

Conroy was nervous. It had been some years since he had been inside a rectory. He sensed that this could turn out to be a ghastly mistake.

Tom Denning walked in, the familiar grin set in a heavier face and the dark hair graying. "Frank, you look terrible," he said, grasping Conroy's good hand. "How do you feel?"

"It looks worse than it is. A nuisance mostly, not much pain."

"Sit down, Frank. Can I get you anything? A drink?"

Conroy wanted a drink, but now his main desire was to leave as quickly as possible.

"No, thank you."

"I read about you in the newspapers, Frank. It must have been terrifying."

Conroy nodded. "It isn't the sort of thing you'd want to go through twice."

"I'm truly glad to see you," the bishop said. "I've missed you."

"Well, I've meant to . . . well, under the circumstances, I just never—"

"You mean leaving the Church?"

Conroy's eyes dropped away from Tom Denning. "I felt that it might be embarrassing for you."

The bishop, who was wearing an old-fashioned floor-length cassock but with the neck open, pulled a pack of small cigars from a pocket and offered one to Conroy, who declined.

"Listen, Frank," the bishop said through a cloud of smoke, "some of my best friends are lapsed Catholics."

"But not failed priests, I'll bet."

Tom Denning's eyes were serious. "You might be surprised. Anyway, I'm delighted you came to visit. What's up?"

Conroy smiled. "Oh, just looking up old friends. I haven't seen you for a while, so I thought I'd drop by."

Denning drew on the cigar before speaking. "So you got up out of a sickbed, all trussed up like a turkey, and taxied out here just to say 'Hi,' is that what you're trying to tell me, Frank?"

"No law against it."

"No, there isn't, but I think something else brought you out here. Come on, it's me, Tom Denning. What's up, Frank? And don't give me any cock-and-bull stories about old times, eh?"

Conroy extracted a cigarette with his good hand. The bishop bounded out of his chair to light it for him. "Come on, Frank, let's hear it."

Conroy started to laugh. "Up until now I could never figure why they made you a bishop."

"Exactly. I have the knack of getting priests to tell the truth."

"I'm not a priest anymore. I'm excommunicated. I left it all, Tom."

"Go on." The bishop leaned back in his chair, obviously relaxed, but very interested.

"As you probably know, I just walked away. I didn't try to get the pope's okay or anything. One day I just decided there was no God, and that made being a priest a little silly under those circumstances."

"I'd say so," Denning agreed.

"So I walked off. I kicked around at a few things for a while, then I got my present job as a probation officer. Tom, I never regretted leaving, because I felt there was no God, do you understand?"

"I understand," the other man replied easily as he knocked the tip of his cigar into an ashtray. "Tell me, Frank, how about sex? I mean, how did you do in that regard? If you don't mind me asking, that is?"

Conroy forced a smile. "I made love once."

"Just once!"

Conroy felt himself color. "Yes, once. Maybe it's my age, but it really isn't all that it's cracked up to be, at least not as far as I'm concerned."

The bishop laughed. "You're not saying that just to make me feel good, are you? I mean, that's just the sort of thing a celibate likes to hear."

Conroy laughed. "No, that's the straight goods, Tom. I'm afraid I'm not much of a sex fiend."

"Well, how about the other interesting things in the outside world—gambling, graft—get in on any of those things?"

Conroy shook his head. "I'm a big disappointment to you, I'm afraid."

"Yes," the bishop said. "Doesn't sound like you changed a hell of a lot."

"Drink more. I get drunk every so often. It may be becoming something of a problem," he said, remembering the old record of the Mass.

"Drinking is a problem in the Church as well as out," Denning said. "You know, they say they didn't know how many priests were drunks until they started saying the Mass in English."

Conroy laughed. "That's another thing. I just couldn't adjust to the liturgical changes."

"Ah, ha," the bishop said, "so when we stopped with the Latin, you stopped with the believing, is that it?"

"I don't think so, Tom," Conroy said, a bit irritated that the bishop was treating the matter so lightly.

"Why are you here, Frank?" The tone suddenly changed, subtly commanding. "Give it to me, one friend to another."

Conroy breathed deeply. "I honestly believed there was no God until that incident at the court. I prayed, Tom. I really prayed. You see, if I didn't believe, I wouldn't have prayed. But I prayed, and my prayers were answered."

Denning studied him. "You're not getting superstitious in your old age, are you, Frank?"

Conroy shook his head. "No, not really. Perhaps my prayer wasn't in fact answered, maybe it was just a co-incidence. But the fact that I prayed and believed has shaken me. I don't know where I stand now. I just wanted to talk it out with someone."

"If you believe in God, then there's really no reason for your not returning to your duties as a priest, is there?"

"They'd never take me back, Tom. Even if I wanted to come back."

"Do you?"

It was the question that Conroy had been afraid to ask himself. His face was somber, reflecting his thoughts. "I . . . I really don't know. Perhaps I would. But even if I did, they wouldn't—"

The bishop held up his hand. "Whoa! You forget you are talking to 'they' right now. I am a bishop with the full powers of that office, Frank."

"I just wanted to talk, Tom. I thought maybe if I could open up to someone, I might be able to get things straightened—" Conroy's eyes widened in surprise.

Bishop Denning had taken the stole from a pocket of his cassock. It was the traditional vestment of confession. Denning kissed the cloth and then placed it around his neck.

"Frank, we might as well get this over with. You are a priest forever, and I can square all raps, as they say. Now, let's hear your confession, Father Conroy. Toss in the sin of pride, Frank. I think you might be a little guilty of that. And start with when you got laid; that sounds like the most interesting part."

Frank Conroy had come home.

the information desk

A detective leaned against the information desk and listened to the ever-talking, never silent Red Mehan.

"You know, if there's one thing I've learned in this life, it is don't fuck with fate. You know, if you think about it, we are all marching toward our end. Shit, old Tingle come down here like a dog in heat, thinking this was the greatest thing in the world that ever happened to him. Same thing with that asshole Harbor. Every one of them rushing toward his own fate.

"I suppose those people who blew this joint up thought the same thing. Even that burglar—what was his name—Simes. Christ, what was a practical, veteran burglar doing with a bunch of kooks, eh? Fate, that's what it was. That jackass was doomed to die here the day he was born.

"Kind of makes you wonder, don't it? You wonder what those cards might hold for you, ya know?

"I remember when I got this arthritis. God, I thought it was the worst thing in the world, I honestly did. Even thought about blowing my brains out, what little I have anyway. But, hell, I end up with the best damned job in the world.'

"No shit, I'd pay money to sit here. This is the damned-est show in the world. It's a zoo, and it's full of animals. They smell, they're lousy, they're wacky, but they are interesting. I mean, really interesting.

"I just love this fuckin' job!"